Vampirates

IMMORTAL WAR

by Justin Somper

LITTLE, BROWN AND COMPANY

New York   Boston

Also by Justin Somper

VAMPIRATES: Demons of the Ocean
VAMPIRATES: Tide of Terror
VAMPIRATES: Blood Captain
VAMPIRATES: Black Heart
VAMPIRATES: Empire of Night
VAMPIRATES: Dead Deep (e-book exclusive)

Text copyright © 2011 by Justin Somper
Cover hand lettering by Leah Palmer Preiss
Interior illustrations by Jon Foster

Little, Brown and Company

Hachette Book Group
237 Park Avenue, New York, NY 10017
Visit our website at www.lb-kids.com

Little, Brown and Company is a division of Hachette Book Group, Inc.
The Little, Brown name and logo are trademarks of Hachette Book Group, Inc.

The publisher is not responsible for websites (or their content) that are not owned by the publisher.

First U.S. Paperback Edition: January 2013
First U.S. hardcover edition published in 2012 by Little, Brown and Company
First published in Great Britain in 2011 by Simon & Schuster UK Ltd

Library of Congress Cataloging-in-Publication Data

Somper, Justin.
Immortal war / by Justin Somper ; [interior illustrations by Jon Foster]. — 1st U.S. ed.
p. cm. — (Vampirates ; bk. 6)
Summary: When the Pirate Federation and Nocturnals form an alliance to battle the renegade Vampirates, twins Connor and Grace Tempest each have important roles to play in the war — he as a pirate warrior and she as a powerful healer working with the war-wounded.
ISBN 978-0-316-03324-4 (hc) / ISBN 978-0-316-03325-1 (pb)
[1. Pirates—Fiction. 2. Vampires—Fiction. 3. War—Fiction. 4. Seafaring life—Fiction. 5. Twins—Fiction. 6. Brothers and sisters—Fiction.] I. Foster, Jon, 1964– ill. II. Title.
PZ7.S69733Im 2012
[Fic]—dc23
2011019641

10 9 8 7 6 5 4 3 2 1

RRD-C

Printed in the United States of America

Book design by Alison Impey

For the Nocturnals.
Thank you for making this such a memorable voyage.
No captain could ask for a more supportive crew.

FIVE HUNDRED YEARS AGO

The Vampirate captain stepped into the room, dressed in his familiar garb of mask, gloves, and cape. He bowed to Mosh Zu, who acknowledged him politely.

"Cardinal North."

The two of them turned toward the doorway, waiting for the others to arrive.

Now an identically dressed figure arrived at the threshold and strode over to greet them.

"Cardinal East," Mosh Zu proclaimed, before he and the first captain bowed at the new arrival, who tilted his head reciprocally.

Mosh Zu's assistant, Olivier, moved from the center of the room over to the doorway as a third, then fourth, figure arrived. They nodded perfunctorily at Olivier, then joined Mosh Zu and the others.

"Welcome, Cardinals South and West," Mosh Zu said. "Now that all four of you are assembled, it is time for the ceremony to begin. Cardinals, please take your positions."

At these words, the four captains moved to stand on the points of the mosaic compass on the floor—North, East, South, and West, in accordance with their title. Mosh Zu remained inside the circle. He was surrounded by the four Vampirate captains. They each raised their arms and joined their gloved hands, forming an unbroken circle. Their four capes began to billow. As they did so, they sparked with light, as if the joining of their hands had created a power surge. The light crackled for a moment, then diminished to a flicker. The capes continued to move but more gently now, like sails in the breeze.

"I shall not waste any time," Mosh Zu said. "It is rare for you to come together, but I had to call you here tonight." He paused. "A prophecy has been revealed to me, one I must share with you. If I have interpreted it correctly, this prophecy has the power to change everything."

"What is the prophecy?" The captains spoke as one, their voices rolling over one another like soft waves, in a strange whisper.

"A time of war is coming to the oceans," Mosh Zu announced.

"War?" answered the captains, their voices once more united in that strange, watery whisper. "War between us and the pirates?"

"No," Mosh Zu said. "War within our own realm. Our

precious union will splinter and the greatest threat will come from within."

"What is this threat?" asked the captains. "Give it a name!"

"I do not know its name," Mosh Zu said. "But the chief warmonger belongs to one of your crews. Be alert to him or her."

"When will this war commence?" the captains asked Mosh Zu.

"Soon, I think," Mosh Zu replied.

"Soon?" There was a note of scorn in the captains' whisper. "Soon is an unhelpful term for immortals like us."

"Agreed," Mosh Zu answered. "But it is time to make plans."

"What more does your prophecy tell us?" asked the captains.

"Our hope rests with twin children, who have yet to be born."

"What are their names?" inquired the captains.

"Their names are not yet clear to me," Mosh Zu said. "But they are the children of this warmonger and their powers will be unprecedented. Their role in the future of our realm will be great, and, when war comes, they and they alone will have the power to deliver our victory."

"We must find these twins, these children of the warmonger," the captains said. "We must search for them across the oceans."

"I repeat," said Mosh Zu. "They have yet to be born.

When the time is right, *they* will seek *us* out. That will be the sign that war is imminent."

There was silence for a moment; then the captains spoke once more. "Is this the end of your prophecy?"

"There is one more thing," Mosh Zu said. "In order to bring about peace, one of the twins must enter the void. I saw darkness surround one twin, and auguries that signified death."

"The death of mortals or our immortal death?" pressed the captains.

"I cannot be sure," Mosh Zu said. "But my sense was that though the child will be born of a Vampirate and will therefore be immortal, he or she will have to journey to the realm of the mortal dead in order to achieve peace. That is as much as I could ascertain."

"We thank you," the captains said, their whisper more haunting than ever. "We will take our leave now and ponder these portents."

At these words, their capes began to undulate more strongly and to spark with light once again. A mist began to circle around them. Soon it had completely surrounded them and it was no longer possible to discern their outlines.

As the mist receded, Mosh Zu found himself alone in the center of the mosaic compass.

The Four Cardinals had taken their leave. They would not meet again for a very long time.

1

TICK-TOCK

The ancient offices of Mizzen, Mainbrace, Windvane, and Splice, "lawyers to the pirate community, by appointment to the Pirate Federation, since 2015," were at the top of a cliff and took the form of the upper three decks of a pirate galleon, which had been braced directly onto the rock itself. The impression was of a ship sailing—indeed flying—right off the peak into the bay far below. The main conference room of the famous maritime firm of solicitors had once been a pirate captain's cabin and possessed floor-to-ceiling windows. Once these windows had looked out onto a seeming infinity of ocean; now they afforded a queasily vertiginous view down the cliffs.

It was before these windows that old Mr. Mizzen currently stood, his back turned—though with no intention of rudeness—to the other inhabitants of the room. Mr.

Mizzen's still-keen aquamarine eyes traveled from the similarly colored waters of the bay below up to the ticking clock on the conference-room wall. There was reassurance to be found in the tick and the tock, but also a warning. Old Mr. Mizzen was under no illusion—the clock was always ticking. Whether fate decreed that one was gently eased out of this life by natural means or snatched from it in the cruelest terms possible—as Molucco Wrathe had been—it was advisable to make the necessary preparations for that final voyage.

A not entirely discreet cough sounded close by Mr. Mizzen's right ear. A sudden arctic chill caused the profusion of white hairs protruding from said ear to stand on end. Turning away from the window, Mr. Mizzen saw that he had been joined by Trofie Wrathe. The glamorously intimidating deputy captain of *The Typhon* was dressed from head to toe in black. A lace veil—patterned with skulls—covered her face, while her legendary golden hand was, for the moment at least, encased in a long black glove, as was her other, regular, hand. It was not uncommon for visitors to wear black to attend these offices—but though de rigeur for funerals, it was not required for the reading of a will. Even through her veil, Trofie Wrathe's penetrating stare caused Mr. Mizzen's old eyes to smart a little. She raised an eyebrow inquisitively before asking in her distinctive accent, "*Must* we wait any longer?"

"I'm afraid we must, Madam Wrathe. It is a matter of some importance that we do not begin the reading of your brother-in-law's will until *all* the beneficiaries have arrived."

"*Whom* exactly are we waiting for?" she asked. "Don't they know that time is short? There's a war on, in case you'd forgotten!"

Mr. Mizzen heard her words but chose, as he sometimes did, to feign deafness. Instead, he surveyed the others, who were also waiting in the room, with varying degrees of irritation, for the formalities to begin.

In the front row, on either side of the chair temporarily vacated by Trofie, sat her husband Captain Barbarro Wrathe and her teenage son Moonshine. Barbarro looked solemn. He was the last Wrathe brother standing—the Vampirates having claimed his younger brother Porfirio's life before finally closing in on Molucco.

Moonshine Wrathe had yet to prove himself worthy of the family name. Still, Mr. Mizzen noted there had been some improvements since last they'd met at his uncle's funeral. Moonshine's skin was now clear and his hair tied back from his face. His locks were as long and black as his father's but without the lightning strike of silver shooting through them. He was neither handsome nor otherwise, and it was hard to believe the young pirate was heir to such fame and fortune as came with the Wrathe name.

On the other side of Barbarro—separated by another empty chair—sat Matilda Kettle, owner of the eponymous tavern, which had been drawing in the pirate hordes for as long as anyone could remember. Once, "Ma" Kettle's beauty had been the feverish talk of the oceans. She was still attractive, granted Mr. Mizzen, but *tick-tock*...He smiled ruefully. No, he thought, it was not the tick and the tock that had stolen away Ma Kettle's looks. Molucco's exit had done that. It was no secret that Ma Kettle had been close to the rebellious captain for many a year, and Wrathe's sudden death seemed—if a maritime metaphor might be forgiven under the circumstances—to have taken all the wind from her sails.

Where once she might have worn a fur stole or a feather boa, now Ma Kettle sported something equally colorful but rather more unusual. Wrapped about her sinewy neck was Scrimshaw, the dead captain's beloved pet snake. Ma had taken the snake into her keeping since the captain's demise. The reptile's glassy eyes were like two mirrors, reflecting the woman's lost expression back at her.

Mr. Mizzen's own eyes migrated to Matilda Kettle's traveling companion—a decidedly exotic creature who went by the name of Sugar Pie. Some kind of barmaid-cum-burlesque artist, according to the notes young Mr. Splice had prepared for him. Faced with the general mood, Mr. Mizzen found Sugar Pie to be a veritable oasis in the desert. True, her face was solemn—her eyes darting frequently to her aged companion—but a dazzlingly pure light seemed to emanate from those eyes. It seemed to Mr. Mizzen as much a cause for hope and celebration as sunlight.

To Sugar Pie's side was another empty chair. Seeing this, Mr. Mizzen was brought back to the matter at hand. His smile faded. He glanced again at Trofie Wrathe, who was still pacing back and forth. Catching his glance, her eyebrow lifted inquiringly once again. *Tick-tock*, he heard, *tick-tock*. Perhaps he would have to start after all.

Just then, there was the sound of footsteps out in the corridor. Trofie stopped pacing and turned toward the door. Mr. Mizzen's eyes traveled in the same direction as the door opened and the young and breathless Mr. Splice entered the room, nodding reassuringly at his superior while holding open the door and addressing someone in the vestibule.

"Please, come this way. The others are waiting in here."

All eyes turned toward the open doorway.

A figure stepped into the room, then paused, turning to face the others.

"I'm so sorry we kept you waiting," said Catherine Morgan, Molucco's deputy captain, most often known as Cutlass Cate. Her trademark russet hair brought to mind a dramatic sunset.

"It's good to see you again, Cate," boomed Barbarro Wrathe, rising to greet her. Taking her arm, his fingers briefly brushed the black armband she had sported for the past several months. She was a woman in mourning, too, but not, primarily, for Captain Molucco Wrathe.

Releasing Cate's hand, Barbarro indicated the vacant chair between himself and Ma Kettle. Nodding and smiling politely at the others, Cate took her seat, as Trofie sighed with relief. But, as the captain's wife adjusted her skirt, she had a sudden realization. Cate had said, "Sorry *we* kept you waiting..."

As she thought this, a young man strode through the door. A man of equal years to her own son but whose journey had been charted across far different waters. It was Connor Tempest—the shipwreck victim who had become a pirate but, more than that, the closest thing Molucco had had to a son. Their relationship, like so many of Molucco's, had hit the rocks and ended when Molucco burned Connor's articles. Yet here he was, as dependable as the tide, come to take his seat beside the others. Smiling minimally, Trofie turned to face the front.

"Connor." It was Ma Kettle who spoke first. "Of course. We should have guessed you'd be here."

Connor looked awkward as he stepped into the room, hovering before the others as if recognizing that he was the last and least welcome guest.

"Mister Tempest," said Mr. Mizzen, lifting his eyes from Mr. Splice's excellent notes. "I believe there is a spare chair for you, to the right of Miss, er, Pie. Please sit down and we will commence our business."

"About time," hissed Trofie to her husband.

Yes, thought old Mr. Mizzen, once more attuned to the merciless rhythm of the tick and the tock. *When all is said and done, it's always about time.*

2

MOLUCCO'S HEIRS

"I, Molucco Osborne Mortimer Wrathe, being of sound mind and disposition..."

A cackle from Ma Kettle caused Mr. Mizzen to pause and glance up from the scroll of paper in his hands. "Sound mind and disposition! That doesn't sound like the man *I* knew these past forty years."

Mr. Mizzen smiled indulgently then began again. "I, Molucco Osborne..."

"Wait!" Trofie Wrathe raised her right hand and, as Mr. Mizzen glanced up once more, she removed her black glove. The solicitor found himself momentarily dazzled by the sight of her burnished gold fingers and shimmering ruby fingernails. Seizing her advantage, Trofie spoke. "I'm sure no one would mind if you skipped some of the unnecessary formalities and cut to the chase." A row of shocked faces turned toward her, but Trofie was unabashed. "As I said before, there *is* a war on."

"War or no war," answered Mr. Mizzen, "certain ceremonies must be observed."

Now Barbarro entered the fray. "My wife has a point," he said. "We are somewhat late beginning and several of us are due at the Pirate Academy for a Council of War this evening." Barbarro glanced carefully at Cate, then back to Mr. Mizzen. "I think we all want to ensure that we leave here in good sailing time."

"Very well," said Mr. Mizzen with a sigh. "I shall, as you say, *cut to the chase*." He observed his audience through his spectacles with cool detachment. "Who gets what. Of course, that's what you all came to find out."

There was a moment or two of uncomfortable silence while Mr. Mizzen glanced down the scroll and then began to read once more.

"To my dear Ma Kettle, the most beautiful and exciting siren I ever had the good fortune to know across the Seven Seas. A goddess, who has been more of a comfort and balm to me over the years than she will ever know. To you, I leave the sum of five million..."

"*Five million!*" Trofie exclaimed loudly. To her exasperation, Barbarro was beaming broadly, as was Sugar Pie. Ma herself was speechless, her moist eyes trained on Mr. Mizzen as he continued.

"It was," he read, "my hope that we would spend this money and our twilight years together but, if circumstances have decreed otherwise, then I see no reason why you, darling Ma, should not enjoy such comfort and pleasure as I can offer you. It is my one regret that I cannot be here to toast our future in oyster champagne."

"Mine too," said Ma, gratefully accepting the handkerchief proffered by Sugar Pie.

Mr. Mizzen reddened as he continued. "The very best of my days and nights—ahem—were those I spent with you. Remember to spend this money as recklessly as you know I would!"

This last sentiment prompted a throaty chuckle from Ma. She nodded, smiling. Sugar Pie reached out and clasped Ma's hand in her own. "I knew he'd take care of you," she said.

"He always did," answered Ma, with a squeeze of her hand. "In his way."

Mr. Mizzen's tone now grew more businesslike. "Molucco did not specify whom he wished to look after his beloved pet, Scrimshaw, after his demise, but it seems, Madam Kettle, that you have taken this upon yourself?"

"Oh, yes," said Ma with a nod. "Scrimshaw will always have a home at the tavern." Her free hand stroked the snake's scales tenderly. "We have a connection, me and Scrim. I, too, have shed many a skin in my time."

"Well," said Mr. Mizzen. "Molucco set aside a further ten thousand to cover Scrimshaw's rather particular gastronomic tastes."

"Ten thousand?" Trofie mouthed to Moonshine. "For

pet food!" Moonshine grinned at his mother's disbelief, then glanced over at Ma, who was nodding once more.

"Scrim shall never go short of honeyed dates or rosewater-dipped pistachios as long as he's in my care," she assured Mr. Mizzen.

The solicitor scanned Molucco's will once more, then resumed reading with renewed vigor. Barbarro wondered whether he was imagining it or if Mr. Mizzen was actually trying to impersonate his dear departed brother.

"My ship, *The Diablo*, has been my home for many years—one of the few constants in my life. I have thought long and hard as to who should be the heir to my ship and I have decided to entrust it to my nephew, Moonshine Wrathe."

All three attendant Wrathes listened carefully as Mr. Mizzen forged on. "Moonshine, I hope this ship is the making of you as a pirate captain. If rigging and cannon and old deck boards could talk, this old galleon would have plenty of tales to tell under my captaincy and—I've no doubt—under yours, too! Take good care of her, my boy. I trust you will make me proud."

"Thanks, Uncle Luck," said Moonshine breezily. "Though I'd have preferred a ship that wasn't in Vampirate hands..."

"Presumably," Trofie interrupted, lifting her veil as she addressed Mr. Mizzen, "the ship comes with a signifi-cant financial bequest?" Her ice-blue eyes bore into the lawyer's.

"No doubt all will be revealed as we proceed," said Mr.

Mizzen firmly, turning from her. He was enjoying himself now, back in his stride.

"To Cate Morgan, who has served with me in varying capacities for the majority of her maritime career and proved herself to be one of the finest piratical minds of her generation. To Cate, I leave five million..."

"*Another* five million...?" Trofie's golden hand gripped her husband's arm. "Are you doing the math here? I don't like the way this is stacking up..."

"To Cate," Mr. Mizzen resumed more loudly, "I leave five million, but with a small condition attached. I have gifted *The Diablo* to my nephew Moonshine, and it is my hope that this ship will be the making of him—but timber and sailcloth alone cannot accomplish a task of this magnitude. Cate, I had the great privilege to know you as my deputy aboard *The Diablo*. Now I ask you to resume that position, as deputy to Moonshine, for a period of three years. That should be sufficient to give him the support and grounding he needs. I hope you might stay on for longer than that, but, even if you choose not to, at the end of the three years, my gift of five million will be yours."

Barbarro laughed. "I'm sorry, Cate," he said. "I'm not laughing *at* you. Just thinking how my brother was an inveterate deal-maker to the very end."

"And beyond," Cate said. She could feel both Trofie's and Moonshine's eyes upon her. No doubt, they were trying to read her thoughts and emotions. She studiously avoided glancing their way, looking instead directly at Mr. Mizzen.

"May I take some time to consider this proposition?" she asked.

Mr. Mizzen nodded. "Captain Wrathe allowed for that. He knew that you would want to weigh the pros and cons."

"Pros and cons!" snapped Trofie with irritation. She felt her husband's warning touch. It drew out some of her sting. "Well, really! He's given her a fortune and all she has to do is mentor our son." Barbarro was silent but reflected that, in Molucco's position, he might have upped the ante still further to sweeten the deal.

"To my dear brother Barbarro," Mr. Mizzen continued, "I leave you . . . nothing."

Nothing. The word seemed to ricochet around the conference room. The tension and surprise were almost audible.

"I leave you nothing," repeated Mr. Mizzen, "because you are as wealthy as me in your own right, and there are others who will benefit far more from a leg up. I trust you will not think ill of me on this account. Brother Barbarro, it was one of the deepest sadnesses of my life to lose our brother Porfirio. And one of the greatest joys to be reunited with you in the twilight of my days. We wasted so much time. I learned the lesson, but a little late, that blood is thicker than all the oceans."

As Mr. Mizzen paused to draw breath, Trofie inquired, "Is there a personal message to me?"

"Only this," said Mr. Mizzen pointedly, as he cleared his throat and found his place once more. "My precious family, my dear, dear friends, if you have been doing your sums—and knowing certain amongst you, no doubt you have—you will know that there is still the whale's share of my fortune to apportion. My accountants can confirm the total sum, though I estimate it to be in the region of…"

"Twenty-eight million!" Trofie finished the sentence for him.

"Twenty-eight million, eight hundred thousand," corrected Mr. Mizzen with a smile. "And I am passing on this wealth, which I have built over many years and all seven of the oceans, to my friend, Connor Tempest."

All eyes turned to Connor. Both Moonshine's and Barbarro's faces registered surprise. Trofie looked in urgent need of medical help. Ma Kettle was smiling, as was Sugar Pie. Cate's expression was harder to decipher. As for Connor himself, he had no idea how to respond to what he had just been told. When he'd been asked to come to this office, he had expected to leave with a token gift—if that. His last meetings with Molucco had been awkward, and the captain had left him in no doubt that any relationship they had once enjoyed was now over. Yet, according to Mr. Mizzen, he was about to inherit nearly thirty million. The figure was so far beyond his reality that his brain was simply numb.

"Connor," read Mr. Mizzen, "I'm sure this comes as a surprise to you. To be honest, it's something of a surprise to me. You came into my life by chance and soon became a valued member of my crew. But, more than that, my lad, you became the son I never had. Because of the deep affection I felt for you, you had the power very few others ever possessed—the power to hurt me. And you did. When you asked to be released from my command, you might as well have run your rapier through my heart. I responded, as I often did, with anger. I burned your articles and vowed to eradicate every trace of you from my life." Mr. Mizzen paused and took a sip of water, gratified to know all eyes were fixed on him.

"I couldn't cut you out of my life, Connor, any more than I could cut you out of my heart. I know why you did what you did. I saw your confusion and guilt—more clearly, I daresay, than you did yourself. So now, I reach out from my grave and ask to shake your hand..."

"I've heard enough," Trofie barked, rising to her feet, eyes flashing fire. "This will is a travesty—the rantings of a sick, deluded man who, in his decrepitude, became vulnerable to the worst kind of strumpets and con men and..."

As she sought out the next insult, Mr. Mizzen cut her off. "I can assure you, Madam Wrathe, that your brother-in-law was of sound mind and disposition when, in my presence and that of Messrs Mainbrace, Windvane, and Splice, he signed this last and final testament."

"Spare me," snorted Trofie derisively. "My husband and I will challenge this farce in every court on the land and oceans."

"No." It was Barbarro who spoke, rising to stand alongside his wife. "No, we will not. It was my brother's fortune to distribute as he thought fit. He has made his choices and, though we may not agree with all of them, we must respect them." He extended his hand toward Mr. Mizzen. "Thank you, sir. And now, we really must get going. We have a war to win—and a ship to reclaim." Barbarro looked at Moonshine, who obediently rose to his feet.

Trofie stood, still shaking her head in disbelief. Barbarro grabbed hold tightly of his wife's hand and escorted her briskly toward the door. "Come, *min elskling*. We must make haste for Pirate Academy."

Moonshine hesitated, grinning at the others. Then he, too, headed for the door, pausing before Connor for a moment.

"Well, old sport, looks like you scooped the jackpot today." Moonshine grinned. "Congratulations, Connor. Mazel tov! For a shipwrecked slumdog, you've made out like a bandit."

He paused to give Sugar Pie a wink, then, smirking, strode off after his parents.

3

KILLING PIRATES

Three ships coursed through the dark ocean, like a school of killer whales on the hunt. *The Blood Captain* was a nose ahead, flanked on its port side by *The Redeemer* and, on starboard, by *The Diablo*. The three Vampirate vessels were closing in on a pirate galleon.

Sidorio stood at the helm of his ship, hands on hips, surveying the figures racing back and forth across the target deck. Mortal eyes would have required night-vision goggles and an optical zoom to zero in on the scene. Sidorio's visual acuity was such that he could see far across the ocean, *his* ocean, with crystal clarity.

"Can't you get us there any faster?" he asked the man at his side.

His question was met by a shake of the head. "Regretfully, no, Captain. We're making good speed but ours is a large ship. Besides, you wanted *The Redeemer* and *The Diablo* to keep pace with us."

The mention of the other two ships made Sidorio instantly nostalgic for their captains—Stukeley and Johnny Desperado. One of the few drawbacks of the ultra-rapid expansion of the Vampirate fleet was having to release his trusted deputies and bring up others from the ranks—like this *babbo* at his side.

Well, thought Sidorio, Stukeley and Johnny might have their own ships now, but they remained his joint deputies within the empire.

Turning away from the imbecile at the wheel, Sidorio's fiery eyes sought out Stukeley, standing poised at the helm of *The Redeemer*. The always reliable Stukeley turned and saluted his commander in chief, awaiting instructions.

Smiling with satisfaction, Sidorio turned to his other side and found the reciprocal gaze of Johnny Desperado, captain of *The Diablo*. He, too, was ready to do his master's bidding.

"Follow me!" Sidorio commanded.

"What?" The man at his side jumped nervously and glanced at him in confusion.

"Not *you,* Lieutenant Jewell!" Sidorio said, venting his impatience.

"Sorry, Captain!" Lt. Jewell lifted one hand from the wheel to make a salute. With only one of his shaky hands on the wheel, the vast ship began to reel. They were never going to catch the pirate ship at this rate!

Sidorio pushed the trembling lieutenant away from the wheel and took over. Immediately, the ship steadied itself, like a wanton horse brought under control by an expert rider. The captain turned and shouted over his shoulder. "Is there *anyone* here capable of steering while I attend to business?"

"Yes, Captain!" A young-looking Vampirate—all ripped muscle and attitude—eagerly strode across the deck.

"What's your name?" Sidorio inquired.

"Caleb McDade," the Vampirate replied, saluting him. "At your service!"

Sidorio smiled at the young man's eagerness. "You've just been promoted, Caleb McDade," he said. "Take over from me."

As he stepped aside, Sidorio bashed into the lately demoted Lt. Jewell. The captain surveyed the useless excuse for a Vampirate.

"With regret," Sidorio said, "you're fired!"

He lifted the bewildered lieutenant up by his armpits and stepped toward the very edge of the ship. Sidorio released his hands, and Lt. Jewell made a hasty descent into the briny waters below.

At the wheel, Caleb McDade grinned from ear to ear.

"I see we share a sense of humor," Sidorio said. "Righto, time I was going. Keep your eyes on the ocean and your hands on the wheel, *capisci*?"

"Yes, Captain!"

Sidorio felt satisfied that this one was up to the job.

He glanced back to Stukeley, on board *The Redeemer*, then to Johnny, at the helm of *The Diablo*. "On the count of three!" he said. "*One... Two... Three.*"

He propelled himself up into the air, flying high above the deck and next the dark, churning ocean itself. It was as if he were drawing the target ship effortlessly toward him, like a kite. Glancing swiftly to either side, he spied Stukeley and Johnny soaring through the night air in the same direction.

Sidorio let out a satisfied roar. *Game on!*

━ ⌣ ━

On the deck of the pirate ship, Captain Jack Fallico was held fast in the clutches of Mimma and Holly, two of the feistiest Vampirates on Lola Lockwood-Sidorio's crew. Captain Fallico was the only pirate left standing. The others lay scattered across the deck like so much flotsam and jetsam, their prostrate bodies silvery-gray in the meager light of the ship's lanterns. Lola's crew—dark-cloaked shadows—was busy at work, harvesting the blood of the newly dead.

The pirate captain had put up a fight for a time, lashing and spitting at his captors. Now, at last, he seemed reconciled to his fate. His eyes gave a final flash of fire at the deliverer of his doom. Lady Lola Lockwood-Sidorio.

"If you're going to kill me, just kill me," said the pirate captain bravely.

Lola arched an eyebrow, giving nothing away. Feeling pleasantly giddy, she sniffed the air. The aroma of different blood types commingling on the deck was utterly intoxicating. She was already contemplating the intriguing blends she could create from tonight's harvest.

"Look here," Captain Fallico snarled, "I've had enough of this! You've massacred my crew and taken my ship. You're obviously going to kill me, too, so stop playing games and just get on with it, you vile, bloated vampire!"

"*Bloated?*" Lady Lola stepped closer to her prey, the heels of her thigh-high sharkskin boots drumming on the bloodstained deck. "*Bloated?* How dare you! I'm not bloated, you mortal fool. I'm eight and a half months pregnant!" She lifted her cloak and proudly displayed her belly, snug under her maternity suit. Rubbing it proudly, she stepped forward and seized Captain Fallico's rapier from where it had fallen onto the deck in front of him.

"Live by the sword..." Lola began.

"Captain!" exclaimed Mimma.

Seeing the look in her deputy's eyes, Lola paused. Killing a captain was a moment to savor—like uncorking a bottle long stored in the cellar and breathing in its heady perfume. Mimma must have good reason to interrupt her at a moment like this.

Behind her, Lola now heard the whistling of air, followed by a thud.

Turning, she saw her husband land on the deck, a few

meters from her. Her face froze in dismay as Stukeley and Johnny dropped down on either side of him.

Rapier still poised, Lola frowned at Sidorio. "What are *you* doing here?" she asked, no trace of warmth in her cut-glass voice.

Sidorio's jaw hung open. "What are *you* doing here? It's almost your due date. You're supposed to be taking it easy." His eyes glanced protectively at his wife's bulge.

Lola rolled her eyes. "Must we have this conversation *again*? There are two types of pregnant women," she declared. "Those who lie around for months reading magazines and demanding foot rubs, and the other category, to which I belong, who continue to attend to business."

With that, she turned away, lifted her sword, and skewered Captain Fallico.

As he fell meatily to the deck, Holly swiftly plugged in her draining apparatus and began bottling his blood. It was the last of a good haul. From the edges of the deck, others of Lola's crew now came forward, stepping over their victims. Each carried the standard-issue black case, which now held half a dozen bottles of recently harvested pirate.

"Good work, ladies!" Lola said, standing proudly before her crew as Holly snapped shut her case and strode into position beside her. "Holly, Camille . . . next job for you. You know that quaint tradition the pirates have of putting a Nocturnal on each of their ships?"

The girls nodded.

"Doubtless, he or she will be hiding belowdecks," Lola said. "Find them and bring them up to me."

"Dead or undead?" Camille inquired.

Lola laughed lightly. "Undead, if you please. We're going to play a little game with the opposition." Her eyes searched the crowd. "Jessamy, Nathalie — fetch the package from *The Vagabond*, if you please. The rest of you can start clearing up the deck."

At her words her crew sprang into action. Jack Fallico's husk of a body was the first to hit the water.

"What's going on?" Sidorio asked.

"I'll explain later," Lola said, hurling a set of keys toward him. As he caught them in his thick palm, she continued. "A gift to you, husband. Another ship for your burgeoning collection. Number one hundred and one, if I'm not mistaken? It was supposed to be a surprise but you've rather blown that."

"Thank you," Sidorio said, cradling the keys in his hand. He stepped forward to kiss his wife, but, at the last moment, Lola twisted her face and Sidorio found his lips thudding against her taut cheek, smooth and cold as marble.

Stukeley, Mimma, and Johnny averted their eyes. Even so, Sidorio flushed with embarrassment.

"Are you angry with me, wife?" he inquired, a dangerous edge to his voice.

Lola sighed, her breath sending a sharp spiral of smoke

through the black air. "I'm *furious* with you," she said. "I'm having a baby, Sid, not a lobotomy. I'm perfectly capable of taking care of business both before and after the birth."

"*Births,*" Sidorio corrected her. "You're having two babies, Lola. Our twins. The heirs to our immortal empire."

"Yes, yes," Lola said briskly. "Please be assured I know there are two budding Sidorios in my belly. I'm the one who gets kicked and nipped at all hours of the day and night. It seems big feet and sharp teeth run in the family."

Sidorio smiled and extended his hand to his wife's neck. It was as elegant as a swan's, deceptively fragile-looking. "I'm sorry," he said. "I acted rashly. I know I'm overprotective sometimes, but I just care about you so much." His voice became husky. "I almost lost you once before. I can't imagine how I'd go on if something happened to you."

Lola's dark eyes met her husband's. "If something happened to *me* — or to your precious twins?"

The brutal barb did not throw Sidorio off track. "You know how much these children mean to me," he said. "But you'll never know how much *you* mean to me, because my love for you is a thing which defies all measure."

At these words, Lola at last softened. "That's very sweet," she said, running a fingertip along the flat of Captain Fallico's sword and bringing the bloodstained tip to her mouth. She tasted it, then nodded approvingly. The blood was surprisingly complex. She'd enjoy a glass of that later. Full of health-giving nutrients for the twins.

"Are you truly sorry, Sid?" Lola asked. "Do you promise to mend your ways?"

Sidorio nodded. "I only wish there was some way I could prove it to you."

"Actions speak louder than words," Lola announced decisively. She reached out and took back the ring of keys. They glimmered in the moonlight as she extended them toward the girl by her side. "Mimma, you've shown excellent leadership qualities of late. I think it's high time you commanded a ship of your own."

"Wow!" Mimma said, clearly taken by surprise. She gripped the keys tightly.

Stukeley swept her up in his arms and kissed her. "Congratulations, Captain!"

"Gee, thanks," Mimma said, beaming broadly. "Look, here come the others!"

The captains and their deputies turned. The rank-and-file members of Lola's crew were busy tossing dead pirates into the ocean and swabbing the deck. Through the melee strode Holly and Camille, strong-arming a terrified-looking Nocturnal. Further in the distance, Jessamy and Nathalie were also making their approach, carrying over their shoulders what looked very much like a body bag.

Holly and Camille came to a standstill, presenting the

ashen-faced Nocturnal to their leader. Lola stepped forward to make a cursory examination of the man.

"You're a poor excuse for a Vampirate," she declared.

"I'm not a Vampirate," he rasped. "I'm a Nocturnal. I serve Obsidian Darke and the—"

"Enough!" Lola raised a gloved hand and slapped him viciously. "You are a traitor to your kind!"

"Shall we finish him off?" Holly inquired hopefully.

Lola paused as Nathalie and Jessamy deposited the hefty package they had been carrying onto the deck.

"No," Lola said. "No, we'll take the little traitor with us. I'm sure we can think of some ways to bring him back to the right, true path. Take him away to *The Vagabond*!"

Holly and Camille dragged the helpless Nocturnal away.

Now Lola turned her attention to the body bag lying before her. It was black, with a long gold zipper glinting in the moonlight.

"Open it!" she commanded.

Jessamy crouched down and released the zipper. The others all leaned forward to see who—or what—was inside. As the mutilated body was revealed, there were gasps.

"Who *was* that?" Johnny inquired.

Lola smiled. "Don't count him out just yet, Cowboy. He's in a bad way, but I'm sure the Nocturnals can patch him up with their healing magic."

"What's all this about?" Stukeley asked.

Ignoring him, Lola addressed Nathalie and Jessamy once more. "Throw this one over the side to join the others."

The two Vampirates swiftly embarked on the task.

"Jacqui!" Lola called across the deck. "Do you have the flares?"

"Yes, Captain!" Jacqueline raced forward, flares and matches in hand.

"The girl who played with fire!" Lola giggled as Jacqueline lit the flares. There was a whooshing noise, then a pop, and suddenly the whole deck was suffused with red light.

"Time to make ourselves scarce," Lola said, taking her husband's arm. "You may take me home now. I think I shall have a little nap. And perhaps a foot rub wouldn't be so bad."

Sidorio drew his disarmingly beautiful, unboundingly vicious wife close in to his side and escorted her swiftly across the deck. It was almost deserted now as the others, having executed their business, had returned to *The Vagabond*.

Holly came marching across the deck to rejoin Mimma and Sidorio's two deputies. She and Mimma exchanged a high five, as Stukeley inquired, "Do either of you know exactly what Captain Lockwood is up to this time?"

He was met by two shaking heads.

"But I got myself a ship," Mimma said, smiling and twirling the keys around her finger.

Johnny brought his own arm around Holly's waist. "I reckon this calls for a drink."

Holly glanced at her antique fob watch. "It's still happy hour at the Blood Tavern."

"Sugar," said Johnny, grinning and rolling his eyes, "since they franchised that joint, *every* hour is happy hour!"

"Well, either way, we'd better make ourselves scarce," Stukeley said. "Here comes one of those Alliance ambulance vessels."

"They must have seen the flares," Johnny said, his eyes sparkling. "This is all kinda crazy...but fun!"

Mimma turned to Stukeley. "Can you give me a quick lesson in how to steer this behemoth?" she asked.

Stukeley nodded, stretching out his hand. Giggling, the four young Vampirates raced hand in hand toward the steering column, their feet slip-sliding on the newly swabbed deck.

4

EMPTY CHAIRS

Connor felt a knot in his chest as he saw the iconic stone arch that marked the entry point to the Pirate Academy harbor. His mind had been so busy since the will reading, he'd failed to perform the one task he needed to complete. Soon they would be heading into a Council of War with the pirate captains and there would no longer be an opportunity.

Cate was on his side of the boat, expertly steering the vessel toward the center of the arch. On either side, flaming torches hungrily licked the ancient stones and illuminated the engraved words of the school's famous maxim:

> PLENTY AND SATIETY,
> PLEASURE AND EASE,
> LIBERTY AND POWER.

"Cate!" Connor said, immediately aware that the tone of his voice was all wrong. Too loud. Too urgent. He'd rehearsed this scene so many times in his head but now he knew he was going to mess it up.

Her face met his instantly, unnerved by his expression and sudden awkwardness. "What's up, Connor?"

"There's something I need to tell you." He frowned. "Before we arrive at the jetty."

Cate smiled at that. "You'd better be quick about it, then. We've got about five minutes' sailing time, max."

Five minutes! He should have stepped up to the plate when he'd had the chance. He'd let Cate down—and not just Cate. He reached his hand into his pocket, his fingers searching for the tiny but potent object inside.

"Connor!" He could hear the impatience now in her voice.

"I'm sorry," he said. "It's about Bart."

"What about Bart?" Cate asked, her tone of voice at once profoundly different.

This was too big, too important a conversation to cram into a few minutes, but now that he had started, Connor had no option but to forge ahead. "When he came to find me on *The Blood Captain* he told me something. Something important..." Here, at last, were the right words. Suddenly he found himself distracted by the sight of figures clustering on the jetty and the trail of torches lighting the path up the hill.

"Connor, what exactly are you trying to tell me?" Cate's

voice drew him back to her eyes. In them, he saw a depth of emotion he had never seen before. Not even when she had heard the news of Bart's death — the confirmation of her worst fear.

Connor looked straight into Cate's eyes. "Bart was going to ask you to marry him," he said. "When he came back. He was going to give you this." Connor drew his fingers from his pocket but kept his eyes fixed on Cate. "It was his grandmother's ring."

He lifted out the tiny circle of metal and passed it to Cate. Instinctively, she reached out her finger. Connor had been expecting to place the ring in her palm and, taken by surprise, he let the metal band fall to the deck boards below. He dropped down onto the floor, searching in the darkness for the tiny band. This was going from bad to worse. If he had lost the ring, he'd never forgive himself.

Above him, Cate stood stock-still. "He was going to ask me to marry him," she rasped. "After all this time."

"He always loved you," Connor said, still desperately trying to recover the ring. "He wanted to spend the rest of his life with you." There it was! He reached out with relief and grabbed the tiny ring between his thumb and forefinger. Rising to his feet, he saw that they were now only meters from their mooring. Grace was standing on the jetty. She smiled to see him and raised her hand.

He lifted his own hand and nodded, then swiftly turned and placed the ring carefully in the center of Cate's palm.

Her fingers closed tightly around it. Besides that small movement, she remained as still as a statue, her shock of red hair buffeted in the harbor breeze.

"I'm *really* sorry not to have told you before," Connor said. "I know how important this is to you. And it was to Bart, too. I've been trying to work out the right moment to tell you but I've completely messed this up. I'm so—"

"It doesn't matter," Cate said, cutting him silent with a voice as brisk and efficient as her sword. "Connor, we haven't really talked about Bart's death. About our loss, yes, but not how it happened…who was responsible." Her eyes met his, imploringly. "Connor, I need to know. Give me a name."

He shook his head. "What good would it do?" He could hear voices nearby now. Grace and Jasmine talking. The thought of them discussing him together was distracting.

"I need a name, Connor," Cate insisted, commanding his attention. "It's not much to ask, under the circumstances."

He turned away for a moment, unable to bear the emptiness in her eyes. As he turned, he caught sight of Jasmine. She smiled at him and stepped forward to help moor the boat. Smiling back weakly, Connor turned again to Cate. "Let's talk later," he said. "After the Council."

Cate's eyes held his. "A name, Connor. That's all I'm asking for." She was standing at the end of the boat now. There was no way down onto the jetty without stepping past her. Sighing, Connor lowered his eyes and gave her her answer.

"Lola."

Cate's expression didn't change. She simply nodded, then turned and stepped down onto the jetty. He saw that her fist, which enclosed Bart's ring, was still tightly clenched. Connor heard her saying hello to Jasmine and Grace, her voice now normal or some valiant imitation of it.

Now he, too, stepped down onto the jetty, greeting first his sister, then Jasmine. As Grace fell into step with Cate, Jasmine held back for a moment, looping her arm through his.

"Did you do it?" she asked, gently.

"Yes." Connor sighed. "But I made a complete fist of it."

Jasmine squeezed his arm. "It was never going to be easy. But you've told her now. And she has the ring."

Connor could hear Cate's voice inside his head. *I need a name.* Well, now she had one. But he feared it would do her no good.

Lorcan Furey—once a midshipman, next a lieutenant, now a commander—stood on the deck of *The Nocturne* as the ship made its final approach toward the Pirate Academy harbor. Not so long ago, the sight of a Vampirate ship approaching pirate territory would have been the cause of deep concern and evasive action. In the past six months, however, everything had changed. This time, they were coming in peace and partnership for a Council of War. It still seemed incredible to Lorcan that he found himself in a state of war and yet on the same side as the pirates.

"We're almost there," Lorcan said, turning toward Obsidian Darke. The commander in chief of the Nocturnals stood a few meters away, across the lighted deck, talking with several other of the ship's officers. At Lorcan's words, Darke glanced up and nodded. As he turned back to his conversation, Lorcan took the opportunity to appraise his leader.

The once nameless Vampirate captain had undergone a profound transformation to become Obsidian Darke. In many ways, his own metamorphosis encapsulated that of the Vampirates as a whole. Gone were the mask and cape that had kept his face and body hidden all these years. Now, his face was visible to all, its rugged features made still stronger by the moonlight and its complementary shadows. In place of his gloves and cape, Darke now wore close-fitting body armor. In a similar way, *The Nocturne*, which had formerly steered a discreet course across the ocean, now sailed proudly alongside pirate galleons. For so long, the captain had spoken in a mysterious, watery whisper. Now, his voice was loud and, when occasion called for it, gruff. He had found his voice in more ways than one. The partnership with the Pirate Federation was an equal one, and though the pirate side of the Alliance was far more numerous in terms of ships, Darke still stood shoulder to shoulder with his opposite number, Ahab Black, the commanding officer of the Pirate Federation.

As *The Nocturne* slowed and cruised into its dock, Lorcan lingered at the deck rail, watching the pirate ships alongside them. It was a peaceful night—or at least it had that veneer. The sky was velvet black, punctured by diamond stars. It took him back to nights when he had stood on this same deck and held Grace in his arms. Such times seemed a world away now. Lorcan rarely got the chance to visit Grace at Sanctuary, and, when he did, he often found that she was engrossed in her work or exhausted after an intense healing session. But tonight she would be at the Council of War and he would be able to snatch some precious time with her.

As he gazed out into the night, Lorcan thought back to special moments when they had simply wandered on deck, holding hands and naming constellations. It seemed hard to believe there had ever been times of such innocence; harder still, to have faith that they might return in this time of war.

"Commander Furey!" Darke's voice drew him away from his fantasies. "Come, we are about to disembark!"

Lorcan took his place among Darke and his comrades as they walked across the gangplank and onto the dock. The first to greet them on shore was Ahab Black—not the most engaging or likable of men but a steadfast leader. He was followed by Barbarro and Trofie Wrathe and their son, Moonshine.

Lorcan now greeted each of the pirate elite in turn. He was filled with respect for all of them and grateful for the chance this war had delivered, to get to know them. He shook hands with René Grammont and exchanged a salute with Pavel Platonov. He bowed before Lisabeth Quivers and Kirstin Larsen. Commander Lorcan Furey was on a cordial basis with each and every one of them, but at the end of the line were the pirates whom he called his real friends: Captain Li and the key members of her crew, Cate Morgan, Jasmine Peacock, and Connor Tempest.

"Good evening, Commander Furey." Cheng Li took his hand but also proffered her cheek. Perhaps it was only his imagination but, as his lips brushed her skin, she seemed to shiver, though she did not recoil. Lorcan thought once more of Grace, remembering that she had once said his lips were often as cold as ice.

As Cheng Li moved on to greet Lorcan's colleagues, Cate stepped forward and clasped him firmly by the hand. Lorcan and Cate had become close comrades since they had been thrown together to plot a groundbreaking combat strategy for the Alliance. Lorcan knew that Cate was not given to physical demonstrations of affection. At first he had thought this might express her unease at being in such close and prolonged proximity to a vampire, but he had come to realize that it was simply her nature. Since Bart Pearce had been killed, Lorcan had watched Cate withdraw further into herself, like a flower bud closing to protect itself against a rainstorm. She still executed her responsibilities in an exemplary fashion; if anything, she seemed more obsessive about her work than before. But it was clear to Lorcan that a certain light was missing from Cate's eyes; that though she strived for victory in the war, she had given up any hope of a happy future for herself.

He saw something of the same haunted look in the face of Jasmine Peacock, who now stepped forward. Jasmine had also lost her boyfriend to the war. Jacoby Blunt had been a young man of immense promise, cut down in his prime. So many good, brave men and women lost already. As Jasmine moved along the reception line, Lorcan shook his head. *How many more would be lost before this war was won?*

Connor Tempest stepped forward and reached out his hand. Lorcan smiled at his girlfriend's brother. "Good to see you again, Connor," he said.

"You, too." Connor returned an amiable smile.

Theirs was the friendship Lorcan had had to work hardest at—partly because it mattered to him the most. He knew how difficult it had been for Connor to discover that he was Sidorio's son. The fact that he was a dhampir was a closely guarded secret. Neither Cate nor Jasmine knew, though they lived and worked alongside Connor. Lorcan had never spoken directly to Connor about his secret but he had sent word via Grace that he was always there if Connor needed someone to talk to. So far, his offer had not been taken up. Though brother and sister, Connor and Grace were profoundly different.

"Come, my friends and allies!" Ahab Black's voice now boomed across the grass. "The meeting chamber awaits us. We have a brief ceremony to conclude before we can begin, so we must make a start."

The assembled military leaders followed him as he strode back toward Pirate Academy. As Lorcan brought up the rear, he watched the Nocturnals following the pirates and marveled at just how much had changed. The pirates were voluntarily welcoming the Nocturnals into the heart of their world. *Would the Nocturnals so easily do the same?*

—⁓—

As they approached the Rotunda, the single most important building in the Pirate Academy complex, Connor couldn't help remembering the first time he had walked this path. It had been morning then and sunlight had danced on the waters of the fountain. Now the same fountain was bathed in moonlight, while flaming torches lit the way up the hill from the harbor below.

The first time Connor had visited the Rotunda, Commodore John Kuo had been his guide. Now Kuo was gone— one of the many pirates slaughtered by Lola and the Vampirates—and much had changed for Connor, even in such a relatively short space of time. He had earned his pirating stripes. He'd made his first kill. He'd discovered that he was a dhampir and that his biological father was none other than Sidorio, self-styled King of the Vampirates. Now he had also found out he was Molucco's main heir and rich beyond his wildest dreams. Yet, on some level, Connor still felt like the same naive kid who had listened with undisguised awe as Cheng Li had explained how the vast, carved wooden doors to the Rotunda had been plundered by one of the academy's founding captains, during a daring raid in Rajasthan.

As his palm made contact with the ancient Indian wood, Connor remembered what Cheng Li had said that first time: *Whenever I see these doors, I feel as if I am coming home*. He doubted he'd ever share her feelings about the academy. His own history with this place was rather more ambivalent. Nonetheless, each trip back to the academy seemed to mark a staging post on his own personal journey.

Now, following Cate, Grace, and Jasmine inside the Rotunda, he saw that the vast circular room was packed. The dome of the building was punctuated by glass portholes in varying shades of blue. Moonlight filtered through them, sending shafts of light down upon all those gathered beneath. It was as if they were convening at the bottom of the ocean.

There was amphitheater seating all around the room, save for the center, where a raised platform had been set up. Around the platform itself was a ring of seats, soon to be filled by the great and the good of the pirate world. As Connor walked along the plush blue carpet toward the front, he saw that two glass cases, each containing a sword, were resting on the central table. Glancing up to the ceiling of the Rotunda, he felt a shiver of electricity race up his spine.

High above the platform, suspended by thin steel wires, were glass cases just like those on the table below. Each of the cases contained a sword that had once belonged to one of the most celebrated pirate captains of all time. Most of those pirates were dead now, but somehow their swords kept their presence within the room, a sign of the power they once wielded and the rich history that bound together all those gathered here now.

"Come on, Connor." He felt Jasmine's hand on his arm. "It's time to take our seats."

Drawing his eyes away from the glass cases, he followed Jasmine along the row. Cate was already sitting down, her eyes fixed ahead, staring at the two swords on the central table. Scanning the crowd, Connor noticed Grace taking her seat a couple of rows in front of him, alongside Lorcan Furey and Obsidian Darke. It was a sign of the strength of the new alliance between the Pirate Federation and the Nocturnals that key Nocturnal personnel were attending tonight's Council of War.

Connor noticed there were four empty seats next to Barbarro Wrathe. They were not for Trofie and Moonshine, as they both now sat down at the end of Connor's own row. Moonshine grinned at Connor. Connor nodded, then turned toward the stage. Commodore Ahab Black, chief officer of the Pirate Federation, had just taken to the platform and a hush had descended upon all those in attendance. Yet still, four empty chairs remained on the dais.

"Where's Captain Fallico?" Jasmine whispered in Connor's ear. "It's unlike him to be late. Especially for such an important event."

Connor shook his head, distracted from Jasmine's words by her perfume. Shaking her head softly, she leaned away again as Commodore Black began to speak.

"You have been called here for a Council of War, but before we begin, we have an important ceremony to conduct. Some of you may feel that a war such as we are currently engaged in allows us no time for this. But, ladies and gentleman, pirates *and* Nocturnals, it is my belief that, in the current climate, a ceremony such as this is more important than ever." His expression somber, he stepped forward to the table and stretched out his hands to indicate the two glass cases.

"Here lie two swords belonging to pirates who have given their lives in the current conflict. This sword was wielded by John Kuo, one of the most famous names of his generation, the former headmaster of this academy and a pirate who shaped the Pirate Federation into what it is today." Black lifted his eyes to address the congregation directly. "Commodore Kuo's famous Toledo blade has hung in a case here in the Rotunda for many years, brought down for the commodore himself to use on special days. He last used it when Cheng Li became a captain, in the Captains' Race that formed part of the celebrations. John was the firm favorite to win that race." Black shook his head sadly. "But events proved otherwise. That day, Commodore Kuo lost not only the race but also his life. His sword was stolen by his killers, and it is only thanks to a young pirate who has already made quite a name for himself—Connor Tempest—that the Toledo Blade was recovered and will tonight be returned to its rightful place, in the firmament of weapons above our heads."

Commodore Black paused to glance up above, then brought his eyes down once more. "It will not surprise you that we come together to honor the achievements of a pirate like John Kuo, whose deeds are legendary in our world. But, perhaps you are surprised that we would even add this other sword to the cases above. *This* sword did not belong to a famous captain or, in fact, any kind of captain. This sword belonged to a foot soldier in our navy—one Bartholomew Pearce, a loyal member of Captain Molucco Wrathe's crew aboard *The Diablo*." Black turned to face Barbarro. "At this point, I should like to acknowledge Captain Barbarro Wrathe and his brothers, Porfirio and Molucco, both of whom were victims of the Vampirates. Tonight, we have set chairs for these two former comrades, just as we have for John Kuo, in order to help us more strongly feel their presence and their power."

Connor leaned over to Jasmine. "So maybe the fourth empty chair is for Bart," he whispered.

"No," Jasmine said. "They only put out chairs for the captains. Jack Fallico should be sitting right there. Which begs the question, where is he?"

Black's monotone voice boomed out once more. "We have lost some of the leading lights of our generation in this conflict," he said, "but we have also lost great pirates of the future. Pirates like Bart Pearce, whose best days doubtless lay ahead of him."

Connor glanced to his side and saw that Cate's face was pale and contorted. She was struggling not to cry. Instinctively, he reached out for her hand and took it, then turned his eyes to the front as Black warmed to his theme. "War is the great leveler," he said. "It is indiscriminate, taking away our leaders and our foot soldiers. Tonight, we honor just two of those we have lost but, as their swords are raised aloft to join those above, I want you to think of the many others who have given their lives to this war. A war we are endeavoring to bring to an end. These swords, which once belonged to John Kuo and Bartholomew Pearce, serve as constant reminders to us all of the battles we have endured and, more important, of the battles that lie ahead."

Black gave a nod to indicate he had come to the end of his speech, and from each side of the platform stepped forward a somber-looking academy student. They joined Commodore Black at the table and waited as he clipped the sword cases to the steel wires that would support them up above. Then each of the students took the steel wire in his hand and pulled at it, working in perfect unison, so that the swords began to rise together.

As the swords made their slow journey upward, the academy orchestra played the Federation anthem. The crowd rose to its feet and began to sing. Connor, like most of the others, was transfixed by the two swords floating up through the watery blue light. Turning to look at Cate, he saw tears rolling down her face. Suddenly she stood up and slipped past him, then stumbled away down the row.

Connor moved to follow her, but Jasmine held him back. "Let her go," she said.

The music died away. Connor turned back and saw that the swords had reached their final resting place.

5

NEW ALLEGIANCES

Out on the hillside, overlooking the harbor, Cate sat on a bench, sobbing for Bart. Why now? She had been stoic from the time she had been brought the news of his death to the moment earlier that evening when Connor had revealed the name of Bart's killer. Somehow, seeing Bart's sword in that case had made her realize the finality of his death. She knew that Connor had buried their comrade-in-arms at sea. But the glass case that held Bart's sword might as well have been his coffin.

She was momentarily interrupted from these thoughts by a figure arriving at her side and hovering, gawkily, above her. It was Moonshine Wrathe.

Cate looked up at him through her tears.

"What are you doing here?" she asked.

"They say misery loves company," answered Moonshine. "And, right now, you look decidedly miserable."

"I just miss him," Cate said to Moonshine. "It's as simple and complicated and painful and irreversible as that." She slumped back on the secluded bench. The night air was scented with oleander, and sweet pomegranates hung ripe and low just above their heads. Moonshine stretched out on the seat. "You know, my Uncle Luck had a maxim. A pirate's life—"

"Should be short but merry." Cate cut him off. "Yes, Bart was wont to say that, too. It's a downright stupid maxim, if you ask me."

Moonshine smiled. "I'd have to agree with you. The merry part is fine, but let's marry that with a long life, please...Though of course I wouldn't want to be an immortal like *them*." Shuddering, he pointed at a couple of figures making their way up from the dockside toward the hall. "What's with their long faces? Sheesh—they don't look like *they'd* be any fun at a party."

Cate gave a hollow laugh. "I'm not really in the party spirit myself right now," she said.

"You know what? Maybe that's *exactly* what we should do!" Moonshine said, his eyes bright. "Put a hefty chunk of your inheritance behind the bar at Ma Kettle's, send out invitations far and wide and have ourselves a party— nothing better than getting filthy drunk with your buccaneer mates!"

Cate shook her head. "Do you really think that would make me feel better?"

Moonshine grinned. "How would I know? We're little more than strangers. Besides, I'm not old enough to consume hard liquor. Prescription drugs, on the other hand..."

Cate rolled her eyes. "In any case, I don't get the inheritance unless I agree to be your deputy." Her eyes met his. "And there's no chance of *that* happening anytime soon."

Moonshine shrugged. "Hey-ho. No party for you then, CC. Just the *almost*-widow's armband for another few months and, I fear, more of those lines across your forehead. Of course, Uncle Luck's bequest could also buy you some timely Botox. I'm sure my mother could recommend someone."

Cate shook her head. "You're really not a very nice person, Moonshine, are you?"

"No, I'm not." A sliver of starlight broke through the branches overhead and bisected his face. "But let's face facts: There are more than enough nice people in this world," he said. "You've got nice Connor Tempest and nice Jasmine Peacock and oh, that lovely Lorcan Furey, and... well, the list goes on. Nice, nice, nice. What the world needs right now is characters, more like Uncle Luck. He wasn't always nice but he'll be remembered as a legend."

Cate nodded. "And you're planning to step into his shoes, are you?"

Moonshine shrugged. In his hand was a pomegranate, which he'd just grabbed from the branches above them.

He sliced it in two with his pocketknife and began intently removing the seeds—every last one of them. Cate watched him with renewed interest.

"Do you have OCD?" she asked.

"I have pretty much everything." Moonshine continued worrying away at the fruit. "You name it. Lots and lots of baggage, all personally monogrammed of course!"

"Poor little rich boy," Cate said. "Where did it all go so wrong for you?"

"Oh, Cate," Moonshine said. "Dear, sweet Cate! I know that it's easy to romanticize being born into fabulous wealth, but I'm here to tell you, it doesn't stop you from having this big gaping hole of empty inside."

Cate snorted. "Try being born into abject poverty. When I was a kid, the big gaping hole was the one inside my stomach."

Moonshine offered her the deseeded half of pomegranate and got to work on the other half. "Well, now you need never go hungry again," he said. "Not with the money Uncle Luck has left you." He flicked away another seed with evident disgust.

"You really expect me to come and be your deputy?" Cate said, shaking her head. "For three years?"

Fireflies seemed to dance in Moonshine's eyes. "Can you imagine *anything* worse?" he asked.

Cate laughed at that. "I really don't get you," she said.

"Of course you don't *get* me," Moonshine said. "I'm far too much of a riddle for the likes of you to unpick. I've confounded some of the finest psychiatric minds on each of the seven oceans. Their voyages to the bottom of my psyche have cost my parents a pretty penny, but let's face it, Trofie and Pops have got plenty to spare." He looked at her strangely. "You're smiling at me," he said. "Please don't do that. It's unnerving."

Cate shrugged. "I know one thing, Mr. Nasty," she said. "You followed me out here, for reasons I can't quite fathom, to make sure I was okay."

"Oh nooo," Moonshine said, seemingly horrified at the thought. "You couldn't be more wrong. I came out here to bug the hell out of you. I saw you were vulnerable, Cate, and I closed in for the kill. *That's* the kind of guy I am."

Cate couldn't help but notice that, however harsh his words, Moonshine was now smiling broadly back at her.

"Come on," said Moonshine. "Better get back inside. I've got a plan I want to put to the Council and I think you should hear it."

Cate raised an eyebrow at him questioningly, but he just tapped his lips and beckoned her to follow him. Shrugging, she did as he requested. It sounded as if things were about to get interesting.

Even before they set foot inside the hall, Cate and Moonshine could hear raised voices. The two Nocturnals they had seen earlier were exiting as they came to the doors.

"What's going on?" Cate asked.

"*The Evening Star* has fallen to the enemy," said the first of the messengers.

"What of Captain Fallico and the crew?" inquired Cate.

"Dead," confirmed the second messenger. "Only the onboard Nocturnal survived, and he has been taken to Sanctuary. His wounds were very severe, though. He may not endure the night. The Federation is discussing a counterattack right now."

"No time like the present, then!" Moonshine said, gathering himself. Cate looked at him questioningly as he pushed open the doors and stalked to the front of the Rotunda, leaving Cate trailing in his wake.

There were shouts from different factions within the room: some calling for retaliation against the Vampirates; others expressing fear that the enemy was gaining significant ground.

Ahab Black was trying to restore order to the proceedings. He seemed almost relieved when Moonshine leaped onto the stage and raised his own hand to quiet the baying crowd.

6

MOONSHINE'S PROPOSAL

"I have a proposal, if I may beg your attention," Moonshine said, standing firm under the gaze of so many experienced captains.

The roomful of pirates and Nocturnals looked at the teenager with interest and waited for him to go on.

"You may have heard that I've lately been promoted to the rank of captain. My uncle, Molucco, bequeathed me *The Diablo*, but it is currently in the possession of the Vampirates. So I'm a captain with no ship. The Wrathe family, as you are all aware, has had its fair share of wounds at the hands of our common enemy. I have lost both my uncles. I have lost the ship I would have captained. My parents' ship has been targeted and my mother personally assaulted.

"But this war isn't just about my family. It's about all of

us, all of our families. Many pirates have lost their lives." His bright eyes surveyed the crowd as he added, "And many Nocturnals, too. But I can assure each and every one of you that many more lives will be destroyed if the Vampirate threat is allowed to forge ahead unchallenged. We must stand united and be brave enough to take the fight to the enemy.

"And that's why I'm standing here. I'm rather hoping to persuade my fellow captains to help me recapture my uncle's old ship. As a symbolic first attack."

"You plan to recapture *The Diablo* from the Vampirates?" said Lisabeth Quivers, her interest piqued.

"That is what I would like to propose, yes."

There were gasps around the room. Commodore Black spoke first. "Do you think you're ready for such a mission?" he inquired.

Moonshine nodded. "I do. Though I would like to consult with Commodore Li and Commander Furey, among others, about the detail."

At the sound of her name, Cheng Li turned to study the young man in front of her. He was a teenager on the precipice of manhood. His face, long hidden under an unruly fringe, now boldly proclaimed his lineage. His strong features made her think of both Barbarro and Molucco, though Moonshine's face was rather more angular than those of his father and late uncle. This might be on account of his youth or perhaps the genetic gifts of his boundlessly beautiful mother. But the lad had the Wrathe eyes; of that there could be no doubt. It was as if they were precious booty shared out among the key members of the clan. And, right now, Moonshine's eyes were wide and bright. He caught her gaze and walked directly over to her.

"Commodore Li," he said, stretching out a hand. "Will you help me?"

Cheng Li's intense almond-shaped eyes calmly appraised Moonshine Wrathe, the newest captain in the Federation. "I'll hear you out," she said coolly. "What exactly do you propose?"

Moonshine spoke out. "I'd like to put a team together to take back *The Diablo* and I want you...*all* of you on it." He spread his arms wide to include the rest of Cheng Li's crew, who sat around her: Connor, Cate, Jasmine—even Bo Yin.

His words and ambitions were swiftly digested by all those assembled. Each began considering the key challenges posed by his proposal.

"Do we know where *The Diablo* is right now?" Cheng Li asked.

Jasmine nodded. "Affirmative, Captain Li. We have their route mapped on the diorama on board *The Tiger*."

"Okay," Cheng Li said, "but we'll need to corroborate when we last received digits on the vessel from the tracking teams."

"The location of *The Diablo* was last confirmed at twenty-two hundred hours last night," Bo Yin announced confidently from the audience.

"Thank you, Bo," said Cheng Li, as the young pirate sat back down.

Connor spoke up with a question. "*The Diablo* was taken by Johnny Desperado, aka the Cowboy, wasn't it? Sidorio's joint second-in-command?"

Lorcan spoke up now. "That's right, Deputy Tempest," he said, his face grim. "Desperado masterminded the assassination of Molucco Wrathe and has now taken the ship as his own."

"So," Connor said, "*The Diablo* is right at the heart of the Vampirate fleet?"

"Yes," answered Cheng Li. "Both symbolically and in practice. According to our latest information, the four key Vampirate vessels—*The Blood Captain*, *The Vagabond*, *The Redeemer*, and *The Diablo*—are all sailing in close formation."

Commodore Black nodded ruminatively. "It will be hard to take out *The Diablo* so long as they remain so close." The other captains nearby nodded in agreement.

Lorcan rose to speak. "It's not unheard of for the Cowboy to break away from the others and head off on a jaunt," he said. "Captain Li, I'm sure tracking can supply you with the data to back that up. Can I propose you sit tight and wait for Johnny to next go rogue? It's only a matter of time before he does."

Moonshine spoke again now, his eyes bright. "If we *do* succeed in taking *The Diablo* back, it will be a major morale boost for the Alliance."

All those around him nodded. Cate looked thoughtfully at the young pirate. He was certainly full of surprises.

"We *will* succeed," said Cheng Li, resolute. "For all those reasons, and more besides."

"So are you in?" Moonshine said, his bright eyes circling the room. "It sounds like you're in!"

There was a moment's pause as Cheng Li glanced around at her young comrades. They each nodded. "If this Council of War ratifies our plan, then yes, Captain Wrathe, you have yourself a deal," she said.

Commodore Black put his hand on Moonshine's shoulder but addressed Cheng Li directly. "Commodore Li, I charge you with making this proposal a reality. As for everyone else, we have some attack strategy to work on ourselves. Time for a quick break, then key personnel should rendezvous in the bunker at twenty-three hundred hours."

As the ceremony audience began to break up, Moonshine smiled gratefully. "Thank you," he said. "Thank you all." His eyes settled on Cate. She nodded formally, then glanced down to write something in her notepad.

As he stepped down from the stage, Jasmine caught Moonshine's attention. "I have a question, Captain Wrathe."

Moonshine smiled. "Shoot," he said.

"Why us? Surely there are plenty of other pirates you could employ—from *The Typhon*, for instance?"

Barbarro looked up at this. He had come over to shake his son's hand, but he, too, was intrigued by Moonshine's decision.

"Fair point, Deputy Peacock," Moonshine said, nodding, "but consider my position. I'm a young buccaneer trying hard to stand on my own two feet. I've been given something of a break and I intend to capitalize on it. It wouldn't say much about my leadership potential if I simply asked Mom and Dad to sort it all out for me, now would it?"

"I suppose not," Jasmine said, pleasantly surprised by his answer and the direct way in which he gave it.

Barbarro beamed proudly and gripped Trofie's gold hand as she came to stand beside him. Their boy was doing well.

"Besides," Moonshine continued, "everyone knows that you guys are the experts on the Vampirates. You were the first dedicated Vampirate assassination ship to be commissioned by the Federation." His eyes zeroed in on Connor. Trofie scowled. "You have some of the most talented pirates in the whole Alliance on your squad. Plus..." Now his gaze returned to Cate. "You have the best military strategist of her generation. When you consider those salient facts, of *course* I had to come knocking on your door."

Unmoved by his flattery, Cate looked Moonshine square on. "We also have the key tactical and operational advantage of working hand in hand with Commander Furey and the Nocturnals."

Turning to Lorcan, she said, "This is a dangerous mission—attempting to take back *The Diablo* from such a high-ranking Vampirate as Desperado. Is it worth the risks involved?"

Lorcan nodded calmly. "We've done dangerous many times before, Cate."

"So tell us what you have in mind, Moonshine," said Cheng Li.

The young captain took a deep breath. "I was thinking an attack undertaken by a pirate force alone, during daylight hours."

"An attack by daylight?" Cheng Li said, surprised. "That's a highly unusual move for our alliance."

"Exactly," said Moonshine. "But I think that's the time the Vampirates are at their most vulnerable, no?"

Lorcan nodded, surprised at the young pirate's perceptiveness. "Yes," he said. "They'll be as disoriented as snakes who've just shed their skins. If you time it right, you should have at least twenty minutes to take back the ship. And, of course, if the attack is taken up onto the deck, your advantage could prove decisive."

"Just what we need at this point in the war—some surprise tactics," Cheng Li said. She glanced at Moonshine, the flicker of a smile playing on her lips. "Good work, *Captain* Wrathe."

Moonshine flushed at this, surprised and grateful for the response he was getting.

Connor looked at him in disbelief. What had happened to the Moonshine he had known to date? This didn't seem like the same person. But then, he knew that *he* was not the same person either, since he'd first set out from Crescent Moon Bay. The world of piracy had forced him to grow up. War had forced him and Moonshine to become men.

＊＊

Grace was getting ready to leave when she felt a hand on her shoulder. She knew exactly who it was before she turned around.

"Lorcan!" Smiling, she saw that she was right.

"I'm afraid this is only a brief hello," Lorcan said, his dazzling blue eyes meeting hers. "I have to head into the bunker for the strategy meeting, but I wanted to catch you before you headed back to Sanctuary."

Grace sighed. "We've barely had a chance to say two words to each other, have we?"

Lorcan shook his head sadly. "I know. I think I've been introduced to every last pirate in the building when all I really wanted was five minutes alone with my sweetheart. It feels like all we ever get to say these days is hello and good-bye, but..."

"...these are the times we live in." Grace completed the sentence, well acquainted with the refrain.

Lorcan opened his arms and drew Grace into a hug.

Feeling the familiar lean but comforting terrain of Lorcan's chest and shoulders, Grace held him close, grateful to have even this brief moment of solace. She closed her eyes for a moment, willing time to stand still, but knew it was futile. Opening her eyes again, she found that Obsidian Darke was staring over in her direction. He nodded at her and she returned the gesture—one born more out of respect than warmth.

"I know what's really going on," Grace said fiercely, as Lorcan reluctantly released her. "It's Obsidian's will that we should be kept apart—you on *The Nocturne*, me up at Sanctuary. He doesn't want anything or anyone to distract you from your mission—or me from mine."

Lorcan rested a hand on one of her shoulders and brought his other to lift her chin. "Now, now, Grace, you're being just a little bit paranoid."

"No," she said. "Ever since he returned, he's been utterly single-minded about it."

"Maybe he has to be." Lorcan frowned. "These are strange times," he said, "with new allegiances." His frown melted away. "But I'll make you a promise," he said. "We'll find some time, somehow, for a *proper* catch-up, just the two of us."

Grace hugged him once more. "Yes," she said, feeling more rational. "I'd love that. You know I would."

CASUALTIES

The all-too-familiar bell woke Grace instantly. It seemed barely a moment since she had fallen asleep and, in truth, it hadn't been more than a handful of hours since she had returned from Pirate Academy. She opened her eyes and pulled herself upright on her bed. The bell meant that the first of the dawn ambulances were already making their way up from the harbor. She glanced over to the other bed just as Darcy Flotsam blinked open her wide brown eyes.

"Bells!" Darcy exclaimed, sitting up and shaking her sleek dark hair into place. "Sometimes I feel that my whole life is framed by bells!"

Smiling, Grace got up from the bed and walked into their small adjoining bathroom and scanned her reflection in the mirror. She looked a mess! She splashed some water on her face and ran a comb through her hair before pulling it back into the utilitarian ponytail she had adopted of late. There was no time for vanity under the current circumstances.

Coming back out of the bathroom, she lifted her blue healer's uniform from the chair and dressed quickly. As she fastened the last button, she turned and saw that Darcy's appearance was flawless—as always. Grace shook her head in admiration. "I don't know how you do it! One minute, you're dead to the world. Next, you look fresh and ready to go."

Darcy gave a wry smile. "I've had plenty of practice," she said, opening the small closet the girls shared and reaching inside. She held out a pale gray cardigan to Grace. "Would you like to borrow this? You know how brutal the wind can be out there."

"But what will you wear?" Grace said, without thinking. Realizing her mistake, she shook her head. Darcy, of course, would not be joining her out in the light, but waiting inside the compound to receive the freshly wounded. Though Darcy could withstand daylight while in the wooden form of *The Nocturne*'s figurehead, she was unable to do so in mortal shape, like any other Nocturnal or, indeed, Vampirate.

Grace took hold of the butter-soft cardigan gratefully and draped it over her shoulders. Darcy nodded, with evident satisfaction. "We can't have our lead healer catching a chill."

"I'm *not* the lead healer," Grace said, following her

roommate out into the corridor. She was not unaware of the feverish talk around the compound of her considerable—and growing—powers; the rumors that her abilities were now only surpassed by Mosh Zu's and that, any night now, she might gain the edge. To Grace, this talk seemed silly at best. She was just doing her job and following Mosh Zu's expert training. Every single member of staff at Sanctuary played his or her part in the healing process: from the tag teams of pirates and Nocturnals who went out in the ambulance boats to rescue the wounded; to those who brought them up the hillside in a convoy of ambulances; to Darcy and the other nurses and the healers like Mosh Zu and herself.

As Grace stepped out into the crisp early morning air, she saw that many of her colleagues were already waiting at the open gates. She felt a sense of pride and belonging as she joined the group. Sanctuary had always been a place of healing, and it had only been natural to extend this with the advent of war and transform the compound into a field hospital for the Nocturnal and pirate alliance.

The mountain air was as chilly as Darcy had predicted and, as Grace watched the first ambulance make its final approach, she hugged her arms to her chest to generate further warmth. Two of her nursing team, Evrim and Noijon, strode over to join her.

As she waited for the ambulance, Grace could sense the buildup of adrenaline that seemed to always flow through her at these times, no matter how tired she felt. She knew that, in part, she was fortifying herself for the arrival of fresh horrors. Over the past four months, Grace had been faced with the grisliest of sights—severed limbs, exposed arteries, and blood. So much blood. This from the pirates they brought here—the ones too badly injured to be taken to the other field hospital, set up in the infirmary at Pirate Academy. But if the pirates were in really bad shape, the sight of the wounded Nocturnals was somehow even more terrifying.

."Here they come, people! Get ready for a busy night!" Mosh Zu's trusted assistant, Dani, strode out to meet the ambulance, clipboard in hand.

The back doors of the ambulance opened and two pirates jumped out, exchanging the briefest of pleasantries with Dani before turning to business. They began lifting a black body bag from the back of the vehicle. The wounded Nocturnals had to be completely covered in order to protect them from even the briefest of exposure to the light.

Reading the tag on the bag, Dani called out to the gaggle of nurses and healers, "Patient severity Silver. Team three, please."

At her words, a healer and two nurses came forward with a stretcher on a trolley. The ambulance crew set the body down upon it and the medics lost no time in trundling it inside.

There were eight levels of severity, each aligned to a precious metal. Silver meant fourth-level wounds: either severely wounded pirates or, as in this case, a lightly wounded Nocturnal.

"Patient severity Osmium," called Dani, as a fresh bag was lifted out from the ambulance. "Team six, please."

"That's me!" said a young woman behind Grace. Stepping forward, she squeezed Grace's arm reassuringly as she and two nurses walked forward to receive the body.

Grace watched her friend Tooshita go. Osmium was the severity level above Silver. The patient was a Nocturnal with some complications. Grace had no doubt that Tooshita and her team would give the patient whatever healing he or she required.

"Patient severity Gold," Dani called now. The word immediately caught the attention of the remaining teams. Gold was the highest level of severity. Usually, these cases went straight to Mosh Zu. He was not out here waiting for his case to be assigned, however. Grace knew that Mosh Zu *could* venture into the light if he chose to. Nonetheless, he always preferred to wait for his patients inside his healing chamber.

"Team one," Dani said. This was indeed Mosh Zu's team. Grace felt a flash of envy as two nurses hastened past her. She was under no illusions, despite the rabid talk, that Mosh Zu's powers outstripped her own. Still, she would like to work on a Gold case—to test herself and see what she could do to help. She watched as Mosh

Zu's team propelled the thick black body bag with its gold zipper past her.

"Patient severity Platinum," Dani called now. "Team seven." Grace felt her adrenaline surge to a new level as she stepped forward, flanked by Evrim and Noijon. Platinum was the next level down. She had almost got her wish. She had been assigned Platinum only a couple of times previously.

"Think you can handle this?" Dani asked, as Grace approached the ambulance's open doors.

"If you think I can," Grace said.

"I *know* you can." Dani's placid face lifted into a smile. Dani's smiles were rare, Grace reflected, but they brought out a hidden light and beauty within her. As Dani turned her attention back to the ambulance, Evrim and Noijon were already wheeling the patient toward the entrance of the compound. Grace hurried alongside to join them.

"Patient is male, Nocturnal," confirmed Noijon as they wheeled the stretcher-trolley down through the Corridor of Lights. "Age indeterminate at this juncture. Main wounds located in the head area..."

Now that they were safely inside, they paused momentarily to unzip the top of the bag. Grace glanced down at the patient's face, what little there was left of it. It—*he*—was not a pretty sight. The eyes were still there, though hazy and distant. They spoke of confusion and fear and pain. Around the eyes, the skin was riven with lesions. Grace was accustomed to this kind of sight, though this was even more severe than usual. When Nocturnals got this bad, the fabric of their skin literally disappeared, leaving deep fissures and giving a vertiginous glimpse into the infinity of darkness below. It had been an early adjustment for Grace, during her time on board *The Nocturne*, to see the deep pits of fire visible in a blood-hungry Vampirate's eyes—or rather a Nocturnal's. But this was nothing compared to the sight of the stripping away of the wounded's being so that you saw through their fragile shell into an oblivion with an insatiable hunger all its own. This Nocturnal patient's eyes seemed to be hovering in a dark void.

There could be no question—he had come close to the very brink of destruction.

Grace tried her best to push away such negative thoughts as his eyes at last met hers, pleadingly. Although he must be in unbearable pain and very likely disoriented, still he seemed to know that it would be up to Grace to bring him back from the brink.

"Don't worry," she said, her voice sounding much calmer than she felt. "We can heal you here. You're in good hands."

"The best hands," agreed Noijon, smiling reassuringly at the patient and nodding at Grace, who rested her hand on the edge of the stretcher to keep pace as she walked.

Suddenly, Grace felt something icy cold grip her. The patient had reached out to clasp her hand. Nocturnals tended to have cold hands at the best of times, but this felt like touching sheet ice. Smiling, though it was an intense effort under the circumstances, Grace refused to let go. The strength of his grip was a good sign. It meant that despite the broken appearance of his outer shell, some vital life force remained deep inside. Whatever horrors he had lately endured, this Nocturnal was not yet ready to give up and let go. Grace gritted her teeth at his ice-cold touch. Every healing procedure was like embarking upon a journey together with the patient. She had the sense that this was going to be a difficult and painful journey for them both.

8

THE NOCTURNAL PATIENT

As her team lifted the patient from his stretcher onto the healing bed, Grace stepped back out of their way. The violet-clad nursing staff moved swiftly, talking in low voices as they began cleaning the worst of the patient's wounds and removing any torn vestiges of clothing. Grace watched, unable to keep her eyes from the gaping splits within the fabric of his skin. She knew the extent of the work to come.

Each of the healing chambers had a small anteroom adjoining it. As the nurses continued their work, Grace retreated inside the small chamber and drew the flimsy curtain. The curtain was little more than a symbolic separation from the other room but it was an important part of her preparation to enter another space—one of stillness and silence. There was a pitcher and basin of water beside her, drawn from the spring closest to the peak of the mountain. Grace began the ritualistic washing of her hands, at the same time practicing a series of rhythmic breaths. She was now so well versed in the healer's art that it did not take her long to prepare.

Grace drew back the curtain and stepped into the main room. Although her eyes were closed, she felt intensely attuned to the needs of the patient. She was aware of the nurses parting before her as she approached the healing bed and reached out her hands.

She began by lightly touching the patient's feet. Through this contact, she could feel the unevenness of his breaths. They were abrupt and jarring, like waves crashing against jagged rocks. The first stage of the healing was to calm the patient and induce more regular breaths—in effect tranquilizing him so that he could enter the optimum state of relaxation during the treatment.

Grace nodded and was instantly aware of ribbons being bound around each of her hands, fastening them to the patient's feet. Their work done, the nurses swiftly stepped back.

Cupping the patient's feet very gently, Grace began to draw out his agitated energy and to replace it with her own sense of calm. He responded well, better than she had expected. There was no doubting the impact of the vicious attack he had been subjected to, but his spirit had remained strong. Grace waited, letting his energy flow and release, flow and release. It did not take long for him to slip into a relaxed slumber.

Satisfied that the patient's breathing was now more regular, Grace nodded again and the nurses stepped forward to unfasten the ribbons. Grace released her touch as fresh ribbons were placed in each of her hands. She let the ends of these new ribbons brush the patient's blood-stained fingers.

"Take hold of these ribbons," she instructed. At her words, the patient reached up and tightly gripped the end of each ribbon.

"That's good," Grace said softly. Drawing the ribbons taut, she began to chant, remembering with ease one of the most powerful healing incantations Mosh Zu had taught her.

The ribbons helped her to connect and communicate with the patient. Grace prepared for the onslaught of his pain as it began releasing into her. It was slow at first but, as she continued to chant, she felt it begin to move. The pain came first as shallow waves, but grew steadily more intense. As each wave of his pain entered her body, Grace grounded herself in readiness for the now familiar body shocks. The ribbons drew out a certain amount of the sting, but, even so, this Nocturnal had been deeply wounded. If he was to make a full recovery, she had to release every last toxin from his body. She chanted more quickly, and more loudly, keeping her fingers firmly connected to the ribbons, though the powerful energy flowing between them threatened to tear them apart.

In moments of reflection, this part of the healing

process made her think of trying to ride a wild horse—the ribbons themselves rather like reins. It drew upon not only all her mental capacities but also her physical strength. But she had become a master of these arts, and, as she continued to chant and finely adjust her breathing, she was able to temporarily absorb and swiftly neutralize the high-voltage current of the Nocturnal's pain.

Eventually, she felt the patient's toxic energy slow. She waited, continuing to observe its ebb and flow. At last, certain that he was settled, she nodded. The nurses came forward and helped ease the patient's hands down onto the table, then removed the ribbons, which fell from Grace's fingers.

Throughout all of this, Grace's eyes had remained closed. Now she stepped around the other side of the bench and held out her hands to receive a fresh ribbon. This she placed over the patient's closed eyes. This would give her a window into the Nocturnal's mind. As she took hold of each end of this shorter ribbon, she waited to make a connection. Sometimes it happened swiftly; at other times, like now, contact proved elusive. Chanting, Grace continued to wait patiently. She was inside the Nocturnal's head but she could see only darkness. She continued to chant.

Very gradually, the darkness began to lift like a thinning mist and Grace discerned shapes coming into focus. She had a unique window into the diverse inner workings of the patients she treated. It was a rare privilege to inhabit another soul's space in this way, if only for a short time.

As the vision became clearer, Grace recognized the familiar corridors of Sanctuary opening up to her. This in itself was not a surprise. It was not uncommon for her patients' visions to commence in this way. On his journey to the healing chamber, the Nocturnal patient had been wheeled first along the Corridor of Lights, next the Corridor of Discards, and then the Corridor of Ribbons. He had been conscious during his journey and, she noted now, had experienced his surroundings in an unusual amount of detail. Holding the ribbon just above his flickering eyelids, she waited for the vision to move on.

As it did, she found that they remained within Sanctuary but were now turning a corner deep inside the main building. Grace stayed anchored in the vision but could not help but be puzzled. The patient had *not* been wheeled through this part of the compound.

She realized that in the vision the Nocturnal was *walking* along the corridor—a corridor that she herself had come to know very well. And now she observed that he was slowing his pace and approaching a door. With complete clarity, the door opened and they moved inside a familiar suite of rooms, commonly known by the healers as "the lab." Moving past a closed doorway, they entered the main room, which was dominated by a large bench, its counter smooth and uneven with age and use. Behind the central counter were floor-to-ceiling shelves groaning with jars of herbs, roots, seeds, and other items used to create a healer's many potions and medicaments. There was no longer any doubt in Grace's mind. For the patient to picture this scene so well, he must have been here before. Probably more than once.

The angle of the vision shifted, and the door once more came into view as someone else stepped inside the chamber. Grace continued to breathe rhythmically and chant calmly as she watched her younger self enter the room. Now, she knew for certain the patient's identity.

She let go of the ribbon and, as the nurse stepped forward to remove it, Grace opened her eyes. She stared at the upside-down head before her. She was gratified to note that as a result of her healing, his face was now patched together again. Where there had been fissures, now there was flesh, and the fibers of his skin were already beginning to knit themselves back together. Despite the wounds, despite the fact that his face was the wrong way up, she knew she had seen this face many times before.

"Olivier," she said softly. "Welcome back to Sanctuary."

The Nocturnal's eyes were closed, and he appeared to be in a deep state of relaxation and recovery. Nevertheless, as Grace looked down upon him, she was convinced she saw his cracked lips form the crescent of a smile.

She nodded silently to Noijon and reached out her hand once more. Understanding that Grace wanted the ribbon back, he passed it to her. She laid it across Olivier's eyes again and took hold of the two ends. Instantly, she was back in the lab, watching her younger self exit the room. For a moment afterward, everything was still. Then Olivier crouched down under the main counter. His hand reached out as if tracing the lines and knots on the wooden panel below. Then his fingers came to a rest and he pressed the panel gently. A section of wood moved and a small opening appeared under the bench. Olivier reached in his hand and withdrew a compact, rectangular object. As it came into the light, Grace saw that it was a book, bound in dark blue cloth. At first it seemed to her that the cloth binding was unadorned, but then gold lettering began to appear and she was able to read the book's title: *The Way of the Dhampir*. Grace frowned. Why would Olivier have such a book? And why, when he had lately been at the very brink of oblivion, was this little book right there at the forefront of his mind?

9

DEPUTIES

"Enter!" called Cheng Li, pouring a second bowl of tea as Jasmine shut tight the door behind her and walked over to sit opposite the captain.

"It's a beautiful day, isn't it?" said Cheng Li, glancing out the porthole.

Jasmine nodded perfunctorily, but Cheng Li knew her deputy well enough to realize that her mind was elsewhere.

"I still can't believe the news about Jack Fallico," Jasmine said.

Cheng Li nodded grimly. "When he failed to turn up at the Council of War, I think we knew to expect the worst."

"I gather Lola led the attack," Jasmine said. "The casualties were terrible. The Nocturnal aide was in an especially bad way when they found him."

"Well," Cheng Li said, glancing at her clock, "he should have arrived at Sanctuary by now. If anyone can bring him back, it's Mosh Zu and his team."

After this discussion, it was a relief for them both to turn their attention to the quotidian business of procedures and personnel. Cheng Li had no doubt that her exceedingly capable deputy had everything completely under control. Some had thought it a bold move to appoint such a young deputy as Jasmine. How wrong they had been proved. Like Cheng Li herself, Jasmine had been a straight-A student at Pirate Academy, but, since taking to the oceans for real, she had seamlessly integrated the lessons she'd learned during her ten years at the academy with a fresh vision, exceptional people skills, and a mind sharper than any of the weaponry in *The Tiger*'s onboard armory.

"We're running low on swords again," Jasmine informed the captain now. "I've made up a fresh order for Master Yin." She passed the list over to Cheng Li to approve.

"Are we covered if we proceed with the proposed attack on *The Diablo*?" Cheng Li inquired.

"Yes," said Jasmine. "But we shouldn't lose time getting this order under way. Not the way things are gathering pace now."

Cheng Li scanned Jasmine's immaculate handwriting and precise instructions, then glanced up again. "This all looks in excellent order to me. Let's send Bo Yin to collect the new weaponry. Master Yin will be glad of the chance to see his pirate daughter and hear all she has achieved in such a short time span."

Jasmine smiled and nodded. "I was going to suggest the very same thing. It will do Bo good to see her home and father again."

Her report delivered, Jasmine began to collect her various papers. She never presumed to impose on her commander's precious time. But, on this occasion, the captain was in no rush.

"And how are *you*, Jasmine?" Cheng Li inquired now, in a deceptively casual tone.

"Fine," Jasmine replied automatically. As the two young women's eyes met, the lie was exposed.

"You are fulfilling your role brilliantly," Cheng Li said. "I want you to know how impressed I am. The way you have held things together since Jacoby's disappearance has been truly inspiring. We all know how close you two were."

Jasmine frowned. "I think we should stop calling it a 'disappearance' and start admitting that Jacoby is dead," she said. "He's never coming back, and, if we're to have any hope of moving on with our own lives, we have to accept that."

"That's very brave of you," Cheng Li said, noting that it was highly unusual for Jasmine to let her guard down in this way. "In that case, we ought to plan some kind of memorial service for Jacoby."

"No!" Jasmine exclaimed loudly. Then she resumed in a more controlled voice, "Well, maybe. I don't know."

Jasmine's volley of responses was further proof to Cheng Li of the conflict raging within her deputy's mind and heart. She smiled reassuringly. "Why don't you give it some thought? There's no rush."

"I will," Jasmine said with a nod.

"I'll leave you to your work, Deputy Peacock," said Cheng Li.

Jasmine collected her things and headed for the door. Cheng Li strode forward to open it for her. "Remember," she said, "it's always easier to fight the demons out there than the ones in here." She tapped the crown of her own head.

"I don't have any demons," Jasmine said.

"Yes, you do," Cheng Li replied. "We all do. And the more we try to deny them, the bigger and more dangerous they grow." Her voice became more businesslike. "Keep me posted on any changes to *The Diablo*'s position."

Jasmine nodded. "I will, Captain."

Looking over Jasmine's shoulder, Cheng Li could see that Connor was already making his way along the corridor toward them—ready for his own meeting with the captain. Cheng Li turned around discreetly and stepped back inside her cabin. She hovered just inside the doorway, listening carefully to the exchange between her two deputies.

"Hi," said Jasmine.

"Hey," answered Connor. "How are you?"

"Okay," she said, her voice seeming to suggest the very

opposite. Then, "Connor, I really need to talk to you. We spend all day racing around this ship, but we never get the chance to talk to each other—not properly."

There was a pause, then a sigh. "I know," he said. "I feel the same. Let's try to make some time tonight, okay?"

"Yes," she said, more brightly. "I won't keep you from your meeting. See you later!"

Their words were prosaic enough, but Cheng Li knew that the two of them were embroiled in a close and often challenging relationship. She suspected that had Jacoby Blunt still been around, Jasmine would have broken up with her long-term boyfriend and declared her true feelings for Connor. As it was, with Jacoby's situation still a mystery, his presence lingered like a restless ghost.

Cheng Li walked soundlessly back across her cabin and sat down once more at her conference table, ready to greet Connor.

Between sips of mango juice, Connor confidently led Cheng Li through all his areas of responsibility. Since Jacoby's disappearance, Cheng Li had made yet another daring decision in appointing Connor as her joint deputy. He lacked the formal training from which she, Jasmine, and Jacoby had benefited at the academy. Nonetheless, Connor possessed a rare instinctive gift for piracy, which was all the more startling given how new he was to this world. It was less than twelve months since Cheng Li herself had rescued him from certain death in the ocean.

Now he was utterly changed; the transformation from shipwrecked orphan to full-fledged pirate was complete.

He was, she reflected as she listened to him now, something of a throwback to the old days of piracy. Another Molucco? The thought crossed her mind. *No*, she thought. *No, we've caught him in time to prevent that.*

One of Connor's greatest gifts was the goodwill he inspired in almost all those around him. This had first struck Cheng Li through the strong bonds he had formed with his crewmates. Lately, she had found a new way to harness this gift of Connor's. Since the beginning of war, Cheng Li was no longer merely captain of one ship but overseer of a further twelve. And it was Connor who acted as the chief point of liaison with the other twelve captains.

"Captain Gresham's crew was particularly badly hit in the last battle," Connor told her now. "Over thirty of them are still in recovery in the field hospital at Pirate Academy. I've talked direct to Nurse Carmichael and she says she won't release them for at least another week." He smiled. "Actually, I negotiated her down from ten days."

Cheng Li returned his smile. "So we're caught between the Scylla of Christabel Carmichael and the Charybdis that is Wilberforce Gresham. What do you suggest?"

"I thought we could lend Captain Gresham some crew members from the other ships until Nurse Carmichael gives his lot the all clear." Cheng Li nodded approvingly as Connor continued. "I was going to suggest offering ten of our own pirates and five each from four other ships in the fleet, but, with our plans for *The Diablo*, I think we should keep our crew intact for now. I've prepared a transfer list for you to approve when the time comes." He passed the document across to her.

Captain Gresham's dilemma resolved, there were only a couple more items on Connor's list. As he finished talking, Cheng Li leaned back in her chair. "Before you go, there's one more thing to discuss," she said.

"Sure," he said, looking up from his sheaf of papers. "Shoot!"

"Molucco's will," Cheng Li began.

In response, Connor held up his hand. "I'm sorry you had to hear about my legacy from somebody else. But really, there's nothing to talk about," he said. "It doesn't change anything."

Cheng Li toyed with her fountain pen. "It will change everything, Connor. And the more you push it away and ignore it, the more of a tidal wave will hit."

"All right," Connor said, barely reining in his impatience. "Then I'll just give the money back to the Wrathes. I'm sure they won't say no."

Cheng Li shook her head. "It doesn't work like that. There's Federation revenue and taxes to deal with, for one thing."

Connor frowned, annoyed that there seemed to be no way out of this conversation. "Okay then," he said. "I'll donate it all to the Federation itself. For the war effort."

Cheng Li smiled. "That's a noble thought, Connor, but please don't be rash. Molucco's bequest has the power to change your life."

"I still don't know why he gave it to me," Connor said. "We were enemies when he died. He said so himself."

Cheng Li gritted her teeth. She'd done plenty of cleaning up on behalf of Molucco Wrathe when he was alive and she had been his deputy. It was galling, to say the least, to find herself in the very same position six months after his death. But Connor had become too important to her for her to let this go without a fight.

"Try not to let your thoughts of Molucco or of the rift between the two of you cloud your thinking about this incredible gift. You were an orphan with nothing but the rags on your back when we met. Now you have the chance to do whatever you want with your life."

Cheng Li could tell that her words had hit home.

Connor sat staring at her, silently, for a time. Then he shook his head. "I appreciate what you've said. I mean it. But, Captain, you—alone of everyone on this ship—know the truth. You alone know who and what I really am. And no amount of money on this blue earth can change that."

So, thought Cheng Li, *at last we come to the heart of this.* "I know that you are still coming to terms with being a dhampir," she said. "But it isn't in any way impeding you from being a valuable member of my crew or of playing a central role within this conflict." She paused. "Indeed, given that we are now in strategic alliance with the

Nocturnals, you might say that it's a positive advantage that my joint second-in-command is immortal."

Connor shook his head. "You and I both know that this alliance is only born out of pragmatism. Once the threat of Sidorio is eliminated, the old dividing lines will soon reemerge."

Cheng Li frowned. "You underestimate what a revolution in thinking there has been at the heart of the pirate world. And, in so many ways, you and your sister are responsible for it. Before you and Grace came onto the scene, all we knew of the Vampirates was that old shanty and a slew of bogeyman stories. We were guilty of lazy thinking. But as the cracks began to emerge in the Vampirate world, with your father's ... with Sidorio's rebellion and his allegiance to Lola Lockwood, well, we've seen a truer picture not only of the evil that stalks the oceans but of the goodness, too. Over the past six months, I have come to know Obsidian Darke as a trusted ally. I won't lie to you—he can be frustrating as all hell to work with— but I have no doubt whatsoever that he is a good man."

Connor shook his head once more, pushing back his chair. "He isn't a man," he said. "Nor is his deputy, my sister's great love, Lorcan Furey. And nor am I. We're none of us men. We're monsters, demons!" Tears welled in his emerald green eyes.

Cheng Li rose calmly from her own chair. "You are *all* men," she said. "Whatever else you may or may not be, you are all good men."

At these words, to her surprise, Connor leaned toward her. Then, to her even greater surprise, she found herself opening up her arms and drawing her deputy into a hug. As her arms gripped his shuddering body, she realized that a terrible tension had been building within him. "Let it out," she found herself saying. "Connor, let it all out."

"I'm sorry," he said, drawing back from her arms.

"Here," she said, passing him a handkerchief. "Dry your eyes."

"Thanks."

Cheng Li watched him, then caught his attention once more. "Connor," she said softly, "you *are* taking that berry tea that Grace sends over, aren't you?"

He nodded.

"Good. Because Obsidian assured me that it was—"

"I'm taking it," he said. "Every night. Just like Obsidian and Grace said to."

Cheng Li nodded. She had no desire to come across as any more maternal than she had already. "Keep taking the tea," she said. "And keep up the excellent work!" Her eyes brightened. "Not one of us knows quite what this voyage has in store for us, but I happen to think that life would be pretty boring if we did."

Connor finally cracked a grin. "Right now, I could handle a big bowl of boring," he said, offering her back the now-sodden handkerchief.

Cheng Li wrinkled her nose. "You can keep it." She glanced once more at her clock. "Well, I think we're both up to date. Do you want to go and ask Cate to join me? We've got an attack to plan."

Bo Yin was just about to finish her shift in the crow's nest. As she glanced below once more, she saw a lanky figure jump up onto the deck of *The Tiger*. She scanned the deck to call for reinforcements but saw, to her horror, that it was empty. She wanted to cry out—*There's a war going on, people!*—but she kept her cool. She was just going to have to deal with this situation herself. Stealthily, she climbed to the edge of the crow's nest. Then, letting out a piercing war cry, she somersaulted down to the deck, landing perfectly on her toes, with her sword outstretched toward the intruder.

The trespasser—a tall teenage boy—laughed. "So it's true what they say about you lot. Slash first and ask questions later."

Bo Yin's eyes narrowed. "You!" she said.

"That's right, pookachoo," he said. "Me! I'm a bit of a legend in pirating circles. The Next Big Thing! I'm not surprised you've heard all about me."

Bo Yin nodded. "Nothing good, though," she said, unable to suppress a smile.

"Cheeky!" Moonshine grinned back at her. "What's your name?"

"I'm Bo Yin," she said. "You may have heard of my father. *He* is a genuine legend in pirating circles."

"Indeed he is." Moonshine nodded, clearly impressed. "For my fifth birthday, my dad took me to Lantao to watch your dad make me my first sword. It was the best birthday gift ever."

"You've been to my father's workshop?" Bo said, somewhat disconcerted.

Moonshine nodded. "Yes, I have." He smirked. "Hey, I remember this crazy little kid racing about all over the place, wanting to play-fight with me. That wasn't you, was it?"

"Maybe." Bo blushed. "I don't remember."

Moonshine's eyes bore into hers. "Well, Bo Yin, it's nice to catch up with you after all these years. Now, will you spare me the cutlass so I can beg an audience with your esteemed leader? Or should we have a duel right here and now?"

"So!" exclaimed Moonshine, prowling around Cheng Li's cabin. "This is the nerve center of the Alliance war effort."

Cheng Li folded her arms and nodded. "Pretty much," she said.

Moonshine seemed utterly transfixed by the many charts, crew lists, and diagrams pinned to the wall. Cheng

Li studied him, thinking that despite his latest growth spurt, he seemed like an excitable kid feverishly exploring a playroom of new and amazing toys.

"Isn't it risky to keep information like this on display?" Moonshine asked. "What if one of those scumbag Vamps managed to force its way in here?"

Cheng Li arched an eyebrow. "I hardly think that crew lists and navigation charts, though vital to us, are sensitive documents. Rest assured, the really important stuff is kept in my safe."

Moonshine's eyes bulged with interest. "And where's that?" he asked.

"Need-to-know basis," said Cheng Li with a smile.

Moonshine scanned the room. "My guess is behind the family portrait," he said, gazing at the portrait of Chang Ko Li, Cheng Li's father, which hung above the captain's desk. It was clear that his interest lay less in the picture itself and more in the possibilities that lay behind it. Cheng Li remained insouciant though he had guessed correctly. Shrugging, Moonshine turned away, his attention soon alighting elsewhere. "And what's *this*?"

Moonshine had walked over to a round diorama. The central display was made of turquoise glass and bordered by a silver rail. The turquoise glass was rippled, evidently to represent the ocean. Leaning against the silver rail to scrutinize the display more closely, Moonshine saw that through the glass ran red lines of latitude and longitude. The undulating glass ocean was covered with small models of ships—roughly half of them red; the other half blue.

Cheng Li came over to join him. "This," she said, "shows to our best knowledge the latest recorded positions of all the key Alliance and Vampirate vessels. Ours are the blue ones; theirs, for reasons I'm sure you can fathom, are red."

Moonshine let out a breath and gazed at the display as if it were the best toy ever. "You mean you can pinpoint exactly where *The Diablo* is right now?"

Cheng Li nodded. "Look for a red ship numbered five." She passed him a miniature telescope. "This might be useful," she said.

As Moonshine stared through the eyepiece, he felt his spine begin to tingle as each of the blue and red ships came to life, charting their urgent paths across the swelling ocean. He felt his heart begin to race. This moving multitude of vessels was both terrifying and thrilling; an epic conflict and here he was, right at the epicenter of it.

"Any joy?" Cheng Li asked.

"What? Oh, er, no." Moonshine brought his excitement under control. The ships ceased their motion, becoming painted models once more. He scanned their tiny sails for the all-important number. At last, he saw it.

"There she is!" he cried. He removed the telescope from his eye and used the small instrument to point out the model to Cheng Li.

"Ah, yes," she said. "Well spotted!"

Moonshine frowned. "She's red."

"Of course," Cheng Li said. "We have the ships dipped in color when they change possession from one side to the other."

"And she's surrounded by a lot of other red ships," Moonshine observed.

Cheng Li nodded. "Yes. That's to be expected."

Moonshine spoke through gritted teeth. "I hope you have some blue paint ready, because you're going to be in need of it very soon."

Cheng Li smiled. "Trust me, Captain Wrathe, we have a truckload of blue paint. Our every waking breath is directed toward painting every last ship on this ocean bright blue."

It was Moonshine's turn to smile. "I'm still getting used to being called Captain!"

Cheng Li nodded. "It's your official rank now. The fact that you are not currently in possession of a ship has no bearing on that."

Letting go of the silver rail, Moonshine drew himself up to his full height, squarely facing Cheng Li. "Have you thought any more about my proposal?" he asked. "Will you really help me put a team together to take back *The Diablo*?"

For a time, Cheng Li's intense almond-shaped eyes coolly appraised Moonshine Wrathe, the newest captain in the Federation. There were *so* many reasons to decline his proposal, yet Cheng Li felt something in her gut that she couldn't quite explain. She found herself nodding once more. "Yes," she said. "I'll help you, Captain Wrathe."

"That's awesome, Captain Li!" Moonshine punched the air. "This calls for a drink! I heard you have your own bar in here. Why don't I whip us up a couple of Coraltinis to celebrate?"

Cheng Li smiled softly. "I suggest we hold off on the celebrations until *The Diablo* is back under Alliance command. For now, I think some hot seaweed tea would be more appropriate." She gestured toward her conference table. "Take a seat."

Moonshine obediently pulled out a chair while Cheng Li poured two bowls of the pungent tea. As she did so, there was a knock at the door.

"Enter!" Cheng Li called, without glancing up.

The door opened and Connor and Jasmine strode into the room, closely followed by Cate. Bo Yin lingered behind the others, in the doorway.

"Right on time," Cheng Li said with satisfaction, then watched as, to her surprise, Lorcan Furey followed the others into her cabin. She smiled as he approached her. He had lately taken to wearing a steel-gray uniform, which made his blue eyes shine all the more brightly. "Commander Furey," she said, struggling as she always did in his presence to retain her composure. "How good to see you again."

Lorcan nodded, somewhat formally, but smiled warmly back at his ally. "You, too, Captain Li. I came over to discuss some strategy matters with Cate. I gather my visit may have proved opportune timing."

Cheng Li nodded. "Most opportune," she said. Reluctantly drawing her eyes away from him, she gestured around the table. "Please take a seat, everyone." She glanced over to the doorway. "You, too, Bo Yin! Come and join us."

Clearly thrilled to be included, Bo stepped inside and shut the twin panel doors of the captain's cabin behind her. As she made her way to take her seat beside the others at the captain's table, she noticed that Moonshine Wrathe was staring at her. Without the others noticing, he gave her a cheeky wink. She turned away, blushing furiously.

"Well now," Cheng Li said, "I think you all know Moonshine Wrathe, except perhaps for you, Commander Furey?"

Lorcan smiled. "It's true we haven't been formally introduced." He stood up and extended his hand toward Moonshine. Moonshine rose to his feet and they shook hands.

"Commander Furey is one of the most senior-ranking Nocturnals within the Alliance," said Cheng Li. "He is joint director of military strategy with Cate."

Moonshine gave the Alliance salute to Lorcan. "It's a pleasure to meet you, Commander Furey."

Lorcan returned the gesture. "You, too, Captain Wrathe."

As the two young men sat down, Cheng Li addressed her comrades once more. "As you know, Moonshine has come up with an intriguing proposition, and I want to garner your opinions on it." She turned to Jasmine. "If we have any chance of success, the tracking team needs to focus its attention on if and when *The Diablo* breaks from the Vampirate fleet."

Jasmine nodded. "Already on it."

"But also," Cheng Li added, "if any Vampirate ships start moving in a similar direction once our plans are under way"—she turned from Jasmine to address the rest of the group—"Cate and I have listed the personnel who will be involved—and you all have a key role to play during the attack. That is, except Commander Furey. Cate will commence training drills from tomorrow morning." Cheng Li now locked eyes with Lorcan's baby blues. "Our preferred hour of attack is 0600 hours, Commander Furey. What do you think?"

Lorcan nodded. "Yes, at that point the Vampirates' recovery time will be at its slowest. They will return to full strength, but this will give you your best chance to infiltrate the lower decks with minimal casualties to the Alliance."

"Provided nothing goes wrong!" Jasmine said.

Lorcan nodded once more. "Yes, provided nothing goes wrong, Deputy Peacock. But I have some suggestions of what to look out for. Stealth is going to be of the utmost importance."

As the others started to leave, Cheng Li rose from the table and approached her desk. There was plenty of work waiting for her there and no time like the present to get stuck in.

Bo Yin strode over to her. "Thank you for including me in the meeting tonight, Captain Li."

"You're very welcome, Bo," Cheng Li said, shuffling through her papers. "You should know that you have fast become an invaluable member of this team."

"Thank you," Bo said, swelling with pride. "Can I do anything further for you? Perhaps you'd like a fresh pot of tea?"

"No," Cheng Li said, "no, you go and get some rest. You've done more than your share today."

Bo Yin turned and followed her comrades out into the corridor. Moonshine Wrathe still lingered in the captain's cabin and Bo left the doors slightly ajar for him.

"I'll be going then," Moonshine said.

"Oh, yes." Cheng Li glanced up, removing her glasses. "How silly of me. For a moment there, I forgot you weren't one of my crew!"

Moonshine smiled. "That's good, I think."

Cheng Li shrugged.

"I'd like to work closely with you," Moonshine said. "And I thought perhaps we could find a way to share Cate—assuming she was interested."

Cheng Li folded her glasses contemplatively. "Cate is perfectly capable of making her own decisions about her future."

"But you're her captain," Moonshine said. "And I know that she has this vital role in military strategy. But if we put our heads together, I'm sure we could find a creative solution to this."

Cheng Li smiled. "Don't push your luck, Captain Wrathe. I think you got what you came for today. Let's leave it there for now. When you have a ship under your command, we can address the issue of who's going to be your deputy."

"Fair enough," Moonshine said. Then, grinning playfully, he added, "If Cate proves unwilling, perhaps your feisty little Bo Yin could take up the post?"

Cheng Li unfolded her spectacles, slipping them back over her nose, and bowed her head to resume her business. "Good night, Captain Wrathe," she said, her tone leaving him in no doubt whatsoever that he had been dismissed.

—~~—

Later that same night, a lone figure stepped ashore at the Blood Tavern. He entered the vestibule and approached Lilith's dome.

"Back again?" Lilith said, looking at the young man curiously. "You're a thirsty lad...third night on the trot, isn't it?"

The young customer wasn't keen to be engaged in conversation. "I'd like a pint, please," he said, pushing his money across the counter.

Lilith's hand clamped down on the notes. "I've been trying to place your face these past few nights. Didn't you first come in here months back with a friend of yours?"

Connor shook his head. "You must be thinking of some other guy," he said.

"Wait a mo! You wanted blood for him back then, not yourself. Said you were a pirate. Your name was... oh, it's on the tip of my tongue...Connor! That's it— Connor..."

"Smith!" Connor said. "Connor Smith is my name."

"Really?" Lilith arched an eyebrow.

"Which room?" Connor interrupted, anxious to bring this conversation to a close as the shame crept up on him again.

"Room Seven," Lilith said.

"Thanks." Connor immediately made for the velvet-covered doorway. He had no desire to linger here, where he might be spotted or, worse, run into someone he knew. He slipped through the doorway, making his way toward Room Seven. He knocked, then took a deep breath and stepped inside.

10

MIND GAMES

It was late in the afternoon when, having performed two other healings and managed to grab the briefest of cat-naps, Grace returned to the ward to check up on the patient. She coughed discreetly to make her presence known, her hand resting on the muslin curtain that surrounded the patient's bed.

"Come inside my cocoon," called a voice she instantly recognized, though it was hoarse from all he had lately endured.

Grace slipped around the curtain and found Olivier sitting up in bed. His face looked markedly different now to when he had been brought in. The deep fissures that had opened up the path to oblivion were now merely wounds. His flesh had patched itself together, and he looked, more or less, as she had remembered him from their former encounters. It was a truly remarkable transition. Grace knew that in large part this metamorphosis was due to her expert healing. But the healing process was a joint journey undertaken by patient and healer, and Olivier had played his part in this impressive recovery. There was a long road ahead, but now at least he was strong enough to answer some of the questions that had been bugging her.

"What happened to you?" Grace asked.

His mouth opened but he hesitated.

Grace smiled gently. "There's no need to tell me if it's too painful."

He shook his head. "It's not that. It was entirely predictable, really. War is brutal, isn't it? And this war is rewriting the book on brutality, wouldn't you say?"

She nodded. The cases she had dealt with every single night and day since the outbreak of war were testament to the truth of his words. "But I don't understand," Grace said. "When I last saw you, you were heading off with Sidorio's crew. How did you end up here? I assume it *was* the Vampirates who did this to you—not our own forces?"

"It was indeed the Vampirates," Olivier acknowledged bitterly. "You're right—I did flee from here in the company of Sidorio. I've always been drawn to power. And as great as Mosh Zu's powers were...*are*...I sensed that Sidorio's would prove even greater." As he spoke Sidorio's name, Olivier's eyes met her own. She wondered if he knew the true nature of her relationship with Sidorio. She hoped not, but suspected that he might.

"Of course," Olivier continued, "you might say that my assessment of the situation was correct—that Sidorio's powers will ultimately prove unstoppable."

Grace frowned. "That's a matter of opinion. But I still don't understand—if you were part of Sidorio's crew, why would the Vampirates attack you?"

Olivier shook his head sadly. "Grace, let me share with you what I've learned about powerful people. They have a habit of stepping on others in order to achieve the giddy heights. Sidorio used me to help instill unrest here at Sanctuary, but, once that was accomplished, he didn't have sufficient vision to find further use for me." There was an awkward pause between them. Grace found herself thinking about the book she had glimpsed in Olivier's vision: *The Way of the Dhampir*. Why would Olivier have had it? Could he be a dhampir himself? If so, couldn't he have better protected himself from attack? And if he wasn't a dhampir, then why was he so interested in them? Did he know about her and Connor? Had he known about them before they had found out the truth for themselves? She must not forget that Olivier had been extremely close to Mosh Zu and therefore privy to many closely guarded secrets. All of which made his ultimate betrayal so explosive.

The thought flashed across her brain again. Could Olivier be a dhampir? He had always claimed parity with Grace during their previous encounters, on the basis that they were neither Vampirates nor donors but "in-betweens." Had that been his way of saying that they were both dhampirs? She hadn't even known what a dhampir was back then. How he would have loved being a step ahead of her. Always a step ahead.

She was aware of his eyes upon her. They were so much sharper now than when he had arrived to be healed. Now they were like needles, just as before. She took a breath. She wouldn't let him intimidate her. She had come a long way since their last meetings. She met his gaze. Had he somehow managed to key into her thoughts? If he was a dhampir, he might well be capable of that. But no, when he resumed speaking, it seemed that he had been brooding further—not on her but her father.

"Sidorio isn't what you'd call a forward-thinker. I had so much to offer him." Olivier smiled pointedly. "So much knowledge and skill to share. But he was only able to focus on the two *boys* he had already made his deputies— Stukeley and Desperado." He spat their names as if expelling a lump of gristle. Grace could tell there was no love lost between the three of them.

"So," Olivier continued, "having lured me away from this place, Sidorio cut me adrift. I found myself without portfolio, as it were." Again, his dark eyes met Grace's. "I couldn't very well come back and beg Mosh Zu for forgiveness."

"You should have come back," Grace said. "Mosh Zu would have forgiven you."

Olivier shook his head. "You're wrong, Grace. I've known

him a lot longer than you. And I know full well that, once he is crossed, mercy is not one of his finer qualities."

Though it galled her to admit it, Olivier spoke the truth. But this was not a line of discussion Grace was keen to pursue.

"So where did you go?" she asked.

"I disappeared for a time," Olivier said. "To lick my wounds." He lifted his bandaged arms. "Not that my wounds then compared to these! I watched from the shadows as the changes coursed through the Vampirate world, and it gradually fractured into one of Vampirates and Nocturnals. When war came, I joined up like all good Nocturnals."

Grace was surprised by this. "You're a Nocturnal?" she said.

"Why, yes," Olivier said. "Do try to keep up, Grace. I told you before. When I left with Sidorio, he sired me."

"No," she said, firmly. "You didn't tell me that."

"Did I not?" He shook his head, then shrugged. "Fancy that. Well, I suppose I'm not thinking as clearly as I might. Understandable, perhaps, under the circumstances."

Grace nodded but reflected that Olivier was thinking very clearly indeed. She was fairly confident he was playing mind games with her. Did he want her to think he was a dhampir, or had she framed that thought for herself? Whichever, it seemed she now had her answer—he was a Vampirate, converted by Sidorio, even though he had referred to himself as a Nocturnal.

"You know, of course," Olivier resumed, "how the Alliance has installed a Nocturnal on every pirate vessel, to work with the pirate crew on attack strategy and so forth."

Grace nodded once more. This had been Lorcan's idea—one born out of the effectiveness of his own joining of forces with Cate.

"Well," Olivier continued, "there you have it. I was assigned to Jack Fallico, captain of *The Evening Star*. And there I stayed, playing my part, until Lola Lockwood and her vile acolytes decided to pay us an unexpected call. They made short work of the crew and the captain. As for me, well, I hardly think I need furnish you with the details."

"No." Grace found herself shuddering at the brutality of Lola and her crew. Worse still was the thought of how close she herself had come to being one of their pack.

"I'm bored with all this talk of me and my dreary journey," Olivier said now, though he never seemed bored when talking about himself. "Much more interesting to talk about you and how you've changed beyond all recognition from that wide-eyed little girl I led across the mountain, foraging for berries."

"It wasn't that long ago," Grace said. "A few months at most."

"It was a world ago, Grace," Olivier said. "And I speak as an immortal when I say that. Time passes rather differently for us."

"I know," she said in an impassioned voice, once more irritated by his superior tone. She realized he was staring at her curiously now. "I know," she said, rather more gently. "I've been around Nocturnals and Vampirates for some time myself."

"Indeed," Olivier acknowledged. "You know, I was a little jealous of you when you first arrived here."

"Yes, I realized that," she said.

"In some ways, it's your fault that I betrayed Mosh Zu. I was always his favorite before you arrived on the scene."

Grace was surprised by his candor but infuriated by his attempt to implicate her in his rebellion.

"You said we were 'in-betweens,'" she reminded him. "You always implied we had a particular bond."

He looked at her with obvious disdain. "Oh, I tried to bond with you, because those were my instructions. But, really, I had my own work to do and—to be honest—it was so tiresome having to stop and explain everything to you."

Grace bit back her anger. This was not at all how she remembered their time together.

Olivier nodded. "Remember when I showed you how to make the elder salve for your ailing boyfriend?"

She nodded.

"And look at you now. I expect you could knock up a vat of the stuff in your sleep." Before Grace could think of an appropriate response, Olivier continued. "I'm impressed, Grace. It's clear that Mosh Zu's faith in you was more than justified, though I don't say that easily. You do have the makings of a healer."

Grace had allowed most of his barbs to wash over her, but she had too much pride to let this one pass. "I *am* a healer," she said, fixing him with her eyes. "*I* healed *you.* When the ambulances arrive here, all patients are classified according to the severity of their wounds. You were a Platinum case — the second-most-severe kind. That's why they assigned *me* and *my* team to treat you. Otherwise, well..."

Olivier nodded. "Yes, yes, I've heard the feverish whispers that you are Mosh Zu's second-in-command these days. And I'm grateful to you, I truly am."

This paltry offering was clearly as close as he would come to thanking her. He had turned away from her. His hand stretched toward the muslin drapes around his bed. He pushed back one of them and peered out at the ward. Holding the curtain open, Olivier turned back to face Grace. "This is quite a setup you have here. Tell me, how many patients do you treat each night?"

Grace shrugged. "It varies," she said. "Last night was particularly busy — though we've had worse. Sometimes the bell just keeps going and we don't get much rest between arrivals."

Olivier nodded and looked once more through the gap in the curtain before letting it drop. "Does Mosh Zu know that I'm here?" he asked.

Grace paused. "Perhaps, though I haven't seen him

myself since I healed you. As I said, it's been a busy night and day and we've all had a lot to contend with." She paused. "But, when I see him later, I'll be sure to tell him."

Olivier shrugged. "As you wish. Just don't get your hopes up for a bedside reunion."

Grace couldn't help but smile. Olivier was so eaten up with bitterness, and more egocentric than ever. "We're in the middle of a war, Olivier. I'm just here doing a job. You were brought to me on a slab, on the verge of oblivion. I caught you and brought you back. You must rest now, and, in a matter of nights, you should be well enough to go on your way." She smiled, sensing that at last she had gained the upper hand. "And now, if you'll excuse me, I must check on my other patients."

Olivier nodded. "I've taken up enough of your precious time, I know. Besides, I'm tired now. It was intriguing to catch up with you, but, as you say, I need my rest." With that, he closed his eyes and turned his bandaged head to the wall.

Grace's eyes lingered on him for a moment. Then she turned to make her exit from his stifling cocoon. As her hand reached out to the muslin, she couldn't shake the feeling that he had somehow engineered this return to Sanctuary. To have done so, he would have had to inflict those injuries upon himself or, more likely, had others do so. It seemed inconceivable, but where a mercenary like Olivier was concerned, you just couldn't apply normal rules.

What could his reasons be for undergoing such physical punishment? Could he still be working for Sidorio, despite his story to the contrary? Was he some kind of spy?

As she strode through the center of the ward, her path bordered on either side by other cocoons of white muslin, Grace found herself back inside Olivier's vision. Once more she saw him waiting for her to depart, then crouching down and reaching for that book. Could it be that that slim, cloth-bound volume was still here at Sanctuary, hidden under the counter on which she and her fellow healers created their healing potions? Had Olivier endured all this to come back and reclaim the book? If so, it must be extraordinarily powerful. She couldn't let it fall into the wrong hands.

11

CAMP DECIMATION

VAMPIRATES' TRAINING CAMP, ATAFUTURA ATOLL

Sidorio stood at the edge of the atoll, watching the jewel-like surface of the ocean. He could feel the burning heat close around him. The night was warm, and the whole atoll had been ringed with flaming torches to facilitate the night's training. As he and Lola had sailed in on *The Vagabond*—the last of the ships to drop anchor around the atoll—it had seemed to him that the ocean itself was on fire. The sight had pleased him—a portent of the deepening conflict. Once, thanks to the scaremongering of others, he had been afraid of fire. Now he knew that, like so much else, it was nothing to be afraid of. He was beginning to realize there was nothing he could not overcome if he put his mind to it. Perhaps one day soon he would break the ultimate taboo and walk out proudly into the daylight. At last, after so much wasted time, he felt he was finally coming to understand what being immortal really meant. That he felt these things, he knew, was all thanks to one extraordinary person.

He could see her now, still some way away, walking toward him across the surface of the water. Burnished by a strip of moonlight, it appeared as if the ocean itself had rolled out a golden carpet for Lola to walk to shore upon. As she strode nearer, Sidorio smiled, seeing her familiar black-heart tattoo and the beauty spot at the side of her mouth as if for the first time. Her face was as luminous as the moon. Every time he gazed upon her, it felt like a miracle. Or, rather, two miracles: the first to have found her at all; the second to have succeeded in bringing her back from the void.

Lola was followed by two of her closest aides, Nathalie and Jacqueline. Each was a rare beauty, but Sidorio only had eyes for his extraordinary wife. She was looking lovelier than ever tonight, in a flowing gown in many shades of blue. As she stepped from the water onto the sand, it seemed as if she had fashioned her clothes from the ocean waters themselves. She stood there for a moment, catching her breath after such an intense effort of showmanship, and smiled to see her husband waiting for her. Though she had walked some distance across the surface of the ocean, her boots were still bone dry.

"Ready to inspect the troops?" Sidorio inquired, extending his arm.

She nodded, looping her own arm through the crook of his. She glanced over her shoulder to check on Jacqueline and Nathalie's progress. Reassured that they had now joined her on the sand, she allowed Sidorio to lead her off into the melee.

The whole atoll was alive with movement and noise as the swarm of Vampirates got stuck into their nighttime training session. The air rang with the clashing of swords and other noises—cries, roars, and the ominous, more subtle, sound of weaponless combat. The crews of some twenty Vampirate ships had disembarked here tonight for this latest bout—designed to sharpen their fighting skills and also their bloodlust.

As Sidorio and Lola strode among them, followed close behind by Jacqueline and Nathalie, the warring Vampirates were careful to make room for their revered leaders. Sidorio slowed his pace to observe a particularly vicious duel.

"Go on, my son!" he called out. "In for the kill! Show no mercy!"

Lola laughed. "This *is* only a training session," she said. "You don't *actually* want them to destroy their own comrades, do you?"

Sidorio turned to face his wife. "Darling Lola, Camp Decimation is based on principles derived from the Roman Army. By the close of play tonight, I want the weakest ten percent of our troops destroyed. *That's* how you keep your army on its toes." Smiling, he added, "If you want a solution, always look to Rome."

Lola raised an eyebrow and reached out her hand to toy with the line of chunky medals pinned across his chest. "No one could argue that the Romans didn't leave us a potent legacy." She smiled. "I'm impressed, husband. It seems you've been making some interesting changes."

Sidorio nodded, his eyes turning from his wife back to the duel being enacted before their eyes. "War is a state of constant change," he said. "And I intend to *win* this war."

Suddenly the Vampirate Sidorio had urged on before broke free and attacked his opponent from a new angle. As he did so, he opened his mouth and bit off his opponent's middle finger.

Lola and her aides gasped in surprise. Sidorio only laughed. "There you are, ladies. I give you the principle of decimation in practice. Removal of a tenth."

Lola shook her head fondly. "Sometimes I forget what a brute you are, Sid." She stroked his serge sleeve tenderly as they continued on their way. "Thanks for the reminder."

"Commander!" came a cry. Johnny marched out of the fray to greet Sidorio and the others.

"Stetson!" Sidorio exclaimed, pulling his comrade into a warm bear hug. "How's it going with the new recruits?"

"Same old, same old," Johnny said, bowing courteously to Lola and her aides. "The landlubber Vampirates are still coming to grips with the rudiments of swords-manship. But there are a few stars in the making. Take a look at these two over here." He pointed to a muscled young man locked in a fight with a lithe older woman.

"What's their story?" Sidorio asked, his arm draped casually over Johnny's shoulder.

"The blond guy, Skawen, is an old vamp," Johnny said. "Viking stock, so no stranger to fighting, pillaging, and the like. He's been landlocked for centuries but he was made to be on our team."

"And his sparring partner?" Sidorio inquired.

"Martha Corey," Johnny said. "She's an interesting one. American by birth. Hanged in the Salem witch trials but didn't go gentle into that good night."

"Good for her!" Lola said. "Look at the fire in her eyes. If you hadn't already recruited her, Johnny, I'd take her for *The Vagabond*."

"She's yours if you want her," Johnny said, in no doubt of the hierarchy.

"That's very kind of you," Lola replied. "But I'm happy enough with my current crew. She's all yours, Johnny. Cherish her!"

Johnny nodded. "I will."

"How's it going with the newly converted pirates?" Sidorio asked him now.

Johnny nodded. "Stukeley's got them in hand over there." He pointed diagonally across the atoll. "I'll leave him to give you the debrief. But don't forget, I'm heading off this week to begin a new recruitment drive among land-based vampires. Have to keep our numbers strong!"

"Very good, Stetson," Sidorio said. "Catch you later for a pint or two on *The Blood Captain*?"

"Sounds great!" Johnny said, grinning at the ladies, then racing back into the fray.

Sidorio and Lola led the others on around the atoll, observing with pleasure the sparring on all sides.

"Isn't this thrilling?" Lola exclaimed. "Camp Decimation! How ingenious you are, Sid!"

Sidorio smiled at her praise. He glimpsed Stukeley close ahead, and his spirits soared even higher.

Stukeley extricated himself from the battle zone to greet the others. "Good evening, Sidorio. And Lady Sidorio."

Lola smiled prettily. "I think it's high time you started calling me Lola," she said.

"Absolutely," Stukeley said. "Lola it is."

Sidorio leaned forward confidentially. "Stetson said that you'd been training up the newly crossed pirates. How are they performing?"

"Pretty well," Stukeley replied. "Yes, on balance, I'd say that the freshly crossed pirates are more of an asset to us than the landlubber vamps. Johnny has his work cut out with them!"

Sidorio nodded. "He said as much."

"Still," Stukeley said, "it makes sense to keep both recruitment streams going."

"Absolutely," Lola said, stepping forward. "Every recruit

to the Vampirate army is one less recruit for the blood-hating Alliance."

Stukeley nodded. "That reminds me," he said. "I wanted to talk to you both about something." He paused as their eyes met his. "Have you noticed that although we seem to be so much more aggressive at recruiting, the Alliance army always seems to outnumber ours?"

"Things are changing," Lola said. "Fast."

"Lately we have triumphed over them in one battle after another, yet their numbers seem to remain constant," Stukeley continued. "Maybe they're recruiting more actively than we thought. Either that or they have found a way to bring their fallen troops back from the dead."

Sidorio laughed, his eyes bright. "That's more our territory than theirs, surely?"

Lola looked thoughtful, then turned to Stukeley. "Rest assured, it's under investigation," she said.

Stukeley gave a precise salute, turned, and marched back into the melee.

"That boy is like a son to me," Sidorio said.

Lola smiled. "I confess I didn't take to him at first. Neither him nor the Cowboy. But now I find my feelings have shifted."

Such words were balm to Sidorio's ears. His group had now completed a full circuit of the atoll. Their inspection of the troops was concluded. Everything appeared to be in order.

Lola pointed to a row of ships illuminated by the moon.

"Do you remember when we first met, Sid? We only had but two ships to our name. Now, consider our growing fleet."

Sidorio nodded, smiling and feeling a river of warmth run through him. He noticed that Jacqueline and Nathalie had fallen back, allowing their two leaders a rare moment of privacy.

"Over a hundred Vampirate ships and more recruited by the night!" Lola gazed up at Sidorio, her eyes bright. "At last, my dear, you have the empire you always craved."

"I couldn't have done this without you," he said, truthfully. "I was nothing but a lonely drifter before I met you."

Lola shook her head. "Don't sell yourself short, Sid. I hate it when you do that."

He circled his arms around her, his hands caressing the small of her back as he gazed at her in love and awe. "What I mean to say is, all this"—he gestured from the line of ships to the horde of skirmishing Vampirates— "everything we have now, is because of you."

"No," Lola said. "Because of *us*. We planned all this— on our honeymoon. During those long, deliciously bitter Siberian nights, when the virgin snow ran red with the blood of our victims. Remember? Then we came home and made it happen. That's the wonder of us, Sid. Others merely dream but we know the alchemy that turns dreams into reality."

She moved one of his hands around to place it on her swollen belly. Beaming at her, Sidorio waited until he felt the now familiar tremors of movement beneath her clothes and skin.

"Not long now," he said.

"Not long indeed," she said, "until your two boys are born."

Sidorio's eyes were ablaze. "Boys? Our babies are both boys?"

"Why, yes," Lola said, her dark eyes narrowing. "I thought I'd already told you that?"

He shook his head. His mind was racing. For some reason, he had expected the twins to be one boy and one girl. Now he realized the folly of his thinking. Why should history repeat itself so precisely?

It was a mental adjustment to think that he would soon be the father to two sons; two true heirs to this empire he and Lola had built. He thought of Johnny and Stukeley. His deputies had become like sons to him, but blood heirs were different. In twenty or so years' time—no more than an inhalation and exhalation to him—he could watch his own sons spar with each other as they warmed themselves up for the fight. He could watch his boys command equal fleets that circled the oceans. Such thoughts made his heart burst with pride and anticipation.

Turning back to Lola, he was ambushed by an unexpected emotion. It took him a moment to recognize it as sadness. Sadness that Lola was not having a girl. Because he would have loved to have seen Lola's rare beauty replicated in a daughter. Perhaps, he reflected, it was better this way. Lola was one of a kind. After her, the mold was broken.

"What is it, my darling?" Lola's eyes looked up at him, questioningly. "Aren't you happy to know you will soon have two blood-hungry sons?"

He smiled down at her. "Lola, you have made me the happiest man in the realms of the undead."

Lola stared deep into her husband's eyes. "You can't keep things hidden from me, Sid. You know that, don't you? I see all your secrets."

He knew her words were the truth. "I couldn't be happier at this news," he said. "If my deep joy is countered by a small sadness, it is simply that I would have loved to have created a daughter with you."

Lola's face dissolved into a smile. "My darling, I understand — of course I do. But don't you see? These twins are only the *first* fruits of our eternal union. There will be many other children in the years to come. Our own empire within an empire."

Sidorio found himself beaming from ear to ear, positively swelling with happiness. "I almost forgot," he said. "I have a gift for you."

"A gift?" Lola's eyes twinkled in the moonlight. "Not more jewelry, surely?"

"Well, it does *involve* silver," Sidorio said, excitedly. "Wait here!" He ran off across the sand. Lola watched him, thinking how puppyish he sometimes seemed. She folded her arms as he made his way back to her. In his huge hands was a sleek and shiny crossbow.

Lola smiled as he extended the streamlined weapon, a pouch of arrows, and a pair of gloves toward her. "For me? It's absolutely beautiful, darling!" She weighed the crossbow in her hands. It was surprisingly light but Lola was instantly alive to its deadly power.

"I thought it would come in handy against the Nocturnals," Sidorio said. "All the arrows are silver, of course. So you'll need to wear these gloves whenever you handle them. Rest assured, they are deadly when shot with precision."

Smiling, Lola lifted the sight to her eyes. "Oh Sid, how marvelous. Shall I have a little practice?"

"Why not?" Sidorio nodded.

Lola gazed through the sight until it settled on a coconut tree. The moonlight illuminated a ripe coconut at the center of her sight. Lola was about to fire the arrow when, feeling rather more playful, she adjusted her position so that the crossbow was directed at one of Sidorio's weaker crew members. A moving target was so much more of a challenge.

Lola took aim and sent the silver arrow on its deadly trajectory. As the surprised Vampirate slumped to the ground, causing a hubbub around him, Lola turned and kissed her dumbfounded husband. "Thank you, darling. It's a truly wonderful gift. And *so* much more practical than another pair of earrings!"

12

THE TURNING OF THE TIDE

The Tiger, The Typhon, and *The Muscovite*—the last having lately been brought out of retirement—were all moored together. On the top deck of *The Tiger,* the crews of three of the most valued Alliance vessels were still engaged in combat training as night closed in around them. The sky was full of stars and the sea seemed the calmest it had been in recent memory. Standing outside her cabin, Cheng Li was flanked to her port side by Barbarro and Trofie Wrathe and to starboard by her former teacher Pavel Platonov. They each watched with relish the dazzling skills of their crews. Each of these leaders seemed to be lost in thought when Trofie broke the silence.

"As terrible as this war is, it has brought about some pleasing changes." She lifted her golden hand to gesture to the deck. "Commodore Li, I must commend you. The work you have done to raise our fighting skills is nothing short of extraordinary. Your close contact with the Nocturnals has certainly borne fruit."

"Thank you, Deputy Wrathe." Cheng Li nodded graciously. "Yes, you're right about these changes." Her eyes narrowed in on one combatant in particular. "Look at your son, for instance. He is utterly transformed."

Trofie nodded, smiling softly as she, too, observed Moonshine's almost balletic maneuvers as he clashed swords with Connor Tempest.

There was a discreet cough at Cheng Li's side. She turned to find Jasmine.

"Captain, I have important news from our tracking teams." All the leaders' eyes turned to Jasmine as she continued. "*The Diablo* has finally separated from the Vampirate fleet."

Calmly, Cheng Li nodded. "We must cut short this training session." Her eyes met Cate's in the midst of the melee. The captain gave a signal that Cate immediately understood and acted upon. Across the deck, swords fell and the drumming of footsteps softened.

Barbarro turned to Cheng Li. "Is there any way we may be of assistance?"

Cheng Li smiled softly. "No, but thank you. We have the optimum trained crew at the ready."

Minutes later, the other captains had assembled their crews and begun the swift return to their ships.

Meanwhile, Jasmine had gathered up the key personnel of *The Tiger*. Cheng Li, Jasmine, Connor, Cate, and Bo Yin were all standing at the prow of the ship. They were joined by Moonshine Wrathe, not strictly a crew member but nonetheless a key comrade in the battle that lay ahead. The rest of *The Tiger*'s crew lingered on the deck, weapons down, catching their breath and mopping up the sweat endured by their long workout. There was a heady sense of expectation in the air.

"Are you certain that *The Diablo* is now cut off?" Cheng Li asked Jasmine.

"Yes," answered her trusted deputy. "It has broken away from the other key ships of the Vampirate fleet, and, when last tracked, had moored on the shore. Intel believes that the Cowboy is on a mission to recruit land-based vampires to his crew."

Cheng Li shuddered at the thought. He had to be stopped. Kill two birds with one decisive stone.

Bo Yin, standing at Jasmine's side, spoke now. "If we leave now, Captain, we can be in position by 0600 hours." Bo, Cheng Li realized, was another example of metamorphosis. She had transformed herself into a key member of the team—matters of navigation and liaison with tracking and Intel were her specialty, under the watchful mentoring of Jasmine.

Cheng Li nodded gratefully at his talented and committed crewmates. "It seems that the moment we have been anticipating has come. Jasmine, instruct the navigators of our target coordinates and tell them to make haste. Bo, I want you to maintain an eye on the rest of the fleet. We don't want any nasty surprises! Cate, I will of course leave you to go through the weaponry allocation and checks. Plenty of aconite solution tonight, if you please!" Now Cheng Li turned to face Connor and Moonshine. "We three will, as discussed, lead the vanguard attack. Jasmine and Cate will follow. Talk to your teams. Ensure they are ready for what lies ahead."

"Yes, Captain!" declared Connor and Moonshine in unison.

Addressing the whole group, Cheng Li had but one final set of instructions. "After these preparations are concluded, please ensure everyone who is not on duty returns to their cabins and gets a few hours' rest. We'll reconvene on deck at 0400 hours, ready to commence Operation Scrimshaw."

Connor smiled to himself. It had been his suggestion to name this mission after Molucco's beloved pet. He thought that his former commander would have appreciated the touch.

"Wait!" Moonshine Wrathe broke from the ranks and stood at Cheng Li's side. The captain seemed momentarily disconcerted as Moonshine began to directly address the rank-and-file members of the crew. "I want to thank you all for joining me tonight on this mission to take back my ship, the legendary pirate vessel, *The Diablo*."

Connor watched with growing interest as Moonshine

continued, his eyes bright, his voice strong and surprisingly sonorous. "If fortune smiles upon us and grants us this much wished-for victory, I pledge to stand each and every one of you brave pirates a tankard of grog at Ma Kettle's Tavern tomorrow night."

There were cheers at this. Connor shook his head. Pledging tankards of grog and intoning the sacred name of Ma Kettle were easy wins. Nonetheless, he was impressed. No question, Wrathe junior had inherited the family gift for working a crowd. As if to prove his point, Moonshine's expression changed and a sudden hush fell upon the deck. "Make no mistake," he said, his voice lower than before but no less potent. "This mission is not simply about helping me take back what is rightfully mine. This is about tipping the scales of victory in this war. It was a war we didn't want, but which we had no option but to engage in. Tonight, every last one of you will play your part in turning the tide and firing a shot right into the heart of that dirty Vampirate fleet."

He had spoken with such vigor that his face was red and dotted with beads of sweat, but his eyes shone starbright as he reached for his sword and raised it aloft.

Across the deck, each and every pirate mirrored Moonshine's gesture. Connor found himself reaching for his own sword and saw that Cate, Jasmine, and even Cheng Li had done the same. The deck of *The Tiger* was a deadly field of sharpened silver blades.

"To victory!" cried Moonshine.

"To victory!" echoed the crowd in unison. The troops began stamping the deck boards as they continued the cry. "Victory! Victory! Victory!"

Connor watched, fascinated, as Moonshine lowered his sword. Once more, the crowd was hushed, as if they were his puppets.

"Thank you," Moonshine said, turning, "but, most of all, thanks to Captain Li for agreeing to join me in this fight. May our actions tonight prove a decisive moment in this war."

———

Back in Cheng Li's cabin, Connor, Cate, Jasmine, and Moonshine joined her in drinking to victory. They slammed together their glasses of cuttlefish grappa and drank to a successful mission.

As the fiery grappa slipped down Connor's throat, he glanced across at Cheng Li's clock. It was a full ten minutes ahead of his watch. He felt a cold wave of panic. Which was the correct time? Had he missed his rendezvous?

"I have to go," he said, suddenly striding toward the exit. "I'm expecting a delivery."

As the doors banged shut behind him, Jasmine's eyes turned curiously toward the captain. "A delivery?" she inquired. "At this time of night?"

Cheng Li nodded. "That's right! We arranged a special

courier earlier. For some of Master Yin's aconite potion. We're running low—remember?" Her dark eyes seared into Jasmine's, eliminating any possibility of challenge. "Thank goodness Connor has his wits about him."

"Time I was off, too," Cate said. "There's a passage from Marcus Aurelius I always like to read before I go into battle. It helps me to center myself."

Cheng Li smiled. *"And thou wilt give thyself relief, if thou doest every act of thy life as if it were the last."*

Cate nodded. "I'm impressed," she said. "How did you know?"

"Just a guess," Cheng Li said. "Those words have great resonance for me, too."

"Come on, Cate. I'll walk with you," said Jasmine, her eyes glistening in the candlelight.

As the twin doors of her cabin swung shut once more, Cheng Li turned to Moonshine. "Just us captains, then! Care for another glass of grappa?"

Moonshine shook his head. "You know the old saying, Captain Li. One shot keeps you sharp, a second keeps you up all night. I intend to follow your advice and avail myself of a power nap before action commences."

Cheng Li nodded, impressed by his newfound discipline.

Moonshine rolled his empty glass between his palms. "You're an amazing role model, you know," he said. "The way you are with your crew—and them with you. I want to be just like that when I have my own ship."

Smiling, Cheng Li brushed aside his flattery. "All being

well, this time tomorrow you will be in possession of your ship. But, make no mistake, there's something of a journey between inheriting a ship and forming a solid crew."

"I know," Moonshine said, with genuine humility. "I'm just at the beginning of my piratical career. But I'm eager to learn from the greats...like you." His eyes glanced from her to the portrait behind her. "And your dad."

Cheng Li nodded. There seemed to be no stopping Moonshine once he was on a roll.

"I meant what I said out there," he continued. "I'm so grateful to you for agreeing to help me. I know your relationship with my family—my uncle especially—has been a bit of a roller-coaster ride, so I especially appreciate—"

"This has nothing to do with your uncle," Cheng Li said briskly. "You came to me as one pirate captain to another, asking for help." She glanced up at the portrait above her desk. "Sometimes our inheritance can be a mixed blessing. All my life, I have lived in the shadow of my father's reputation."

Moonshine's eager eyes skimmed the portrait. "Chang Ko Li," he said in reverential tones. "He's a complete legend. The best of the best."

"If only I had a ruby for every time I've heard that," said Cheng Li. "Yes, my father is a legend. Chang Ko Li, John Kuo, your uncles Porfirio and Molucco—each one of them may justifiably be called a pirate legend." She turned to face her companion once more. "But their time is over now. You and I can be spurred on by what they have taught us, and, to a greater or lesser degree, by their example. But when we enter the fray, it will be *our* wits and reflexes that determine the fight and prove decisive in this war. Legends they may be, but now they are no more than dust—their swords either rusting or impotent in their display cases at the academy." Her almond eyes bore into Moonshine's. "Be your own man," she said. "That's what matters now."

He nodded ruminatively, still gazing at the portrait.

Cheng Li leaned closer and lowered her voice confidentially. "I'll let you in on a little secret, one captain to another. Chang Ko Li was, without question, one of the greatest pirates to have ever traversed the oceans. But a good father?" She shook her head. "Not so much."

"You took your time," said the mean-faced courier. "That'll cost you. I don't like to be kept waiting."

Connor frowned. "Keep your voice down," he said, glancing nervously up at the deck. He leaned out from the ladder toward the courier's small lightboat. "Hand over the goods, mate, and we'll decide your price."

"That's not how it works, *mate*." The courier shook his head, retreating farther into the shadows of his small craft. "Money first. Then we'll see about your blood."

Fire burned in Connor's eyes. "Just give it to me," he

said, the deep hungry need consuming his insides. He reached out to grab the man's arm.

The courier cried out in pain. "All right! Get your filthy Vampirate hands off me and we'll proceed with the transaction."

Connor composed himself once more. "I'm sorry," he said, seeing the already livid bruise forming on the man's arm.

"Here!" The courier thrust a flask toward him.

At the sight of it, Connor felt a wave of calm course through him. He reached into his pocket for the roll of money. "Here you are. Take all of it. With my apologies for making you wait." He glanced at the bruise once more. "And for the way I acted before."

The courier's hand closed tight around the notes. "You lot are all the same. Full of fire and brimstone until you get what you want. Then sweet as treacle and overflowing with fancy words. You make me sick." Stuffing the money into his purse, he lost no time in steering away from *The Tiger*.

"Thank you," Connor said, cradling the flask as carefully as if it were a baby. "I *really* needed this."

There was a look of pure revulsion in the courier's eyes. Then the night thrust a cloak of darkness between the two men and they set off on their separate ways.

13

THE LOST BOYS

Connor strode briskly across to the door leading toward his cabin. Hearing voices up ahead, he dropped back to wait for the others to pass. He was taken by surprise to see Jasmine and Bo Yin step out onto the deck. There was no avoiding this encounter.

"Connor Tempest," Bo Yin said, smiling with pleasure. She never seemed to tire of running into him; nor he of her. There was something puppyish about Bo Yin, which brought out Connor's warmth and also his protective nature. He returned Bo's smile.

Jasmine's eyes immediately fell to the flask Connor gripped tightly in his hand. "I see your delivery has arrived."

"This?" Connor said, cracking a careful smile. "Oh, no, this isn't my delivery. Just a flask of tea I took with me while I was waiting. The guy never showed up. We won't be using that courier company again." Shaking his head, he brushed past them and forged on inside.

Jasmine waited until he was safely out of earshot before turning to Bo Yin. "He spends so much time lying these days, you'd have thought he'd be more accomplished at it."

Bo Yin frowned, pained at this further evidence of the animosity between two people whom she cared for deeply. "What makes you think Connor Tempest is lying?" she asked Jasmine.

"I don't *think* it," Jasmine said, "I know it. Plus, we made a plan to meet up tonight and talk, but he's totally forgotten. I don't believe anything he says anymore." She sighed. "Come on, Bo Yin. Let's get this inspection done and dusted. We could all use some sleep."

Jasmine and Bo Yin had almost completed their tour of the deck when they came to the foredeck. There, sitting atop one of the cannons, looking out into the star-filled night, was Cate. She was as still as a statue and didn't notice them at first.

"Cate," Jasmine said softly, reaching a hand up gently to Cate's shoulder.

As if drawn out of a deep trance, Cate shuddered, then turned to acknowledge her comrades.

"I thought you were going back to your cabin to read," Jasmine said.

Cate nodded. "I did and then I tried to take the captain's advice, but I can never sleep before an attack. These days, I'm not sleeping too well in general."

"Because of Bart," Bo Yin said. She spoke with such tenderness and innocence that her words didn't seem the invasion of privacy they might have been from other mouths.

Cate nodded, her eyes turning to the distant horizon. "I keep thinking that he's coming home. How stupid is that? Of course, I know it's impossible, but my mind keeps playing tricks on me." As she spoke, she gently twisted the slim engagement ring, which she had taken to wearing on the fourth finger of her left hand.

Jasmine nodded, sitting down beside her. "I understand. I feel the same way about Jacoby. Every logical instinct tells me that he's gone and yet, every morning, I wake up thinking that today might be the day he comes back to us."

"You should hold on to that hope!" Bo Yin said, leaning against the deck rail, facing her two older comrades. "One day, you could be proved right."

Jasmine smiled and shook her head. "I hope experience doesn't change you, Bo. You're so full of hope and optimism."

"Yes, I am!" Bo Yin nodded vehemently. "For all of us."

Cate's eyes moved from Bo Yin to Jasmine. "Perhaps

she's right. I know that Bart is dead and gone. Connor told me he buried him at sea." She shuddered, as if holding back tears before continuing. "But Jacoby's body has never been found. There's every chance he could still be out there, only wounded, waiting for the right time to return."

Jasmine felt the now familiar heat of budding tears pricking the backs of her own eyes. "Every night, scores of pirates' bodies are washed out to sea," she said. "If he *was* only wounded, he'd have been picked up by one of our ambulance boats and taken to the field hospitals at the academy or Sanctuary." She reached for Cate's hand, gripping it tightly. "I'll never forget watching that ship of Vampirates sail away with him that night and feeling so powerless to help him." Her eyes met Cate's. "I think we have to let them go," she said. "For our sake as much as theirs."

Nodding, Cate turned back, desolately, toward the horizon.

14

BROUGHT TO BOOK

All that night, Grace waited for a chance to go to the lab and see if Olivier's book was still hidden there under the counter. She had no doubt of its power and importance and was intent on discovering for herself what lay between its blue cloth covers. Nor did she doubt that, as soon as he was capable, Olivier would set off to retrieve the book for himself. She was sure now that this was one of the reasons he had come back to Sanctuary—perhaps the main reason. Fortunately, he was not yet strong enough to rise up from his bed. But he would be soon enough. He was making a surprisingly swift recovery, given the severe state he had arrived in. The clock was ticking.

But it was one of those nights where everything seemed to be conspiring against Grace. First, there had been the arrival of more ambulances and a fresh healing procedure to conduct. Then Tooshita had asked Grace to take on an extra ward round while she was immersed in another healing. It was a favor Grace could not deny her friend and fellow healer. Just as Grace was at last heading off in the direction of the lab, she was assailed by Darcy, in an obvious state of distress.

"Do you have five minutes free to talk?" Darcy managed to stammer out before her face crumpled into tears.

Nodding, Grace put her arm around her friend's waist and swiftly steered her along the corridor and out into the open air. Once outside, they embarked on the short walk to the small herb garden with the water fountain. There, Darcy told Grace how a Nocturnal patient they had thought was making a strong recovery had taken a turn for the worse and they had lost her—despite their best efforts.

Grace took Darcy's hand as tears streamed down her friend's cheeks. "I completely understand why you're so upset," she told her, "but, remember, we're successful in the majority of cases we treat. We're healers, not miracle workers, Darcy—we can only do our best. You know that as well as I do."

Darcy nodded, lifting a handkerchief to dab at her eyes. "I know, Grace. You're right, of course. I don't know why this one patient affected me so much. I didn't even get to know her, like you sometimes do."

Grace smiled. "You're a wonderful nurse, Darcy," she told her. "Don't forget that. All the healers say so. Everyone fights to have you on their team."

"Really?" Darcy's wide eyes were filled with hope once more.

Grace nodded. "You're right to put your blinders on a bit. We all need to do that, I guess. If we dwelled on the horror and pain every time we began to treat a new casualty, we'd be next to useless." She paused. "But every once in a while, the horror—the enormity of it—does strike you. It's inevitable. And it's not a bad thing. But these feelings will pass." Grace stroked her friend's arm reassuringly. "I'm sure you did everything you could to help her recover. It's very sad that she wasn't strong enough to make the journey back, but it's not your fault."

She couldn't help thinking then of Olivier. His wounds had been the worst she'd ever seen and yet his recovery had seemed effortless. She wasn't so arrogant as to attribute this solely to her own healing powers. More likely, Olivier was a dhampir and therefore able to heal himself. But that didn't explain how he had been so badly injured in the first place. She was starting to strongly disbelieve his tale of his suffering at the hands of Lola's squad— plausible though it was. Perhaps, on reflection, it was rather *too* plausible.

Returning her gaze to Darcy, Grace saw there were fresh tears in her friend's eyes.

"You should get some sleep," Grace said. "I'm not saying that things will be significantly better when you wake up, but I've seen the hours you've been keeping, and you're in danger of running on empty."

"Thanks, Doctor!" Darcy said with a forced grin. "Is that your prescription, then?"

Grace nodded. "Yes," she said. "Give yourself at least six hours, none of these so-called power naps. Put in your earplugs and forget about the bells. And go and see Jim. I think you could do with some blood, Darcy. You look like you're at a low ebb."

At the mention of her donor, Darcy brightened. "Yes, that's a good idea," she said.

"Why don't I walk you over to the donor block?" Grace suggested.

Darcy smiled but shook her head. "No, that's okay, Grace. I can make my own way. I might stay here for a bit, anyhow. It's always peaceful in this garden, whatever craziness is going on around us. Maybe I just need a little quiet time." She squeezed Grace's hand. "Thanks for being here for me, Grace—as always."

"We're best friends," Grace said. "It goes with the territory. You've always been there for me, ever since we met."

"And I always will be," Darcy said, her voice suddenly full of passion. "Now off you go, Grace. I'm sure you have a hundred things to be getting on with."

Grace smiled to herself. There was just one further thing on her list tonight. She rose to her feet and smoothed down her skirt, then turned and took her leave of Darcy and the sweet-scented night garden.

Back inside the compound, Grace made her way through the corridors, intent on getting to the lab without any further diversion. Miracle of miracles, it seemed that this might at last be possible. The corridors were empty. Everyone was getting on with their business. Now was her moment to investigate under the counter and see if that book of Olivier's was still hidden there.

As she approached the door to the lab, Grace's heart was hammering. As much as she tried to calm herself, she knew—somehow—that the book was really important. Not just to Olivier, but also to her.

She pushed open the door, excited to think that in a matter of moments she would have the book in her hands and be able to start uncovering its secrets. But as the door swung forward, Grace's heart sank. She was not alone.

"Good evening, Grace." Mosh Zu looked up from the central counter, where he was busy preparing a potion.

"Hello," she said, trying to inject some brightness into her voice. She didn't want him to think that she wasn't pleased to see him. "It's been ages since I've seen you in here."

Mosh Zu shrugged. "It has been a while. We've all had our hands full with the wounded." He turned his face to her. "I thought it would do me good to come and handle something other than wounded flesh." As he spoke, he lifted a pestle and began grinding seeds into the base of a mortar. He smiled softly at her. "There's a fresh batch of berry tea over there, by the stove. Why don't you pour yourself a draft and keep me company?"

Grace nodded automatically. Then, as Mosh Zu returned his gaze to the pestle and mortar, her eyes skimmed the base of the counter. Was the hidden panel on this side? It was tantalizing to be so near, yet so far from the moment of discovery.

Before she might arouse Mosh Zu's suspicions, Grace moved over to the stove. Next to it was a small counter, on which sat a crate filled with metal flasks. Above the counter were shelves crowded with crockery and cooking utensils. Grace reached up and retrieved an enamel mug and a thermometer, just as Mosh Zu had trained her. She lifted one of the flasks out of the crate and unscrewed its double cap carefully before inserting the thermometer and watching closely as the level rose to thirty-seven degrees Celsius. Body temperature.

She inhaled the familiar smell of berry tea—the brew of seven rare mountain berries that Mosh Zu had created as a substitute for blood. Grace carried her mug and the flask over to the main counter. She pulled up a stool at the other end of the bench from Mosh Zu and poured a draft of liquid into the mug. He watched her approvingly. She was dying to inspect this section of the counter, but she couldn't—not yet. Instead, she brought the mug of tea to her lips.

According to Mosh Zu, dhampirs were not dependent on blood in the same way regular vampires were. Yet, slowly but surely, Grace's appetite for blood had been awakened deep inside her. In the latter stages of her sojourn with Sidorio and Lola, she had experienced such a deep hunger for blood that she had attacked a mortal girl and drunk hungrily from her. Even now, she could smell and taste that girl's blood; even now she bore deep shame and regret for her actions.

Grace's happiness at returning to Sanctuary had been tempered by her fear at having to confess her addiction to Mosh Zu. But she needn't have fretted. Mosh Zu had listened carefully and reacted with equanimity. He had prescribed Grace a nightly flask of berry tea—just as he did for the regular Vampirates who came to Sanctuary, struggling to control their dependence on blood. Mosh Zu was, he had confessed, unsure whether Grace would ever lose the taste for blood or if, ultimately, they would need to find a more permanent solution. One possibility under consideration was that she would be paired with her own donor. For now, though, it was a nightly flask of berry tea. As she took another sip, Grace reflected that it was curious to be both an addict and a healer at the same time.

Perhaps having some insight into her thoughts, Mosh Zu glanced up from his work and smiled at her reassuringly. She took another sip, feeling relaxed as the warm tea slipped like liquid velvet down her throat.

When she had first returned, she had asked Mosh Zu if it was even feasible for her to work as a healer when, by necessity, she would often be faced with the open arteries of the wounded. To her surprise, he had declared that it was not only possible but would be part of her own healing process. In any case, she had soon learned that wounded Nocturnals tended not to have a high concentration of blood in their system. For this reason, they did not have a propensity toward bleeding. Instead, their wounds presented themselves as breaks in the very fiber of their flesh—like a building crumbling to dust or a landmass after an earthquake. Looking down at Olivier on the healer's slab, she had seen through the fissures in his desiccating flesh to a dark, infinite void. It had taken all her healing powers to reanimate that dust and patch together his flesh—or at least she had thought it had been *her* healing powers...

"What are you thinking about?" Mosh Zu inquired.

Glancing up, Grace saw that he had cleared up his things. The salve he had been working on was complete. How long had he been watching her? She decided to take a chance.

"I was thinking about a new patient of mine."

Mosh Zu said nothing but nodded, encouraging her to continue.

"We both know him," she said. "It's Olivier."

Once more, Mosh Zu nodded, his face impassive. "Olivier is here," he said—his tone leaving Grace unsure whether this was a statement or a question.

"He arrived last night," Grace went on. "Dani assigned him to me to heal. I had no idea that it was him at first. He was extremely badly wounded—right at the brink of oblivion"—her eyes met Mosh Zu's—"or so it seemed."

Mosh Zu's face remained perfectly placid. Nonetheless, when he spoke again, there was an edge to his voice. "What, I wonder, is Olivier doing here?"

Grace thought of the book. Should she tell Mosh Zu about her suspicions? Her glimpse into Olivier's troubled psyche? She probably should, and yet something warned her to keep this information to herself.

She met Mosh Zu's gaze. "He says he was sired by Sidorio. That when war came, he joined the Alliance and was the Nocturnal on board one of the ships attacked by Lola and her crew. He claims her squad left him in this state."

Mosh Zu remained still and quiet. Grace knew that he was caught up in his own thoughts. "A lie," he said, at length. "Perhaps more than one lie."

Grace's heart was hammering now. Was Mosh Zu referring to Olivier still or to her as well? Was he accusing *her* of being a liar? Once more, her eyes darted to the base of the counter, though she swiftly pulled them away.

"I should like to see him," Mosh Zu said. "Which ward is he on?"

"Is that wise?" Grace asked.

Mosh Zu had stepped away from the bench. Now he looked at her questioningly. She wondered if he felt his authority was being challenged. Under the circumstances, it wasn't the best idea to rile him. But when he spoke, his tone was amicable.

"Whatever we think of Olivier, he deserves the opportunity to be healed, just like our other patients." He nodded. "Complete his healing process, Grace. Then we will get to the bottom of why he is here."

Grace took another sip of tea. "Considering how badly wounded he was, he has already made a surprisingly strong recovery."

Mosh Zu nodded once more. "I think when it comes to Olivier, it is always safe to expect the unexpected." He gave a fleeting smile and took the pot of salve in his hands. "And now, I will leave you to your *tea*," he said.

Mosh Zu padded toward the door and, within moments, was gone. At last, Grace was alone in the lab. She wasted no time. Setting her mug back on the counter and slipping off the stool, she fell to her knees to begin her investigation.

The lab was not well-lit in general and the floor surrounding the counter was shrouded with shadows. Grace pressed her fingers along the wooden panel. Each piece of wood remained frustratingly firm. Grace moved around the base of the counter, praying that none of the other healers would come in and interrupt her before she had completed her mission.

Just then there were fresh footsteps outside in the corridor. *No!* She sat still for a moment, refusing to stand up, though she knew it would look suspicious if one of her colleagues entered the room. She didn't care. She was so intent on completing the search for the hidden panel and the book that—hopefully—lay beyond.

As the footsteps faded away, she let out a sigh and renewed her exploration. She had now assessed three of the four sides of the counter. It occurred to her that perhaps it had changed since Olivier had hidden the book there. Or maybe Mosh Zu had known about the book all along and had already removed it and sealed up the panel.

But now, just as that thought floated through her brain, her fingers found a pliable panel, and, as she pressed it, obligingly it opened. Barely breathing in her excitement, Grace inserted her hand and wrist through the opening and began searching for the book.

She could only feel dust as her hand ventured into the dark interior. She adjusted her position and dipped her arm deeper inside. Her fingers brushed something. Not a book but a piece of cloth. Her fingers pinched the cloth and drew it forward. It had a little weight to it. Feeling she must be on to something, she drew the cloth onward, then eased her arm out of the aperture.

Glancing down, she could see a cloth bundle on the other side of the opening. It was a bag, covered in dust. Could this be it? She brought the drawstring bag out into the light. It was the right shape and size. This must be it!

Heart racing faster than ever, Grace wiped her hands clean on the back of her uniform, then undid the drawstring and reached inside the bag. She took out a small book, bound in blue cloth.

She took the book in her hands. Its cover was blank.

But then, right in front of her eyes, gold lettering began to appear. It was not a trick of the light. One moment, the cover was blank; the next there was gold lettering, reading: *The Way of the Dhampir*.

Grace couldn't believe it. She turned to the first page. It was blank. As was the next. Flipping on through the book, she found that each and every page was blank. She couldn't stem her feelings of dismay.

Then, having a fresh thought, she went back and looked at the first page. It was still blank. She held it open and waited.

Words suddenly began to appear on the page. She waited for the characters to stop swirling and the page to steady, then began to read. She could barely contain her excitement, but, as she absorbed the words, that emotion mutated into cold, dark fear.

The time of the prophecy has come.
The Warmonger has made his move.
And now one of the Warmonger's twin children must die.
Just as Mosh Zu prophesied all those years ago.
One twin must die.

15

SHOWDOWN

Grace sat on her bed, transfixed by the open book on her lap. Once more she read the chilling words:

One twin must die.

There could be no doubt that this prophecy referred to her and Connor. Sidorio was "the Warmonger" and they were his children. Some time ago, Mosh Zu had made a prophecy. Now one of them was going to die! But how? And why had no one told her—or Connor—about the prophecy before? It was not the first time they had had information withheld from them. Everyone seemed to have known that she and Connor were Sidorio's stolen children, but still they had bided their time to reveal *that* bombshell. And Grace reflected, her heart thudding, if

Sally hadn't come back, the truth might never have come out at all.

Now, it seemed there was a bigger secret even than that. Grace couldn't help but feel angry—not with Olivier, who, like Sally, was purely a catalyst to the truth emerging. No, she felt anger toward Obsidian and Mosh Zu, for doubtless they both knew of this prophecy. And what about Lorcan? Was he in on the secret, too? He had known about Sally and Dexter and Sidorio, so there was a very strong chance that he knew about this, too. How could the people you loved—the *person* you loved above all others—persist in hiding things from you?

With this maelstrom of thoughts in her head, Grace turned the page. She needed to be free from the words that predicted her, or her brother's, death. She sat there, the book open on the next blank page, trying to get her breathing back to some semblance of normal.

Glancing down, she realized that words were now forming on the new page. Was there no escape from this prophecy? Were its words somehow imprinted on every page of this book like a stick of seaside rock? But, as the words settled, she saw that it was not a repeat of the first message but new information.

Lorcan doesn't know.

Grace was shell-shocked. It was as if the book was talking to her directly. Scratch that! The book *was* talking to her. It had somehow read her thoughts and given her its answer. She had suspected from the first it was powerful, but this was way beyond her expectations. Breathlessly, she turned the page once more, her eyes resting before new characters began to make their mark. In a moment, the book's latest message became clear.

The patient is up and about, searching for me.

You are my custodian now.

Hide me where he cannot find me, then deal with him.

Grace shook her head in wonder. "He's in the lab," she said out loud. "He is, isn't he?" She turned the page, hoping for confirmation, but the page remained resolutely blank. She decided to try another question, but this time only thought it rather than saying it aloud. *Is Olivier a dhampir?*

She glanced down at the blank page, expecting an answer. Sure enough, after a brief pause, text began to appear. But, as it settled, she was disappointed to read...

Find him and deal with him.

Time is of the essence.

Hide me and go.

"All right," she said with a nod. With some reluctance, she closed the book and slipped it inside her pillowcase.

It wasn't the safest of hiding places, but, given the book's own pleas for urgency, it would have to suffice for now. She had to find Olivier, and she had a strong intuition as to where he would be.

As she pushed open the door to the lab, her suspicions were confirmed. Olivier was down on his knees, scrabbling around the counter, looking demented. As he took note of Grace's arrival, he glared up at her like an angry snake, cornered and ready to unleash its venom.

"You shouldn't be here," Grace said, more calmly than she felt. "Your healing is not yet complete and you need your rest."

"Cut the act, Grace," Olivier snapped. "Where is it?"

"Where is what?" she asked, closing the door behind her and stepping closer to the counter.

"You know very well what I'm referring to. I know you do." Olivier rose to his full height. "You have something of mine and I want it back."

Grace folded her arms. "It isn't yours anymore," she said. "When you betrayed Mosh Zu and fled Sanctuary, you lost all rights to it and any other property you left behind. Besides," she said with a smile, "the book has left me in no doubt that your period of custody of it is over."

His eyes seared into hers with pure hatred. "So you *do* have it. I knew it!" Now he moved closer toward her. "Run along and fetch it," he told her, as if he were talking to the lowest minion. "The book is much more powerful than you realize."

Grace smiled again, pleasantly. "I am completely alert to the book's powers, Olivier. But, like I said before, even if I *wanted* to return it to you, the book does not wish to be returned."

They had reached some kind of standoff, one on either side of the counter. Whichever healer had been here last had left some glass jars of herbs and roots on the countertop. Now, seized by anger, Olivier swept his arm across the table and sent the jars and their contents flying. Grace remained calm and still as the breaking glass chimed around her.

She observed Olivier, seeing that his recovery was continuing apace. It really was remarkable. Either he had not been nearly as badly injured as she had thought or he had simply miraculous powers of recovery. "I think it's time you left Sanctuary," she told him. "You obviously don't need, or welcome, any help with your healing. If you came for the book, you are out of luck, so all in all I'd say it's time to depart."

Olivier could not contain his rage. "I came for many reasons," he spat, then seemed to regret letting that information out. Regaining his composure, he smiled. "I don't know why you're looking so pleased with yourself. If the book has started talking to you, doubtless it has also shared Mosh Zu's prophecy with you."

Grace attempted to remain stoic but it was a step too far.

Olivier grinned. "So it has! It's a loose-lipped book and

no mistake." He stepped around the side of the counter. "Well, now you're in on the secret, first revealed five hundred years ago.

"Yes, that's right, Grace—five hundred years ago. I was here then, along with Mosh Zu and the Four Cardinals. I heard the prophecy with my own ears, in Mosh Zu's meditation chamber."

This information at least gave the lie to one of Olivier's earlier claims. "So it wasn't Sidorio who sired you," Grace said. "You were a Nocturnal from long ago."

"Not a Nocturnal," Olivier snapped. "A Vampirate. I was—and remain—a Vampirate. A very powerful one. More powerful than Mosh Zu or Obsidian Darke or even you, Grace Tempest."

"Show me," Grace said. "If you're so powerful, prove it."

"What?" Olivier clearly hadn't expected to be challenged in this way.

"You want the book. I don't want you to have it. You want to stay here at Sanctuary. I think it's time for you to leave." Grace smiled. "Let's see who gets their way."

He looked at her venomously once more. "All right," he said.

As he spoke, the glass jars on the wall behind Grace began to vibrate. She could hear them chinking against one another. She could not allow him to wreck this room or its contents. The herbs and other plant matter within the jars were the basis of all Mosh Zu's healing remedies. They could be replaced, but not easily or swiftly, and not without the risk of death or oblivion to their mortal and Nocturnal patients in the interim.

Grace focused her powers on the jars. She found Olivier's current and directed her own against it. At first, his was stronger, but then—to his surprise and not a little to her own—she began to overcome him. She knew she had succeeded when the clinking suddenly subsided and the room fell silent once more.

Olivier was down but not out. Reaching to the counter itself, he peeled off the strips of metal around it, wielding the spikes in his hands like deadly *katanas*.

Grace drew on her inner strength once again. She knew she had options. One was to fashion herself one or more weapons with which to combat him. She was pretty confident that her skill at swordplay would surprise and outflank him. But this, she decided, was too obvious. Instead, she sent all her energy onto the metal spikes that he gripped in his hands. Very slowly but surely she attacked the molecular structure of the metal until it began to heat up from within. The ends of the spikes began to glow red-hot.

The fire was reflected in Olivier's eyes. He was little more than a savage now. And she realized that he thought *he* had set the metal alight, turning the spikes from swords into red-hot pokers. How little he knew.

As he gripped the improvised spears tightly, Grace continued to work her superior magic on them. Before Olivier realized what was happening, the heat from the metal became unbearable, searing into the palms of his hands. And now, as Grace concentrated further, the two bands of metal began to coil around his wrists and arms like snakes. The metal hissed as it scalded him, but the sound was soon overpowered by Olivier's cries.

Try as he might, he could not loosen his grip. *Ironic*, Grace thought. *All that time and energy I spent healing this schmuck. And now I go and do this to him.*

"All right," he rasped. "You win." He could barely speak. "Stop it!" he pleaded. "Stop the pain!"

"I'll stop it," she said, "if you go quietly. And you never come back. Do we have a deal?"

Olivier had no choice. His eyes were full of pain and fury. But he managed to nod.

Grace waited a moment, just to drive home her superior power. Then, she reached forward and took the burning spikes of metal from his hands. He watched her with undisguised awe as she carried the pieces of hot metal back to the counter and laid them down, good as new.

Olivier's hands were another matter. They were burnt to a crisp, worse now than when he had arrived at Sanctuary. He looked at them in horror.

"I'd offer you some salve," Grace said. "But you don't seem to value my healing efforts. So I think it's best if you take your leave now."

He nodded.

Suddenly the door opened and Mosh Zu appeared on the threshold.

Olivier shook his head. "Come to gloat?"

Mosh Zu looked sadly at his former deputy. "No," he said. "Not to gloat. Just to remind myself why I must quell any feelings of pity I have for you, Olivier. You have lost your way and there is nothing I can do to change that." As he spoke, two guards moved into the room and approached Olivier. One brought Olivier's arms around his back. The other snapped handcuffs around his wrists. They wasted no time in leading Olivier toward the door.

"I'll go now," he said, his voice brighter again, despite the intense pain he must be experiencing. "I'll leave you two to discuss the book and the prophecy." He smiled now. "I'm sure Grace is keen to know why you have been keeping secrets from her... again." With a glint in his eye, Olivier allowed himself to be led away.

Mosh Zu shut the door.

"I have some questions for you," Grace said.

Mosh Zu nodded. "I'm sure you do." His voice was as composed as usual. Somehow this irritated her.

"The first concerns Olivier," Grace said. "Is he a dhampir, like me?"

Mosh Zu's limpid eyes met hers. "He *is* a dhampir, Grace. But not like you or your brother. A dhampir has the power to be an unparalleled force for good or for evil. You and your brother have chosen to use your powers for good. I think it's clear now that Olivier has chosen otherwise."

"So," Grace said, "his power is for evil. But when we dueled, my powers outstripped his."

"Your powers are very sharp," Mosh Zu said. "Once, Olivier's were *almost* as sharp. But he is dissolute. You must see that. He spends too much time thinking of allegiances and hurts and vengeance. All these impulses weaken him. True, he still has certain exceptional powers, but he is no rival to you—or to me, for that matter."

Grace nodded. "My other question concerns the prophecy."

Once more, Mosh Zu nodded. "You want to know what it means and why we kept it from you."

Grace shrugged. "Those are valid questions, but let's cut to the chase. All I want to know is whether it's me or Connor who will die. I want to prepare myself, or help him to prevent it."

Mosh Zu was silent for a time as he weighed her words. "Perhaps neither of you need die," he said.

"But the book was very clear on the matter," Grace persisted. "It said that the time of the prophecy had arrived and one of the warmonger's twin children must die. Connor and I are the warmonger's children, are we not?"

It was Mosh Zu's turn to nod. "Yes, you are. And it may be that to achieve lasting peace one of you *must* enter the realm of the dead. We are in a state of bitter war now and sacrifices must be made." There was a callousness to his words. It was not the first time she had observed this quality in the Nocturnal guru. When he spoke next, his tone was somewhat softer. "I think your own future is assured now, Grace."

Her eyes narrowed. *What did he mean? Why did he always cloak his words in riddles, just when you most needed clarity from him?* "Are you telling me that it will be Connor who is sacrificed?"

Mosh Zu looked deeply pained. Grace had the feeling he was keeping vital information back from her. "Grace, I have shared with you all that I can. Please try not to worry about the prophecy."

"Don't *worry*? How can you say that when the prophecy predicts a death sentence for either me or my brother?"

Mosh Zu stepped closer toward her. "Please try to be calm. These things all happen for a good reason. This is the direction your life was meant to take, whatever the outcome. Everything is unfolding just as it should." His words were like a key turning in a lock—cold and metallic. "And now, I must meditate. I need to be released of Olivier's toxicity. Join me, if you wish."

Grace didn't want to be anywhere near him. He was supposed to be her friend, her mentor. But she was starting to lose sight of him as both of these. "I'm going back to my own room," she said in measured tones. "It's been a long night and I could do with a rest before the next ambulance arrives."

"As you wish," Mosh Zu said. He opened the door and they went their very separate ways.

Outside, guards hurled Olivier out through the doors of Sanctuary, then closed the tall iron gates against him. They clanged shut with finality.

Olivier took the path down the hill. He lifted his hands up to the moonlight and was gratified to note that they were already beginning to heal.

His return to Sanctuary had been as eventful as he had anticipated. More so, in some respects. He had come with two missions. His first—to recover the book—had failed spectacularly. But his second had been rather more successful. Smiling to himself, he looked forward to bringing Sidorio and Lola fully up to speed with what he had learned.

Back in her room, Grace felt suddenly dog-tired. Darcy was already fast asleep in the bunk beside her, and Grace kicked off her shoes and lay down, too exhausted even to contemplate stripping off her healer's uniform. Before she lay down, she checked her pillowcase and was relieved to find the weight of the book still inside. She took it out and couldn't resist flicking through it again.

She turned to the first blank page and watched as the words began to emerge.

You are an excellent custodian of the book.
Thank you for hiding me from the patient.
You did well to defeat him, but his threat is not yet over.
He has business with the Warmonger and the Fury.

Grace frowned. It was uncomfortable information but not a complete surprise. Yawning, she was about to close the page when fresh text began to appear.

Regarding the prophecy, remember that
Mosh Zu has lied to you before.

No, she thought. He hadn't actually lied. Kept things from her, but not lied. As she reflected on this, fresh lines scurried across the page.

Keep me safe, Grace, and I will return the favor.
Dark times are coming.
Darker than you can ever imagine.
I will guide you as best I can.
Trust no one but me.

Not even Lorcan? Grace waited for the book to answer this thought. But the page remained unchanged. Feeling absolutely shattered, despite everything spinning around her head, Grace slipped the book into a new hiding place under her mattress. Then she extinguished the candle in the glass by her bed and focused all her energy on summoning sleep.

16

SILENT ASSASSINS

Three dinghies made their way stealthily across from *The Tiger* to *The Diablo*. An hour after dawn, the sea was rougher than the pirates had been hoping for. While the bulky *Tiger* was able to maintain a strong and steady course, the smaller, lighter dinghies were lifted high on each swell. The waves were burnished gold, reflecting the intensity of the new day's sun and the halo of cirrus clouds surrounding it.

Connor stood at the helm of his dinghy, fighting the waves' determination to separate his craft from the two others on either side. The conditions were giving both his mind and body a workout and his face and arms were already coated in sweat. Connor's six crewmates worked soundlessly at his side. The only sound was the thundering ocean beneath them and the cawing of gulls above.

Having brought his dinghy back into line, Connor glanced across to check how Moonshine was faring in his neighboring vessel. Connor found it almost impossible to connect this athletic and focused youth to the acne-ridden kid who had hurled starfish *shuriken* at Connor and his buddies, for no apparent reason, the first time they'd met. Similarly, there was no trace here of the self-serving jerk who had endangered the success of the pirates' heist on the Sunset Fort and incited Connor to make his first kill. Moonshine suddenly turned and looked over at him. Their eyes met now not as adversaries, nor thorns in each other's sides, but as comrades and equals.

If he was honest, Connor had been waiting for Moonshine's restrained new persona to crack and the capricious, egomaniacal monster they were all too familiar with to emerge. But, to his surprise, this hadn't happened. It truly seemed that war had worked some alchemy on Moonshine Wrathe, transforming base metal into gold. Raising his hand, Connor gave his comrade the thumbs-up.

Cheng Li's vessel was the first to reach *The Diablo*. As one of her crew secured the dinghy to the ship, the captain moved to the front of the vessel and swiftly calculated the distance to the deck of the galleon. Wasting no time, she took aim and hurled a weight up onto the deck. It met its target first time. Rather pleased with herself, Cheng Li adjusted what looked like two kite strings. As if miraculously, a discreet but strong wire ladder now connected Cheng Li's dinghy to the main deck of *The Diablo*.

Connor and Moonshine had each been supplied with the same equipment from Federation HQ. Simultaneously, the pirates assessed their target points and threw their own weights up onto the deck, a moderate distance to either side of Cheng Li's. Now three ladders led the way up to the deck and the pirates lost no time in climbing them. Connor was the last to go up. The wire ladders were so thin it truly looked as if his comrades were scaling the ship with their hands and feet. As space opened up above him, Connor bid a silent farewell to the one pirate assigned to wait behind in the dinghy, then began his ascent. In all, it had taken less than three minutes for the eighteen pirates to make their way from the dinghies below to the deck of *The Diablo*. The first phase of Operation Scrimshaw was an unqualified success.

Soundlessly, the pirates made their way across the deserted deck. This was new territory for Connor— usually the fight was under way the instant your boots made contact with the enemy ship. This was different. It was as if they were combating an invisible enemy.

Connor glanced back briefly at *The Tiger*. Under the interim command of Jasmine, it was waiting until it was safe to make its approach. Connor imagined Jasmine standing on the bridge, shoulder to shoulder with Cate and Bo Yin. He could conjure every frown line on Jasmine's face. He knew just how intently she would be watching and waiting. Turning back, he hastened to catch up with Cheng Li. She had reached the door leading into the interior, but now she hesitated. Connor was curious to know why, when Lorcan had emphasized time and again that speed was the essence of this mission's success. As he drew nearer, he saw the problem.

Though the deck was deserted while the Vampirate crew slumbered below, a trip wire had been placed across the entrance. The wire was even finer than the ladders by which the pirates had ascended—so fine, it would have been easy to miss, were it not for the sudden gift of a ray of sun. He and his comrades watched as, without uttering a word, Cheng Li pointed to where the wire led to an intricate system of pulleys and, ultimately, a bell. There was no doubting the unholy din that they had avoided by the narrowest of margins. Cheng Li carefully crossed the threshold, then tapped her finger above her eye. Her message was understood by one and all.

Following the captain over the trip wire, the pirates made their way toward the heart of the ship. They had rehearsed their maneuvers under Cate's expert tutelage; now they lost no time putting them into action.

Connor twisted open the cabin door to his right. Just as predicted, two Vampirates were fast asleep here. They didn't even stir as Connor and Moonshine stepped inside. The pirates exchanged a glance, then reached simultaneously for their silver swords, which had been dipped in Master Yin's toxic aconite potion.

No words or sounds were exchanged. With a nod, both drew their weapons at the same time and plunged them straight into the hearts of their sleeping victims. It was the strangest attack in which Connor had ever participated. Their victims did not cry or scream. They did not put up a fight. They didn't even open their eyes. Instead, their flesh began to splinter and crumble to dust. As they did so, Moonshine's face contorted. Of course! Connor was regrettably familiar with the stench as the flesh of many centuries was at last destroyed, but this was new territory entirely for Moonshine. Reaching for his companion's shoulder, Connor pulled him out into the corridor.

Across the hall, Cheng Li stepped out of the opposite cabin. She and Connor exchanged the briefest of glances. It was, nonetheless, loaded with meaning. Cheng Li disappeared into the next cabin along, a member of her crew on either side. Connor checked that Moonshine was with him, then, nodding, opened the next door on their side of the corridor.

Four Vampirates lay sprawled on their bunks in this cabin. Connor leaned out of the doorway to summon two more of his crew. They moved swiftly and, on Connor's silent command, drew their weapons. The four swords plunged into four fresh victims. No cries. No fight back. Just the horrible sight and odor of dying flesh. It was,

Connor reflected, somehow too easy. As he moved along the hallway, Connor felt less like a pirate than like a silent assassin. He knew that war had a knack for rewriting the rules of engagement, but, even so, this battle seemed unequal.

At the end of the corridor was a long communal cabin, which had a particular history for Connor. This was where he had bunked on his first nights aboard *The Diablo*. This was where, on that very first night, Bart had given up his bunk for him. As he opened the door, beckoning his team to follow, Connor's eyes swept the room. Like the previous cabins, it was full of Vampirates, deep in sleep on their bunks or suspended in hammocks.

Connor could see the simple bunk that Bart had ceded to him on that first night. It had been the first generous act in a friendship marked by many more. Suddenly, Connor's thoughts came into focus. This morning's raid was no more unjust than Lola's ruthless murder of Bart. The Vampirates slumped across these bunks and hammocks wouldn't have a moment's pause if the tables were turned. Connor ushered his comrades forward, waiting until Cheng Li and the rest joined them. This was a job for all eighteen of the first attack. It took only seconds for them to be in position, then Connor deferred to Cheng Li.

This time, *she* gave the signal as the pirates raised aloft their silver swords and rammed them through the hearts of their dormant prey. Withdrawing his sword, Connor wiped it clean in preparation for his next kill. His eyes skimmed his old bunk as he left the room. War, he reflected, was no place for fairness. Cate and Lorcan had left the attack squad in no doubt as to what they had to do. *You need to move as quickly as you can. In their weakened state, there's a much higher ratio of kill to regeneration.* It hadn't taken long for the team of pirates to rid the upper deck of *The Diablo* of its erstwhile Vampirate crew. The recapture of Molucco's legendary ship was well under way.

Cheng Li's almond eyes met Connor's. He nodded. Everything was going according to plan, so now he would take the attack down to the next stretch of cabins while she journeyed on toward the captain's cabin and an encounter with Johnny Desperado; captain to captain. She didn't go alone, of course—that would have been foolhardy, even allowing for the pirates' advantage. She proceeded with grim determination and two trusted escorts.

Meanwhile Connor and Moonshine descended the stairs, side by side. Connor could sense that Moonshine was unsettled by what he'd experienced so far. He knew that as much as Wrathe junior wanted to take possession of his uncle's ship, he hadn't completely comprehended what it would involve. It wasn't simply a matter of naivete. Nothing could inure you to the smell of a Vampirate hurtling toward oblivion.

Connor strode along the lower deck, thinking how strange it was to be walking along these familiar corridors and finding strangers behind every door. It was rather like returning to your past and discovering that every trace of you had been eradicated—as if you had never been there in the first place.

At his side, Moonshine pushed open the first cabin door on this level. Connor turned to follow suit but, hearing Moonshine curse, hesitated. There was a sudden deafening tolling of bells from the very belly of the ship. Moonshine had missed the trip wire strung across the officers' cabin, and now the Vampirates' alarm system had been activated. The pirates had been lulled into a false sense of victory and lured deeper into the ship by the sword-fodder above. Connor could see the raw horror in Moonshine's eyes. Anyone could have made such a mistake, but Connor found himself wishing that it had been he, not his comrade, who had tripped the wire.

In each of the open cabins, the crew was waking. And you could bet that the same was happening in each and every remaining cabin. Once again, Lorcan's words sounded in Connor's head. *When you rouse them, they'll be as weak as snakes who've just shed their skin.* The pirates still had the advantage, but it would no longer be quite so clear-cut. From this point on, the battle would be more evenly balanced. And, no question, a hell of a lot nastier.

17

DEADLY EMBRACE

Cheng Li ran toward the captain's cabin, her escorts at her side, as the deafening alarm reverberated around them. As she pushed open the cabin door, she saw that darkness lay beyond. It was broken only by a flash of white, which Cheng Li realized was Johnny's naked torso as he leaped out of bed. Talk about sleeping on the job!

"Wakey, wakey!" Cheng Li cried, striding into the familiar cabin. "We've come to take back our ship."

Johnny barely had the chance to leap into his pants as Cheng Li and her two escorts entered the cabin. Cheng Li kicked the door shut behind them, her eyes now adjusting to the dim as she made out the silhouette of the Cowboy.

"This is my ship now!" he asserted huskily.

"Only if you believe in squatter's rights," said Cheng Li.

Drawing her twin *katanas*, she strode purposefully toward the blackout blinds. "Time to let back in some light!"

"No!" Johnny wailed as Cheng Li's escorts closed in on either side to restrain him.

— · —

Vampirates streamed out of their cabins. Some were disoriented at having been woken too soon from their sleep. These were swiftly dispatched by the silver swords brandished by Connor, Moonshine, and the rest of the pirate vanguard. The corridor soon became a minefield of putrid Vampirate dust — a hazard in more ways than one. And now other Vampirates entered the corridor, still sluggish but bearing weapons and able to fight. The battle had shifted. Finding himself in greater danger but on more familiar turf, Connor gripped his sword and hurled himself into the fray.

As ever, Connor found the focus required for one-on-one conflict a relief. He was able to achieve *zanshin* — the legendary higher consciousness of the Samurai warrior, which Commodore Kuo had once lectured about. In this heightened state of awareness, he could fend off direct attacks while maintaining strong peripheral vision. This enabled him not only to protect himself from secondary assaults but also to look out for his comrades. Even as his sword clashed with his own adversary, he was aware of

Moonshine, fighting with genuine flair and professional-ism and claiming a fresh victory.

The corridor became still more crowded as Vampirates from the lower decks, roused by the bell and the concerto of cries and footsteps above, came up to join the fray. The pirate vanguard was now locked in a confined area with no way to open up more space than through slaughter. This phase of Operation Scrimshaw had been predicted by Cate, and she had identified her strongest swordsmen and -women accordingly.

Connor knew that the pirates' key advantage—sur-prise—was now lost to them. The sense of jeopardy had roused the Vampirates like a hefty dose of caffeine, and the blood from the wounds inflicted on their pirate attack-ers had awakened their hunger, too. Connor could see the fires of hunger stoked in his enemies' eyes. Thankfully, he himself was still sated from the blood he'd scored the night before—otherwise, this would have been an unwel-come distraction.

He could see the change in his own adversary. With every clash of their swords, the Vampirate seemed to grow stronger. For the first time in the attack, Connor felt he was engaged in an equal fight. He found himself lifting his own sword skills. The duel was a close-fought one, but at last he outmaneuvered the Vampirate and claimed victory.

To his side, one of his comrades had not proved so lucky. Goran fell to the floor with a crash, a dead weight.

Goran had been a popular member of the crew, and Connor saw momentary hesitation in his ranks.

"Come on!" he urged the others. "He played his part. Fight on! Clear this corridor!"

At his words, the pirates took to their mission with fresh vigor. But they no longer had the advantage of numbers. Vampirates from belowdecks were surging toward them, pushing them back along the corridor.

Cheng Li enjoyed the pleasing sound of her *katanas* slicing through Johnny's blackout blinds and watched as the morning light burst into the cabin.

"No!" Johnny cried once more.

As Cheng Li turned around to witness his imminent destruction, she saw with horror that both her escorts lay on the floor, motionless, blood pooling around them. How on earth had he done that? Evidently, he had a rare gift for killing. But these would be his last kills. He was already trembling as he faced the light, as if he were experiencing a terrible chill—when in fact the complete reverse was true.

"No," he cried once more, his voice obviously weaker now.

The light seemed to have rooted him to the spot. His eyes were closed, but his face nonetheless expressed the terrible pain he was experiencing. Cheng Li could smell burning. It was not an unfamiliar smell to her these days, but she would never become used to it. Stepping closer, she watched with horrid fascination as the skin on Johnny's handsome face began to char and blister. She reached out, tentatively, to his bare shoulder and found that his flesh crumbled to ash in her fingertips.

This, she thought, was all part of the mystery—how creatures so strong in darkness could crumble to nothingness when faced with the light. She almost felt sorry for him. Then she reminded herself that he had been instrumental in murdering Molucco and was one of Sidorio and Lola's most trusted operatives. The blood of countless pirates lay on Johnny's hands. Cheng Li's eyes fell to her own two fallen comrades. The Cowboy had certainly wasted no pity on them. Turning her gaze back to the desiccating Vampirate, she pushed aside any instinct of pity. She slipped her *katanas* back into their sheaths. Folding her arms, she watched Johnny cry out with pain as the light burned deeper into his core.

As the Vampirates claimed another of the pirates and paused to feast on her blood, Connor saw a flash of fear in Moonshine's eyes.

"Fight on!" Connor cried. "This is your ship we're fighting for!"

The words were enough to jolt Moonshine back into action. Just then, a greater jolt sent the ship rolling in the ocean. The battle zone was thrown into immediate confusion as the floor rose up by sixty degrees on the starboard side. The confusion intensified as pirates and Vampirates were thrown across the narrow corridor. As they landed and came to their senses, the floor shifted again, but in the other direction. At last, the ship slumped back to where it had started, but the various combatants were now scattered and squaring up to different adversaries. Nevertheless, the Vampirates resumed the fight.

Connor and the pirates knew that the jolt signaled good news. It meant that *The Tiger* had drawn up alongside them and it wouldn't be long before reinforcements arrived.

—◦—

The force of *The Tiger* ramming into *The Diablo* threw Cheng Li and Johnny across the cabin and—*slam*—into each other. Face-to-face, they were both momentarily disoriented. Johnny's scorched hands locked around Cheng Li's narrow waist.

She tried to push him away, feeling suffocated by the toxic smell of burning. "Let me go!"

Johnny smiled grimly at her. "If I'm going down in flames, sugar, you're surely coming with me!"

Although pieces of his charred skin were now floating around the cabin like ticker tape, still his inner strength remained. Cheng Li was unable to break free of his grip.

Now, he reached behind her and extricated the *katanas* from her back. "You won't be needing these where you're heading!" he declared as Cheng Li's trusted weaponry clattered onto the cabin floor.

Cheng Li felt naked and vulnerable without her *katanas*, but there was nothing she could do. It was as if, close to the edge of destruction, Johnny was possessed with a final surge of strength. She found herself being pushed toward the glass of the vast porthole that, until recently, had been covered with blackout blinds. "No!" she cried out, drawing on all her own strength to defy Johnny. But his strength was far superior despite his injuries, and he succeeded in propelling them both with such force into the cabin window that the glass shattered around them and they fell through the broken porthole. Locked in a deadly embrace, Johnny and Cheng Li tumbled through the morning air and down into the water. He was burning and she was bleeding, and yet the ice-cold water offered neither of them any kind of release.

⌒～⌒

Connor's momentary relief at the arrival of *The Tiger* was short-lived. His vision was blurred. He was seeing double. His first thought was that he must have taken a blow when the two ships had braced against each other. But, as he experienced the most violent headache ever, he realized that he was seeing two places at once, like two pictures overlapping each other—the first this crowded corridor, the second a large cabin on the corridor below.

"Which one?" asked a voice. It took him by surprise as he realized that the voice was his own.

Now, he saw Vampirates on the attack in both rooms.

"Choose, quickly!" the voice said again. His own voice.

"Down," he answered numbly and, as he said the word, he found that he was already in the downstairs cabin, fending off an attack from two Vampirates. His headache had gone and his *zanshin* seemed stronger than ever, as he sent the first adversary flying and thrust his sword into the second. The Vampirate crumbled to dust before his eyes.

"Result!" said his own voice. Suddenly, he was back upstairs, in the thick of the corridor battle, dispatching another Vampirate adversary.

Just as suddenly, he was back downstairs, taking on a fresh opponent and calling for reinforcements. As he did so, he was up above, hearing his own voice. How on earth was this happening? He was in two places at once, fighting two battles simultaneously. It was disorienting at first. Both Connors felt queasy. Even to think of himself as "both" made him yet more nauseous. But from somewhere came an iron resolve. Each Connor focused on the battle at hand, and somehow the queasiness gave way to pure adrenaline.

In the upper corridor, Connor was thrilled to see Cate and Jasmine entering the fray, leading the rest of *The*

Tiger's attack squad. For a time, the battle intensified, but with their new numbers and greater fighting prowess, the pirates once more gained the advantage and claimed the second corridor for their own.

Connor considered racing downstairs but knew his other self was already there, claiming the upper hand in a fresh duel.

"Connor!" Moonshine cried, entering the downstairs room. "How did you get down here so quickly?"

He didn't answer, too confused and not wanting to lose his concentration now.

With the fresh influx of pirates, the battle was soon contained within the main cabin, and it didn't take long for the pirates to gain the upper hand here, too. The remaining Vampirates, and they were still numerous, had been pushed to the back end of the ship. Not all of them were armed, and even those that were now recognized the odds were against them.

Connor stood shoulder to shoulder with Cate and Jasmine. Wiping a stray hair from his forehead, he gave the command. "Take them!"

The pirates were poised. But Jasmine raised her hand. "They're not all armed," she said. "Shouldn't we at least offer them clemency?"

Connor shrugged, then turned to Moonshine. "There's no sign of Cheng Li, and since this is your ship, Captain Wrathe, you better make the call."

Moonshine assessed the situation. Connor, Jasmine, Cate, Bo Yin, and the others waited on his word.

"Take them!" he cried, raising his own sword aloft.

At this command, the pirates moved in for a coordinated endgame.

But now one of the Vampirates pushed to the front and raised his arm, bearing a handkerchief that was just about recognizable as white, though somewhat bloodied.

"Cate! Mistress Cate!" he cried out. "We surrender."

"Wait!" Cate called out. She stepped forward, curious to know who had addressed her.

"Who are you?" She beckoned the Vampirate forward.

"Don't you remember me, Mistress Cate? I served under Captain Wrathe, and latterly your good self, for many a year."

Cate stared at the Vampirate for a time then clicked her fingers. "Antonio?"

The man nodded, smiling suddenly and revealing two oversize canines. "That's right, Antonio." He stretched out his arms to either side. "And this here is Lukas, and over there Jack, who used to be called Toothless, and De Cloux."

Cate surveyed the men. Connor did, too. He recognized each and every one of them, and others besides. They had been loyal crew to Molucco—to the very last it seemed. The Diablo had been taken when the ship was docked at Ma Kettle's. The first assumption had been that it was largely deserted at the time, but evidently that was not the full story. Johnny and his troops must have found plenty of Molucco's original crew and "converted" them. For there was no doubt that these pirates were now Vampirates.

"Please, Mistress Cate," Antonio said now. "We beg you for clemency. Not one of us was a willing recruit to the Vampirate force. We had no choice in the matter."

Glancing at her comrades on either side, Cate nodded. "We accept your surrender," she said. Her eyes turned to Moonshine. "*The Diablo* is once more under the command of a Wrathe. Captain, it's your command now."

There was no time to savor the victory. Moonshine swiftly organized his team to secure the vessel.

"Connor, take the pirates you need and secure the prisoners! Jasmine, I want you and your team to check the rest of the lower cabins and ensure we've achieved one hundred percent success here." Jasmine gave Moonshine the Federation salute and led Bo Yin away.

Moonshine turned to Cate. "Come with me," he said.

"Where?"

"To the captain's cabin," Moonshine said. "Cheng Li should have dispatched the Cowboy by now. It'll be ready for us to take over command."

"Us?" Cate said, surprised to find Moonshine nodding and smiling at her.

Down beneath the surface waters, Johnny still clasped Cheng Li in a viselike grip. Clearly, he had no intention of letting her go. She was finding it harder and harder to keep the air in her lungs. Her body felt weak in a way that was utterly alien to her. She no longer had any doubt. She would not be making it back from this.

It was as if Johnny had read her thoughts. For now he turned his eyes to her and all the pain and fury she had seen there before was gone. Instead, he looked peaceful. Her first thought was that perhaps the water had quenched his burning, but she saw that this was not the case. If anything, his disintegration was gathering momentum. Yet still his face—his eyes—were suddenly peaceful and, in a way, quite beautiful. Feeling on the verge of delirium, she thought of Lorcan Furey. Beautiful Lorcan Furey. If only he were here to save her now.

At last, she felt Johnny's grip loosen, though she realized that this was involuntary. It seemed that his strength was finally being depleted. He seemed to shrug at her as his arms set her free. She found herself floating away from him and her heart leaped. She was floating up to safety. But it had better be quick. Her lungs felt as if they were about to explode.

— ⁀ —

Connor watched as Cate and Moonshine set off. Once, he might have felt envy at Moonshine's sudden prominence, but now he felt only satisfaction at a job well done and a certain confusion as to the events of that morning. One of his men, Scott, came over to his side. "Want some help?" he asked. Connor nodded gratefully.

They called forward their teams and rounded up the prisoners, leading them out into the corridor and up to the higher deck. "Obviously they can't go outside while it's light," Scott said. "Let's contain them in the dormitory cabin upstairs for now."

Connor nodded, letting Scott go on ahead while he took up the rear. As he followed the prisoners up the stairs, he saw a door push open on the upper corridor. No one but him noticed as a figure stepped out.

Connor found himself looking at his own self. They were identical in every way. Now the second Connor slipped his sword back into its scabbard and lifted a finger to his lips. He stepped closer to Connor, closer and closer until... Connor felt another searing headache. The pain drove him to close his eyes for an instant. When he opened them again, the ache was gone and so was his other self. He shook himself, feeling suddenly energized, and followed the prisoners up to their holding bay.

"Well?" Cate asked as she and Moonshine crossed the threshold into the captain's cabin. "How does it feel to be a full-fledged captain?"

Moonshine's face was streaked with blood and sweat, but he smiled from ear to ear and punched the air. "It feels great!" he exclaimed. Then his face grew more serious and his voice husky. "What's happened here? Where's Cheng Li?"

They both assessed the scene of devastation—the torn blinds, the broken timber, and the shards of broken glass. The air was still thick with ash. Moonshine found the soles of his boots were sticky with blood. Taking another step, he glanced down at the bodies of Cheng Li's slaughtered escorts.

His eyes met Cate's once more, but he no longer looked as if he was claiming a victory. "I don't like this, Cate. I have a bad feeling about what went down here."

Cate nodded. Her own blood was running cold as she stepped forward and looked out through the broken window. She didn't know what she expected to see. Cheng Li treading water? Her body floating on the waves? Cate saw neither—only the mirrorlike surface of the callous ocean. "Cheng Li!" she cried out. "Has anyone seen Captain Li?" Her question was met only by silence.

Suddenly Moonshine pushed past her. "I'm going in," he said.

"No!" Cate reached out a hand to restrain him.

"I'm a strong swimmer," Moonshine declared. "If she's down there, I'll find her."

Before she could do anything to stop him, Moonshine had climbed out through the broken window and jumped down into the icy water below.

"Be careful!" Cate cried as he dipped beneath the water's surface. A strong beam of sunlight suddenly struck Cate directly in the face. It made her raise a hand to her eyes and turn away from the window. She found herself looking into the cabin once more. The cabin floor was now further illuminated by the stark glare of the sun. Light reflected off two spikes of silver on the floor. Cate recognized them immediately. She had seen them many times before.

Cate's heart hammered as she knelt down and reached out her hands toward Cheng Li's twin *katanas*. Both of her hands were soon covered in blood and ash, but she was past caring. She gripped the hilts of the *katanas* in her hands. There was no way Cheng Li would have willingly been separated from her beloved weapons. A horrible sense of foreboding washed over her, and she dashed to the porthole, terrified of what she might see in the waters below.

Oblivious to the scenes above, Jasmine and her team worked their way systematically through the lower cabins. Some of the stuff they found made for grim viewing.

"Are you sure you can handle this?" she asked Bo Yin as they came across a fresh skeleton.

Bo Yin nodded. "I'm tougher than you think," she said.

"Yes." Jasmine nodded. "I guess you are."

"That's about it, Deputy Peacock," announced a gruff voice at her side. "We have this level locked down, with the exception of this cabin here."

Jasmine glanced deeper into the gloomy cabin. "It doesn't look like there's anything we can't handle here," she said. "You can go up and join the others. Report to Captain Li and see if she has fresh duties for you."

"Yes, ma'am!" The officer saluted Jasmine, then turned on his heels.

Jasmine pushed open the creaking door to the final cabin and stepped across the threshold. Bo Yin followed close behind. Glancing up ahead, Jasmine narrowed her eyes.

"Is that a cage?" she asked, stepping closer and seeing the bars and the thick chain that looped around the door.

"What's inside it?" Bo Yin asked.

"Probably just more bones," Jasmine said with a shudder. "I don't want to know what went on down here."

"Me neither," Bo Yin agreed. "Wait! Did you see that?"

Jasmine froze to the spot. Yes, she had seen it. Behind the steel bars, there was a movement.

"There's something in there," Bo Yin said.

"Not something," Jasmine corrected her. "Someone." Her heart hammered as she stepped closer and knelt down before the cage. A pale, skeletal hand reached forward. The bony tips of the fingers pushed through the gap in the cage and made contact with her own flesh. It— *he*—seemed to want to make contact. Jasmine shuddered but did not retreat. A thin face hovered in the darkness beyond the bars. It lingered there, as if afraid to come any farther forward, but she willed it to keep coming—as if she were luring a frightened kitten out from a hiding place.

Finally, the face leaned forward, atop a scrawny neck. The flesh was drawn and gray in color and the head had been shorn of hair. Despite this, Jasmine would have recognized those eyes anywhere.

"Jacoby!" she exclaimed with a gasp. "Oh, my God... Jacoby, what have they done to you?"

Cate was still standing at the broken window when she heard Moonshine's cries.

"I found her! I've found Cheng Li!" Moonshine was bobbing on the water's surface with Cheng Li in his arms. The captain's eyes were closed and there were lacerations all over her pale face.

"Help me!" Moonshine cried. "Her heartbeat is weak, but I think we can bring her back. She's a fighter."

Cate shook her head in amazement, then jumped into action. Ripping an ornate tapestry off the nearby wall, she sliced it to ribbons with her sword, then tied the pieces together to form a makeshift rope. It wasn't the best method, but it was certainly the quickest.

Cate threw the rope out of the porthole and down to

Moonshine. He grabbed at it with one hand as he paddled desperately to keep them afloat with the other.

"Thank God," said Cate to herself. Then, tentatively, she tugged at the rope. It held, so she pulled again, harder this time. Securing her end to a chair, she called down to them. "Hang on in there; I'm going to get help to pull you in. But just so you know, Cheng Li, we've won back *The Diablo*!"

"We did?" Cheng Li's voice was recognizable but weak. Moonshine grinned at her. "You bet your sweet *katanas* we did. Turns out we're quite a team, Commodore Li!"

Under normal circumstances, he might have gotten a slap for that. As it was, Cheng Li smiled and sank back into his arms as he swam her back to safety. In the distance, ambulance boats were already heaving into view.

18

PLANS INTERRUPTED

Darcy stepped inside her room, closing the door behind her. "Grace," she said in surprise. "What's going on? You look terrible. And why are you packing that bag?"

"I'm going away for a bit," Grace said, drawing the zip across the top of the bag.

"Where are you going?" Darcy asked. "For how long? And why now?"

She watched her friend's face as she registered each of the questions. Grace was flinching as if she were being assailed by gusts of biting wind.

"I don't know how long I'll be gone, exactly," she said, sitting down on the edge of her own bed. "I need to see Lorcan, Darcy. I'm going back to *The Nocturne*."

"What's brought this on?" Darcy inquired. "I know you miss him, but there's more to it than that, isn't there?

There must be for you to desert your patients, and Mosh Zu, and..."

"There's a prophecy," Grace told Darcy. "Mosh Zu made it five hundred years ago."

"What *kind* of prophecy?" Darcy asked.

"A remarkably accurate one, in many respects," Grace answered. "He foresaw a time of war and that the threat would come from within the Vampirate realm — from a warmonger..."

"Sidorio!" Darcy exclaimed.

Grace nodded. "There's more. Mosh Zu foresaw that the warmonger would have twin children and that they..." At last she faltered. "That *we*, Connor and I, would play a key role in resolving the conflict."

"Which you are!" Darcy exclaimed protectively.

"Yes," Grace agreed, tears now flowing. "But there's a price to be paid, Darcy. One of us must die. That was part of the prophecy."

"How do you know all this?" Darcy asked.

"It's all here," Grace said. "In this little book." She reached into her bag and passed the book across to Darcy. Grace watched as her friend turned the pages, and saw the understandable confusion in her eyes.

"It's blank," Darcy said.

Drying her eyes, Grace smiled wryly at her friend. "It's blank to you because you're not its custodian. I know it sounds crazy, Darcy, but it speaks to me."

Darcy closed the book. She knew Grace well enough to

believe her story, however far-fetched it might seem. "I presume you've talked to Mosh Zu about this?"

Grace nodded. "I did, when I first found the book. And he told me not to worry."

"Well, then..." The relief was evident on Darcy's face.

"The book told me to trust no one. And when you think about it, Darcy, Mosh Zu has kept things from me before. So has Obsidian. They both conveniently forgot to tell me that I was Sidorio's daughter, though they knew it from the very first."

Darcy's eyes fell. "To be fair, Lorcan knew it, too."

Grace shrugged. Maybe she was even more alone than she had figured. "I didn't want to believe the prophecy," she said. "I've tried to shut it out of my mind and focus on my work here, but I can't do it. I think the time is coming when either me or Connor *is* going to die."

Darcy pointed to the book. "Has it said something else to you to make you think that?"

Tears coursing down her cheeks, Grace nodded.

"What did it say?" Darcy asked, putting her arms around Grace. "You have to tell me."

Grace bit back her tears. "It said that we're approaching the end of the war. That when Lola's twins are born, the end is in sight." She trembled in Darcy's arms. "I have this feeling I can't seem to shake that, for some reason, the world cannot contain both pairs of Sidorio's twins."

Darcy felt a sudden tightening in her chest. Usually, Grace was so strong and resolute. Despite everything she had been through, it was rare to see her so vulnerable. She had offered Darcy comfort on many occasions and now, more than anything, Darcy wanted to be the strong one, but she wasn't sure what solace she could offer. She had a sudden vision of the first time she and Grace had met, on the deck of *The Nocturne*. She had been lighting the lamps when she'd become aware of this strange girl staring at her. Grace had been wide-eyed with wonder back then. Now, her eyes were shadowed with deep fear.

"I don't want you to go," Darcy said, "but I think you're right. You need to see Lorcan."

Grace nodded, crumpling into Darcy's embrace.

Just then, there was the familiar sound of bells. They both registered it like a shock of icy water. They stood, locked in each other's arms, frozen for a time as the bells continued, summoning the healers and nurses to their positions.

"You can still go," Darcy said as Grace began shaking her head. "Yes, you can, Grace. Let the other healers take the brunt this time. You're in no fit state to heal, anyway."

Grace drew herself back upright and dusted herself down. "I can't do that," she said.

Darcy was resolute. "Sometimes, you have to put your-self first," she said.

Grace hesitated, catching sight of the book. She was desperate to see Lorcan, but could she really abandon her colleagues at this time?

She stood stock-still on the floor, unable to commit to a

movement in either direction. Just then, there was a loud knocking on the door.

"Grace! Grace, are you in there?" It was Tooshita.

Grace darted to the door and opened it. She saw Tooshita's relief, then surprise at seeing Grace in tears.

"I'm glad I found you," Tooshita said. "It's all hands on deck, I'm afraid. We have some bad casualties coming our way."

Darcy came to the doorway and asked Tooshita, "Another attack?"

Tooshita nodded. "A victory for us, though," she said with a smile. "The Alliance has taken back an important ship. *The Diablo*, I think..."

"*The Diablo!*" Grace exclaimed. Immediately, she thought of Johnny. "You say the Alliance was successful?"

Tooshita nodded. "Come on, Grace, we'll walk and talk."

Grace found herself propelled along the corridor. Darcy hurried after her and Tooshita.

"Do you know any other details?" Grace asked, unable to prevent herself from asking the next question. "Do you know if the captain of *The Diablo* escaped?"

"The Vampirate incumbent, you mean?" Tooshita asked.

Grace nodded. Johnny, she thought. Kind, handsome Johnny. Poor, misguided Johnny. The most contrary man she had ever met. Her enemy. Her friend. He was so many things to her. *What if*... She found herself unable to complete the thought.

Tooshita's eyes were dark. "There was a terrible fight," she said. "A duel between him and one of our leaders, Commodore Li. They crashed through his cabin windows and into the ocean together. But only one of them came back up for air."

They had walked so fast that they were already at the entrance to the compound. Grace was aware of Darcy hanging back behind them as Tooshita pushed open the doors into daylight. The other healers were already waiting outside.

"Who came back?" Grace asked as she and Tooshita strode out into the bracing light. "Cheng Li or John— Cheng Li or *the Vampirate*?"

Tooshita smiled softly at her friend. "Good news," she said. "Commodore Li is making an amazing recovery. He tried to take her down with him, but he failed." Evidently, she didn't notice Grace's expression as she marched on into the waiting area. Grace stumbled after her, feeling suddenly weak. It was an effort putting one foot in front of the other. *Not Johnny. Not Johnny. Not Johnny.* But she knew, deep down, that it must be true. War was raging and its fire would consume them all.

19

REUNION

Grace watched, feeling wretched and numb, as three ambulances arrived at the top of the hill. Three ambulances meant a lot of casualties for her and her fellow healers to attend to. She should have followed Darcy's advice and disappeared when she had the chance. Now there was no escape. Darcy's words rang in her head. *You're in no fit state to heal.* Darcy's words were even truer now than they had been when she'd spoken them.

Although Grace felt numb, she knew that deep within her was a maelstrom of turbulent emotions. She was in profound mourning for Johnny—for everything he had been and everything he might have been. She had always felt that, with time, she could save him from himself. Now it seemed that time had run out. How could she possibly heal the wounded from the battle to regain *The Diablo* when all her thoughts and feelings were with the man they had killed?

Grace watched the scene in front of her with a sense of disconnection. Moments of crisis like this had somehow become commonplace. The rescue workers made up a well-oiled team; they all knew their places and responsibilities. The ambulance doors were opening, and there was Dani, clipboard in hand, ready to classify the casualties and assign them to the healers. The staff began passing the patients over to the stretcher-bearers. Grace waited, with a mounting sense of dread, for her patient to be assigned and her name to be called.

She started when she recognized an ashen-looking Jasmine stumbling out of the back of one of the ambulances. *What is Jasmine doing here?* Obviously, she would have been involved in the attack on *The Diablo*. *Is she wounded?* Grace watched as Jasmine walked purposefully toward her. Other than a few cuts and grazes, Jasmine looked fine. It was clear that she was not here as a patient. Grace's hands clenched into protective fists. Jasmine was Connor's comrade and girlfriend. *Had Connor been wounded in the battle?* Her thoughts had been so much with Johnny that she hadn't even stopped to think of her brother. The words of the prophecy came back to her in sharp relief. *One twin must die.* No, this was too much—not Johnny *and* Connor. *Please, no.*

Standing before Grace, Jasmine's face broke with evident relief. "Thank goodness you're here, Grace," she said. "He's in a really bad way. I thought that they'd take us to the infirmary at Pirate Academy, but they said he was...that he was too far gone for that." She managed to get the words out but only just before she started to sob.

Grace stood before her brother's girlfriend, barely daring to ask the question. "Jasmine, are you talking about Connor?"

Jasmine shook her head, her face pale, her eyes wet with budding tears. "No! No, Connor's fine. It's Jacoby!"

Grace felt ashamed at the relief that flooded through her. Suddenly things were coming back into focus. "Jacoby? But that's wonderful. He's alive after all!"

"Barely," Jasmine said with a shudder. "Wait till you see what they did to him. It's a good thing Commodore Li killed that despicable Johnny Desperado before I could get my own hands on him. He kept Jacoby in a cage!"

Grace didn't know where she found the strength to squeeze Jasmine's shoulder reassuringly and tell her, "Let it go, Jasmine. All that matters is that Jacoby's safe." She smiled softly. "He's in the right place now. I'll do everything I can for him."

Grace moved toward the stretcher and flinched as she saw Jacoby borne aloft. She was shocked, but not in the way she had expected to be. She knew that, whatever else, she had to remain calm. Turning, she saw Jasmine watching the unfolding scene intently. Grace's eyes sought out

Noijon. As if reading her mind, Noijon moved swiftly across to Jasmine and drew her away across the courtyard. Grace turned back to address the rescue team in a low but firm voice.

"Why wasn't this patient bagged?"

The ambulance man looked at her in confusion. "He's a pirate. Or what's left of one. We don't bag pirates."

"Look at him!" Grace commanded, her own eyes falling upon the livid burns covering Jacoby's face and arms. The burns were fresh, but they were also familiar. She had seen them before on Lorcan's face—after he had stayed out too long in the light.

"Hmm, that's strange," admitted the ambulance driver. "I don't remember him having those when we brought him off the boat. He must have taken a turn for the worse." Grace frowned and shook her head as the man continued. "Anyhow, my job is to deliver them to you to fix up. He's your problem now!" So saying, he actually smiled at her as, helped by his mate, he passed Jacoby's ravaged body across to the nursing team. They clamped the patient onto a stretcher-trolley.

"I'm going with him," Jasmine said, breaking away from Noijon.

"Wait!" Grace called to them both. "He's in a bad way, and we can't lose any more time in beginning his treatment." Seeing the raw terror in Jasmine's face, her voice softened. "Of course you can come with us, but I can't let you into the healing chamber."

"He will be okay, won't he?" Jasmine asked in a voice little more than a whisper. Before Grace could construct an answer, she heard her name being called again.

Turning, she found Dani beckoning her over to another of the ambulances. Grace hurried over, then saw that she was standing over a zipped-up patient bag.

"I need you to take another patient," Dani told her. "It's a Nocturnal, severity Gold. He or she—it's not possible to tell which—is in a *very* bad way." When Grace didn't answer, Dani continued. "I'm sorry to ask, Grace, but I've already assigned cases to all the other healers. I've sent two of the most badly wounded to Mosh Zu. Frankly, you're the only other healer capable of handling two of this severity."

Grace didn't want to waste precious time thinking about this. Her earlier numbness had drained away and she felt filled now with a powerful energy and the urgent need to get started on her work. She nodded at Dani, then turned to her team.

"Noijon!" Grace called out. "Come over here, please, and bring another trolley. We're taking on a second patient. Evrim, take Jacoby down to the healing chamber and prepare him for me." Seeing Jasmine hovering nearby, she added, "And someone please make Deputy Peacock comfortable in one of the anterooms."

Everyone did exactly as Grace instructed. They all had the utmost faith in her.

With Jasmine settled outside, Grace gazed down at Jacoby's lifeless body and the livid burns on his face and arms.

"Evrim," she said softly, "I need you to begin treatment while I get started on the other patient. It's a close call, but he, or she, is in more urgent need of my attention."

"No problem," Evrim said, gratified by this sign of Grace's trust in her.

"You've prepared a Nocturnal for treatment many times before," Grace said. "You know what to do."

Now Evrim turned to Grace, her dark eyes wide with confusion. "But Grace, I thought he was a pirate," she said.

"*Was,*" Grace repeated. "Past tense. Look at these burns! What more information do you need? He's been converted—and none too willingly by the looks of it." Their eyes met as Grace continued. "It's imperative that Deputy Peacock knows nothing of this. Not yet. She needs to hear it in the right way and from the right person, understand?"

Evrim nodded. "I'll start with some salve for his burns."

Nodding, Grace gave her colleague's arm a reassuring squeeze, then pushed back the gauze curtain to attend to the patient on the other side of the healing chamber.

Noijon had made all the necessary preparations, and, as Grace took her place at the foot of the bed, he lost no time in passing her the first set of healing ribbons. Glancing down at the wounded Nocturnal, Grace shuddered. There was no question. This was the most extreme case she had ever been confronted with. Poor, beaten-up Jacoby was going to have to wait his turn.

—◦—

For all Grace's earlier doubts, she found herself rising to the challenge of the healing process and grateful for the complete concentration it demanded from her. Maybe this was exactly what she needed, to distract her from her nascent grief. She soon found her own thoughts and feelings floating away as she became deeply immersed in the uniquely intimate dance between patient and healer.

Noijon was with her every step of the way. They had worked together so often now that he anticipated her every move. It was clear, too, that he took pleasure at being challenged in this way. The healing was slow and arduous at the beginning, and Grace knew that, even if they were successful, this was going to be a long journey. But they persisted, and, slowly but surely, Grace began to sense intermittent but strengthening signs of the patient's returning vitality.

She knew now that the patient was a man. His body was ravaged with lesions, and the burning—which she now knew to be the prime cause of his wounds—had gone deep. His extremities began to patch themselves back together. His hands were too charred, and in any case too weak, to hold Grace's healing ribbons. Taking this into consideration, Grace instructed Noijon to bind the ribbons through the patient's hands—securely enough that they would not break free but loose enough that the ribbons would not rub against the sensitive skin there. Noijon swiftly attended to these preparations, then stepped back, presenting Grace with the other end of the ribbons.

Her eyes were closed now, and, as she took hold of the ribbons, she felt a faint but building rhythm. It called to mind the drums that signaled the beginning of Feast Night. The drumming grew louder and more frequent. This was a good sign. Grace knew that the patient's heart was beginning to repair. Now the beats made her think of the ocean lapping against the shore or the side of a ship. She continued her work, tuning in to the nuances of the patient's heartbeats. The drumming grew progressively louder and louder until its beats became horses' hooves, thundering across the sand.

Her full attention given over to the patient, Grace had a powerful vision of night on a beach and a horse cantering across the shoreline. She realized, with a start, that she was still thinking of Johnny and of their midnight horseback rides. She had allowed herself to become distracted—something that must never happen during a healing. She pulled herself back from the vision, tempting as it was to linger there, and focused once more on the strengthening heartbeat.

But, as she returned her focus to the patient, the image of night and the beach came into even sharper focus. Bewildered, she found she had no choice but to stay with it. Now her own heart began to race. It was the exact same beach she had ridden across with Johnny on that midnight ride. But now she was seeing it from his point of view. And not just seeing it, but hearing it, too—the crashing waves and the taste of the salt-spray. She was feeling it all from his point of view and was aware of the intensity of his happiness. Her own heart felt as if it might burst. It could mean only one thing.

The patient was Johnny. There could be no doubt. There must have been the most almighty mix-up, but the cocksure ambulance crew had brought in "the immortal enemy" for treatment. Before, she had wanted to punch the ambulance man's lights out. Now she would have hugged him in gratitude.

She pushed aside these thoughts and allowed herself to return to the beach of the vision. The drumming was louder now—of Nieve's hooves and Johnny's heartbeat.

"He's back." She heard Noijon's soft voice in her ear. "You've brought him back, Grace."

Opening her eyes, she saw that the patient's face had returned from the abyss. His eyes were closed, but there was now no doubt about it. She'd know that handsome cowboy's face anywhere. A soft smile played on his blistered lips. It was a good thing Noijon was here or she might do something foolish.

"Great job!" Noijon whispered.

Grace nodded. She was smiling, too. She passed the ends of the ribbons to Noijon. "I need you to continue my work," she said. "I must attend to Jacoby now."

Nodding, Noijon stepped into position and took hold of the ribbons.

Grace drew back and stared down at Johnny. She was so grateful that she had been able to heal him. But Sanctuary was not a safe place for him. As soon as she had healed Jacoby and made both her patients comfortable, she needed to find a way to get Johnny out of here— undetected and fast.

"No one is to come into this healing chamber besides you or me," she told Noijon. "Absolutely no one, understand?"

He nodded, eyes closed, as he began his own healing practice. Grace watched the rise and fall of Johnny's abdomen. Knowing he was in safe hands, she slipped back to the other side of the curtain, where she knew Jacoby was waiting for her.

20

A GREAT LOSS

"Care for a top-up?" Lola asked her guest, moving toward him, decanter in hand.

He smiled at his hostess genially. "Why not?" Turning to Sidorio, he said, "You certainly have a nice setup here."

Sidorio nodded, leaning forward, eager to conclude their business. "Yes, we do. Of course, this isn't our primary ship..."

Lola chuckled as she refilled Sidorio's glass. "What my husband means to say is that *his* ship, *The Blood Captain*, is the engine of our burgeoning empire. This ship, *my* ship, is very much reserved for the inner sanctum of friends and allies."

Their guest nodded and lifted his glass aloft. "A toast, then! To friends and allies!"

Sidorio raised his glass and drank it down in one. Lola

bit her lip, disappointed to see old habits resurface. She filled her own glass and took a discreet sip. As she did so, she noticed that their guest was watching her closely. She was not overly perturbed by this. She had never been surprised by this kind of attention.

"Is something amiss, Lord DeWinter?"

He met her stare and held his glass between two hands. "No, not really. It's just that you're pregnant, aren't you?"

Lola giggled, proudly displaying her bump. "Indeed I am, sir. I can assure you that's the only reason for my enormous belly."

"Indeed," said Lord DeWinter. "My point is, should you be drinking blood while pregnant?" He shrugged, seeming embarrassed to have raised the matter.

Lola smiled, confident that she had him exactly where she wanted him. "Actually, I have it upon good authority that blood is vital for my babes at this point."

As she spoke, Lola turned toward Olivier, who was sitting unnoticed in the corner of the cabin.

As if on cue, he rose to his feet and walked over to join them. "Blood is full of all the nutrients Lady Sidorio's babies need to come out kicking and fighting," he said, sitting down beside them.

"And you are?" Lord DeWinter inquired.

Before Olivier could answer, Sidorio spoke on his behalf. "Olivier here is in charge of our healing center — for treating war-wounded Vampirates."

Lola chimed in. "We discovered that the Nocturnals

had two healing centers, and so we sent in Olivier to research their facilities and then establish our own, infinitely superior, version."

"It seems you really have thought of everything," Lord DeWinter said, clearly impressed, and he lifted his glass once more. "I wish you and your kin the best of health," he said.

"Talking of kin," said Lola, exchanging a glance with Sidorio before turning the full beam of her stare back upon their guest, "do you feel ready to make an alliance with us? Are you ready to join our family, so to speak?"

Lord DeWinter set down his glass and rose to his feet. "My Lord and Lady Sidorio," he said, "you have made an impressive case. It seems as if your power over the ocean rivals mine across the land. A lot of what you say makes sense to me. I can see the virtue in an alliance between our two empires."

"That's marvelous!" Lola exclaimed, rising to her own feet and gesturing to Sidorio to join her. "Isn't it simply marvelous, darling?" she said.

"Yes," Sidorio agreed, extending his hand to Lord DeWinter. "You won't regret this."

Lola reached for a small gold bell resting on a matching salver. She lifted up the bell and rang it. "In the hope of this happy outcome, I took the liberty of having some papers drawn up to formalize the arrangement."

Lord DeWinter beamed. "You're not one to let the grass grow under your feet, are you, Lady Sidorio?"

She laughed coquettishly and shook her head. There was a knock at the door.

"Enter!" Lola cried, and Holly came into the room, carrying a golden salver bearing the contract, a fountain pen, and a glass inkwell.

Lord DeWinter dipped the pen in the ink and then placed the nib on the parchment. As he signed his name in crimson, he chuckled. "Nice touch."

Lola nodded appreciatively. "You have made the right decision," she said. "Our power over the oceans is unquestionable. With allies like you, we will be able to forge on, relentlessly, until the oceans are red with the blood of our victims."

Sidorio coughed discreetly. "I think you've started to repeat yourself, my dear," he said, in a husky whisper. It was not sufficiently husky that Holly, Olivier, and Lord DeWinter could not hear. Lola shot her husband an icy stare.

The door opened once more and Mimma strode into the room.

"Mimma!" Lola said, surprised but grateful for the distraction. "Allow me to present you to Lord DeWinter. You'll know him by reputation, of course. He is the Overlord of the Land as far as the eye can see. And, as of two minutes ago, our newest ally."

Mimma waited for Lola to finish but seemed unmoved by her words. She turned to Lord DeWinter and nodded. "I have heard of you, sir, and it's good to meet you."

He nodded, smiling, but Mimma turned straight back to Lola.

"Captain, I have important news."

"News?" Sidorio said, his voice booming across the cabin. "What news do you have?"

Mimma bit her lip, turning to Lord DeWinter.

"Don't worry about him," Sidorio said. "He's our ally. We share news with our allies."

Mimma seemed unsure but Lola, seeing no other option, nodded. "He's right. Do share with us."

"It's *The Diablo*," she said. "It's been taken...by the pirates."

"*The Diablo*!" Sidorio's voice was no more than a whisper.

"Doesn't that ship belong to one of your deputies?" Lord DeWinter asked.

"Johnny!" Sidorio exclaimed, striding toward Mimma. "How is Johnny?"

Mimma shook her head. "The ship was taken over, Captain. According to our sources, there was a high fatality rate."

Sidorio's face was grim.

"When did this happen?" Lola asked, all business.

"An hour or so after dawn," Mimma answered.

Lola was incredulous. "Dawn...but that was eons ago! Why are we only finding out about this now?"

Sidorio strode toward the door, his hands clenched like claws.

"Where are you going?" Lola called after him.

"To find out about Johnny," he said, lingering at the doorway, his face evidencing his deep loss. "My apologies, Lord DeWinter."

"You can't leave now," Lola said. "It's light outside."

Sidorio faced her. "I can't be a prisoner of the light anymore," he said. "Not at a time like this."

Lola threw herself at her husband. "I know how upset you are, but you can't go out into the light. There are too many people depending on you."

"But Johnny," Sidorio said, suddenly defeated. "I have to know what happened to him. And I have to tell Stukeley. They were as close as brothers."

Lola nodded. "I know how close-knit you all are," she said. She turned back to Lord DeWinter. "You talked of family before. Sometimes I think that neither I nor my unborn children can compete with my husband and his two deputies." She smiled, but this time, Lord DeWinter did not return her smile. He seemed preoccupied.

Lola faced Sidorio. "Of course you must talk to Stukeley, but you must wait, my darling, just until darkness comes."

"Actually," Mimma said, "Stukeley is here, on *The Vagabond*."

Lola arched an eyebrow questioningly, but Sidorio grabbed hold of this fresh information eagerly. "Bring him here. Now! On second thought, don't—take me to him!" He ushered Mimma out into the corridor and strode after her.

Lola's eyes turned from them to Lord DeWinter, who had salvaged the contract from its tray and now held it in his hands, his thumbs meeting at the midpoint of the pages. Olivier and Holly were both watching him curiously.

"Please don't be hasty," Lola said, but, unheeding, Lord DeWinter's eyes fell to the pages. He made a gesture as if to tear them, but, instead, the pages began to burn. As the flames licked their way up toward his fingers, Lord DeWinter dropped them on Lola's antique rug and stamped out the fire with his boot.

Lola winced but Lord DeWinter was in a merciless mood. "You put on a good show," he said. "And I'm grateful for the drink. But your claims just don't stack up. You can't possibly claim to be an invincible army when the Allied forces can sweep in and take over your deputy's ship just like that."

"Now wait a moment," Lola said, raising her hand and trying to remain calm. "It's unfortunate timing, I'll grant you—"

"It's a little more than that," he cut in, the coldness in his voice undermining his smile. He clicked his fingers and his two bodyguards rose to their feet. Lord DeWinter made for the door, flanked by his retinue.

"Wait!" Lola implored. "You are no more able to travel in the light than my husband."

Lord DeWinter paused, turning to face her once more. "I think you're forgetting that when our ships moored, we locked covered walkways. Mercifully, I'm able to walk off this ship and back onto mine, without risking the light. I don't want to lose any time in disengaging from you and your delusions of grandeur."

As he made his exit, Lola found herself uncharacteristically lost for words. Taking her empty glass, she threw it at the closing door, where the antique crystal of a thousand years' pedigree smashed to smithereens. The action failed to quell Lola's anger.

"That bloody cowboy!" she cried. "If he had to die, so be it, but not tonight of all nights!"

Her words were met with a sob from across the room. Surprised, Lola turned and saw Holly was still there.

"Pull yourself together, woman!" Lola said. "You can do better than a washed-up rodeo star!"

Behind them, Olivier found himself unable to suppress a throaty chuckle. Lola really was a hoot!

21

INVISIBLE WOUNDS

The first phase of Grace's second healing successfully completed, Evrim had started to tidy up the healing chamber. Evrim's meticulousness was one of the things Grace most valued in her.

"You said you know this patient?" Evrim asked as she carefully stored away the ribbons.

"His name is Jacoby Blunt," Grace said with a nod. "I first got to know him when Connor and I visited Pirate Academy for the first time." She could see Evrim was hungry for more information. "Jacoby was the most popular kid at the academy. Kind of the school jock—but smart too—and, of course, he was dating the academy equivalent of Homecoming Queen..."

"Ah, yes, the charming Deputy Peacock," Evrim said.

"She's sitting outside, as still and as beautiful as a statue—waiting for news."

Grace nodded, deciding to leave out the fact that Jasmine was now dating Connor rather than Jacoby. She had some considerable sympathy for Jasmine under the circumstances. "I'll go out and talk to her in a minute. He's in a comfortable state of sedation now." She looked down at Jacoby's now tranquil face. "He was captured by the Vampirates six months ago, and presumed dead."

"And so," said Evrim, "it falls to us to imagine what happened to him during those six months."

"I think we have a pretty good idea," Grace said. "He's lost a significant amount of weight since his capture by the Vampirates. A good proportion of that was muscle. He looks like he's wasting away. I think he was found just in time." She paused, extending her hand so that her fingers were tracing the air just above Jacoby's face. "Look at these lesions," she said. "I'm sure he acquired these scars during his journey from *The Diablo* to Sanctuary. I've seen the effect of daylight on Nocturnals before," she continued. "The first time I came to Sanctuary was with Lorcan, when he had stayed out too long in the light and had gone temporarily blind. His face was covered with similar burn marks to these. Mosh Zu allowed me to change his bandages and prepare the salve for his wounds."

"You've come such a long way since then," Evrim said softly, feeling very proud that she was Grace's colleague.

Her eyes returned to the patient. "I don't understand, though," she admitted. "If they converted him, why was he found caged up like an animal? And why is he so weak now?"

Grace had already thought that through. "I think our Jacoby has been a most uncooperative Vampirate," she said. "They may have converted him, but I strongly suspect they were unable to persuade him to take blood."

"He's going to have to change his stance on that," Evrim said. "For a Nocturnal, it simply isn't a viable option to refuse blood. For a short time, perhaps, but not in the long term."

Grace nodded. "When he wakes, we'll need to talk to him about his need for blood, as a matter of urgency." She frowned. This was not a conversation she relished having. And, even before she came to that, she had another pressing conversation to navigate through first. "What on earth do I tell Jasmine?" she found herself wondering aloud.

At that moment, the muslin curtain that separated the two sides of the healing chamber was brushed aside and Noijon stepped through. Seeing Grace's worried look, he was quick to reassure her. "He's doing well, Grace. He's sleeping deeply now."

Grace nodded, suitably reassured, though her head was buzzing with fresh anxieties. She looked over, fondly, at her two dedicated nurses. "You've both been absolutely brilliant today," she said. "Together, we have saved both of these men. And please be in no doubt, I could not have done this without you."

Evrim had a sudden thought. "Do you have any idea who the Nocturnal—I mean—who the *other* Nocturnal is?"

Grace lifted her hand to cut off this line of inquiry. "We don't have time to discuss this now. I need to ask you a further favor. I can't explain to you why I'm asking, but I just need you to trust that it's the right thing, okay?"

Noijon and Evrim both nodded. Grace felt enormously grateful that she had established a complete circle of trust with them both. She was going to have to push that trust to its limits now.

"I need to have a potentially difficult conversation with Deputy Peacock," Grace said. "While I do that, I want you to remove the other patient from here."

Evrim looked confused but Noijon was more practical. "Where would you like us to remove him to?"

"He needs to be off the main ward in a private recovery room."

Noijon nodded in understanding as Grace continued. "His trauma was very intense. I want him completely isolated for the time being. No one but us three should know where he is. Not Dani, or even Mosh Zu."

"I know the perfect place," said Noijon.

"It would be best," Grace said, "if no one saw you taking him there. Is that possible?"

Noijon nodded again. "I'm on it, boss. Don't worry! You

go and talk to Deputy Peacock. Evvie and I will take care of this...situation."

"We will?" Evrim still looked confused.

"Yes, we will," Noijon said with complete confidence.

Grace smiled, breathing a sigh of relief. Then she took a moment to gather herself before stepping outside for her encounter with Jasmine.

———

"What do you mean, I can't see him?" Jasmine's intense dark eyes were wide with concern. She gazed up at Grace from the other end of the wooden bench in the anteroom adjacent to the healing chamber.

"I didn't say you *can't*," Grace corrected her. "I just think the best thing for him now is to rest, undisturbed, until we have him on a steadier footing."

"But you said he was already in a steady condition," Jasmine said, her eyes narrowing. "Why do I feel like you're lying to me, Grace?"

Grace smiled sympathetically. "Because you're tired and worried and angry and there's no one but me to lash out at?"

Jasmine nodded, her face softening. "You're right," she said. "I'm so sorry."

Grace put her hand over Jasmine's. "I've made him as comfortable as I can. There's a long journey ahead of him, but I'm confident he's going to make it." She chose her words carefully. "You know you're welcome to stay here at Sanctuary tonight, Jasmine. I can find you a room. You can stay as long as you want, but you might prefer to go back to *The Tiger* and be among your friends. I will see to it myself that you are kept regularly informed of Jacoby's progress."

Jasmine nodded. "I really should go back," she said. "It's not a matter of choice. I have duties on *The Tiger*. The war has reached a turning point and I can't let Connor shoulder my work and responsibilities on top of his own."

Grace smiled. "I'm sure Connor will want to support you at a time like this. He's your boyfriend, but he knows how much you cared for Jacoby. How much you *still* care."

"Thanks, Grace," Jasmine said. "You're good people— you and Connor." She smiled. "I knew that from the first."

Grace glanced at the ticking clock. "I wish I had more time to spend with you," she said, "but there never seems to be time for anything anymore. I have another patient to check up on now." She stood up but, seeing Jasmine's deflated expression, she added, "There's a garden just outside the complex. Turn right at the main exit and you'll soon come across it. You might want to go and sit there for a while. It's a peaceful place."

"Thanks, Grace," Jasmine said, already sounding more composed. "But my ordeal is nothing compared to Jacoby's." She rose to her feet.

Grace felt a sense of sisterhood and the desire to protect her brother's girlfriend. "We're all casualties of this war," she said. "It wounds each of us in different ways. But often the invisible wounds are the ones that hurt the most."

As she stopped speaking, Jasmine put a hand on her arm. Grace realized that Jasmine was crying, albeit very quietly.

"Thank you," Jasmine said, once again. "Thank you for helping Jacoby and me. Thank you for everything you're doing for the pirates."

Grace nodded. She felt a wave of guilt run through her. Jacoby Blunt's time as a pirate had been brought to a sudden end, and, while Grace might not have lied to Jasmine—not in so many words—nor had she told her the whole truth. She realized that Jasmine might not be quite so thankful toward her if she knew who else Grace was treating.

Glancing left and right to check that no one had seen her, Grace inserted the key in the lock and twisted it. It made her think back to her first days aboard *The Nocturne*, when Lorcan had kept her locked up inside her cabin. He had told her it was for her own safety. She had been dubious about that but now she completely understood as, key in hand, she darted inside the room and closed the door swiftly behind her, then locked it again.

In front of her was—how had Olivier described it?—a *cocoon* of gauze. Grace approached the bed and drew back the curtain to enter the cocoon. As she did so, Johnny opened his eyes in wonder.

"Hello," he said, his voice cracked and low.

"Hello," she echoed, reaching for his hand. She only cupped it gently but still thought to ask, "Sorry, does that hurt?"

He shook his head, but only slightly. She could tell that it still wasn't entirely comfortable for him to move. "No," he said. "Doesn't hurt. Feels nice."

Grace smiled, gazing down at him. "Do you know where you are?" she asked. "And why?"

Again, he made the smallest possible movement with his head but she could see he was trying to nod. "Your nurse guy...the one with the funny name, he told me. I'm back at Sanctuary. And you saved my life, Grace."

His fingers brushed hers gently. The smallness of the movement and the simplicity of his words drew tears from her eyes.

"Hey, don't cry!" he said.

"Sorry." She brushed her free hand across her face, trying to mop up the tears. "I'm just so relieved that you're back, that you're going to make it through."

"It's all thanks to you," he said. "I wouldn't be seeing or touching you if you hadn't worked your healing magic on me, sugar." He paused to summon up more energy. "For that, I will be eternally grateful. In fact..."

Grace held up her hand. "You're still in critical condition, Johnny. You mustn't tire yourself through talking."

Once more, he attempted a nod. "All right, I'll shut up and you can do the talking. I like it when you talk to me."

He smiled and, once again, she noted how blistered his lips were.

"You can't stay here," Grace said. "If the Alliance has the merest suspicion that you survived the attack, they'll dispatch someone else to finish the job. We need to get you away from here."

"Okay," Johnny said. "But where? How?"

"I don't want you to worry about that," Grace said. "It's all under control. I just need you to concentrate all your energy on recovering." She let go of his hand. "I'm going to conduct a fresh healing session with you now. It will send you into a deep sleep. When you wake, you might already be on your way home."

"Home?" he said, as if the word had no meaning for him.

"I know your ship is . . . gone," Grace said. "But you're going back to your comrades." She began to stand up.

"Wait!" His voice was hoarse. "Can't I stay here with you a little longer?"

Grace thought about it. For so long, she had hoped that he would choose the Nocturnals rather than the Vampirates. But, whatever he might say now, in truth that decision had been made long ago. Now it wasn't safe for him to stay. Sadly, she shook her head. "I'll always be here for you, Johnny, but, for now, I think it's best you go back to Stukeley and the others as soon as possible."

Johnny tried to sit up in bed but found the movement too much for him. "I don't understand, Grace. If I'm still the enemy, why did you bother saving me?"

Grace shook her head once more. "You're not *my* enemy," she said. "And you never will be. You're on the wrong side in this war and I hope with all my heart that your side loses. But some things are more important than battle lines."

"Like what?" he asked.

"Like dear, old friends," she said, lifting his hand and very gently kissing it. "Now, I need you to be quiet and still and let me do the job I'm here to do."

Johnny smiled and his dark eyes sparkled momentarily. Grace knew then that she'd done the right thing. Whatever anyone else said. Whatever the repercussions.

❧

After Johnny was settled into a deep, restorative sleep, Grace slipped back out of his room and into the corridor. Checking once more that she hadn't been seen, she locked the door behind her, pocketed the key, and strode briskly away along the corridor.

The second healing session had left her thoroughly depleted of energy and she knew that it was vital she now got some rest. She pushed open the door to her room, grateful to find that Darcy had not yet returned from her own labors. But, though it was tempting, she did not settle down to bed right away.

There was one more thing she had to do before she could rest.

On board *The Albatross*, Stukeley lay in Mimma's arms.

"I can't believe he's gone," he said. "Johnny and me, we were like brothers. Blood brothers." His body began to shake. It was a familiar sensation. "I can't bear it, Mim. I've lost too many others. But not Johnny. Not John..."

"I know," Mimma said, stroking his hair tenderly. "I know how close you were and I can imagine how I'd feel if I lost Nathalie or Jacqui."

Stukeley rearranged himself on the bunk and pulled Mimma in closer to kiss her. As their lips parted, he held her close. "Thank you for agreeing to stay," he said. "I'm not sure I could get through this without you."

"Hush now!" Mimma said. "Don't say such things. We'll get through this, together." As she spoke she interlaced her fingers with Stukeley's. She was strong, like a force of nature. Stukeley looked into her fiery eyes, then found his attention diverted. If he wasn't very much mistaken, Grace Tempest was standing at the foot of his bed, dressed in a very strange pinafore creation.

"Grace," he blustered, starting to sit up. "What on oceans are you doing here?"

Mimma turned around, equally dumbstruck to find Grace in the cabin. *How come they hadn't heard the door open?* "Howdy, stranger!" she said. "I'd like to say you're looking good, but, honestly, I don't think that's a great look for you, sweetie."

Grace's eyes coolly met Mimma's, then turned back to Stukeley.

"I'll fast-track this," she said, "because time is of the essence. I'm not physically here. This is an astral visit..."

"Of course!" Stukeley nodded in understanding. "Johnny told me you could do that." His face fell. "Are you here because of him? You've heard the news, then? That he's dead?"

Grace shook her head. "He's not dead," she said.

"What?" chorused Stukeley and Mimma, both clambering out of bed, while trying to protect their modesty.

"He's here at Sanctuary," Grace said. "I'm sure you know by now that we have a treatment facility here for wounded Nocturnals. One of our rescue squads picked Johnny up by mistake this morning, after the attack on *The Diablo*." She paused, wanting to be sure they'd understood what she had said.

"I've begun his healing, but he can't stay. Stukeley, I need you to come and fetch him tonight."

Stukeley was already standing up and buttoning his shirt. "I'll come right away," he said.

"Come alone," Grace said. "And don't try anything clever. I'm doing this for Johnny's sake, you understand? Don't make me regret this."

Mimma couldn't believe her ears. "*You've* certainly grown up since we last clapped eyes on you, Gracie."

"I didn't have any choice," Grace said, turning her attention back to Stukeley. "Now listen carefully. This is what I need you to do..."

22

BRIEF ENCOUNTER

At the appointed hour, Grace and Noijon walked side by side along the Corridor of Ribbons, then turned into the Corridor of Discards. As they passed Dani, Grace nodded politely and exchanged a relieved glance with her trusted nurse. Noijon smiled back at her. She rather thought he was enjoying their clandestine mission. She wasn't—not in the slightest. It had set all her nerves on edge. And, as they turned into the Corridor of Lights, an unwelcome surprise lay in wait.

"Grace!" exclaimed Darcy. "And Noijon." She nodded in greeting. "Where are you both off to?"

"Just out to get some air between shifts," Grace said as casually as she could muster under the circumstances.

"You know how rare it is to get any free time around

here," added Noijon. "And even the quickest draft of fresh air does wonders for your concentration and stamina. Wouldn't you agree, Nurse Flotsam?"

Darcy nodded. Already, she smelled a rat. She could read Grace's body language pretty expertly by now and she knew something was amiss. Was it possible that Grace was making another attempt to leave Sanctuary, only this time without a bag and without letting Darcy in on the secret?

"You know, I could do with some air myself," Darcy said chirpily, "and, as luck would have it, I'm on a break, too. Mind if I come along with you?"

Grace wanted to protest, but she didn't want to create any more of a scene. Nor did she want to miss their appointed rendezvous.

"Of course," she said. "We'd be happy to have your company." She really ought to give Darcy some warning of what—or rather who—lay in wait in the courtyard, but she could hear footsteps behind them in the Corridor of Discards. There was simply no more time.

Noijon pushed open the door and the three healing staff strolled out into the courtyard. In the distance, the security guards were changing over shifts—Grace had timed this very precisely. She continued walking across the courtyard, where she caught sight of him, leaning against the wall outside, lost in the shadows. Seeing Grace and her companions, Stukeley stepped forward.

Darcy gasped in surprise, then said in cool tones, "What are you doing here?"

He lifted his head and looked at her rather nervously.

Grace spoke up. "I asked him to come."

Once he overcame his own shock, Stukeley smiled at Darcy warmly. "It's great to see you again," he said.

Darcy shook her head, finding herself completely wrong-footed. "Please, will someone explain what he's doing here?"

There was a brief but awkward silence as the others exchanged a glance. Then, softly, Grace whispered in Darcy's ear. "He's come for Johnny. He was brought here by mistake after the attack on *The Diablo*. I've been healing him in secret."

"Grace!" Darcy exclaimed, shocked. "How could you? He's our sworn enemy! If Mosh Zu found out…"

Grace turned to face Darcy square on. "He's not going to find out," she said firmly. "We are the only ones who know. And it's going to stay that way. Noijon and I will bring Johnny out to Jez and then they'll go on their way."

"How's our boy doing?" Stukeley asked Grace now. "I can't wait to see him."

"He's still in a bad way," said Grace. "I've started his healing, but he can't stay here. It's too dangerous for all of us."

Stukeley nodded. "It's okay. We have our own treatment facility now."

"I'm sure you do," Grace said, somewhat bitterly. "And I'll bet I know who's running it."

Before Stukeley could answer, Noijon interrupted. "We shouldn't lose any more time. There's movement over at the guards' station."

Grace nodded, suddenly all business once more. "Darcy, why don't you take Stukeley to the kitchen garden and wait for us there? We'll bring Johnny out to you."

Darcy turned to Grace. "I'm not sure I'm comfortable being an accomplice in this," she said. "You know I'd do anything for you, Grace, but…"

"Please," Stukeley said. "Would you do it for me, Darcy? Look, I know I'm not in any position to ask a favor of you. But would you do it for what we once were to each other—before I destroyed that?"

Darcy looked across at Stukeley. It had been a long time. There he stood, framed by moonlight. She couldn't deny that he was still handsome—perhaps, to her chagrin, even more so than she remembered. He was dressed in the Alliance uniform—all part of Grace's master plan, no doubt—and it lent him a new gravitas.

"All right then," she said with a sigh. "I'll do this." Turning to Grace and Noijon, she added, "But be quick."

As Grace and Noijon headed back inside, Darcy turned to Stukeley, catching him gazing at her a bit too dreamily for her liking.

"Are you at all pleased to see me?" he asked. "Have you thought about me much?"

Darcy shook her head. "I'm far too busy to dwell on the past," she said. "My work here is very important to me."

"You always did have a strong sense of duty," he said. "It's one of the things that I loved most about you."

Despite the "L" word, she didn't crack. "Come on," she said. "We can't dawdle here. I'll take you to the garden, like Grace said."

He nodded, smiling softly. "Lead the way!"

She set off with him at her side. He felt dangerously close. At any moment, he might reach out for her. But he didn't. He was the perfect gentleman.

When they reached the kitchen garden, he smiled. "Well, this is a pretty spot and no mistake. What do you say we sit down for a moment by this fountain, while we wait for Grace and the others?"

Darcy shrugged, and, as she did so, her cardigan slipped from her shoulders. She reached out behind her to catch it but Stukeley was already there. His hand met hers. The touch sent shivers along her spine. She removed her hand and allowed him to settle the soft fabric of the cardigan back on her shoulders.

"There you are," he said, remaining close.

"Thanks." Darcy stepped away from him and sat down on the wooden bench.

"So, you're a nurse now?" he said.

"Yes." She nodded. "But I think it's best not to discuss my work here with you. I'm sure you understand."

He nodded. As he did so, she saw the deep sadness in

his eyes. Once more, she was struck by how handsome he was. And how vulnerable. She'd forgotten this quality but it was one of the things that had drawn her to him in the first place. He had always seemed a little unsure of his place in this world, just like her.

"Is there anyone special in your life?" he inquired. "Because, though it would hurt me a bit to think of it, I do want you to be happy, Darcy."

"My work comes before everything right now," she replied.

He nodded, seeming rather pleased by her answer.

"How about you?" she asked. "Are *you* seeing anyone?"

"There's a lovely girl," he said, his honesty taking her by surprise. "One of Lola's officers. She's Italian by birth, from the South. Full of spirit..."

Darcy was unnerved by the wave of sadness that swept over her as he talked about this other girl. She drew on all her strength to prevent it from showing. Whether Stukeley had seen it or not, he reached out his hand for hers and this time she did not resist his touch.

"She makes me laugh," he said. "But you take my breath away, Darcy. You always did and you always will."

Darcy slipped her hand free from his and rose from the bench. She took a few steps toward the fountain, feeling its spray dampen her face like raindrops—or tears.

When he spoke again, there was a note of pleading in his voice. "I wonder," he said. "Do you think you could ever entertain the possibility of giving me another chance?"

His eyes sought an answer in hers, but Darcy kept her expression veiled.

Stukeley sighed. "It gets lonely, don't you find? I realized that, when I thought Johnny was...gone, there are so few people I trust these days. I know you have your work, and so do I, but there's all this eternity stretched out before us. It scares me sometimes."

"I won't be your cure for loneliness," she said sharply, staring into the fountain.

"No," he said, standing close beside her, his face glowing in the light of the moon and its reflection in the water. "You'd be so much more than that."

Darcy felt a fresh wave of sadness break within her. "We can never be together," she said. "Your words are like diamonds, Jez. They always were, but your actions fall short." He looked at her forlornly as she continued. "The reason I didn't run away with you that night was because of the hideous way you treated the captain—the very man who'd rescued you from the abyss." It pained her to think of that night but now that Pandora's box was open, it could not be closed. "You whispered sweet nothings to me, but after you'd gone I learned that you had murdered Shanti in cold blood." She paused but he didn't deny it. "I'm sure you've murdered many others since then. And now you're one of Sidorio's trusted deputies, so you're just as responsible for this war as he is. It's your fault your best friend is in the state he's in."

Stukeley frowned. "That's not fair. You've never liked Sidorio."

"There's very little to like," she said. "But at least Sidorio knows himself. I think you look in the mirror, Jez, and you see someone quite different staring back at you."

She turned from him and drew her cardigan more tightly around her. The cold sadness inside her was now equaled by the chill of the night. Once every dream of hers had been bound up with Jez Stukeley. Now all she wanted was to go back inside and bury herself under her bedcovers. Perhaps this was the saddest part of all—that he, whom she had once thought to be her Mr. Jetsam, might now mean so little to her.

"Is that it, then?" Stukeley asked. Now there was bitterness in his voice. "Is that all the time you'll deign to grant me before I leave with Johnny?"

She turned to glance over her shoulder, perfectly poised. "I think I've been more than generous, all things considered," she said. "And now, I think I'd best get back inside. If I stay out any longer, I might catch a chill. Or worse."

Darcy turned away and, bowing her head against the night breeze, made for the Corridor of Lights. Walking back into the compound, she was surprised how weightless she felt—as if a heavy burden had been lifted from her shoulders. She walked beneath the butter lamps, finding their distinctive smell homely and grounding. Turning the corner into the Corridor of Discards, she felt as if she were seeing the place for the first time. Her eyes were assaulted from all sides by the shapes and colors of the trinkets so many Nocturnals had left here in order to journey deeper into the compound and on toward a state of peace.

Darcy paused in the middle of the corridor and reached into the pocket of her nurse's uniform. With trembling fingers she retrieved a small brooch in the shape of a shooting star. It was the first gift Jez had given her, and she had kept it close all this time—a kind of talisman. Now she placed the brooch here where it belonged— among all the other discarded things. She had been on the verge of placing it here before, when Grace and Noijon had surprised her. But she had found herself afflicted by doubt. Now that doubt had evaporated. Feeling lighter having disposed of the last token of her toxic relationship with Jez, she continued on her way.

She felt sure that Grace and Noijon could handle Johnny, and she didn't want to play any further part in their misguided plan. She decided it was best, all things considered, to keep out of their way. Up ahead, the door leading to the inpatient wards was open. She slipped through the door and into the ward. It seemed deserted; the other medical staff must be on a break. Darcy immediately fell back into duty mode, picking up a sheaf of papers that had been dropped on the stone floor and adjusting the muslin curtains around one of the beds to retain the patient's privacy. She continued on her way, noticing that within one of the muslin tents, there was a light.

Stepping closer, she saw that on the other side of the curtain, the patient was awake and moving. He was whispering to himself and waving his arms about. Thinking that he might be in some kind of distress, she pushed back the curtain and stepped inside.

"Are you all right?" she asked gently.

The patient, a young-looking man with shiny black hair shaped into a pompadour, froze and smiled at her. "Never better," he said.

"What were you doing just now?" she asked. "Whispering and waving your arms like that?"

He winked at her. "I was just playing my guitar," he said.

"Your guitar?"

He nodded and brought his hands up to mime strumming an invisible guitar. Darcy smiled but couldn't help wondering how badly concussed he must have been to be experiencing such delusions.

"Don't look so worried," he said. "You're much too beautiful to have frown lines."

She smiled at the compliment, taking a closer look at his face and noticing that his eyes were almost as dark as his hair.

"My actual guitar was lost when we were attacked," he said. "The band and I were entertaining the troops, you see. We all made it out in one piece, just about—except my 1954 Fender Strat Sunburst." He smiled. "Now *that* guitar had the Mojo. Big time! In fact, she pretty much saved my life, you know."

"She . . . you mean *it* did?"

The patient nodded, patting the seat beside his bed. Darcy sat down, setting the sheaf of papers she had picked up earlier on her lap and turning her full attention to the young man at her side.

"This merciless Vamp was bearing down on me with this evil-looking, double-headed ax doohickey. So I took hold of my Fender Strat and staked him clean through the heart with it. He disintegrated into itty-bitty pieces but so, sad to say, did my Fender Strat." He shook his head sadly but then shrugged. "And that's why I'm reduced to playing air guitar," he said. "But it's probably a good thing because that way I don't wake up any of the others when I'm practicing my set."

"Ah!" Darcy nodded in understanding. "*That's* why you were whispering."

He nodded. "No flies on you, nurse," he said.

"So you're in a band?" Darcy said. "Would I have heard of it? What's it called?"

The young man's eyes twinkled as he strummed his imaginary guitar with a flourish. "Jet Jetsam and the Jets," he said.

Darcy barely dared to ask the next question. "And you are . . . Jet Jetsam?"

"The one and only," he said, putting her out of her misery with the biggest, most beautiful smile she had seen in centuries.

23

WALKING WOUNDED

Johnny leaned heavily on Grace and Noijon as they walked him out across the courtyard and into the kitchen garden. Seeing them appear, Stukeley jumped to his feet.

"Johnny!" he cried, jumping up and running over to his old buddy. "It's *so* good to see you!" Stopping short beside him, Stukeley took a proper look at his friend and comrade. "Man, you look like—"

"I feel worse than that!" Johnny said, hanging his head.

"Where's Darcy?" Grace asked Stukeley.

"She had to go," he said. "Or, to be more accurate, she felt she had to get away from me."

"Oh." Grace nodded. "Well, I suppose you two should be on your way, too. Noijon and I will go and distract the guards." She was about to set off when Johnny reached out and softly caught her arm.

"Hey," he said. "Don't I get to thank you for saving my life?"

Grace shrugged awkwardly. "You've already thanked me," she said. "Hundreds of times."

He smiled at her, opening his arms and drawing her into the gentlest of embraces. "I owe you," he said. "If you ever need me, if I can ever help you, I'll be there in a flash."

"Thank you," she said. It was a kind offer but she couldn't imagine what set of circumstances would send her running to him. "You really should get going now."

"Sure thing, sugar. I just want to say one more thing. If you ever change your mind about Lorcan...I know that ain't likely any time this millennium, but if you ever do, I'll be waiting."

Grace remembered how during her first healing session with Johnny she had felt the tangible sense of his happiness during their midnight horseback rides. In another lifetime perhaps they could have made it work, but not now, not the way the die had been cast. It was on the tip of her tongue to tell him not to wait for her but she decided, on balance, that it was kinder to say nothing. Instead, she let him stand back on his own two feet, then addressed Stukeley. "Take good care of him, Jez, or you'll have me to answer to."

Stukeley nodded. He didn't even call her out for using his long-forsaken mortal name. "I'm grateful to you, Grace. More than I can say."

"Come on," Noijon said. "Time for the final phase of our plan."

~—~

It all went without a hitch and soon the two comrades were on the other side of the Sanctuary gates — Stukeley leading Johnny back down the mountainside.

"Guess you know what happened to my ship?" Johnny said mournfully.

Stukeley nodded. "Those scumbag pirates came under cover of the dawn light and stole it from you."

Johnny's eyes were wide and sorrowful. "That was *my* ship, *mi hermano*. My ship and my crew." He shook his head. "Hell only knows what they did to my men and women if they did this to me."

Stukeley spoke gravely. "Word on the water is that the oblivion toll was high." He squeezed Johnny's shoulder. "But you'll get another ship."

Johnny's eyes were cast down. "Truth be told, I'm not sure I deserve one. I let my team down, Stuke. We shouldn't have been caught unawares like that." He lifted his eyes once more to meet his friend's.

"You know who was behind this attack?" Stukeley asked.

"The unholy Alliance, of course."

"Yeah, but I mean who *specifically*."

Johnny shook his head.

"Lorcan-freaking-Furey," Stukeley sneered. "Seems like Captain Sanctimonious is directing military strategy for their side now."

"Really?" Johnny shrugged. "Well, it ain't no surprise when you think about it. The self-hating Vampirate needs something to keep himself warm on those long, cold winter nights."

Stukeley grinned. "The way you were talking to Grace back there, I thought you were all going to be friends."

"Nah!" Johnny shook his head. "I'm done fighting him in love, but I sure ain't letting him get away with anything in war."

"That's the spirit!" Stukeley said as they navigated a particularly treacherous section of the cliff path. Thankfully, the moon and stars were there to guide their footsteps. "You know, I've been worrying about you all day long and thanking every one of these stars that you survived."

"Thank you," Johnny said, more touched than he could say by Stukeley's words.

"*De nada, hermano*," Stukeley said, smiling at his friend. "Sidorio was out of his mind with worry, too."

"He was?" Johnny said, his eyes brightening at the thought.

"More than you can imagine. He had to be physically restrained not to go out into the light and search for you himself."

Johnny's eyes went wide. "He'd have done that for me?"

"We're family now," Stukeley said. "And family looks out for one another."

"Brothers to the end!" Johnny said, reaching out a hand to his comrade.

Stukeley felt the tears budding in his eyes as he gripped Johnny's hand tightly. "Brothers to the end!"

24

RETURN FROM THE DEAD

"Ready?" Stukeley asked Johnny as they waited outside Lola's cabin on *The Vagabond*.

His companion nodded, so Stukeley knocked on the door.

It was Sidorio who called out in response, "Enter!"

Smiling in anticipation, Johnny pushed open the door and stepped gingerly inside, followed by Stukeley.

"Stetson!" Sidorio immediately rose to his feet and strode toward Johnny. He opened his arms to him but a voice, from deeper inside the cabin, caused them both to freeze.

"So, the cowboy has risen from the dead!"

Sidorio immediately glanced over his shoulder. "I thought you were having a little rest, dear."

Lola emerged from her private salon, clad in a voluminous layered nightgown, holding a compress to her fore-head. She was followed by Camille and Holly, whose face instantly brightened on seeing Johnny. Sadly, the same could not be said for Lola. Her features brought Stukeley to mind of lowering skies before a thunderstorm finally breaks.

"How's your headache?" Sidorio asked.

Lola ignored the question, brushing past him to focus squarely on Johnny. "Welcome back, Cowboy," she said, affecting a Texan twang. "We sure are stoked that you made it home to the range!"

"Thank you," Johnny said, tipping his hat and misjudging the mood of the chamber entirely.

"Did you have fun, flirting with the enemy?" Lola inquired, back to her usual clipped tones. At her side, Holly looked perturbed by this line of questioning.

"Not really," Johnny said, wising up to the general mood. "I was too sick for that, sadly."

"What a shame," Lola said. "For everything your actions have cost us, you might as well have had a few laughs."

Johnny glanced over Lola's shoulder to Sidorio. "I'm really sorry about losing my ship," he said. "I feel just terrible about my crew. I was no kind of captain to them."

Lola's lips made a smile but there was no levity in her voice as she took a step closer to Johnny. "You speak the truth, Desperado. You are no kind of captain. But frankly, my dear *vacquero*, your ship and your crew are as insignificant as you are."

"Lola!" There was warning in Sidorio's voice and in his eyes, too, but, when Lola raised her hand, he fell silent again. Lola resumed her attack on Johnny.

"Do you have any *idea* what you've cost us? My husband and I were meeting with the most influential Vampire leader in this quadrant this morning. We were in the middle of signing an accord that would have extended our power beyond the oceans and across the land for as far as the immortal eye can see." She paused momentarily to grab her belly, then swiftly resumed. "The blood was drying on the contract when news of your defeat and presumed death arrived." Her eyes narrowed. "How disappointing that the intelligence transpired to be only fifty percent accurate."

Stukeley had heard enough and now stepped in to defend his comrade. "Johnny fought hard to prevent the pirates taking *The Diablo*—he was nearly killed in the process. I think he deserves a little more gratitude. Now, I know how important that alliance was to you—to all of us—but Eternal DeWinter was always going to be an unpredictable ally. There are others that Johnny has been working on for months now..."

"Too slow!" Lola said. "That's the problem with all of you men. You plot and you plan and you scratch your... heads, but you just can't get the job done! You were flailing about on *The Blood Captain* until I arrived and turned you into a force to be reckoned with."

"We were doing just fine until you came along," Stukeley said huskily.

"*What* did you say?" There was hot lava in her voice. It left no doubt in anyone's mind that Mount Lola was about to erupt.

"I said..." Stukeley began, feeling suddenly liberated from caution.

"She heard you," Sidorio said, his voice utterly commanding, as he stepped forward. His eyes took in all of those gathered in the room. "You all have a right to your own opinions, but this isn't helping matters. The events of the past twenty-four hours have stretched our emotions as taut as piano wire. Our feelings are running high. But what kind of an army are we if we fall apart at the first sign of trouble?" His imperious eyes swept the room once more. "No kind of army, that's what! We all need some time out to take stock. Johnny, you lost your ship and your crew this morning. You nearly lost your life—again. That shouldn't have happened but it did. We learn from it and we move on." Now his eyes settled on Lola. "Lola, we lost momentum in a key alliance today. Again, it's regrettable, but our power grows all the time. We can still win this war—Stukeley's right when he says there are other, better, allies just waiting for us to call."

He brought a reassuring hand to his wife's shoulder. There was a strange look on her face, impossible to decipher. She opened her mouth and from her lips came an earsplitting scream. It lasted well over a minute. Sidorio, who hadn't merely heard the scream but felt it tearing through every fiber of his being, turned toward her.

"Please, darling, try to keep things in perspective. I know Johnny messed up, but..."

Lola seemed a little unsteady on her feet. She stumbled, reached both hands to her belly, then opened her mouth once more. The others all braced themselves for a second scream. Mercifully, it did not manifest.

"My labor has begun," she said, with quiet composure. Pushing past Sidorio, she reached out her arms for Holly and Camille. They immediately offered their support and led her back inside her bedchamber.

25

BIRTHING PAINS

The deck boards of *The Nocturne* glowed red under the light of the lanterns and the stars. All around the deck, Nocturnals were engaged in their nightly bouts of combat practice. As usual, an array of weaponry was employed. Over the past six months, this largely pacifist crew had transformed itself into a mean, merciless, and often highly inventive fighting machine. At the center of the deck, right at the heart of the clashing metal, were the two men responsible for this metamorphosis—Obsidian Darke and Lorcan Furey. As had become their custom, the two men were sparring with each other.

"A good blow," Darke said, nodding circumspectly in acknowledgment as Lorcan withdrew his sword and readied himself for a fresh bout.

Darke and Furey circled each other for a time. Of all the

Nocturnals, they were the finest fighters and therefore the most closely matched. Lorcan had benefited from intensive training by Cate since the commencement of the Alliance. Darke, on the other hand, was a strong and instinctive swordsman who could pull seemingly impossible moves out of thin air.

It was Darke who struck now, his rapier clashing against Lorcan's in a sharp succession of volleys as they moved back and forth through the limited space they had carved out for themselves on the deck. As he pushed forward, Darke spoke. "I thought after the recapture of *The Diablo* you might have granted yourself a rest. On the contrary, it seems it has only sharpened your desire for the fight."

Lorcan's eyes remained steadfastly trained on Darke's as he fought back. "This is no time to rest on our laurels, Captain," he said. "The taking of *The Diablo* may have given the Alliance fresh momentum, but it came at great cost. I for one cannot allow that to go unpunished." So saying, he swung his sword hard at Darke's. The captain was momentarily unsettled. Lorcan took full advantage and pressed in closer.

"We need to talk again about the other ships in the Nocturnal fleet," Lorcan said. He had Darke cornered up against the mast. He stared into his opponent's face. It was impossible to read. It was still an adjustment to be able to look at the captain's face, rather than at the opaque mask he had hidden behind for so many years. It was a fact both curious and frustrating that, though his features were now visible to the eye, if anything his thoughts and moods were harder to read than ever.

Darke met Lorcan's stare, keeping his counsel, his eyes giving nothing away. Then the captain executed a seemingly impossible turn and regained the advantage. "There is no need for us to discuss this matter again," Darke said, his sword whistling through the air, close to Lorcan's shoulder.

"I disagree," Lorcan responded, turning his own sword expertly to derail Darke's attack. "Now is the best chance we have for victory—but we must boost our force. By calling on the additional ships in the Nocturnal fleet, you could ensure lasting victory."

"You know nothing of this," Darke said, biding his time, assessing his options. "You must heed me when I tell you that calling upon my former comrades is not an option. You would do well to stop this line of questioning."

"I'll stop asking when you give me a valid reason," Lorcan said. His sword met Darke's and steel clashed upon steel with the force of both men's wills.

"No," said Darke, gaining the advantage once more. "You'll just stop asking or we will be in danger of becoming legitimate adversaries."

Lorcan shook his head. He couldn't accept the captain's stance on this matter. The Alliance was not in the luxurious position of having many cards up its sleeve. The mysterious fleet of other Nocturnal ships was a key advantage and it was surely time to play it.

"Every time I raise this, you just shut me down," Lorcan said.

"Yes," answered Darke, "and I will continue to do so. And so, Commander"—he paused and then raised his sword aloft once more—"you would do well to let this matter rest."

The captain's intransigence had lit the touchpaper on Lorcan's anger. Their swords met once more but now Lorcan put aside all knowledge of this man as his ally. To him, this was no longer a training fight, and he renewed his attack for real.

Obsidian realized the change and lifted his own game accordingly. As Lorcan pushed in with renewed urgency, the captain drew on all his reserves to power Furey's sword away. The strength of his blow was such that the rapier was dislodged from Lorcan's hands. As he turned to recapture it, Darke's sword swung past Lorcan's shoulder and the razor-sharp steel sliced through his hair and the skin of his neck.

Lorcan turned, stunned, letting his sword fall to the deck. It fell alongside his fallen locks. Looking at Obsidian Darke with new wariness, Lorcan raised his hand to the back of his neck. As he drew it away again, it was bright with blood.

This turn of events was sufficiently unusual to send shock waves across the deck. The fighters on either side of them drew down their weapons and turned to stare at their two leaders.

"I'm sorry," Darke said. "Believe me, it was never my intention to wound you." Immediately he dropped his own weapon and leaped forward, laying his hand across the back of Lorcan's neck, right across the cut. Darke kept the contact with Lorcan's neck for a minute or so. As he did so, his eyes met Lorcan's once more. When Darke withdrew his hand, the wound had already sealed itself.

"Are you in pain?" Darke asked Lorcan, his voice softer than before.

"No," Lorcan said, shaking his head. He smiled. "If you thought I was overdue a haircut, you might just have said."

Darke smiled back at him, his hand resting on Lorcan's shoulder. "For a moment there, I think we each forgot we are allies, not adversaries."

"Yes," Lorcan admitted.

"We should work hard to ensure that does not happen again," Darke said, extending his hand.

Lorcan nodded, extending his own palm. They shook hands. The relief across the deck was palpable. Suddenly, aware of the level of attention upon them, Lorcan turned and shouted to his crew. "Combat session is over for tonight. Thank you all for your time and effort."

As the deck began to clear, Darke's eyes met Lorcan's once more. "You have become a fine commander," he said. "When I think back to the midshipman I knew, not so long ago, I draw great pride and pleasure in your metamorphosis."

Lorcan acknowledged this praise with a formal nod.

But, as the captain turned and made his way across the deck, he found himself unable to repay the compliment.

⌐◆⌐

Lola's bedchamber had become a foreign realm, Sidorio thought as he gingerly poked his head around the door. Lola was propped up in bed, on what seemed like a thousand crimson pillows. She was surrounded by her most loyal crew members—Holly, Camille, Jacqueline, and Nathalie.

"How's she doing?" Sidorio inquired.

"Who's *she*? The devil's mother?" cried Lola, her dark eyes rolling toward him.

She looked quite mad and was, no doubt, experiencing intense pain. Sidorio watched as Holly dipped a napkin in cool water and mopped his wife's brow.

"Can I do anything?" he asked.

Holly did not respond but Lola did. "I think *you've* done *quite* enough. It's because of you I'm in such pain. And yes, Sid, it *is* excruciatingly painful. I bore two children in my mortal span and their births were agony enough but they were as nothing compared to *this*..." She broke off and began wailing, a new fear in her eyes.

"You must focus on your breathing," said Jacqueline, who sat at the foot of the bed. "Come on now, just like we practiced."

Lola nodded, her matted hair snaking across the pillows. As Sidorio watched and listened, his wife began making a series of strange noises. It was unsettling, seeing her like this—hearing these unusual sounds emanating from her. Suddenly, they stopped and her head rolled around to face him once more. It made him think of their incredible reunion when he had returned her decapitated head to her body.

"Are you still here?" she inquired now, coldly.

"If you'd prefer me to go, I will," he said, despondent at this strange gulf that had emerged between them—at this, of all times, when she was birthing his twin sons.

Lola's dark eyes seared into his. "Yes!" she cried. "I'd prefer you to go. We have no need of men here, not now. Bringing infants into the world is women's work." She cried out in fresh agony.

"Breathe!" Jacqueline rose from her seat. "Really, you must focus. The breathing will help."

Holly turned to Sidorio, smiling reassuringly at him. "Everything's under control," she said. "Perhaps you had better go and wait on your own ship. This could go on for many hours."

He nodded, finding himself disproportionately grateful for the girl's kindness. He blew a kiss to his wife but it fell unnoticed as her head thrashed from one side of the pillow mountain to the other. Feeling utterly at a loss, Sidorio, King of the Vampirates, backed sheepishly out of the birthing chamber.

Grace opened the door carefully and padded soundlessly toward the patient's bed.

"It's okay," Jacoby said. "No need for the Scooby-Doo walk. I'm awake."

Smiling, Grace carried a chair over beside his bed. As he sat up, she reached behind him and began plumping his pillows.

"Thanks," he said. "I'm going to miss this level of twenty-four/seven care when I'm discharged."

"I wouldn't worry," Grace said. "*My* care may be coming to an end, but I'm confident others will pick up the reins when you return to *The Tiger*."

Jacoby frowned at the mention of his ship. "You really think I can go back there?"

Grace nodded. "Of course, why *wouldn't* I think that?"

He cradled his hands in his lap. "Let's not beat around the bush, Grace. We both know what the Vampirates did to me. We both know what I am now."

"Oh, sure," Grace said. "You're a Nocturnal. And, as you may remember, there's a war going on in which the pirates and Nocturnals are fighting in alliance. *And*, as you may also remember, it is Alliance policy to place a Nocturnal on board every pirate ship." She paused. "In the case of *The Tiger*, I guess they just increased the percentage."

Jacoby chuckled, closing his eyes for a moment, his long lashes casting shadows in the lamplight. "You're doing a very good job of making it sound easy, Grace," he said, opening his eyes again. "I imagine that's all part of the training, eh?"

She shrugged.

"Let's consider the small but related matters of me needing blood and not being able to venture out into the sun anymore," Jacoby said, the lightness of his tone belying the import of his words.

Grace nodded but she was matter-of-fact as she answered him. "You're right. You'll be better off confining your trips outside to the hours between dusk and dawn. It'll play havoc with your tanning regime, but, trust me, your skin will thank you for it." She paused. "As for the blood thing, well, of course you're right. We do need you to start drinking blood if you're to become the big, strong Nocturnal we all want you to be."

He shook his head, sadly. "I can't do it, Grace," he said, his eyes tearing up. "It's just not in me. I don't want to die but I can't kill another living being just so I can endure."

Grace put her hand on his shoulder. "Of course you can't. But you're not going to die, Jacoby. You really haven't done your homework, have you? How many times have you met Lorcan and the others? Every Nocturnal is paired with a donor. The donor provides blood on a weekly basis but it doesn't weaken them, let alone kill them. When you leave here, your donor will travel with you to *The Tiger*."

"*My* donor? I don't have a donor."

Grace rose from her seat. "Actually, you do, you just haven't been introduced yet."

She walked over to the door and pushed it open, calling softly out into the corridor. "You can come inside now. He's ready for you."

"Can I come in?" Jasmine's head poked around the door.

"Hey!" Jacoby called out to her. "This is like the best night of my life. I've had one cute visitor after another."

Jasmine smiled with relief. "Sounds like you're back to your old self." She closed the door behind her and stepped closer.

"Not exactly," Jacoby said. She could see the telltale signs of tension etched across his forehead.

"Tell me about your cute visitors," Jasmine said, keen to lighten the mood. "Go on, make me jealous. I don't mind!"

"All right, then," he said, smiling once more and reaching out his hand for hers. She took it and gave it a squeeze. "Well, first there was my nurse, Evrim. She's incredibly foxy, with these big, smoky eyes. She comes to read to me when she has the time — in Italian. I don't understand a word of it, of course, but I nod sagely at regular intervals."

"You're shameless!" Jasmine said. "Who else?"

"Next to come calling was Doctor Tempest herself. She's become quite the young beauty, wouldn't you say?"

Jasmine nodded. He was right. In the time they had known her, Grace had emerged like a butterfly from a chrysalis. "But I'm not sure she's officially a doctor."

"No," Jacoby agreed. "She's far more powerful than that. She's a *healer*. But, pretty as she may be, I can't do the flirt thing with Grace. It would be too weird."

"Because she's Connor's sister?"

Jacoby shrugged. "Not so much that. More the fact that she's been down deep into my psyche during the healing process."

"Ah, yes," Jasmine said. "That makes sense. So, who came after her?"

Jacoby was suddenly tongue-tied. "Her name is Luna," he said. "She's...she's...Mexican."

Jasmine nodded matter-of-factly, squeezing Jacoby's hand once more. "And this Luna, is she another looker?"

Jacoby smiled and let out a whistle. "Seriously, you have no idea." He took control of himself. "*Almost* as pretty as you but just not quite."

Jasmine smiled at the compliment, then, in the same bright and breezy tone, asked, "And is Luna your donor?"

Jacoby froze, then turned to Jasmine, his eyes wide and questioning. "You know?" he said.

She nodded, squeezing his hand more tightly. "Yes," she said. "I *know* and so does Captain Li, and, Jacoby, I promise you, everything is going to be fine." So saying, she leaned across and kissed him on the forehead.

Jacoby's head was racing. "Man!" he said. "This really is a red-letter day. You're really cool with me being a Nocturnal? And Cheng Li, too?"

Jasmine nodded. "We all want you back on *The Tiger*, Jacoby, just as soon as can be. It's where you belong."

26

AFTER MIDNIGHT

Lilith, mistress of the Blood Tavern, sat inside her glass booth carefully applying a fresh coat of emerald polish to the nails of one hand. A young male Vampirate entered the reception area. At the sight of new customer, Lilith lifted the hand with wet nails. A half-smoked cigarette burned low between two nicotine-stained fingers. No one could say Lilith wasn't a proficient multitasker.

"You again?" she said as the young man approached her booth. "My, you're a thirsty lad! Not that I'm complaining, mind. It's customers like you have made my business what it is today. Allowed for all my extensive franchising and whatnot." She took a pull on her cigarette, thinking how cleverly she had surfed the wave of the Vampirates' rise to power. It paid to have connections, and little Lilith's went right to the very top of the Vampirate command.

Exhaling leisurely, she thought of Sidorio. She'd always known he was destined for greatness.

The customer pushed his money across the counter. "I'd like a pint, please," he said, matter-of-factly but with a familiar undertone of urgency. They were always in a hurry, these immortals, when it came to blood.

Lilith's dry hand clamped down on the notes.

Connor glanced around the vestibule, grateful to see that it was empty, save for a woman in huge fashion glasses too intent upon reading a magazine to even notice him. Perhaps she was waiting for her companion to finish up. Connor remembered waiting on that same ratty sofa during his first visit here with Jez. That had been many months ago, and the magazines were still no more current. Out of the corner of his eye, he saw the woman over on the sofa turn the page of her magazine, oblivious.

"Which room?" Connor said, anxious to be on his way.

"Number Six," Lilith said, her lips raised in a wry smile. "Off you pop, Mr. Smith."

"Thanks."

After he had disappeared through the velvet-covered doorway, Lilith finished up her cigarette and twisted the cap back onto the bottle of nail polish. She slipped down from her stool and pushed open the door at the back of her booth, padding over to the sofa area. Whistling a rather saucy old shanty—it quite made her blush to think of the lyrics—she began sorting through the magazines.

She made neat piles of them, watching the glamorous young woman on the sofa all the while.

The woman, still wearing her oversize sunglasses, continued to read her magazine article. At last, she closed the journal and placed it carefully on the coffee table. Standing up, she smoothed down her jacket, lifted her purse, and nodded at Lilith. "Thank you," she said. "You've been very helpful." She removed a crisp roll of notes from her purse and held them out toward Lilith.

Lilith's eyes were wide, but her hands closed over the notes as tightly as a clam. "Are you sure you wouldn't like a drink yourself while you're here?" she offered. "On the house, of course."

The glamorous visitor shook her head. "It's sweet of you to offer, but I'm going back to my ship now. There's no rest for a captain!" She smiled, pleasantly, and removed her sunglasses. As she did so, Lilith gasped.

"Oh, now look at your heart tattoo! Isn't that fetching?"

Mimma gave a wink with her right eye so that Lilith could appreciate the full effect.

"Oh, yes!" Lilith said, her own eyes bright beneath her crème-de-menthe sparkle-effect eye shadow. "Love it! I'm going to do one of those hearts around my own eye."

Mimma chuckled at her girlish enthusiasm.

Encouraged, Lilith inquired, "And why is that young Vampirate lad of such interest to you, I wonder?"

Mimma smiled. "Loose lips sink ships," she said, raising

a finger to her mouth. She winked again, then turned and sauntered back out the way she had come in.

Grace took the flask of berry tea and her cup and walked over to the counter. As she sat down, she realized she was no longer alone in the room. She looked up with some surprise to see Sidorio closing the door behind him and stepping toward her. She set down her cup carefully, determined to remain in control. Was there any point in even asking how he had managed to evade the fortress-like security here at Sanctuary?

"What are you doing here?" she inquired instead, her tone neutral.

"I came to see you, of course," Sidorio answered brightly, approaching the counter. "You haven't forgotten what day it is, have you?"

Grace glanced at the wall-clock, which read twenty after midnight. She turned back to Sidorio, puzzled. "It could be Tuesday or Wednesday. I'm so busy here, one day bleeds into another."

Sidorio smiled at her and, despite everything that had happened between them, there seemed to be genuine warmth in his smile. "You've forgotten," he said, producing a package from the folds of his coat and setting it down on the counter. "It's your birthday, Grace." He tapped the package. "And this is your gift from me."

It was a tubular shape, wrapped roughly but evidently with some care and finished with a dark red ribbon, tied in a bow.

Grace was taken aback. She had genuinely forgotten that it was her and Connor's birthday. It was a sign of just how hectic things had been at Sanctuary. This war didn't take a convenient break for birthdays—this war *which,* she reminded herself, the man in front of her had initiated.

As if reading her mind, Sidorio's eyes met hers. "I know there's a vast gulf between us," he said, "but when all is said and done, you *are* my daughter. Biologically speaking, at least." He looked suddenly awkward. "Look, I know that this is the first birthday since your dad died. I'm not trying to replace what he meant to you, but, still, I wanted to do something for you."

Grace nodded. She was unsure how she was supposed to react. There were no familiar rules to her relationship with Sidorio; it was far too extraordinary to be forged along conventional lines. Biding her time, she took a sip of the tea.

"What's that you're drinking?" Sidorio asked.

"A blend of seven mountain berries. It's a temporary substitute for blood."

He grinned at that. "Come off it, Grace. There's *no* substitute for blood."

Shrugging, she took another sip. "I think we both know there are some things we will never agree on."

Sidorio tapped the package on the counter again. "Aren't you going to open my gift?" His eyes were wide, like a child's somehow. He still hadn't sat down. How long was he planning to stay?

She reached forward and took the package in her hands, unlacing the bow and then slipping off the brown paper wrapping. Inside was a roll of canvas. She began unpeeling it, wondering what on earth it could be.

"It's the portrait we all sat for," Sidorio said. "For Lola's arty friend. Whatsisname...Caravaggio, that's it!" His momentary elation soon dissipated as his eyes fell to the torn canvas. "Well, what's left of it after your brother set about it with his sword."

Grace opened up the remains of the painting, which someone—could it have been Sidorio himself?—had gone to some trouble to patch together. It wasn't the whole portrait. Perhaps out of sensitivity, Sidorio hadn't patched Lola back in. Instead, it was just Sidorio and his two children. It was a shock to see it again, especially the image of her own eyes filled with the fire of hunger.

"I wanted to give you something to remind you of your family," he said. "Whatever you think of me, I helped bring you into this world. Surely that has to count for something."

Grace was speechless. She couldn't ever imagine putting this canvas in a frame and hanging it on a wall. Not like the beautiful picture of Dexter and Sally, in the early throes of romance, which Lorcan had given her. And yet, though this portrait was utterly grotesque, she couldn't help but feel touched by Sidorio's tortuous thought processes in bringing it to her. It was not at all the kind of gesture she would have expected. She looked up from the rather imperious rendering of Sidorio in the portrait to the real Vampirate and found he was smiling at her tenderly.

"You think I'm a brute," he said. "Now, don't bother denying it, you know it's true. You believe me to be a monster and, mea culpa, many of my actions might have led you to that conclusion. I'm a Vampirate and I'm the commander of a vast empire. But that's not all I am, Grace. I also happen to be your father, and Connor's, too. And that matters to me."

"Are you planning on paying Connor a visit tonight, too?" Grace asked.

Sidorio shook his head, his eyes downcast. "No, things didn't end well between us," he said, his finger tracing the slashes on the surface of the portrait. "He's going to need a little more time." He raised his eyes again. "You were always more open-minded."

Grace looked at Sidorio. "I am open-minded about many things but, all the same, I know which side of this war I'm on."

Sidorio nodded. "I'll allow that," he said. "After all, it's clear you owe your stubbornness to me. It certainly wasn't part of Sally's character. I know we're on opposite sides, and I know there's probably nothing I can do to change that, but I'll ask this one thing of you, Grace. Just the one. Please never forget that I am your father and that I do have feelings for you."

Grace looked him in the eye. "You could change everything by agreeing to a truce. I could summon Obsidian Darke to join us right now. We could end this war here, tonight." She took a breath. "Now that would be a truly amazing birthday gift—one that you, and only you, could offer me."

For a moment, Sidorio was silent. Was there even the remotest possibility he was considering her proposal?

At last he shook his head. "The painting and the chance of a family is my gift, Grace. I know both are a little ragged, but, well, they're all I can give you right now."

She nodded. She hadn't realistically expected him to say anything different. "Thank you again," she said. "I'll tell Connor about this when I next see him."

Sidorio glanced at the clock. "I had better be going. Lola is in the midst of labor."

Grace's mouth gaped open. "Lola is about to give birth to your children and you've left her to come here?"

Sidorio shrugged. "I already have two children," he said. "Besides, I'll be back at her side in time to cut the cords."

Grace closed her eyes for a moment. Somehow, she was transported to the scene on board *The Vagabond*. She could visualize Lola lying on her bed and the eager faces and hands circling around her. Opening her eyes,

Grace looked back at Sidorio. "You'd better hurry," she said. "It will be soon now."

"It's funny," Sidorio said. "All four of you will share the same birthday."

"Yes." Grace nodded. "I suppose we will." She had another thought. Surely Sidorio's new kin would count her and Connor as half siblings. It was strange to contemplate. But the thought was soon pushed away by other urgent matters. "Are you aware of Mosh Zu's prophecy?" she asked.

There was a silence between them and she wondered if she had made a mistake by bringing it up. If Sidorio didn't know and he asked her about it, wasn't she in danger of disclosing important information? Well, it was too late now.

"Yes," he said. "I know about that prophecy. Olivier was very eager to share the information with me."

Of course he would have been! Grace shook her head, unsure how to frame her next question. But Sidorio seemed to have anticipated it.

"You're wondering how much store to set by it, aren't you? You think the prophecy foretells your death, or perhaps Connor's?"

Grace nodded. "It does foretell someone's death. One of the twins, so me or Connor. Though I suppose it might equally refer to your new children." As the words came out, she rather regretted them. Still, he didn't seem perturbed.

Sidorio shrugged. "I don't set much store by prophecies

and portents, Grace," he said. "Now Lola, she *loves* all that hocus-pocus. And that's fine by me—it keeps her entertained, gives her plenty to chew over with Olivier and her girlfriends. But here's the fact of the matter as I see it. People like me—people like *us*—we write our own destinies. I've defied mortal death and immortal oblivion many times already. The more others try to cut me down, the stronger I become." He smiled at her. "I'm sure the same is true of you and Connor, and it will be true for Lola's twins when she brings them into the world. The Sidorio clan was born to rule—not to be ruled over." He stepped closer toward Grace. "It's time you understood that your powers now outstrip Mosh Zu's, just as Connor's rival those of any other pirate's. Don't let a prophecy conjured up hundreds of years ago put the frighteners on you, daughter. Someone of your lineage, of your rare gifts, truly has nothing to fear."

As he finished speaking, he pulled her toward him and folded her into his arms. Grace gazed up at her father. What an endlessly surprising creature he was. It was, she reflected, a good thing they were both immortal. It might take all eternity to understand him and get their relationship on anything like a workable footing.

Releasing her from his arms, he nodded once more, then turned and stepped out into the corridor. The room felt more deeply silent after he had gone. Grace knew his stirring words had been intended to give her strength and support. Nonetheless, she could now think of only one thing: Lola's going into labor signaled the time of the prophecy. The war between the Alliance and the Vampirates was reaching its endgame. And either Grace or Connor would soon die!

———

Inside Room Six, Connor sat at one end of a chaise, staring through a hole in the rotting floorboards. He was fairly sure he'd just seen a mouse dart across underneath. At the other end of the chaise lay a "tav"—Vampirate parlance for a tavern girl, or indeed boy. A girl in this case. Her shirt was unbuttoned, her arms cupped softly in her lap. Her eyes were fixed on the ceiling, her mouth slightly open.

"I'm sorry," Connor said, his own eyes still on the floorboards. "Could we just talk for a bit?"

She didn't answer, and, after a short wait, he turned to face her. He realized she was out cold. Connor felt a sweep of panic. He had been beside himself with hunger tonight. Had he taken too much blood? They didn't usually pass out after only a pint.

"I'm sorry," he repeated, leaning closer and taking the girl's pulse. To his relief, it was still beating, albeit slowly. She'd come back to life soon enough. He decided to wait here until she did—for his sake as much as hers. His own pulse was racing now. The new energy he had drawn from her was fizzing and snapping through him.

What was her name? Had she even told him? Names were of little importance here, especially at the outset of an urgent transaction. But now, seeing her properly for the first time, rather than through the red mist of his hunger, he wished that he'd paid more attention. Noticing the almost dry puncture wounds on her thorax, he drew the sides of her shirt back together to protect her modesty. As he did so, he saw that a tarnished gold necklace hung around her neck. The chain was askew and he reached forward and carefully straightened it. Suspended on the chain was something he first assumed to be a random pattern. Then he saw that it was a name. *Petra*. He smiled.

His attention was diverted by the old clock, ticking on the mantel. The light in this room, like all the others, was meager. Lilith kidded herself it was all in the cause of "mood-lighting," but more likely it was a matter of simple economics. Connor squinted to read the clock face through the gloom. As he did so, he smiled with wry recognition.

"After midnight," he said. "You know what that makes it, Petra?" He turned back toward her. "My birthday. Not much to celebrate today, however."

He gazed at Petra, wishing that she would respond. He experienced another wave of panic and guilt and reached for her wrist again. The pulse was stronger than before. Good. But he was in no doubt now. He'd fed too hard. Just how much *had* he taken to bring her to this state?

He kept hold of her hand, reluctant somehow to let her go. "Of course, I don't know if birthdays really mean anything to me anymore," he mused. "Now that I'm a dhampir, that is. Now that I'm immortal, do birthdays even count? Maybe next year, I won't even bother marking it." He paused, aware once more of the ticking of the clock. "Does time have any meaning at all now?" He squeezed Petra's hand for comfort, but the cool limpness of her hand made him feel lonely and he released it, placing it back on her diaphragm.

"Birthdays are a time for friends," he said now, eyes seeking out the clock face once more. "I should get back to *The Tiger*. Maybe Jasmine will make a fuss over me." He smiled at Petra. "Jasmine's my girl," he said. "The thing is, she doesn't know about me. About me being a dhampir, I mean." He suddenly smiled. "Maybe it's time I just sat her down and told her. That could be my birthday gift to myself. Jasmine's a really amazing girl. If anyone would understand, she would. It'd be such a weight off my mind. That really *would* make it a birthday to remember."

"Birthday? Whose birthday?" Petra's speech was slightly slurred.

"Petra!" Connor turned to face her and saw life blooming in her eyes once more. It was a huge relief to see that she was all right. She began drawing herself up straight on the chaise.

"Can I get you anything?" he asked. "Some water, maybe?"

She shook her head slowly.

"Well, then." He stood up. "I think I'd better go. I've

taken up enough of your time." He couldn't wait to get out of this dingy room. He strode toward the door, then, having second thoughts, returned to the chaise, reached into his pocket, and took out a roll of notes. He placed them in Petra's pale hand.

"Here's some extra," he said. "I may have taken more than I paid for, but Lilith doesn't need to know, does she?"

Petra smiled softly and shook her head again. "Whose birthday is it?" she asked once more.

"No one that matters," Connor said, then turned and slipped out through the door.

THE VORTEX

There was a spring in Darcy Flotsam's step as she made her way along the passageway. In her hands was an old guitar she had found in the Corridor of Discards. She realized she must have walked past it a hundred times or more but today it had seemed to be calling out to her, winking beneath the light of the butter lamps. The guitar would make the perfect present for Jet now that he was firmly on the road to recovery. It might not be the Fender Strat '54 he talked about with the fondness of a lost love, but he could certainly make music on this, and, as one musician to another, Darcy felt sure this would be solace enough. She would give it a good cleanup and then surprise him with it when she visited him again that night.

As Darcy turned the corner, she found Grace striding

toward her. It took Darcy only an instant to notice the familiar bag in Grace's right hand.

"So," Darcy said. "This time you're really leaving."

Grace nodded, pausing before her friend. "You know that I have to."

Darcy nodded, too, her eyes already wet. "Yes, but weren't you even going to say good-bye to me?"

Grace placed the bag on the floor and reached out her hand to Darcy. "I was just coming to find you," she said.

Darcy looked at her askance for a moment, then shook her head. "I'm sorry, Grace. It's just I'm going to miss you so much. We've been through so much together, especially these past few months. You're the one who's gotten me through." Tears began to fall. "It's selfish, I know, but I just don't know how strong I am on my own."

Grace gripped Darcy's arm tightly and pulled her friend toward her. "You're so much stronger than you realize," she said. Then they hugged, holding each other tightly for a time, as if their very lives depended on it. When they finally broke apart, both young women had tears in their eyes.

Darcy, of course, was equipped with a lacy hankie. "I guess I hoped you'd change your mind about leaving," she said as she blotted away her tears, then passed the hankie over.

"I've been torn," Grace said. "If I had left the other day, I wouldn't have been here to heal Jacoby or"—her voice dropped lower—"Johnny. I know someone else would have done the job perfectly well. It's just that everyone is being pushed to their limits right now. The thing is..." She paused, handing the hankie back to Darcy. "The thing is, my father paid me a visit last night."

"Sidorio!" Darcy exclaimed. "Here at Sanctuary?"

Grace nodded, shrugging. "It's no surprise really. He comes and goes as he pleases now. Whatever we may want to believe, his powers only seem to be growing. He knows no bounds."

"You say he came to see *you*?" Darcy asked.

"Yes." Grace nodded. "And to bring me this."

She unzipped the bag and retrieved from within it the canvas, which she held up in front of Darcy.

"Hmm," Darcy said, clearly none too taken with it. "It's not my kind of artwork, though I suppose it's a reasonable likeness of you and Connor."

"I don't think I'll be getting it framed anytime soon," Grace said, folding it up again and putting it back in her bag. "But the portrait is unimportant, Darcy. You remember the prophecy: that one of us, Connor or me, must die?"

Darcy nodded, shuddering. Of course she remembered that prophecy, though she had hoped never to hear of it again.

"I think..." Grace began. "Or, it would be more accurate to say, I *feel*, that the time is drawing near."

Darcy's eyes were riveted to Grace. "Has the book said something to you?"

Grace nodded. "Today is my birthday. Connor and I

turn fifteen today, though to be honest, I feel about a century older."

"Oh, Grace!" Darcy said. "I wish I'd known. I'd have gotten you a gift. Though I don't know what exactly."

Grace smiled. "Well, whatever it was, it would have been better than Sidorio's. That horrendous painting was his idea of the perfect present." She shuddered. "Sidorio had to go back to *The Vagabond* because Lola was in labor with their twins. Strange, don't you think, that a second pair of twins should be born on the very same day as me and Connor?"

"And when the twins are born," Darcy said, "the end of the war is near—and either you or Connor will..." She could barely get the words out. "One of you will die?"

Grace nodded. "Yes," she said, her voice a barely discernible whisper. She drew herself together and looked straight into Darcy's eyes. "I haven't told Mosh Zu I'm leaving. In fact, we're barely on speaking terms at the moment."

"What should I say if he asks about you?" Darcy said.

Grace shrugged. "I was hoping you'd find a way to cover for me," she said. "Buy me some time. But you can just tell him the truth if you prefer. I'm really past caring what he thinks." She bit back fresh tears. "Darcy, I'm really scared and I need to get to *The Nocturne* right away."

Darcy reached out and gripped Grace's hand. "I can see how frightened you are," she said. "But have you taken time to think this through? If you are potentially in danger, isn't Sanctuary the very safest place for you? Aren't you placing yourself in far graver danger by leaving?"

Grace's voice emerged stronger and more determined than she felt. "I have to get to Lorcan," she said. "You, better than anyone, must understand that."

"Yes," Darcy said. "Of course, I understand. I'll do my best to cover for you here." The two young women hugged again, then Grace stepped back and smiled. "Darcy Flotsam, what exactly are you doing with that guitar?"

"I borrowed it," Darcy said, grinning. "For Jet. I thought it would raise his spirits to be able to make music again."

"I see," Grace said, still smiling through the tears, and, though it was hard, she looked straight into Darcy's eyes. "I hope things work out between you and Jet," she said. "I really hope he's the one you've been waiting for."

Her words awoke fresh alarm in Darcy's face. "You're talking as if you're going away a lot longer than a night or two. Grace, the way you're talking, it's as if we're never—"

Grace lifted her hand. "Don't say it, Darcy. Please! Just let me go." She turned and walked along the corridor, and, despite the temptation, she did not glance back once.

~～～

In Grace's mind, the path down the cliff and onto the ambulance boat had grown more and more tortuous, with fresh obstacles arriving at every turn. In reality, it was straightforward enough to get where she needed to simply by lying. At the gates, she told the guards lie number one. "I'm going to fetch some supplies." Such was their trust in her that no one objected. Instead, they smiled and opened the gates, wishing her a safe trip. Then she had the good fortune to coincide with an ambulance vehicle about to set off down the mountain and told the second lie. "Mosh Zu has sent me on an important mission. Can you take me down to the harbor?" The crew asked no further questions. They were only too happy to help. At the harbor, she found one of the ambulance boats idling and plucked a third lie from thin air: "I need to get to *The Nocturne*. There's a badly wounded Nocturnal on board who I'm going to treat."

So it was that, barely thirty minutes after Grace and Darcy had parted, Grace found herself racing across the sleet-gray ocean, on her way to *The Nocturne* and to Lorcan. It was strange after all this time to find herself traveling in daylight, in the open air, with crew members bustling all around her—albeit at a discreet distance. A shame, perhaps, that it wasn't better weather so she could appreciate the now alien sensation of the sun on her face. But, in many ways, the dreary day suited her mood. Even the sting of the rain on her cheeks was no trouble to her.

"Are you sure you wouldn't like to come inside for a bit?" a kindly young member of the crew asked her. "You can get dry and I'll make you a hot drink if you want."

Grace smiled as best she could, but shook her head. "I'm fine out here, thanks." She turned her head away to watch the trail of churning foam the boat left in its wake. Sanctuary was lost in the mist now and they were surrounded by silvery ocean on all sides. When Grace turned back again, the young sailor had left to talk to his mate.

There was something about being back on the water that instinctively soothed Grace. She knew that Darcy had had a point when she'd said that Grace would be safer within the Sanctuary compound, but what she hadn't wanted to say to Darcy was that the safer *she* was, the more danger she feared Connor might be in. At least this way she was equalizing the threat to them both.

Could the prophecy really be true? Had she and Connor come on this extraordinary journey only to perish now? She let the wind dry her face, thinking back to the voyage they had embarked upon together from Crescent Moon Bay all those months ago. It was almost a year ago now but it seemed like ten or more. So much had happened. Each of their lives had changed so profoundly.

And now this prophecy...Having witnessed so much suffering and death, there wasn't much she wanted more than for this war to come to an end. But she wasn't prepared to die for it. After seeing those who had, it rather shamed her to admit this, if only to herself. She was not ready to die. But nor was she ready to lose Connor. There *had* to be another way.

"Miss!" The young sailor was standing beside her again. She realized that she had lost all track of time, her thoughts circling around and around inside her head like a vortex.

The sailor was pointing up across to where a ship lay moored in the lee of a bay. Grace's heart missed a beat as she found herself looking once more upon *The Nocturne*. Its unique winglike sails billowed in the breeze. Its mast stood tall and strong. The only strange thing about seeing the ship again was the space where Darcy should be as the figurehead. Grace thought once more of Darcy and everything their friendship had come to mean to her.

Staring up at the hulk of the galleon as the ambulance vessel drew alongside, Grace felt as if the ship itself held the key to the mysterious prophecy. She felt calmer simply knowing that Lorcan was here. She would see him again in a matter of minutes, hold him again, and talk to him about these terrible fears. And he would know what to do. Because he always did. Lorcan, dear sweet Lorcan, had never once let her down.

28

RETURN TO *THE NOCTURNE*

As Grace climbed the ladder onto *The Nocturne*, she heard cries and thuds above her. A blur of feet greeted her as her eyes drew level with the deck. She took another step and saw that the deck of *The Nocturne* was alive with movement from prow to stern. Men and women were squaring up to one another with swords and a host of other weapons. Grace lingered at the edge of the ship, taking it all in. So, it had come to this.

The faces of many of the combatants were familiar to her. She didn't know all of their names, but she had seen them often enough during her travels. They were the donors. Stepping onto the deck, clutching her bag in her right hand, Grace surveyed the scene. The very last thing she had expected was to see donors fighting. On a chill day such as this, it was unusual to see the donors up on deck at all.

But she sensed she was not in any danger. She turned to give a thumbs-up to the captain of the ambulance vessel. He nodded and lost no time in giving the orders to sail on. Grace began weaving her way through the combatants, anxious to get inside and find Lorcan without delay. She had the door within her sights when someone jumped across her path. A pair of boots clomped onto the red deck boards and a hand reached out before her.

"Halt!"

Grace felt a wave of adrenaline course through her. Was there danger here after all? But when she looked up, she found herself gazing into a familiar face, lean and tanned. The eyes were jet-black, the smile pure Hollywood.

"Oskar!" Grace cried, dropping her bag and throwing her arms around Lorcan's donor. "It's *so* good to see you again."

"You, too," Oskar said, his eyes brimming with light. "The old place just hasn't been the same without you." He gave her another squeeze, then pulled back from her. "Hey—check out my lately acquired sword skills!" He began whirling his rapier around his head dramatically, then proceeded through an intricate sequence of moves.

Grace was impressed. "Where did you learn to do that?" she asked.

"Right here." Oskar smiled. "From the master himself, aka Lorcan Furey. He was charged with training us all up." Oskar rested the tip of his sword on the decking and mopped his brow. "To begin with all our training sessions were at night, but now that we're getting the hang of it, some us have been deputized to oversee daytime training." His dark eyes seared into hers. "You look surprised?"

Grace nodded. "I am. I never expected to see the donors become a fighting force."

"War changes everything," Oskar said, drawing himself upright and tensing his muscles. "No sense in a fighting machine like this going to waste!"

Grace nodded, smiling but nonetheless concerned. Things must be getting serious if it had come to this. Her need to see Lorcan felt even more pressing now.

"It's so great to see you, but I have to go," she said, already making her way toward the door. "I have some urgent business to discuss with Lorcan."

"Wait!" Oskar called after her.

"I can't," she cried over her shoulder, walking on. "I'll come and find you later." There was an expression on Oskar's face she couldn't quite read, but it evaporated as another of the donors crept up behind him and drew him back into the fray. Turning away again, Grace pushed open the door leading to the ship's interior.

She was aware of the beating of her heart as she made her way down the familiar corridors. It was like coming home. She couldn't be sure if it was the look and smell of the ship itself that made her feel this way or whether it was the promise of Lorcan. Either way, it felt good.

At last, she was standing in front of his cabin. She knocked on the door and waited a moment, longing to see him. There was no answer, and, unable to contain her excitement now that she was so close, she twisted the door handle and pushed it open.

"Lorcan?" she called, stepping inside his cabin. It was dark within and the portholes were covered, as she had expected, with blackout material. The lamplight from the corridor cast a lackluster glow into the room. It was just about sufficient to confirm that Lorcan wasn't here. She was momentarily deflated but reasoned that he must be somewhere else on the ship.

As she turned back toward the corridor, she found that the doorway was now blocked by a silent figure.

"Lorcan?" she repeated, but, as her eyes traced the silhouette, she realized it was not Lorcan but Obsidian Darke standing before her. His imposing frame filled the doorway.

"Grace," he said, his distinctive voice as abrasive as ever. "Welcome back to *The Nocturne*. I'm afraid Lorcan isn't here."

Grace struggled to make out Darke's features through the gloom. "Where is he?"

"With Cate and the crew of *The Tiger*. He helped to mastermind the recapture of *The Diablo* and is now helping them to plan what to do next."

Grace felt the energy draining out of her body at the news that her journey had been in vain. What was she supposed to do now? The ambulance vessel was long gone and it wasn't as if she could just hail a taxi boat and head over to *The Tiger* or back to Sanctuary.

"Why don't you come to my cabin?" Darke suggested. "It's more comfortable in there. There are candles and the fire is lit."

His cabin? It was the last place she wanted to go, and, frankly, he was the last person she wanted to spend time with. It made her sad to think this way. When she had known him as the anonymous Vampirate captain, she had felt very differently. But there was something about Darke she found forbidding. Yet, despite herself, she followed him as he turned and crossed the hallway into the captain's cabin.

"Please," he said, "sit down." He lifted a poker and began agitating the coals in the grate. Grace sat down in the chair she had sat in many times before. She watched Darke stir up the fire, then set down the poker and take his seat opposite from her.

"Well," he said, smiling at her. "I hadn't expected to see you today, but I'm pleased to have the opportunity to wish you a happy birthday in person."

"You know that it's my birthday," she said, her tone neutral.

He nodded.

She had wanted to keep things polite, but he had

unwittingly lit a fuse of irritation inside her. "Of course you know!" she found herself saying. "You and Mosh Zu know everything but you keep things secret from the rest of us, even when those secrets affect our lives in the most profound ways."

It was clear from Darke's tone that he was taken aback by her attack. "What secrets have I kept from you, Grace?"

She couldn't believe she was hearing this. "*What secrets?* Where do I begin?"

She hesitated, feeling the anger bubbling away inside her. Perhaps it was better to shut up and leave now, but the fuse had been lit and there was no going back. "You knew that Sidorio was my blood father and you kept that from me until you had no choice but to tell me. And you knew all about my mother but you hid that information from me, too. Until you chose to bring her back."

Darke raised his hand. "I didn't choose to bring her back. As you may recall, I was very weak and on the verge of oblivion myself." His face was etched with sorrow. "I was no longer able to protect Sally or the other souls I had carried for so long." His eyes returned to Grace. "I know it's small comfort, but at least you got the chance to know her for yourself. I had hoped that would be . . . meaningful to you."

Grace frowned. "I got to watch my mother die. Thanks for lining up that experience!" She was shocked by the anger evident in her own tone of voice. Her voice softened as she continued. "I'm not denying that the time we had together was precious. Whether it was your intention or not, I'm grateful for that time. But you have to know how painful it was to get close to her, only to lose her again."

Darke nodded, his face somber. "I do understand that," he said. "I know what it's like to lose those you are closest to." His eyes met hers. "You and I were close once, but it appears, from your perspective at least, that our friendship is over."

Grace felt a surge of anger. "It's not a matter of perspective," she said. "You've kept too much from me. You *and* Mosh Zu. You both knew that Sidorio fathered me and Connor, and you knew that we were dhampirs, but, for reasons that escape me, you chose not to tell us."

"We were always going to tell you," Darke said now. "But we wanted to wait until you were strong enough to handle the information."

Grace folded her arms. "That's awfully convenient, isn't it?"

Darke shrugged. "It also happens to be true." He looked deep into her eyes. "What other secrets have I kept from you, Grace?" he asked. "Or have you come to the end of your list?"

She shook her head, holding his gaze. "No," she said. "I haven't finished. Because now I've found out about the prophecy. So I know that you and Mosh Zu have both been keeping the biggest secret of all. That either Connor or I must die, in order to bring peace to the oceans."

Darke rose to his feet. "You know about the prophecy?" he said. "How?"

"Not from you," Grace said. "And not from Mosh Zu. No, I had to find out by other means."

Darke frowned. "What means do you speak of?"

"A book I found."

Obsidian looked thoughtful. "I assume you've spoken to Mosh Zu about this?"

"Of course," Grace said. "He brushed it aside and told me it wasn't important—though I've no doubt he lost no time in informing you."

Darke shook his head once more. "He didn't, as a matter of fact. This is the first I've heard of it, though, believe me, I wish that wasn't the case."

"Well," Grace said with a shrug, "at last you know what it feels like to be kept in the dark."

Darke turned his head away. Seeing that the fire was dwindling in the grate, he walked over and lifted the poker again. For a minute, there was silence within the cabin, followed by the hiss, spit, and crackle of the fire as it grew strong once more. Carefully, Darke set down the poker and turned to face Grace.

"I had no idea you felt such anger toward me," he said. "But I'm honestly glad you have shared your feelings with me, and, now you have said things as you see them, I can understand how you feel." He came to stand behind her chair, resting his hand on her shoulder. "I'm so sorry," he said, his voice little more than a whisper. It took her back to a time when he had spoken only in that whisper, but now his voice grew louder once more. "I never thought I was keeping secrets from you and Connor. I was just trying to protect you both. When you set out from Crescent Moon Bay, neither one of you could have anticipated just what you were sailing into."

His hand remained on her shoulder. At his words, Grace found herself back in Dexter's old boat as it splintered around her and she was thrown into the ocean.

"That storm," she said. "Our shipwreck. It didn't happen by chance, did it? None of this happened by chance. It was time to call us back."

He was silent for a time, then she felt his hand lift from her shoulder and he moved around to stand in front of her. "You're right, of course," he said. "After Dexter's death there was no reason for you or Connor to remain in Crescent Moon Bay. It was, as you say, time to call you both home."

Grace froze as everything came into focus. She couldn't believe it had taken her so long to figure it out. "You were drawing both of us back to *The Nocturne* but the plan went wrong. You hadn't reckoned on Cheng Li rescuing Connor."

"Quite so," Obsidian said with a nod. "So—the time

has come to put an end to all the secrets. You are strong enough now to know everything. Where shall we begin?"

Grace had no hesitation. "With Mosh Zu's prophecy."

Obsidian nodded. It took him only a moment to collect his thoughts, then he began to tell the story. "Five hundred years ago, in the time just before the New Flood, my comrades and I were summoned to Sanctuary."

Grace leaned in closer. "Mosh Zu called you?"

"Yes, that's right." Obsidian nodded once again. "Let me show it all to you."

"Show me?" Grace asked, confused.

"You've done this before," Obsidian reminded her, turning to glance at the fire once more. "Look through the flames and I'll take you there."

Her heart hammering, Grace focused her eyes on the veil of flames. At first, her vision blurred as she watched the flames flicker and dance. She waited for the fire to fade and the world beyond to come into focus.

Just as she had anticipated, the fire receded and she found herself gazing into a familiar room: Mosh Zu's meditation chamber. She recognized the mosaic floor with its imposing pattern of a compass. Mosh Zu was kneeling right at the heart of the mosaic design, looking down into a copper bowl filled with water.

As Grace's senses tuned into the scene more deeply, she could hear the motion of the water in the bowl. She watched as its surface became agitated. Mosh Zu kneeled above it, as still as a statue in his orange robes. His eyes were intent upon the surface of the water, which was now spinning in circles. Grace wanted to step nearer, to gain a closer look at the bowl, but she found herself rooted to her seat, as if held by an invisible force. And the first of four masked captains entered the room.

29

CELEBRATIONS

Cheng Li stood in the center of Ma Kettle's Tavern, her back to the vast circular bar. She was taken by surprise at just how busy the tavern was. The whole ramshackle building reverberated with the noise of pirate troops making the most of every last precious moment of their transitory freedom.

"Commodore Li!" called out Sugar Pie, weaving through the crowd. "What a nice surprise! You look amazing, considering what you've been through!"

Cheng Li shrugged. "It takes more than one demented cowboy Vampirate to get this woman down." Her look told Sugar Pie that she had nothing further to say on that particular subject. Smiling pleasantly, she glanced around the crowded tavern. "I see that business is booming."

Sugar Pie nodded. "I hate to say it, but war has been very good for business."

"That must be something of a comfort to Ma Kettle."

"I hoped it might be, Commodore Li." Sugar Pie's expression changed. "I thought seeing the old tavern buzzing like this might bring Ma back to life." She shook her head sadly. "But she's lost all interest in the tavern. Time was, I'd have strained my vocal cords trying to persuade her to take just a little break on a night like this. But tonight, she hasn't even come out front once. She just seems to want to stay in bed, muttering to Scrimshaw about Molucco and the old days."

Cheng Li frowned. "I'm sorry to hear that. I think all you can do is give her time."

Sugar Pie nodded. "You're right. Time is supposed to be the best healer. I'm going to keep a close eye on her. She's been like a mum to me—it's the least I can do." Her face suddenly brightened and it was like the sun breaking through dark clouds. "Enough sad talk! It's no way to welcome you back. I'm going to fetch you and your crew a round of drinks—on the house. And there's no need for you to stand about here with the hoi polloi. There's a VIP booth over there with your name on it."

"Thank you," Cheng Li said. "But I'm happy to stay here for a minute or two. I'm waiting for someone." Her eyes returned to the entrance. "Ah, and here he is!"

Both women's eyes settled upon the arresting young

man in a blue-gray uniform who now shook the hand of Pieces 08, the tavern's trusty security guard, and proceeded past the velvet curtain into the bar.

Sugar Pie nudged Cheng Li. "Now he's a walking definition of tall, dark, and handsome! Though a little pale for my liking."

Cheng Li smiled. "He's a Nocturnal."

"Of course!" Sugar Pie said. "You know, I'm still getting used to them coming in here. Time was, a Vamp stepped past that curtain and we'd be on an all-points alert."

"He's not a Vampirate," Cheng Li said, her voice heavy with feeling. "He's a Nocturnal. It's an important distinction."

"Yes, I know," Sugar Pie said. She was momentarily chastened but soon recovered, as she watched Lorcan stride toward them. "I haven't seen him here before. I'd have definitely remembered such a pretty face."

"Once seen, never forgotten," agreed Cheng Li, raising her hand to signal to Lorcan. Cheng Li noted that many pirates, especially the women pirates, had turned to register the young Nocturnal's arrival. She observed with undeniable satisfaction the envious eyes now turned toward her as Lorcan stood before her and gave the Alliance salute.

Flushed with pleasure, she returned the salute and dared to look once more into his unnervingly blue eyes. "Commander Furey, I'm so glad you were able to join us here tonight."

Lorcan smiled. "I mustn't stay long, Commodore Li, but I was keen to congratulate you all on the victorious return of *The Diablo*."

"As usual, you are much too modest," Cheng Li said, feeling the warm glow she always seemed to in his presence. "You know full well that the victory was, in a very considerable way, due to your inspired strategy." She noted that he received praise a little awkwardly. His momentary unease only made him more charming. She reached out for his uniformed arm, deliciously aware of the daggers of envy being launched in her direction. "Come with me," she said. "There's a VIP booth waiting for us."

Smiling again, Lorcan removed his cap. "Lead on, Commodore Li," he said. "As you know, I'm something of a stranger in these parts."

As they made their way through the crowd toward the roped-off booth, a familiar figure suddenly appeared before them.

"Cate!" Lorcan said, apparently catching her by surprise. She looked lost in her own thoughts but stopped and smiled to see her comrades.

"Lorcan," Cate said. "You're about the last person I expected to see here at Ma's."

"I invited him," Cheng Li said with a smile. "We're on the same side now."

"Yes," Cate nodded. "Absolutely."

"Congratulations, Cate," Lorcan said, clasping her hands. "It was a textbook victory."

Cheng Li was momentarily perturbed by the display of easy affection between her two subordinates, but she recovered well. "Too modest by far," she said, shaking her head. "You two have rewritten the rules on maritime warfare. Your names—*our* names—are now assured of their place in pirate history."

"This war isn't over yet," Lorcan reminded her.

"Indeed not," Cheng Li said. "We must now turn our attention to the next phase in this combat. I believe we are reaching a decisive moment. I thought we could talk further about this tonight."

Cate smiled at Lorcan. "You see, my friend, there's no such thing as a free drink."

They had reached the VIP booth. As the velvet rope was moved aside for them to step forward, Cheng Li lost no time in advancing her cause. "Tell me, Commander, has Obsidian Darke thought any more about strategic alliances with other Nocturnals?"

Lorcan's face was clouded as he replied. "Obsidian and I have talked many times of this, but I'm afraid I have no firm progress to report to you."

Cheng Li shook her head. "I don't understand why he remains so resistant," she said, claiming the prime position at the table. "Surely he must see that we pirates cannot continue to bear the brunt of this war alone? Not when there are potential allies among the Nocturnal realm. He *must* bring them into play—and fast."

"I agree," Lorcan said, sitting down across from her. "But when it comes to persuading Obsidian, he is as obdurate as his name suggests."

Cheng Li frowned. "He *must* yield on this point." She laid her hand on Lorcan's arm again. "Would it help if I talked to him directly?"

"I'm not sure," Lorcan replied. "I'm not doubting your considerable powers of persuasion, but, on this matter, his mind appears to be firmly set."

Cheng Li shook her head. "It's up to you and me to find a way to stir him." She glanced up, expecting to see Cate, but instead found herself looking at Bo Yin.

"Where did Cate get to?" Cheng Li asked her.

"She has a headache," Bo Yin said. "She's gone back to the ship." Over Bo Yin's shoulder, Cheng Li could see Cate's familiar shock of red hair moving through the barroom like a flaming torch. "She might at least have said a proper good-bye—to our guest," Cheng Li said, frowning.

"It's all right," Lorcan said. "I don't think Cate has the taste for social gatherings just now. What with her grief for Bart and all."

Cheng Li watched Cate disappear into the crowd, then returned her full attention to her companion. "You're very understanding," she said. "Perhaps even a little *too* understanding."

"I don't think so," Lorcan said softly, but with steel in his voice. "Give her some time."

"Is that an order?" Cheng Li's eyes met his.

"No," he said, his expression becoming more yielding. "Just a tip from one good friend to another."

Basking in his choice of words and the honeyed brogue that never failed to delight her, Cheng Li sat back in her seat, at last beginning to relax.

―――

Cate had almost reached Pieces 08 and the exit when a hand reached out and caught her arm. Surprised and somewhat irritated, she turned to find Moonshine Wrathe standing before her.

"Tut-tut, Catie," he said. "You've got into this terrible habit of leaving parties early. Don't you believe in the healing power of human company?"

"Not that it's any of your business, but I'm tired," Cate said. "And I've got a splitting headache."

Moonshine reached out his hand. On his palm nestled two oval pills. "Pop these and you'll feel a whole lot better."

Cate arched an eyebrow warily. "What exactly are those?" she asked.

Moonshine laughed. "Paracetamol," he replied. "Though I can understand your suspicion. I have a well-earned reputation as a walking pharmacy."

"Thanks, but no thanks," Cate said, folding her arms. "I'm going to leave now. You stay and enjoy yourself with the others." Fearing she had come across more severely than intended, she added, "You deserve it. You claimed a masterly victory."

"Praise indeed," Moonshine said, shrugging and popping the two pills himself. "Now what's *that* look for?"

Cate shook her head but said nothing.

"I know." Moonshine grinned. "I'm a danger to myself. That's why I need someone at my side to teach me right from wrong and be a good influence on me." He winked. "Though I guess we could just start with teaching me right from left."

Cate stared at him, coolly. "You're no fool," she said. "And nor are you the loose cannon you pretend to be. Oh, you certainly *were*. I haven't forgotten the Sunset Fort debacle. I don't think any of us will in a hurry. But you've changed, Moonshine Wrathe. I can see that. The way you acquitted yourself in Operation Scrimshaw was exemplary—worthy of a pirate of many more years' experience."

Moonshine was uncharacteristically rendered speechless by her praise. Taking advantage of this rare scenario, Cate pressed on. "So the answer to your question is yes."

Moonshine's face moved through a series of contortions as he struggled to find the right words. After a great deal of effort, he managed, "The answer is . . . yes?"

Cate nodded, quietly amused. "Yes," she repeated. "I've worked it all out with Commodore Li. I will retain my role as chief strategist for the Alliance but I'll be based on *The*

Diablo for now. I've already packed my things, so, after you've had your fun and made some interesting shapes on the dance floor, perhaps you can see to it that my old corner cabin is made ready for me?"

"Is that an order?" Moonshine inquired, back to his default cheek. "Because in a conventional captain-deputy relationship, isn't it the captain who gives the orders?"

Cate smiled as her slate-gray eyes locked onto his. "Rest assured, my friend, this isn't going to be a conventional captain-deputy relationship."

"I'll drink to that!" Moonshine said, raising his glass.

"Three drinks at the very most," Cate said. "You'll certainly want to keep a clear head for our strategy meeting in the morning. I'll come over at seven-thirty sharp. Unless that's too early for you?"

Moonshine grinned. "Not at all. You'll catch me just after my morning run. I'll even lay on breakfast. Remind me, how do you like your eggs?"

Smiling but leaving the question unanswered, Cate brushed past Moonshine and slipped beyond the velvet curtain into the night.

—◆—

Seeing Connor seated alone at the table beside him—and Cheng Li deep in conversation with Jasmine and Bo Yin—Lorcan quietly rose up and moved across.

"May I join you?" he asked Connor.

Connor glanced up. "Feel free," he said. "But I should warn you, I'm not great company tonight."

"I'll take my chances," Lorcan said, sitting down opposite Connor. "How come you feel that way, on this of all nights?"

Connor stared at the Nocturnal curiously. "You mean on the night we should be celebrating our epic victory?"

"No," Lorcan said. "I mean because it's your birthday."

Connor looked suddenly tense. "Who told you?" he hissed. "No one's supposed to know."

Lorcan leaned closer, smiling as he lowered his voice. "I was there at your birth, remember?"

Connor shrugged but said nothing.

"I'll come clean with you," Lorcan said. "I'm here under false pretenses. Cheng Li invited me here tonight to celebrate our successful mission. But I'm mostly here to see you."

"Me?" Connor said. "Why would you want to see me?"

"Well, you're my girlfriend's brother," Lorcan said. "Plus, we're comrades now. We don't know each other very well, but I'd like us to be friends."

Connor took a draft of his drink. "I don't have a great track record with friends." He set the glass down again slowly, precisely. His eyes remained downcast. "They tend to die. Though I suppose the fact you're already dead might work in your favor."

"I know how close you were to Bart," Lorcan said. "I'm very sorry for your loss."

Connor did not respond directly, asking instead, "Is Grace worried about me?"

Lorcan shook his head. "I don't know. Truth to tell, we haven't spent much time together of late. Grace is very preoccupied with her work, just now. Well, we all are. I'm sure she misses you, but I'm not here because of her. I can see with my own eyes that something's wrong."

"Really?" Connor threw up his arms. "What could be wrong with me, I wonder? Hmm, let me think! I found out my dad wasn't who I thought he was all those years. And my real father? Why, of course, it's Sidorio, leader of the Vampirate army and—wait—as a bonus, I get Lola thrown in as my stepmother. Plus I'm a dhampir, a fact that none of my crewmates but Cheng Li knows—not even my long-suffering girlfriend."

"Jasmine," Lorcan said, his eyes glancing across to the other table, where Jasmine was still embroiled in a lengthy conversation with Cheng Li and Bo Yin.

Connor nodded, also gazing across at her. "Jasmine," he said. "I fell for her the first time I set eyes on her at Pirate Academy. Everything was simpler back then."

"Was it?" Lorcan interrupted. "Or does it just seem that way to you now?"

Connor nodded. "Good point, Furey. Because even back then she had a boyfriend, Jacoby Blunt—a good friend of mine, as it goes. Sure, he tried to kill me once, but we'll gloss over that." His eyes seared into Lorcan's. "Because, you see, the impossible happened and Jasmine and I realized we had feelings for each other but we fought them out of loyalty to Jacoby. Then Jacoby was captured by the Vampirates and killed and we both felt too guilty to be together so our relationship pretty much stalled." Connor shook his head. "Anyhow, by that time, I was completely sidetracked by the discovery that I was a dhampir, and had a rising hunger for blood."

"But you have that under control now, right?" Lorcan said. "You're drinking the berry tea Grace has sent to you?"

A glazed look came over Connor's face. "One thing at a time, eh? We're talking about me and Jasmine and Jacoby right now. Your not-so-regular love triangle. Well, you'd know how uncomfortable that is, wouldn't you? So, as sad as I was at the news of Jacoby's death, I thought maybe, at last, there was a chance for us. Perhaps not right away, but once we'd both had time to adjust." He sighed. "But, as you know, Jacoby was found on board *The Diablo*. Seems he's alive after all, but here's the real stinger. He's a vampire now. He's just as hungry for blood as I am!"

Connor took a breath, fixing Lorcan with his gaze once more. "Only, unlike me, Jacoby was man enough to tell Jasmine what he is. And, guess what? She's *completely* fine with it. So he's coming back to *The Tiger* tomorrow and I reckon that's the end of any chance I ever had with Jasmine." He raised his glass. "Let's drink a toast," he said. "Happy birthday to me! I have so many reasons to celebrate."

Lorcan hesitated. "Connor," he said. "I was concerned about you, but I had no idea you were going through all this—the situation with Jacoby and Jasmine, on top of your grief for Bart. And there's obviously stuff going on in relation to your blood-hunger."

Connor shrugged. "Nothing a swift pint at the Blood Tavern can't remedy," he said.

Lorcan frowned. "We *really* need to talk," he said.

"No," Connor said. "Talking only makes it worse. I'm done with talking."

"Please," Lorcan implored him. "I genuinely want to help you."

Connor rolled his eyes. "One vampire to another?"

"I know you're having a tough time adjusting—" Lorcan said.

"Understatement of the millennium," Connor said, draining his drink. "I hate it. I despise it. I despise *me*. And you want to know the worst part? I'm immortal now so there's no way out."

He slammed his glass down angrily on the table. The gesture made Lorcan flinch. As he did so, Connor noticed a figure standing behind Lorcan. A familiar face staring at him in all-too-evident horror.

"Jasmine!" Connor said, feeling a wave of nausea, adrenaline, and dread. "How much of that did you hear?"

There was a definite edge to Jasmine's brief answer. "Enough."

"Well, now you know," Connor said, trying to be

matter-of-fact. "Now you know the full story—the real shape of things."

Jasmine nodded.

"Aren't you going to say anything?" Connor asked.

"What do you want me to say?" she asked. "I think you've mustered enough self-pity to drown in." She hesitated before continuing. "Nevertheless, it might interest you to hear that I knew you were a dhampir. I've known for some time."

"You knew?" Connor was aghast.

"Yes," Jasmine said. "I guessed. It was weird knowing, but I knew it would be all right."

"All right?" Connor said, incredulously. "How can it possibly be all right? I'm a monster!"

"Yes," Jasmine said. "Yes, Connor, that's a remarkably apt description. But that has nothing *whatsoever* to do with you being a dhampir. You got there all by yourself."

30

LORDS OF THE SEVEN OCEANS

Sidorio was surprised to find his heart racing as he approached Lola's cabin. He was transported back to the very first time he had boarded *The Vagabond* and interrupted Lola during the ritual of her nightly bloodbath. So much had changed since then. Lola had become his wife, and his partner in a formidable empire. Now she would bestow upon him a further prize—twin children who, in time, would join them at the helm of the empire and ensure its further expansion. Sidorio could not remember a time when things had looked so well for him. It seemed that at last it was payback for the long years of purgatory he had endured aboard *The Nocturne*—when he had allowed his appetites to be subdued and his innate power to be constrained.

He knocked on one of the gilded doors of Lola's cabin to signal his presence, then hesitated for a moment, unsure whether to go inside or wait for her call. It was rare for him to feel so diffident, but he was suddenly stricken with nerves. He was entering this room as one thing—a warrior, of course, but also a father to grown kids who had little need of him now, however much he wished that was different. But when he emerged from this room later, it would be as father to two newborns, with whom his relationship would surely prove markedly different. He was excited but, he realized, fearful too. What if, after everything he had accomplished in this world, he was simply not up to this new challenge?

The doors opened and Sidorio was surprised to find that it was neither Holly nor Camille who greeted him, nor Lola herself. Instead, standing on the other side of the threshold, smiling softly in the candlelight, was Olivier.

"Congratulations, sir," Olivier said, gesturing for Sidorio to step inside. Sidorio felt his anger swiftly rise—as if he needed to be welcomed into his own wife's cabin by Olivier, of all people!

"What are you doing here?" Sidorio asked curtly as the doors swung shut behind him. "You're supposed to be off running our field hospital."

Before Olivier could frame his answer, Lola stepped out from the inner chamber, a swaddled babe in each arm. "Leave Olivier be!" she said. "He has been most helpful to me during the births and after." Smiling beatifically, she walked slowly toward her husband. The way she moved reminded Sidorio of their wedding day. He felt his anger draining away. Olivier was forgotten entirely as Lola stepped closer, bearing their precious twins.

"You look radiant, my dear," Sidorio said. It was true. Lola's exceptional beauty never failed to take his breath away, but she had never appeared more beautiful to him than in this moment. He wanted to capture this image of her now and keep it in his head for eternity.

He stepped forward, beaming down at her and catching his first glimpse of the babes. They both had wide dark eyes, which turned inquisitively toward him.

"This is your father." Lola spoke softly, her eyes looking lovingly upon first one babe, then the other, before meeting Sidorio's gaze once more. "Aren't they the most beautiful creatures you have ever seen?"

Sidorio nodded. He reached a finger toward one of the babies. Instantly, its little mouth opened and clamped itself around Sidorio's fingertip.

Lola laughed and glanced at the clock on the mantel. "He's hungry again," she said. "It must be time for another feed." She turned and made her way to the chaise. Olivier got there first and began propping up cushions for her. "Thank you," she said, making herself comfortable. "Sid, darling, don't just stand there looking uncomfortable. Come and sit with your family!"

Spellbound, Sidorio walked forward and sat down in the chair adjacent to Lola's chaise. In front of the chaise was an antique table. Sidorio remembered Lola's telling him that it had once belonged to a queen of England, as if this might make the artifact more special to him. He had smiled at her misunderstanding—the table was only precious to him by virtue of its belonging to Lola herself. On the table now rested one of Lola's Venetian glasses, full of ruby-red blood. Steadying the babies' plump little bodies, Lola leaned forward and dipped her right index finger into the glass. As it emerged, slick with blood, both babies became instantly alert. Lola leaned across to the babe on the right and his mouth gratefully clamped around her finger. As he did so, the other babe began to wail.

"Now, don't cry, little man," Lola said. "Just be patient and Mummy will fix you up, too." To help her, Olivier stepped forward and brought the glass nearer. Lola dipped her left index finger into the glass and presented it to the other baby. His crying immediately ceased and soon he too was merrily suckling on her finger, just like his brother.

Sidorio watched, mesmerized. Lola was so natural with the babies. Clearly, it had been her destiny to become a mother in this life as well as her past.

"Here, I'll take that," Sidorio told Olivier, extricating the glass from his pale hands. "You may go now."

Olivier stepped backward. "Will that be all, Captain Lockwood?" he asked.

"Yes, thank you, Olivier," Lola said, flushed with a rosy glow and wreathed in smiles. "Thank you for all your assistance. You've been most kind."

Olivier bowed his head, returning her smile.

"Her name is Sidorio," Sidorio reminded him icily. "*Lady* Sidorio to you."

"I stand corrected," Olivier said, bowing before hastening toward the exit.

"Wait!" Sidorio called over his shoulder as Olivier reached for the door. "Give us some time alone, but send word for Johnny and Stukeley to come and see us."

"Yes," Lola said. "And Mimma and Holly, too!"

"Yes, Captains," Olivier said, slipping out into the corridor and closing the gilded doors once more.

"He isn't growing on me," Sidorio said grumpily, offering the glass to Lola, who dipped her fingers once more inside.

"That's plain enough," Lola said as the babes' mouths clamped onto her fingers again. "Be that as it may, while you were away gallivanting, Olivier was here helping me through the worst of my labor."

"I *wasn't* gallivanting," Sidorio said, wounded by the accusation and jealous that Olivier had been here to witness the birth rather than him. "You told me to go," he reminded Lola plaintively.

"Did I?" Lola smiled and shook her head. "Everything before the birth seems foggy to me now. I can barely remember, and, well, it hardly matters now. It feels as though everything began anew for me when these two little birds took flight into the world."

"Indeed," Sidorio said, more than happy to let this constitute a fresh start for them both.

"He's tired now," Lola said, nodding toward the babe in her left arm. "Look at his long eyelashes. They're quite as black as mine."

"Yes, they are," Sidorio said, leaning closer. As he did so, the other babe let out a cry.

"Now this one," Lola said, "he's just like you. His appetite is insatiable. All right, baby! A little patience, please!"

"May I feed him?" Sidorio asked, hoarsely.

Lola paused, her fingers hovering above the glass. Then, smiling, she nodded. "Of course. It will help you to bond."

Sidorio dipped his own right index finger into the glass, then tentatively extended it toward the baby's mouth. The tiny lips instantly parted and then closed around his finger. Sidorio beamed with delight.

"Who's a lucky little man?" Lola said, her eyes upon the baby. "Is Daddy feeding you? Is he? Yes, he is!"

Sidorio beamed broadly. "We should discuss names for our boys," he said.

"No need," Lola said. "I've already named them."

"You have?" Sidorio felt somehow wounded. "I thought we'd do that together."

"This one," Lola pressed on, indicating the sleeping babe, "is Hunter."

"Hunter," Sidorio repeated. As he did so, the boy opened his eyes and seemed to smile at his father.

"You see," Lola said. "Hunter is *very* happy with his name." She placed a finger on the baby's button nose. As she did so, he smiled and closed his eyes again. Lola turned her attention to the other baby, who was still sucking blood from his father's finger. "And this hungry little mite is your other son, Evil."

"Evil?" Sidorio repeated in astonishment. "You don't think that's just a little extreme?"

Lola shook her head. "No, my darling, I don't. What do we want most for this dear little lad? To follow in our footsteps and grow up to be evil incarnate. His name will help guide him on the right path." She smiled. "Besides, it's an old family name on my father's side."

Sidorio took stock. "Hunter and Evil Sidorio," he said. It didn't sound bad, though his own first choice had been Julius.

"Hunter and Evil Lockwood Sidorio," Lola replied. "I think it rolls off the tongue just that little bit better, don't you?"

It hardly seemed worth him considering the matter further. Sidorio knew full well when his wife's mind was completely made up.

"I think Evil has had enough blood for now," Lola said, staying Sidorio's hand above the glass.

"But he's crying," Sidorio protested.

"He has to learn when he's had enough," Lola said, "or we shall never have any peace. Besides, I'm thirsty myself." She lifted the glass to her lips and drained the remains of its contents in one gulp.

Sidorio observed Evil watching his mother enviously. Then he saw the baby's eyes close and the infant drift off into easy slumber like his little brother.

—⁓—

"We were nervous about knocking, in case they were sleeping," Johnny whispered.

"It's all right," Lola said, looking down at the babies in their twin gold cribs. "They *were* having a nap, but they'll be excited to meet all of you." She smiled graciously at Johnny, Stukeley, Holly, and Mimma, who had all come in, followed by Olivier, who lingered near the door.

"Up you get!" Lola said, lifting Hunter into her hands and resting his little head on her shoulder. Holly came over and cooed at him. "He's gorgeous!" she exclaimed.

"Isn't he?" Lola nodded, then gestured toward Evil's crib. "Would you like to rouse this one from his slumbers?" Holly nodded excitedly and reached down into the crib.

Lola carried Hunter over to the chaise and resumed her seat. Holly brought across Evil and offered him to Lola, who had quickly grown adept at balancing one babe in each arm.

"Look at you go, Captain!" Mimma exclaimed. "You're a natural mother!"

"Why, thank you," Lola said graciously. "The thing is I know full well they won't be little for long. I must enjoy being able to hold them both for as long as I can, until it gives me back-strain!" She laughed merrily and the others joined in, too.

Sidorio addressed Olivier brusquely. "Come and pour everyone a glass," he said.

Olivier hesitated momentarily, looking to Lola. She met his eyes, then glanced down to stroke Hunter's cheek. Olivier walked over to the table where a decanter full of blood and six glasses were waiting. As he poured the glasses, Sidorio passed them jovially around the room to his comrades.

"Thank you, Olivier," he said, as his subordinate realized that there was no glass remaining for him. Sidorio breezed on ebulliently, coming to stand beside his wife. "Lola and I are delighted to introduce to you our two dear boys, Hunter and Evil," he proclaimed. "So now, please raise your glasses and join me in a toast to the boys and their beautiful mother." He lifted his glass. "To Hunter, Evil, and Lola!"

"Hunter, Evil, and Lola!" echoed the others, even Olivier, who mimed lifting an invisible glass.

"Who came up with their names?" Stukeley asked, amused.

"I did," Lola said, meeting his eyes. "Do you like them?"

"Oh, yes," Stukeley said. "Highly original. Evil, especially."

"It's an old family name of Lola's," Sidorio informed him.

"Of course it is!" Stukeley said, not daring to meet Johnny's eyes. Instead, he lifted his glass and drank.

Sidorio cleared his throat once more. "In all the years I have roamed this earth, I cannot remember another night of such happiness," he said, his eyes jewel-bright as he glanced at each of his comrades. "We already had a family..." he began.

"Meaning Grace and Connor?" Johnny inquired.

He was met by a cold stare from Lola. "Meaning all of you," she said icily.

"Yes," Sidorio said. "We think of all of you as family." His eyes moved from Stukeley to Mimma to Johnny and to Holly. "And now we have these dear boys who, in years to come, will grow to become your friends and allies."

"And their commanders," Lola added.

"What's that, my love?" Sidorio asked.

"Hunter and Evil will be the commanders of our empire," Lola said, glancing down lovingly at the twins once more. "These dear little boys will one day rise to become Lords of the Seven Oceans."

"Ah, yes," Sidorio said. "Quite so." He saw Stukeley and Johnny exchange a swift glance. "Moments like this fundamentally change the way you feel about things. Lola was saying so herself just before. How did you put it, my sweet? That everything before the twins' birth was a fog." His eyes were like stars shooting across the room. "Everything begins anew tonight."

Lola nodded, her own eyes bright. The others, including Olivier, leaned closer, aware that something major, possibly quite unprecedented, was brewing.

"Lola and I have been talking," Sidorio continued. "And we have decided that it's time to end this war."

The blood caught in Stukeley's throat and he began to choke.

"You're surely not thinking of offering a truce?" said Johnny.

"Hardly," Lola laughed. "What sort of a message would that send out about the state of our camp?"

"That's a relief," Mimma admitted. "You had me worried there, Captain. It sounded like the twins' births had put you both in a sentimental mood!"

"The twins' births *have* galvanized us," Lola said. "But not in the way you all seem to anticipate." She turned to her husband.

Sidorio nodded. "We haven't gone soft. Quite the reverse. We need to step up the fight to ensure these boys' future. We are razor sharp and ready for decisive action. We are charging you now to prepare for the ultimate victory." He paused. "Our next attack will end this war in the most absolute terms imaginable."

"What do you have in mind?" It was, to Sidorio's chagrin, Olivier who posed the question. Nonetheless, Sidorio was not about to be derailed. Instead, he glanced first at his wife, next his twin babes—their black button eyes staring back at him in awe—and then at his four dynamic deputies.

"Our next and final target is *The Nocturne*," Sidorio announced.

31

MINOR ADJUSTMENTS

Jasmine and Cheng Li stood at the open hatch on the third belowdeck of *The Tiger*, gazing out into the morning light. The sky was painted pink and silver, its tones reflected by the unusually placid sea. The early-morning mist imbued everything with a sense of calm and still-ness. It was as if they had stepped out of the raging inferno of war into a precious pocket of peace. As they watched, a silvery shadow appeared through the mist and the Federation vessel bearing Jacoby drew up alongside.

"Wouldn't it have been easier if he'd arrived at night?" Jasmine asked.

"Of course," Cheng Li said, her eyes trained on the reciprocal hatch on the other ship. "That's rather the point." As Jasmine pondered the captain's words, Cheng Li turned and called out to two pirates behind her. "Extend the plank!" At her words, the pirates got busy. As the thick metal plank reached the Federation vessel, hands reached out to clamp it into place.

"I just don't see how this is going to work," Jasmine said.

"It's going to work just fine," Cheng Li said, turning to her side once more. "Ready with the awning, boys?"

"Yes, Captain!"

The pirates engaged a second pair of winches and a black awning began moving across the water, above the metal plank. The awning was curved and its sides brushed the edge of the plank as the pirates sent it over to join the other vessel.

"Final preparations!" Cheng Li commanded. At her words, two more pirates emerged from the corridor and stepped onto the plank. They moved swiftly along, fastening the awning to the base so that the tunnel formed by the awning and the plank was completely lightproof. Staring into it, Jasmine couldn't see a thing. It was only the sound of the young pirates' footsteps that signaled to her their return.

"Everything shipshape, Captain!" announced the first.

"Good work," Cheng Li replied.

Now Jasmine's heart began to beat faster as she glanced once more into the void.

"Is he here yet?" Bo Yin arrived, somewhat out of breath, at Jasmine's side.

"No," Jasmine said, refusing to take her eyes away from the tunnel. "Any minute now."

"Phew!" said Bo. "Everything's ready—but only by the skin of our teeth!"

Bo Yin continued to babble away, but Jasmine had tuned out her voice. Her entire focus was directed on the dark tunnel. At last she heard the sound of footsteps once more, and suddenly Jacoby was standing before her. He had gained a little weight during his time at Sanctuary and, all things considered, he looked remarkably strong and vital—the perfect embodiment of an Alliance officer in his tight-fitting blue-gray uniform, with its adornment of silver braid across his broad chest. He removed his cap, revealing his newly cropped hair, and gave Cheng Li the Federation salute.

"Welcome back!" Cheng Li said, returning the gesture.

Jacoby's eyes turned to Jasmine. He lifted his hand to make the salute once more, but, shaking her head slowly, Jasmine opened her arms. "Come here!" she said, hugging him and feeling tears welling as her hands encircled his shoulders. "It's so good to see you again!" she whispered as he leaned toward her.

"You, too!" Jacoby said, his eyes locking with hers, as they had done so many times before. Jasmine was expert at reading Jacoby's expressions. Now she saw in his eyes deep affection and a certain relief but also something else—a new wariness.

There was a discreet cough at Jacoby's side. He drew himself upright once more and moved aside as a young woman stepped out of the tunnel and onto *The Tiger*.

"Jasmine, this is Luna—my donor and private healer."

Disarmed by Luna's unusual beauty and the way she seemed to hang on Jacoby's every word, Jasmine nonetheless shot out her hand. "Good to meet you, Luna. I've heard great things about you."

"It's mutual," Luna said, smiling pleasantly. Jasmine could see the trepidation in Luna's soft gray eyes.

The young women shook hands, and, as Luna smiled at her with genuine warmth and openness, Jasmine realized she had been foolish to dread this meeting. Luna was simply Jacoby's donor and nurse, and, while both those roles involved a certain intimacy, they would not threaten the long-standing bond between herself and Jacoby—a bond forged in Pirate Academy many years earlier when the eyes of two seven-year-old kids had met in laughter during Captain Quivers's knot class.

"Luna," Jacoby continued, "I'd like to introduce you to our esteemed leader, Commodore Cheng Li."

"Welcome to *The Tiger*," Cheng Li said, nodding at the new arrival as two soldiers arrived out of the tunnel bearing Jacoby and Luna's luggage. They passed it across to their opposite numbers on board *The Tiger*.

"Let's get you both settled in your accommodation," Cheng Li said, taking Jacoby's arm and setting off along the corridor. Jasmine followed, with Luna on one side and Bo Yin on the other.

As they reached the end of the corridor, Cheng Li paused beside a closed door. "I just need to pop into the mess hall for a moment," she said, holding Jacoby close as she pushed open the door.

Before he knew what was happening, Jacoby found himself propelled forward until he was face-to-face with a wall of cheering, clapping pirates. Behind them was a big painted sign bearing the legend WELCOME HOME, JACOBY!

Jacoby turned to Bo Yin. "I suppose I have you to thank for this, do I, you little scamp?"

Bo Yin shrugged, but she was smiling broadly. The cheers and claps kept coming. Jacoby stood, then reached for Jasmine's hand and held it tightly. He hadn't anticipated such a rapturous welcome and he found himself genuinely overwhelmed.

"Thank you!" he said to his comrades, but his words made little impact against the sea of noise. "Thank you!" he repeated a second, third, and fourth time as the cheers and claps kept coming.

—◦—

"Come in!" Cheng Li called, setting her reading glasses down on her desk.

"It's me—Jacoby," came the voice from outside.

"Ah, good," she cried. "Just a minute!" She pressed a recently installed button under her desk and blackout blinds smoothly descended across all the portholes in her cabin. At the same time, the lights within the room accordingly grew brighter.

"Okay," she called out. "You're fine to come in now."

Jacoby stepped inside and closed the double doors behind him.

Cheng Li rose to her feet, smiling. "So, how does it feel to be back?" she asked, meeting him in the center of the cabin.

"Mostly good," he said, glancing at the blinds. "But weird in some ways."

Cheng Li shrugged. "Bound to," she said. "It's early days."

Jacoby's smile gave way to a frown. "I don't want to be a burden—not to you or any of the crew."

"A burden?" Cheng Li asked. "Why would you think that?"

Jacoby stared directly at her. "Arriving under cover of darkness, waiting for the blinds to fall before I enter your cabin—I can't even go up on deck anymore until nightfall."

"A few minor adjustments," Cheng Li said calmly.

"Not exactly minor," Jacoby murmured.

Cheng Li folded her arms. "It's Alliance policy for every Federation vessel to have a Nocturnal on board," she said. "Thus far, *The Tiger* has been the exception due to our close relationship with Commander Furey." She smiled as she spoke Lorcan's name. "But now the time has come to have a full-time Nocturnal on our crew." She unfolded her arms and stepped closer to Jacoby. "And I cannot think of anyone better qualified for that position than you."

Jacoby managed to force a smile but it was clear he didn't quite believe her.

Cheng Li continued more forcefully. "Jacoby Blunt, you are an integral part of my crew and you have a key role to play in winning this war. Whether you fight by day or by night, you remain one of my best warriors. You're still deputy captain of this ship."

Jacoby's surprise was evident. "I thought you'd given that job to Connor."

"Connor took over your responsibilities while you were away recuperating, but, now that you're back, the position is yours again—assuming you still want it."

Jacoby's eyes were wide. "Of course I want it," he said. "I just figured you'd tell me I had to take it easy and give myself time."

Cheng Li shook her head decisively. "I'm not running a greeting card company. I'm a senior commander engaged in the biggest war ever to hit the oceans." Her almond eyes had never gleamed with such conviction. "There's no time for anyone to take it easy. You had the chance to convalesce at Sanctuary. Now that you're back, I expect you to give one hundred percent, just like before. Take the blood you need from Luna, stay out of the sunlight, and work your butt off to justify my absolute confidence in you."

"Yes, Captain!" Jacoby exclaimed, grinning broadly as he saluted her once more.

"At ease, Deputy Blunt," Cheng Li said, shaking her head. "Oh, and if you're looking for a new role model, you could do far worse than to emulate Commander Furey."

Jacoby gazed in wonder at his captain and commander. She was certainly one of a kind.

"If you have any more questions, just come and find me," Jasmine told Luna as they left the mess hall after a tasty dinner of halibut, wasabi mash, and sea vegetables.

"Thank you," Luna said. "You've been so kind."

Jasmine shrugged off the compliment. "And if I'm not available, Bo Yin will be pleased to help you, won't you, Bo?"

Bo Yin smiled brightly. "Absolutely."

"Thank you," Luna said. "Yin," she added contemplatively. "Of course! Your father is Master Yin, the legendary swordsmith. I've heard all about him."

Bo Yin beamed. She never tired of hearing people praise her father. It helped her to feel closer to him while they were apart.

"Well, this is me," Luna said, tapping the door of her cabin. "Good night to you both, and thanks again for making me so welcome."

As she disappeared inside the cabin, Jasmine and Bo

Yin proceeded along the corridor. At last, Bo could ask Jasmine some of the questions that had been building up over the past few hours, starting with...

"So, basically, that girl is here to give Jacoby regular drinks of blood?"

"Yes." Jasmine nodded. "That's about the sum of it. Though I believe she's trained in several kinds of healing, too."

"So she's a donor—with benefits," Bo Yin said, cracking a grin. Jasmine bit her lip as Bo Yin continued merrily on. "I've heard about the donors, of course, but I never thought they'd be so, well, so like us."

Jasmine paused and turned to her friend and comrade. "She's just like us, Bo, when all is said and done. Luna's just another soldier doing her bit for the war effort." As she finished speaking, she saw a figure ambling along the corridor toward them.

"Hello, Connor Tempest!" Bo Yin exclaimed. "Where have you been hiding all day?"

Connor smiled amiably at Bo Yin but did not answer her question. Instead, he glanced cagily toward Jasmine. "Did he make it back okay?"

"Yes, Connor." There was an arctic chill to Jasmine's voice. "Jacoby came home at first light. *Most* of the crew were gathered in the mess hall to give him a rousing welcome," she said. "It was wonderful to witness such a show of support and solidarity."

"I'm glad," Connor said, with genuine feeling. "I've

been holed up downstairs all day, updating the logs." He yawned. "I've been concentrating so hard and long, I can barely see straight." Faced with Jasmine's glacial glare, Connor turned his attention back to Bo Yin. "Who knew there was so much bureaucracy at the heart of war? And paperwork was never my strong suit."

"Poor excuse, Connor—even from you," Jasmine said, careful to avoid the slightest contact with him as she moved onward.

Connor watched her go, the pain evident in his eyes. Bo Yin grabbed his arm. "Don't take it to heart," she whispered. "Much going on in Jasmine Peacock's head right now." So saying, she smiled once more at Connor, then hurried off to her cabin.

Finding himself alone again, Connor headed toward the upper deck. After a long day shut inside, the prospect of fresh air was not just appealing but necessary to him.

The deck was almost deserted, save for those members of Cheng Li's crew on the first phase of the night watch. They greeted Connor as he passed but, to his relief, did not attempt to draw him into conversation. After his latest difficult encounter with Jasmine, he just wanted to be alone with his thoughts, tormented as they were.

He wandered to the prow of the ship, feeling a certain sense of peace restored by the sight of the star-filled sky. In times past, he had searched the heavens for familiar constellations. Perhaps that would soothe him once more now.

But, as he reached the front of the ship, he saw that he was not alone. The starlight illuminated a familiar frame, standing with his back toward Connor. Connor hesitated, wondering if he could conceivably turn around and edge back inside or to the other end of the ship without being rumbled. But it was too late. The figure turned around and Connor Tempest found himself face-to-face with his erstwhile comrade, sometime friend, and occasional rival, Jacoby Blunt.

"You made it back then." Connor's words were awkward. "That's good."

"Is it?" Jacoby said, looking hurt. "I guess I interpreted your absence from the welcome-home committee to mean you had mixed feelings about my return."

"What? No!" Connor shook his head. "Cheng Li had me holed up downstairs with a mountain of paperwork."

Jacoby smiled ruefully. "Almost as though she was trying to keep us apart."

Connor shrugged. "Why would she want to do that?"

"You tell me."

Jacoby's eyes bored into Connor's and sent a chill through his bones. *How much did Jacoby know?*

Connor hesitated, his eyes still locked with Jacoby's. "There's no reason. You know how important procedures are to Captain Li." He smiled. "But, I guess, now that you're back, you'll be taking some of those boring responsibilities back from me."

Jacoby's expression changed. "Are you really okay with that? Me resuming my role as deputy captain...?"

"Sure." Connor nodded.

Jacoby continued. "Things getting back to how they used to be...well, as close as they can be." Once more his eyes bored into Connor's. "Buddy, I have to ask you a question, and it's really important to me that you give me an honest answer. Will you do that for me, as a mark of our friendship?"

"Yes," Connor said, feeling a sense of impending doom. Had Jasmine confessed to their relationship, or had Jacoby been tipped off by another member of the crew? They had been as discreet as they could, but secrets weren't easily kept aboard *The Tiger*; there were eyes and ears all over the ship. Connor's heart was hammering as Jacoby opened his mouth once more.

"Are you really okay with me being a vampire, buddy? Because I know how much you hate vampires, so I could completely understand if..."

Connor let out his breath, the tension receding. "No!" he said. "I mean, yes! I'm *completely* cool with you being a vampire."

"You're sure?" The relief in Jacoby's eyes was evident.

"I'm one hundred percent sure," Connor said, nodding.

Jacoby leaped forward and gave Connor a bear hug. "Thanks, man! You have no idea how much that means to me. You and Jasmine and Cheng Li are the most important people in my world. You guys, well, you're what got me through all those times I came close to giving up."

As Connor listened to Jacoby, his relief soured into the familiar stench of self-loathing. Jacoby clearly thought he was another kind of person altogether. Someone you could depend on; someone who wouldn't betray you. He wanted to do something, to salve his conscience, but he wasn't sure what.

"It's good to have you back," he found himself saying. "A lot's happened while you were away. There are a few things we need to catch up on."

"Sure, sure," Jacoby said. "But not tonight, eh, Connor? I've been waiting all day to get out here, back onto this deck that feels like home." He climbed up onto the deck rail and sat there, perched right at the front of the ship like an eagle. "I'm just going to sit here and look out at the sea and the stars. There were so many times when I was locked up in that prison when I never thought I'd get to see the stars again."

Connor nodded, feeling genuine sorrow for his friend's ordeal. "Do you want to be alone?" he asked. "Or, if you like, I can point out some of the constellations to you?"

Jacoby grinned and patted the spot beside him on the deck rail. "Grab a pew! It's high time I learned my Aquila from my Ophiuchus!"

32

LOVE AND DEATH

Grace sat on her bed, back in the cabin Lorcan had brought her to when she'd first arrived on *The Nocturne*. She remembered waking up, back then, and finding herself dressed in a pretty nightdress that, it transpired later, Darcy had lent her. Grace smiled to herself. That had been the first of many such loans from Darcy. Now she was still dressed in the utilitarian clothes she had fled Sanctuary wearing. Except for her shoes, which lay discarded on the floor, and her coat, which she had thrown over the chair tucked under the little writing desk. The same desk she had leaned against when Sidorio had entered the cabin and threatened her all those months ago. Had he known then he was her father? No, of course not. He had just seen her as a potential blood source.

This room was crowded with memories at every turn.

But they were only distractions. She had to think through everything Obsidian had shared with her. Things were coming to a head and she had tough decisions to make.

The knock on the door was, at first, an annoyance. But as she heard a soft, familiar voice ask, "Grace, may I come in?" her heart leaped and she jumped down from the bed.

"Lorcan!" she cried as he pushed open the door and stepped inside. She ran into his arms and he held her there, pressing her against the folds of his greatcoat. Her face nuzzled the nape of his neck. She realized to her surprise that his hair had been cut short. It was a shock at first, but she rather liked it. "Oh, Lorcan," she whispered. "I've missed you so much."

"And I you," he said. "I'm sorry I wasn't here to greet you yesterday." He smiled and took her hands in his. They sat down, side by side, on the four-poster bed. "As it happens, I was in the company of your brother at Ma Kettle's Tavern."

"You were with Connor?" Grace said, surprised. "Of course! Obsidian said you were with the pirates. I just didn't make the connection. How did he seem to you?"

Lorcan smiled, deciding not to burden her just now with Connor's true state of mind. "He seemed well."

"Really?" Grace inquired, turning toward him.

Lorcan nodded. She seemed to be reassured. "But, as fond as I am of Connor, I knew I was with the wrong Tempest twin on their birthday."

Grace shook her head. "I'm glad you were with him."

Lorcan reached into the folds of his coat. "I brought you this, by way of a birthday gift." He held his hand out to hers. His palm was folded but, as Grace looked down, his fingers opened. Sitting in his palm was a platinum ring, with a small diamond.

"Lorcan!" Grace exclaimed. "It's absolutely beautiful."

He smiled. "Just like you," he said. He had smiled at her many times, but in that instant there was a deeper connection between them than she had ever felt before. Despite all her fears, she suddenly felt calm. It was as if Lorcan were her anchor amid the turbulent sea.

"Shall we see if it fits?" he asked.

She nodded, wondering which finger to offer him. Was this ring more than a birthday gift? Suddenly, she felt flustered. There was so much going on right now.

"This ring?" she said tentatively. "It's absolutely beautiful. But what does it mean?" Her eyes met his. Lorcan Furey's eyes had never looked bluer.

"It means I love you, Grace," he said, smiling once more. "But I have a feeling you may know that already." As he spoke, he lifted her right hand and slipped the ring onto her fourth finger. "It's a perfect fit," Lorcan said, clearly pleased.

"Just like us," Grace said. "Oh, Lorcan, I do love you." As she spoke the words, she could feel tears falling. She tried to draw them back but was powerless to do so. It seemed that no matter how powerful she became, she thought ruefully, she could still not prevent her tears from flowing.

"Hey," Lorcan said, squeezing her hand. "Why are you crying?"

Grace didn't want to voice it but she couldn't prevent herself. "I'm not ready to die," she said.

Lorcan nodded. "You're thinking about the prophecy, aren't you?"

She paused, gratefully accepting a handkerchief and drying her eyes. "You knew about the prophecy, too?"

Lorcan shook his head. "No. I only found out from Obsidian just now, when I arrived back. He knew you might be upset and he thought I ought to know."

"But how come you didn't know before?" Grace asked, surprised.

"It happened five hundred years ago, by all accounts," Lorcan said. "Remember, Grace, that was before I joined the ship."

"Oh, yes," she said. "I keep forgetting that. I think I just assume you were always here. We've never talked about your life before *The Nocturne*, or how you crossed."

"No, indeed," Lorcan said, drawing just slightly back from her. "We will one day, Grace." His eyes met hers. "I promise. I want you to know everything about me. Lord help me, I'll tell you about my brother Cathal and the whole wretched story."

Grace fingered the beautiful ring Lorcan had given her,

confident he would one day tell her his full story. For now, though, they had other, more pressing, things to discuss.

"So," she said. "Obsidian told you about the prophecy. And the Four Cardinals?"

Lorcan nodded. "It didn't come as a complete surprise. Do you remember when Obsidian was away and Mosh Zu called you and me and Darcy together that one time? He mentioned then, just in passing, that once there were other ships in the fleet besides *The Nocturne*."

It was like a switch clicking inside Grace's head. "I'd forgotten," she said. "But yes, I do remember that." Things were coming into focus now. "And those ships were the three commanded by the other Cardinals."

Lorcan nodded. "They divided the oceans between them. Obsidian Darke took the southern quadrant, hence his title Cardinal South." He paused. "Grace, these are highly confidential matters...I know I can trust you not to share what I say with anyone."

"Of course," she assured him, wondering what was coming next.

"For some time now, Cheng Li has been pressuring me to get Obsidian to deliver an alliance with the other Nocturnals. The Vampirates' fleet has expanded, and continues to expand far faster than anyone understands. The Pirate Federation has mobilized all its ships."

"What exactly are you saying?" Grace asked.

"This war," Lorcan said, "has reached a critical point. The scales are just about equal, but if Sidorio and Lola continue to expand, then the balance will be tipped. As I say, there are no more pirate ships to bring into the Alliance…"

"But there are Nocturnal ships that could come in and make the difference?"

Lorcan nodded. "That's what Cheng Li believes. And, for some time now, I've had that throwaway comment of Mosh Zu's in my head. That once, there were other ships in our fleet. I've raised it with Obsidian several times, but each time he has told me that it isn't a viable option. In fact, he has never acknowledged that there even *were* other ships until tonight, when he told me about the prophecy."

"He must realize the severity of the situation," Grace said. "He's changing, just as he had to change before to accommodate the new dangers." Her heart lifted. "He told me that the time for secrets was over. He must have come to a decision to reunite with the other three Cardinals and end this war."

Her heart was racing. But, as she looked once more into Lorcan's eyes, she saw a shadow. "No," he said.

"What do you mean, no?"

Lorcan drew himself forward and climbed off the bed, turning to face Grace from the middle of the cabin floor. "Obsidian told me of the prophecy and revealed to me the existence of Cardinals North, East, and West. He even went so far as to confirm that they are still out there in their quadrants. But he will not summon them back."

Grace was aghast. "But he has no choice," she said. "If what you say is true, if time really is running out for the Alliance, isn't it the only option left?"

Lorcan nodded. "I'd say so, yes. But he says that there is a rift between himself and the other Cardinals and he cannot call upon their help."

"A rift? What *kind* of rift?"

"He didn't say. It was clear that our conversation had come to an end. And I didn't press him any further. I can't continue to push at that brick wall anymore, Grace." For the first time, Grace saw fear in Lorcan's eyes. "I'm scared that this war is turning, Grace, and that the one thing we can do to bring about victory is being denied us."

As she considered his words, Grace was surprised to find her own fear melting away, to be replaced with a wave of calm and clarity. Now she, too, eased herself off the bed and stood up. "All right," she said. "So Obsidian refuses to summon the other three Cardinals. So be it." She smiled. "There's nothing to stop *us* from summoning them, though, is there?"

Lorcan met her eyes. "Could we? How? I wouldn't even know where to start."

Grace smiled. "The prophecy said that it was up to me or Connor to win this war. Well, maybe *this* is how I can fulfill the prophecy. By calling them back."

"But how?" Lorcan said again.

"I'm not sure yet," Grace said, bending down to open her bag and remove the dhampir notebook from inside it.

She held the book out toward Lorcan. "I have the feeling the answer will be in here somewhere," she said.

"What is this?" Lorcan asked, turning the pages.

"I'm pretty sure it belonged to Olivier," Grace said, talking as fast as she was thinking. "I found it hidden in the treatment rooms at Sanctuary. You know Olivier's a dhampir, right?"

Lorcan looked up from the open notebook. "Olivier? A dhampir?"

Grace nodded. "He's much more powerful and dangerous than we thought."

"And he's working with Lola and Sidorio," Lorcan said, grimly.

Grace shrugged. "Big whoop. They have one dhampir on their team. The Alliance has two—Connor and me."

Lorcan glanced back down at the notebook. "You say this book will tell you what to do, but as far as I can see, Grace, it's completely blank."

"To you, yes," Grace said, reaching out her hand. "Because you're not the one it's meant for. Give it back to me, please." As she took it in her hands, text began to appear on the page.

"*Summoning the Cardinals*," she read.

Lorcan shook his head in amazement, watching as Grace sat down again, continuing to read. He didn't think he had loved her any more than in this moment. But then a dark thought came to him. Yes, the prophecy had said that she and Connor would bring peace back to the oceans. But hadn't it also said that one of them must die to achieve this? What if that was the price Grace would pay to bring back the cardinals and turn this war?

"You can't do this," he said suddenly, reaching for the book.

"I think I can," she said confidently, her eyes still on the page.

"But what if it's too dangerous?" Lorcan pleaded. "What's the point in winning this war if I end up losing you?"

Grace looked up at him, realizing she had become the strong one. "We all do what we have to do," she said. "We don't have a choice. Like my dad, *I mean, Dexter*, always used to say, we have to trust the tide."

"I love you, Grace." There was a plea as well as a declaration in his words.

Grace set the book down and rose to her feet once more. "I love you, too, Lorcan. And I don't want anything to stand between us spending eternity together." She wrapped her arms around him once more, seeing the ring he had given her glint in the candlelight. "But I have been given these extraordinary powers for a reason." Her eyes met his. "It's time for me to use them."

33

DIVISIONS

Connor found himself standing in the center of the deck of *The Tiger*. Above him, the ship's distinctive white sails billowed. Connor's eyes traced the line down from the mast to the timber decking below, then out to the sea and sky. The burnished gold of the sky told him it was either the beginning of dusk or the end of dawn. He could see the honeyed light reflected in the blood-spattered blades of the pirates spread out across the deck. Many had lowered their weapons—as if the battle were over. It must be dawn then. No Vampirate would dare venture out into the growing daylight, so it was safe to regroup.

Connor glanced at his comrades' faces. They looked weary. In the lines and scars etched upon their faces, he could see the toll not only of this latest battle but of the longer war. Gradually he became aware that they were all looking at him. And in their eyes were shock and fear and pain. For him. Why? What had he done?

Now, he heard cannon fire and smelled the acrid aftermath. He was finding it harder and harder to breathe. Something was blocking his airway. Glancing down, he saw the problem in all its shocking simplicity. A sword was buried deep in his chest.

The sight was almost comical, despite what it portended. No wonder his crewmates were looking askance at him.

Eyes closing, he slumped down, feeling the deck boards rise up to meet him. The sword wormed its way deeper into his flesh. Every faltering breath was noticeably more difficult than the last.

"Open your eyes, Connor!" a voice commanded him.

Obeying, he forced open his eyes and found himself gazing up at a blur of faces. Nearby, he heard a woman's cry.

"Come...Captain Tempest. He is wounded. He needs..."

Was it Jasmine? It sounded very much like her. Connor was confused. He wasn't a captain! He wanted to call out to Jasmine, but he found he was unable to make a sound. A result, no doubt, of the sword spearing his middle.

Her voice grew more urgent. "Captain Tempest is cut. Please come..." Now he saw her luminous face appear among the others. His eyes sought out hers. If he was on the verge of death, he would take his leave of this world looking into those amazing eyes. He smiled up at her, but she did not return his smile. Lifting her head, she called out. "There's so much blood…I'm not sure how much longer he can last."

He felt hands moving across his chest, in an exploratory fashion. Then he watched as the sword was wrenched out and blood gushed up from his open wound. He saw the blood spatter Jasmine's face. He felt a burning sensation in his chest, which grew swiftly into a pain deeper and more unbearable than he'd ever thought possible. He closed his eyes again and had the sensation he was traveling at a rate of knots through the air or across the ocean. But when he forced open his eyes again, there was Jasmine: her face still stained with his blood, her eyes like dark jewels.

She leaned closer, her hair falling about her face and brushing his. The tips of her hair were clogged with blood, but she didn't seem to care. He felt her cool hand against his cheek. It felt nice. Even nicer as she stroked his cheek. Then two things happened in quick succession. The effort of keeping his eyes open simply became too much. And then he realized he could no longer feel Jasmine's touch. Was this it, then? Was this the end?

His vision suddenly shifted and he saw himself lying on the deck. He could see Jasmine bent over him and others close but moving back, slowly, respectfully. Beneath his supine body, a pool of crimson fanned out across the blond deck boards. Jasmine was still stroking his face but he sensed she knew that he was already gone.

Connor's vision grew dim until he was engulfed in utter darkness. Now he heard a hammering close by. It grew louder and closer. Opening his eyes—surprised that he was able to—he came to with a jolt. He found himself stretched out on his bunk in the familiar cocoon of his cabin. Shards of the intensely disturbing vision remained in his head. The scene had been somehow familiar, but how? The shards were fading fast now, as the hammering grew louder. Then a voice boomed from the other side of the door.

"Open up, Tempest! I know you're in there."

Connor staggered to his feet and opened the cabin door to find Jacoby standing on the threshold, his usually pale face puce, feet tapping the deck boards in agitation.

"What's wrong?" Connor asked, feeling that half of him was still deep in the vision, on the deck of *The Tiger*. It made him an easy target as the full force of Jacoby's fist made contact with his jaw.

"What the..." Connor protested, falling backward onto the boards at the foot of his bed. Looking up, he saw Jacoby towering over him, like the mast in his vision. There was a wildness in Jacoby's eyes as he reached out and grabbed Connor's shirt, pulling him up from the floor. "Get on your feet, Tempest! You're coming with me!"

He dragged Connor to the cabin door.

"Where are we going?" Connor managed to rasp. "And why?"

"Up onto the deck," Jacoby snarled, releasing Connor

and shoving him roughly along the corridor. "To sort out the situation between you and me."

Connor did not protest. He knew this moment had been coming. Jasmine had let him know she intended to come clean with Jacoby, to trust him with the truth about herself just as he had trusted her. She must have just told him. Connor felt sick, partly with trepidation but mostly with guilt. He could understand how Jacoby might want to tear him apart limb by limb; he'd have felt the same in his friend's shoes. Only he wasn't even sure he could call him that anymore. Because, whichever way you looked at it, Connor Tempest hadn't been much of a friend to Jacoby Blunt.

As they reached the door to the deck, Connor opened it and felt Jacoby jostle him roughly from behind. They fell together onto the deck boards, Jacoby pinning Connor down and raising his fist once more.

At the last second, as Jacoby's fist came down, Connor managed to twist his head. The full force of Jacoby's blow sailed into the deck boards. Clearly pained, Jacoby frowned but said nothing. Connor took advantage of his comrade's weakened state to push him back and bring himself to his feet.

Nursing his injury, Jacoby rose to stand before Connor. There was fury in Jacoby's eyes, and, as he opened his mouth, Connor saw — for the first time — Jacoby's enlarged incisors. It was a chilling reminder of what Jacoby had become.

"Save your breath," Jacoby cried, smiling strangely. "You're going to need every last gasp." As he finished speaking, he let out a roar and propelled himself up into the air. As he plummeted down again, he reached his arms around Connor's neck and dragged him across the length of the deck. Where had Jacoby learned to fight like this? He'd always been handy with the sword, but this was something else entirely.

"One of the advantages of being turned," Jacoby rasped in Connor's ear. "Those rancid Vamps left me with a few new tricks."

Of course. It made complete sense, and it was a wake-up call to Connor. He wasn't exactly short on new tricks himself. Focusing himself, he slipped out of Jacoby's clutches and back-flipped across the deck, landing a few meters away and catching his breath. He could see Jacoby was surprised. For a second, he even looked impressed. Then his eyes began to change and Connor saw deep pits of fire there. Connor shuddered. Fire was usually the sign of a hungry Vampirate. Had the triggers between anger and hunger become muddled in Jacoby? He was new to this state and, it seemed, not quite as in control as he appeared.

With a sound much like the whistling of the wind, Jacoby flew across the deck and, grabbing Connor, continued racing toward the mast. Connor felt his back collide with solid oak at an incredible speed. The pain was intense. His head ached and his eyes watered.

Now Jacoby's hands reached out for Connor's neck and

began to squeeze. His strength was considerable but Connor's was a match for it, and, lifting his hands, he began to pry Jacoby's fingers away. With relief, he felt the pressure on his neck release and saw again the surprise in Jacoby's eyes. Then Jacoby smiled and squeezed harder. Connor felt his airway being closed. It took him back to his dream. Was it some kind of omen? His eyes closed, and, just as in the dream, he found darkness. It was something of a comfort. He found himself wondering, is this the end? Was death coming to him not through a sword but simply the hands of a former friend?

Jacoby maintained the pressure on both sides of Connor's neck. Seeing that Connor's eyes had closed, he wanted to release his hands but found himself powerless to do so. Suddenly, he felt someone reach from behind him and tear his fingers away. He was torn between gratitude and fear. Turning, he was shocked to see Connor himself standing behind him. How had he managed to slip out of his clutches in such a weakened state? Then Jacoby realized that Connor was still in front of him, eyes closed. Connor was both in front of him and behind him. Either he was going mad or there were two Connors.

"What's going on?"

Jacoby turned to find Cheng Li striding across the deck. "What *on oceans* is going on here?"

"It's a private matter," Jacoby cried, "between Tempest and me!"

Cheng Li shook her head. "I'm captain of this ship and

you are my deputies," she said. "There *are* no private matters here."

Jacoby turned and saw that Connor—the first Connor—was opening his eyes and feeling his neck for bruises. Jacoby immediately felt ashamed of his actions. Then he remembered about the second Connor and glanced around him. But, to his confusion, he had disappeared. There was now only the one Connor. In his furious reveries, had he simply conjured up the second?

Cheng Li shook her head. "You two are senior officers aboard this ship and within the Federation. You are incredible fighters but you should be saving your aggression for the enemy, not unleashing it upon each other." Her almond eyes narrowed as she looked from one combatant to the other. Shaking her head, she pushed Jacoby away from her. "Go to your quarters and cool down. Connor, I want a word with you."

Jacoby loped off, glancing back at Connor and scowling.

"What exactly just happened?" Cheng Li asked Connor as Jacoby disappeared inside.

Connor looked across at her, bruised and battered. "The whole situation between him and Jasmine and me just exploded..."

Cheng Li raised her hand to silence him. "I'm not interested in adolescent angst," she said. "What interests me, Tempest, is this: When I came out, I saw not one but *two* of you fighting Jacoby. Is this some new power of yours?" She lowered her voice. "Can dhampirs split into two?"

Connor shrugged. "I don't know. I guess so." Suddenly, he remembered. "It's happened before. During the attack on *The Diablo*, I divided. I was in two places at once."

Cheng Li's eyes were wide with wonder. "This could be useful," she said.

"I'm not sure I can control it," Connor said.

Cheng Li was contemplating his words when there was a fresh cry from below.

"Permission to come aboard!"

Cheng Li turned and called into the night. "Who seeks permission?"

"Commodore Ahab Black, commander in chief of the Alliance," came the response.

Cheng Li took a moment to compose herself. "Permission granted," she called.

There was the sound of a bridge being lowered, followed by footsteps.

Connor and Cheng Li watched as Commodore Black strode down from the bridge of the Federation vessel onto the deck of *The Tiger*.

"Commodore Black," Cheng Li said, giving him the Federation salute. "What brings you here at such a late hour? Your business must be urgent indeed."

"It is, Commodore Li," Black said with a nod. "I'm here with a proposal on behalf of the Federation. It concerns both you and your deputy."

"I have three deputies currently," Cheng Li said. "Which of them in particular are you referring to?"

"Connor Tempest," Ahab Black confirmed.

"Me?" Connor said, stepping forward curiously.

"Yes," Black said. "I'm here to make you an offer you can't refuse." His cold eyes drilled into Connor's. "I'm here to make you the Federation's next captain." He punched Connor jovially on the shoulder. "Now what do you have to say about that?"

34

LADY LOLA TURNS THE CARDS

"He's just so darling!" Holly said, swinging baby Evil up in the air. It made the little lad giggle.

"He's a doll," agreed Nathalie. "He has his father's nose, don't you think?"

"Never mind." Lola spoke from behind them. "We can always get that rectified later." She shrugged. "Still, much better he has Sidorio's looks and my brains than the other way around." She moved over to the other bassinet. "Look at dear little Hunter snoozing away. Now *he's* definitely got the looks of a Lockwood! Such a stubborn little jaw!" She turned back toward Holly and Evil, who let out a yawn. "That's a big old yawn for a little man! Are you sleepy? Shall Mummy put you down for a nap?"

With both babies settled in their cribs, Lola led Holly

and Nathalie out from the little nursery into the main part of her cabin. "Ladies, can I offer you a drink?"

"Yes, please, Captain," Nathalie said.

Holly nodded. "That would be nice."

"Make yourselves comfortable!" Lola gestured toward the collection of chairs clustered around the coffee table. "I'll bring them over."

"Thank you!" chorused the two young Vampirates, taking their seats.

"It's I who should be thanking you," Lola said, "for keeping me company while Sidorio and the others are engaged in the attack on *The Nocturne*." She carried over the drinks, then walked over to collect her own glass before taking her seat on the chaise, beside Holly. "It's not in my nature to miss an important attack like this, but Hunter was a bit colicky earlier and I didn't feel comfortable leaving him." She glanced over her shoulder, toward the nursery. "He seems happy enough now, though, doesn't he, my little devil?"

The girls nodded. "Motherhood really suits you, Captain," said Nathalie.

"Thank you." Lola nodded graciously. "Of course, I had children in my mortal days, but that was several lifetimes ago. I thought I might be rusty, but it all seems to be coming back to me." She sipped her drink. "Gosh, this is good!"

"What are we drinking?" Nathalie asked.

"Molucco Wrathe," Lola said, wistfully. "Sadly, we're down to the last couple of bottles. He drinks unusually well, doesn't he?"

Nathalie nodded. "Simply delicious."

"Doesn't he have a brother?" Holly said.

"That's right—Barbarro!" Nathalie exclaimed.

"We could always harvest *him*!" said Holly.

Lola smiled at Holly. "You're an ideas girl."

"Captain," Nathalie said, opening her bag, "since we have a little time on our hands, how do you fancy a game of cards?" She reached into the bag and took out a small velvet pouch with a gold tassel and set it down on the table.

"What a splendid idea!" Lola exclaimed.

Nathalie tugged at the drawstring of the velvet pouch and freed the deck of cards inside. "How's about I set them up and you turn them over?"

"Perfect!" Lola clapped her hands with delight. "What fun!"

"Why do you want me to become a captain?" Connor asked Ahab Black as he faced him across the table in Cheng Li's cabin.

"You've shown great potential," Black said, his bored monotone somehow lacking conviction. "We've reached a crunch point in the war, and, by investing in a young gun like yourself, the Alliance will be making a powerful statement to our enemy. We've got no end of surprises! We fight on! We fight until we win!"

There was a discreet cough from the other side of the table. Both men turned their gaze toward Cheng Li. "As Connor's commanding officer and a key member of the Alliance war cabinet, isn't this something that should have been discussed with me first?" she asked.

"You didn't know about this?" Connor was surprised. Generally, Cheng Li knew about everything before it happened.

"No," Cheng Li said. "I didn't. And I'd have appreciated a heads-up."

Connor knew she and Black had history, and her irritation seemed genuine. What was Black up to?

Commodore Black shrugged. "We're in the midst of the most extreme theater of war either of us will live to see, Commodore Li. Things move darn fast within such a scenario."

"I understand that," Cheng Li said with exaggerated patience. "Even so, there are certain protocols that must be observed..."

As Cheng Li and Ahab Black locked horns, Connor's attention drifted. His eyes glanced up at the picture of Chang Ko Li above the captain's desk. Connor had seen the imposing portrait many times before. Now it seemed different somehow—as if the dead captain were watching these petty human matters with amusement. In the greater scheme of things, what did it matter whether Connor said yes or no to being a captain? What did it matter if a protocol or two were broken? There were bigger forces at work, and, Connor was coming to see, he had no real chance of fighting them, no way of stemming the inevitable tide. He could almost imagine Chang Ko Li nodding approvingly at him.

"Aha!" he heard Cheng Li say. "So *that's* what this is really about. The money Connor inherited from Molucco!"

"My inheritance?" Connor brought his focus back to the conference table.

Cheng Li's almond eyes were sharp with indignation. "Did you miss that, Connor? It appears that the Federation will be only too happy to grant you a captaincy, but there's a hefty price tag attached."

Connor sat back in his seat. "What is the price?" he asked.

Ahab Black took a pen and envelope from his jacket pocket. He scribbled a figure on the envelope and slid it across the table, past Cheng Li's eager eyes, toward Connor. "That should seal the deal," Black said.

Connor reached for the envelope and raised his eyes.

"That's a *lot* of money!"

Lola and Holly watched as Nathalie set out twenty-two cards on the highly polished coffee table. Lola recalled that the hand-painted cards were an antique set passed down through many generations of Nathalie's aristocratic line.

"How about we play sevens, tonight?" Nathalie suggested.

Lola nodded in ready agreement.

"Turn your first card, Captain," Nathalie said.

Lola's bejeweled hand hovered over the table, hesitated for a moment, then settled on one of the cards and turned it over. The others leaned in to see her choice. The card depicted a compass rose.

"The Four Cardinals," Nathalie announced. "An auspicious place to start."

"Who *are* the Four Cardinals?" Holly asked.

Nathalie smiled at her comrade's gaucheness. "Not *who*, dear, but *what*. The four cardinals are the main points on the compass—North, East, South, and West." As she spoke, her finger tapped the card. "Then you have the four ordinals—Northeast, Southeast, Southwest, and Northwest."

"I see," Holly said. "So, what does it mean?"

"The Four Cardinals," Lola said, "represent the expansion of our forces. Once we seize *The Nocturne*, we are poised to lock down the southern quadrant. Then we can move on to gain dominion over the rest of the oceans—North, East, and West."

Nathalie nodded, smiling. "An excellent interpretation, Captain. Why don't you turn your next card?"

Lola was more decisive this time, flipping up a card that showed a ship disappearing under the waves.

"Always an intriguing choice," Nathalie said. "This one is called the Vanishing Angle," she explained to Holly. "In maritime terms, it's the maximum angle at which a boat can heel but still right itself."

As Holly nodded, Lola began to interpret the card. "This card marks the point where everything hangs in the balance. It's a reflection of where we stand in the war."

Nathalie nodded, ruminatively, as Lola continued. "As you say, the vanishing angle is the furthest point from which a ship can still heel. It means that we are pushing the Alliance right to its limit."

"But," Holly interjected, "they can still recover? Is that the meaning of the card?"

Lola's eyes met Holly's. "The cards are warning me that we still have a real fight on our hands. We will, of course, win, but we must not underestimate our enemy. We need to push them to the very limit and then push just that little bit harder." Her eyes sparkled in the light of the many perfumed candles lit about her cabin. "I believe that the cards might be telling us what's going to happen this very night. Tonight Sidorio and the others will take *The Nocturne*, shame and silence Obsidian Darke, and tip the Alliance into disarray."

"Will Johnny be okay?" Holly inquired anxiously.

Lola shrugged. "The Cowboy's a resourceful chap, but,

after what happened on *The Diablo*, who can say? You can always do your own reading after mine. Perhaps the cards will give you an answer."

Not fully reassured, Holly sat back and sipped her drink.

"Turn another card!" Nathalie, enjoying herself, prompted Lola. "Ah! Very good. The Nautical Dawn *or* the Nautical Dusk."

"Which is it?" Holly inquired, her attention returning to the game once more.

"It's a double card," Nathalie said, her finger tapping the card, which was indeed split across the diagonal. It bore two almost identical images. Both showed a sky, suffused with golden light, but no visible sun or moon. On one half there was an addition of the silhouette of a bird flying across the right corner. "The import of this card depends on which end is turned toward the reader," Nathalie explained. "On this occasion, the bird is flying toward the captain. That means it's the Nautical Dawn."

"The point about the nautical dawn, as opposed to the civil dawn," Lola said, "is that the sun is still below the horizon. The light has yet to rise to spoil another night. Instead, there is a powerful golden glow, just as you see depicted here. It's dark enough for those of us averse to light to move about in, but light enough to see the horizon." She paused, taking a moment to reflect. "This card has two possible meanings to me. Firstly, it could quite literally mean that the decisive moment will come during the cusp between night and day." She paused again. "But I think it may also have a more general meaning—that everything we want, everything we've been fighting for, is finally coming into view."

"Yes," Nathalie agreed. "That was my interpretation, too." She turned to Holly. "Do you see how the story flows from one card to the next? You can't read them in isolation."

Holly nodded as Lola, unprompted, turned her next card. It bore a picture of a jaunty sailor. Seeing this, Holly smiled. "He's a jolly fellow!"

Nathalie's expression was more somber. "Not exactly," she said. "He might look that way, but his appearance is deceptive."

"How come?" Holly asked.

Lola answered the question. "It's Jack Tar the Mariner," she said. "Otherwise known as the Death card."

"Death!" Holly exclaimed, then asked, "Mortal death or immortal oblivion?" Lola and Nathalie exchanged a private glance. They had no doubt their comrade was thinking once again of Johnny.

"It all depends," Nathalie said, "on what card the captain turns next."

"Or *cards*," Lola reminded her. "Jack Tar affects all the people cards turned after him until another theme card, like the Vanishing Angle, interrupts his progress."

"Hadn't you better turn the next card, then?" Holly said.

Lola nodded, reaching out and considering her choice. Just then, there was a cry from the nursery. Lola hesitated, waiting to see if the cry was a one-off. It came again.

"It's Hunter," she said. "Perhaps his colic woke him up. I'd better go to him before he gets worse, or wakes up Evil. That's the hazard with twins!"

Staring pensively at the cards, she rose from her seat and walked toward the nursery.

Nathalie took the opportunity to reach for the decanter and refresh all their glasses. Setting down the decanter once more, she returned to the chaise. Before she took her own seat, she squeezed Holly's shoulder. "This is about to get interesting," she said.

"It's too much money," Cheng Li said. "And Connor shouldn't have to buy his captaincy. He's one of the most prodigiously talented pirates of this, or any, generation. He'll soon earn the right to be a captain all on his own." She turned to Connor. "My best advice is to wait this out. You don't need to do anything in a rush."

"I'm afraid I disagree," Commodore Black said. "We're running out of time and we're running out of money. If, as you suggest, Connor sits back and waits this out, there may not *be* a Pirate Federation still in existence by the time he's done waiting." His eyes were severe. "There may, however, be a Vampirate Federation, if that's of interest to you."

"Well," said Cheng Li, "that's an awful lot of pressure to pile on a young pirate's shoulders."

"Understood," said Commodore Black. "And I wouldn't be doing so if we had any other viable options." His voice became more human suddenly. "Connor, I'm not going to dress this up in pretty ribbons: Man to man—we really need your help here."

"I'll do it," Connor said.

"You will?" Cheng Li was indignant.

"You will?" Black seemed as surprised as he was delighted.

"Sure," Connor said, rising to his feet. "I always had a dream to be a captain. I just didn't figure the opportunity would come around so soon." He grinned at Ahab Black. "But, hey, you scratch my back and I'll scratch yours."

"Connor, wait!" Cheng Li said. "I don't think you've thought this through. You haven't had time. You're about to give away more than half your inheritance. Molucco left that money for *you*."

Connor shrugged. "I know that, but it's way more than I could ever use," he said. "I had nothing when I was taken in by Molucco. It's the pirates who made me what I am today."

"Yes," Cheng Li said. "It's your friendships with pirates

like Molucco and Cate, Bart, and me. That doesn't mean you owe a fortune to the Federation."

"Perhaps not," Connor said. "But this war has already claimed the lives of Molucco Wrathe and his brother Porfirio. It's claimed Bart Pearce and John Kuo and hundreds, if not thousands, of others besides. We have to put a stop to this right now. We need to make safe the oceans for the future. I can't think of a better use for Molucco's money than that, can you?"

Cheng Li was, uncharacteristically, silent. He thought he knew what she was thinking—what she would have said to him were Ahab Black not with them in this room. *Connor, you're a dhampir, you're immortal. You're going to need that money!* But he knew better than that. He'd had a glimpse of his own death. And it didn't terrify him half as much as the thought of losing this terrible war. If he had to die to bring about peace, so be it. He'd be joining the ranks of his dear friends and respected comrades. He'd have played his part in pirate history in a greater way than he could ever have imagined.

"Is there something you'd like me to sign?" he asked Commodore Black.

"Absolutely," said Black, sliding a contract across the table, along with his fountain pen.

Connor took Black's pen and, after a cursory glance over the text, signed his signature with a flourish.

"Excellent!" Ahab Black said, taking back the contract, folding it, and stowing it away safely in his pocket. "Okay,

Tempest, well, it's customary for you to kneel at this point..."

"Wait just a minute!" Cheng Li said. "You're going to perform Connor's investiture here and now? Doesn't all his money at least buy him a proper ceremony?"

"Like yours?" Black asked. "I remember that day, before John Kuo's untimely death. The sun was shining and the academy chefs surpassed themselves with their canapés. No, Commodore Li, I'm afraid this is a time of austerity. There won't be any more grand events like that until—*unless*—we achieve peace on our terms."

"It's okay," Connor said, falling to his knees. "I'm not so good on big occasions." He smiled reassuringly at Cheng Li. "You know that."

He'd rarely seen Cheng Li seem so sad or worried. His attention was distracted as Commodore Black unsheathed his sword and began to speak more formally.

"By the powers invested in me by the Pirate Federation, I, Commodore Ahab Black, grant Connor Tempest the title of Captain in perpetuity."

Black lifted his sword and brought its cold metal face flush against the side of Connor's neck.

"Plenty and satiety," Black said, then moved the sword to the other side of Connor's neck. "Pleasure and ease," he continued. Then he moved the tip of the sword to Connor's chest, right above his fast-beating heart, where it abutted the silver braid on Connor's uniform. "Liberty and power," said Black. Then, in a more avuncular voice, "You can get up now, Captain Tempest!"

"Wait!" Cheng Li cried. "What about the *rest* of the investiture? *In your head and in your heart* through to *travel home in peace and harmony*?"

"You're a Federation officer," Black said. "I think I can leave you to fill in any blanks. I've got a check to deposit and a war to win. Congratulations, Captain Tempest! And thank you on behalf of the Federation and the Alliance as a whole. Your role in this victory will not be overlooked." He reached out to shake Connor's hand, then strode toward the door. At the threshold, he gave a quick Federation salute, then continued on his way into the night.

Connor rose to his feet, dazed. His first thought was: *I'm a captain now.* His second: *I've just signed my own death warrant.*

Cheng Li shook her head with irritation. "He didn't even stop to tell us what plans he has to find you a ship."

Connor shrugged. Cheng Li was right, as usual, but he had other, darker thoughts to contend with. Thoughts that were too dark even to share with her.

—◆—

"You see?" Lola said, settling little Hunter on her lap. "He's fine now that he's sitting up with us, aren't you, darling?" She blew a little raspberry in his ear and the infant smiled in delight.

"I think he was just missing his mum," Holly said.

"Shall we continue?" Nathalie gestured toward the cards.

"Yes," agreed Lola. "We mustn't leave Jack Tar hanging." Steadying Hunter on her knee, she reached forward and turned the next card.

The three women stared at the image of a young man, or perhaps woman, attending to a weak soul in his sickbed. "The Healer," Nathalie announced.

"So," Lola said. "Death comes for the Healer. I wonder, who could it be?"

"Mosh Zu Kamal!" Holly exclaimed, getting into the spirit. "He's the most prominent healer we know, isn't he?"

Nathalie nodded. "He's a strong contender." She turned to Lola. "And I don't mean to put a damper on proceedings, but wasn't Olivier his protégé?"

Lola nodded. "You make a good point," she said. "But I think you've both overlooked the most obvious candidate." She smiled before adding, "Grace Tempest."

"Of course!" Nathalie exclaimed, her face suddenly sober. "I'm sorry, Captain. For a moment there, I forgot she's still your stepdaughter."

Lola shook her head. "In name only. Grace had her chance with me but she blew it. If the Mariner is coming to claim her, I'm not going to stand in his way."

"Shall we see if Jack has anyone else in his sights?" Nathalie suggested.

Lola nodded, reaching out her hand once more. The card she turned revealed a sailor standing at the prow of a ship, looking out rather disconsolately across a vast ocean.

"The Lost Corsair," Nathalie said. "Also known as the Lost Buccaneer."

"Buccaneer?" Holly said. "That rings a bell!"

Lola brought her hands together. "It's perfect! Connor Tempest and his two friends called themselves the Three Buccaneers. Do you remember, girls?"

"That's right!" Nathalie said. "There's Connor and his friend Bart. But he's dead now, so it can't be him."

"No," Lola agreed, thinking briefly of the moment she'd claimed Bart's life. "The other candidate is Stukeley."

Holly looked distraught. "Not just Stukeley! Stukeley made that speech when Bart was here. Do you remember... at Tiffin? And Lord Sidorio called Johnny the fourth buccaneer."

"Did he?" Lola said. "I'm afraid I *don't* remember." She shrugged. "But even so, you'd have to figure that Stukeley and Connor are the more likely candidates."

"Agreed," Nathalie said with a nod.

"What if it's Stukeley?" Holly said. "Poor, poor Mimma!"

"The auguries are even better than I expected," Lola said, her voice drowning out Holly's as she turned to

Nathalie. "Victory is within our grasp and death is stalking both Grace and Connor. My dear, I simply couldn't have wished for a better reading!"

"You have only turned six cards," Nathalie reminded her. "You have one left to turn."

"Of course," Lola said, her fingers hovering above the cards once more. Her decision made, her fingers came down and flipped over the card. It was a picture of a constellation of stars, bright in the night sky. The stars had been rendered with silver leaf.

Lola gasped. "No!" she said.

"What is it?" asked Holly. "Is it a theme card?"

Nathalie shook her head gravely. "No, dear, it's another people card. This represents Orion . . ."

"More commonly known," Lola continued, her voice low, "as the Hunter."

"So does it mean death for . . ." Holly's question was left unfinished. All eyes turned to the happy infant smiling and gurgling obliviously on Lola's knee.

"It can't be true," Lola said, tears welling in her eyes.

"It needn't be," Nathalie said. "Remember, the Hunter is also a symbolic card. It could refer to the death of any of the pirates who have been stalking us. In particular, the one who captained the first ship of Vampirate assassins."

"Cheng Li," Lola said. "Yes, I suppose . . ."

Nathalie spoke again, more forcefully. "Captain, even if the card does suggest Hunter may be in danger, we let the cards reveal their story to us as a warning. We can take steps to protect him."

"Yes." Lola wiped her eyes dry. "Yes, dear, of course you are quite right." She hugged Hunter more closely to her. "Nothing must happen to him. I will keep him with me at all times."

"Even in battle?" Holly asked. "Isn't that putting him straight into the line of danger?"

"We can take turns looking after him," Nathalie suggested. "A twenty-four-hour rotation."

"What about baby Evil?" asked Holly. "Shouldn't we protect him, too?"

"The card was the Hunter," Lola said. "He's the one in danger."

"Should you turn another card?" Holly inquired. "Just to check?"

Lola shook her head emphatically. "No more cards."

"We agreed at the outset," Nathalie said. "We were playing sevens. The cards made a pact with us to reveal their story in seven scenes. And so they did."

Holly nodded, her eyes turning once more to Lola's sweet little boy. It was unthinkable that he might be in any danger. This game had been fun at the start, but it had taken a rather nasty direction. The captain and Nathalie seemed utterly confident that the cards spelled victory for the Vampirates and death for Grace and Connor. But hadn't they also placed Olivier and Stukeley in the danger zone? Maybe even Johnny, too. Although the others had seemed to believe the reading, Holly was less convinced. It seemed to her that there were many possible ways to interpret the macabre cards. The whole game had left her with an increasing sense of unease about what lay ahead. But, she reflected—as Nathalie cleared away the cards—she was only a beginner. And, based on this experience, this was not a game she would want to play again anytime soon.

35

THE LAST FEAST NIGHT

Not for the first time, Grace experienced frustration that there was no mirror in Lorcan's cabin. Perhaps there was still time to return to her own room and change her dress. She had made as much effort as she could muster out of respect for the traditions of Feast Night. Nonetheless, she wasn't convinced that, had Darcy been here, she'd have been allowed to step out of the cabin looking like this. She had liberated her hair from its utility ponytail but it still looked rather wild. She had run out of time trying to tame it into submission. Her dress was plain navy blue—a good cut and color but, she had no doubt, too simple for her friend's tastes. She imagined Darcy shaking her head and giving her a few stern words about how standards must not slip, even in the midst of war. The only jewelry Grace was wearing was Lorcan's ring. In this respect, at least, she was confident that she had done the right thing. Nothing could, nor should, compete with the beautiful diamond.

Grace's thoughts of Darcy turned to wondering about how things were going at Sanctuary. Seeing the sleeve of Lorcan's uniform poking out from his open wardrobe door, Grace stepped forward. She felt another flash of guilt at her hasty departure from Sanctuary. She had yet to make an astral journey to Mosh Zu to explain her actions. Her excuse was that she didn't want to disturb him at this crucial time. Well, that was part of it, she thought, as she pushed Lorcan's uniform back inside the wardrobe and turned the key. She reflected on the extent of her journey; when she had first arrived on *The Nocturne*, it was Lorcan who had been the one to lock her in her cabin. Now she was the one with the key, putting away her boyfriend's clothes.

Now Lorcan stepped out of his washroom, smelling of his light woodsy cologne, and walked over to her. He brought his arms about her waist and kissed her neck.

"You look gorgeous," he said. "In case you were wondering."

She twisted around in his embrace and caught full sight of him. It was something of a shock to see him out of his serge uniform and back in the more formal attire of Feast Night.

"So do you," she said as his lips met hers. As they

kissed, her eyes closed. When she opened them again, she was overwhelmed — as she invariably was — by his beauty.

"I guess we should get going," Lorcan said. She could hear the reluctance in his voice and sensed that, like her, he'd be far happier remaining here with her in his cabin.

"Yes," Grace said. "If you still think it's the right thing to do."

There was a flash of weariness in Lorcan's eyes. "I'm afraid I do," he said. "We must at least try to talk to him."

Grace reached out for his hand and squeezed it tightly in her own. They set off along the corridor, walking in the direction counter to the other Nocturnals, who were making their way down through the ship to the large dining room on the lowest deck. Some of the Nocturnals glanced curiously at Grace and Lorcan as the couple moved against the flow. Others were too preoccupied by their own concerns. Grace gazed at the stream of familiar faces. Despite the various cosmetics employed in an attempt to disguise their true state, the Nocturnals looked as frail as they always did at the outset of the Feast. It was, after all, when they were most depleted in blood and therefore at their weakest.

As the rest of the crew continued moving down the ship, Grace and Lorcan reached their destination — the captain's cabin. The door was ajar. Either Obsidian Darke was about to emerge or he had anticipated their arrival.

"Captain?" Lorcan said tentatively.

There was no answer.

Grace realized with alarm that there was a third possibility: The captain's cabin had been breached. She turned to Lorcan in alarm. He squeezed her hand and called more loudly. "Captain!"

Still no answer. Grace felt her heart hammering, wondering what might be waiting for them inside the captain's cabin. She had a deep sense of foreboding about this night, and with every step she took—with every beat of the music—that sense of foreboding only grew more intense.

"Come on," Lorcan said to her, his voice deep and calm as he drew his hand free and pushed open the door to Obsidian Darke's cabin. Her heart still beating wildly, Grace followed him inside.

The first section of the cabin—containing the captain's polished wooden table and chairs and the fireplace—was deserted. In the center of the table was an oil lamp, illuminating a number of charts. It was a sight that Grace had glimpsed before, many times. It took her back to the very first time she had dared to enter the captain's cabin.

Lorcan turned to Grace curiously, asking softly, "Where is he?"

Grace thought she knew. Ahead of them lay a pair of thick curtains. Grace moved toward them and parted the material, beckoning to Lorcan to follow. As she had expected, Obsidian Darke was standing on the balcony outside, his hands resting on the ship's vast wooden steering wheel. This was where she had first seen him, almost a year ago now. Then he'd been clad in a mask, cape, and gloves and had cautioned her "not to be alarmed by my appearance." Now it was his human face that turned to meet them.

"I've been expecting you," he said. There was something in the way he said it that confirmed and intensified Grace's ominous feelings about the night.

"We need to talk to you," Lorcan said.

"I know what you want to say," Obsidian answered. "But it's out of the question."

Lorcan hesitated. "I know how powerful you are, Captain, so it doesn't surprise me if you have read my mind, but I'm still going to voice the words."

Grace looked from one to the other, willing Lorcan to draw upon all his remaining strength. Looking at him now, he seemed weary to her. She couldn't be sure if this was the outcome of a war of attrition with Obsidian Darke over the best way to steer their forces or simply his own urgent need to take blood from his donor, Oskar.

Lorcan stole a quick glance at Grace, then turned back to Obsidian. "It's our opinion that tonight should be the last Feast Night," he said.

Obsidian nodded but was silent. Even if he had predicted their plea, he would grant them the courtesy of listening to it.

"*At least* until this war is over," Lorcan continued. "I know the importance of Feast Night to you, but I think the crew needs to feed more often in order to keep strong in case of attack. And I just don't think it's appropriate for us to give such time to this ritual with everything else that's going on around us right now."

Obsidian waited, as if to ensure that Lorcan was finished. Then he nodded and began his answer. "I knew this was what you were coming to suggest, but I cannot agree. With everything else that is going on, the ritual of Feast Night has never been more *appropriate*, nor more important." He paused. "Feast Night has been at the heart of the way this ship has run since it first set sail. It symbolizes the difference between our way of being and that of those who oppose and seek to undermine us. The only time Feast Night has been disrupted has been when they have sought to do so. I will not—*I cannot*—countenance this kind of change. We might as well sound the bell of surrender and let go of all we have held true for so long."

Lorcan tried once more. "You recognize that these are changing times. The threat we face from Sidorio's troops is unprecedented. You have embraced change before, when you stepped out from behind your mask and showed a human face to the world. Others would have thought that was inconceivable, but you knew you had to do it."

Obsidian's voice was heavy as he replied. "There are others who would still challenge that decision. But you're right. I had to change. I had to become a different kind of leader. I acknowledge that and I take responsibility for it, whatever the consequences. But I do not view Feast Night in the same way. As long as I am captain of this ship and commander in chief of this quadrant, Feast Night remains." His long hair rippled in the night breeze. He turned his dark eyes toward Lorcan. "I trust that, while you disagree with me, I still command your loyalty, Commander Furey?"

"Of course!" Lorcan said, eschewing the Federation salute and bowing formally before his longtime commander. "You command my loyalty and my love."

Obsidian turned his eyes now to Grace. "What about you?" he asked. "Is your loyalty still with me?"

"Yes," she said. "You don't need to ask either of us. The fact that we feel we can bring matters of disagreement to you shows the strength of your command."

Obsidian nodded, smiling softly. "A good point, as usual," he said, stepping away from the wheel, which continued to turn back and forth precisely as if his hands were still guiding it. He placed a hand on each of their shoulders. "Come, my friends, let us go down together to the Feast."

Grace knew Obsidian Darke was doing everything in his power to reassure them, but, despite this, her sense of unease was deeper than ever.

The dark shadows of three ships, drawn from the Vampirates' hundred-strong fleet, made their way across the ocean toward *The Nocturne*. Each of the ship's captains—

Sidorio on *The Blood Captain*; Stukeley on *The Redeemer*; and Mimma on *The Calabria*—monitored their progress from the prow of his, or her, ship. Each captain was backed up by a ruthless and battle-hungry crew. No one was in any doubt that tonight would mark a decisive victory for the renegade Vampirates and, if all went according to plan, the end of the war and the unquestioned expansion of the empire of night.

Sidorio stood squarely on the deck of *The Blood Captain*, Johnny at his right hand. They were both looking ahead. Sidorio was smiling.

"It's in our sights," he said, his adrenaline pumping off the scale. "This is going to be one Feast Night they won't ever forget—those we don't kill in order to take over command." He put his hand on Johnny's shoulder. "I used to be a lieutenant on that ship. Imagine that!"

Johnny laughed. "I *can't* imagine you ever being a mere lieutenant," he said. "On that or any other ship."

"I was," Sidorio said, feeling the might of his ship beneath him. "And no more than twelve months since. Sometimes we immortals pay insufficient heed to time. It's amazing what can change in the course of a year."

Johnny nodded, his eyes focused on the strange, sparking sails of *The Nocturne*, closer and closer now. "You're going back to claim it for your own."

"Yes," Sidorio agreed. "Either that or to destroy it."

36

UNDER ATTACK

The Nocturnals and donors stood facing one another across the long banqueting table, heads bowed as Obsidian spoke the words Mosh Zu had written to commence the Feast.

I am a proud voyager of the night.
No lesser, nor greater, than a being of the light.
I will not hide in the shadows…

Lorcan became aware of Oskar watching him from across the table. He realized his friend was trying to attract his attention. "Is everything okay?" Oskar whispered. "You look…" Lorcan brought his finger to his lips. It was bad form to talk during the Nocturnal incantation.

. . . For blood is a gift above all worldly treasure.
I give thanks for this gift. I embrace my immortality . . .

Suddenly, from nowhere came a loud crash and the room lurched to starboard. Seconds later, before they had the chance to recover themselves, a second crash came from the stern, raising the room onto a slope. Then a third collision from the port side, causing further shock and confusion.

Even after the room stopped moving, it was chaos. Chairs slid away from the table, rolling and crashing into the sides of the cabin. The cutlery began moving along the white tablecloth, like a river gaining momentum, colliding with the crystal glassware as both headed for the floor. Oskar reached out to catch the lit candelabra, just in the nick of time. Farther along the table, another candelabra was rescued, but a third fell to the floor and flames began licking at the deck boards. A fast-thinking donor and Nocturnal pair threw jugs of water over it, quenching the fire. Slowly, the room came back into balance, but it looked as if a bomb had hit it.

"What was that?" Oskar asked Lorcan.

Lorcan was about to answer when, to his amazement, he heard Obsidian continuing with the incantation.

I relish this journey through all eternity.
No lesser, nor greater, than a being of the light.
I am a proud voyager of the night.

The doors to the dining hall were thrown open and two Nocturnals ran into the room, finally silencing the captain.

"We're under attack!" they cried in unison.

Lorcan caught Grace's glance across the table. Her expression was grave. Everything they had predicted had come to pass.

"How many ships?" Lorcan cried at the messengers from above.

"Three!" shouted the first Nocturnal.

"We've already lost men and women!" cried the other. "We need help!"

Their words caused a swell of chatter in the room, which now rose to fever pitch. Still, as Obsidian Darke raised his hand, the room fell silent.

"Attack Protocol," he said in his most commanding voice. "You all know what you have to do."

It was true. They had been preparing for the eventuality of attack for some time now. Within seconds, Lorcan's own team—the elite fighters—had gathered around him.

"Commander Furey!" One of his best men grabbed his arm. "We have no swords!"

Of course they didn't! It was a convention of the Feast that there were no weapons inside the dining hall. Accordingly, the Nocturnals and donors had all left their swords in their cabins. How were they supposed to quell an attack with no weapons?

Lorcan turned helplessly to Grace. "How did we let it come to this?" he cried.

Grace did not answer. Her eyes were closed and her hands outstretched. She was chanting in a language he did not recognize. What on earth was she doing?

Then he noticed fresh movement along the table and on the floor. Once more, cutlery was moving about. Had a fourth ship pulled up alongside to cause a fresh collision? Suddenly, the cutlery began rising from the floor and table and spun, faster and faster, around the room. Lorcan and the others were frozen, gazing in amazement as knives, forks, and spoons whirled about above their heads. Lorcan's eyes turned back to Grace. Eyes closed, arms outstretched, she continued to chant.

There was a blur as the cutlery spun faster and faster. Then it began to slow and Lorcan saw that above their heads were no longer knives and forks but swords. How on earth had she done it? And, of more immediate concern, how were they going to claim the weapons without being sliced in two in the process?

His answer came as the movement above slowed and the swords hovered in the air, hilts facing down. Along the banqueting table there were now two lines of swords, waiting to be claimed. It was nothing short of a miracle.

"Take your swords," Lorcan cried, gazing in wonder and love at Grace, whose eyes remained closed as she held the swords in position.

Each Nocturnal and donor reached above his or her head and took hold of a solid steel sword, which Grace had somehow delivered to them.

"And now," Obsidian cried, leading the charge out of the hall, "we fight!"

It could have been chaos as the crew of Nocturnals and donors streamed out of the sole doorway, but somehow it wasn't. The long nights, and days, of training had paid off. Everyone knew what was at stake and everyone wanted to play his or her part in securing victory.

Lorcan watched as Grace opened her eyes at last. She looked momentarily disoriented, then smiled to see the lines of Nocturnals and donors armed with their gleaming weaponry.

"I don't know how you did that, Grace," he said, "but wow!" He reached for her hand. "Come on!"

"Where are we going?" she asked as they ran out into the corridor. Lorcan realized that, alone among the crew, Grace had not been trained in the emergency drills. It was somewhat ironic, given that she was the most powerful of them all. Still, he didn't want to take any chances.

"I'm going out on deck," Lorcan said. "And you're going back to your cabin to wait this out."

He thought she might argue but was grateful that she didn't. Hand in hand, they ran along the corridor after their comrades. Above them, they could hear steel clashing against steel. There could be no doubt. The fight was under way.

As they came to her cabin, Grace pushed open the door and pulled him inside.

"Grace, I need to go!" Lorcan said, as the door shut behind them.

"You need to be strong," she said, drawing back her sleeve and offering her wrist to him. There was no doubting her intention. He could see the veins pulsating beneath her skin.

"I can't," he said, shaking his head as his heart beat wildly.

"You must," she said. "The Vampirates have been clever, arriving here just when the Nocturnals are at their lowest ebb. You need blood now if you're to put up a proper fight. And, make no mistake, tonight you must put up a proper fight."

Lorcan held her hand in his but shook his head once more. "I'll find Oskar," he said. "I'll drink from him."

Grace shook her head. "There's no time," she said. "Let me do this one thing for you."

Lorcan's eyes met hers. It was something he used to dream of, but not like this. But, if not now, then when?

"All right," he said. "But only a drop."

Nodding, she lifted her wrist to his lips and waited for his fangs to puncture her flesh.

Lorcan watched in awe as the wound began to heal in front of his eyes. He looked up at Grace. Her face was beatific.

"You're wonderful," he said, smiling. "I hope you know that."

"You're pretty wonderful, yourself," she said.

"There's so much I want to say to you, Grace. I thought

we were assured of spending eternity together, but now I see how much time I've wasted."

Grace smiled reassuringly at him and shook her head. "We didn't waste a second," she said, her eyes bright. "And now you must go and win this war."

"All right," he said. "And you'll stay here and wait for me?"

Once more, he expected her to protest, but she nodded and lifted her hand to stroke his hair. He leaned forward and kissed her. It was a brief, urgent kiss. As their lips parted, Lorcan stood there looking at Grace, aware that the clock was ticking and he had to leave her. Despite her words of reassurance, he was conscious of the very real possibility that they had shared their last kiss. He couldn't think this way. Head down, he turned and reached for the door.

"Wait!" she called out to him.

"I can't!" He wanted to, more than anything, but the battle was calling him. He had no choice but to answer its call.

"What should *I* do?" she asked.

"Stay here and keep safe!" he said. "And do everything in your power to ensure we're victorious."

"Everything?" she said, her eyes meeting his across the cabin. He thought he understood what she was asking.

He nodded. "Everything," he repeated then turned and began to run up to the deck.

37

OBLIVION

Lorcan charged up to the deck, feeling boosted physically and mentally by the shot of blood Grace had given him. Though he was accustomed to the fresh influx of energy that followed blood-taking, this was far more intense. He wondered whether, as a dhampir, Grace's blood was more potent than Oskar's, or whether the power stemmed from the electrifying intimacy of sharing her blood for the first time. These thoughts faded the moment he set foot on the upper deck. In their place came panic, fear, and dismay. There was no question that the Nocturnals were outnumbered. Worse still, he alone of the crew had benefited from a shot of blood. The others were at their weakest and it showed in their lackluster efforts. He could still see the signs of their intensive combat training, but they might as well have been fighting with blunt weapons. The

Nocturnals were off their game, just when they faced their most critical fight.

In comparison, the donors had thrown themselves into the battle. Lorcan caught sight of Oskar, far across the deck, squaring up to a young-looking female Vampirate. Judging from her extravagant uniform, Lorcan surmised she must be a captain. Her movements were lithe as a serpent and Lorcan found himself uttering a prayer for his donor and hoping he hadn't overextended himself.

Suddenly a familiar voice boomed in his ear. "Midshipman Furey!"

Lorcan looked up to find Sidorio bearing down upon him, sword drawn. "You're out of touch," Lorcan cried, readying his own sword. "I'm a commander now."

"You?" Sidorio laughed. "Dress it up as much as you like, Furey. We all know that you're a pacifist. Like your captain and the rest of your crew."

"Take a look around!" Lorcan cried, as he and Sidorio exchanged blows. "Does this *look* like a ship of pacifists to you?"

Sidorio did not take his eyes away from Lorcan, but this didn't prevent him from declaring his verdict. "Looks like a ship of losers to me!" They circled each other, their mutual dislike evident in their eyes. "Looks to me like a weakened, dying force," Sidorio continued. "Why draw this out? Why pretend you can fight? Call over your captain and sound the defeat. You never know—I might take pity on you, for old times' sake."

Lorcan shook his head. "We don't want your pity!" he said.

"And by the way," Sidorio continued, "while I've got you on your own, there's something I've been meaning to tell you for a while now. Keep your bloodless hands off my daughter!" He nodded. "I know you've been sniffing around Grace for months now, but she's out of your league, understand?" He smiled unpleasantly. "From this night forward, she won't be having anything more to do with you."

Sidorio was smirking at Lorcan, as he had done many times before. Holding his nerve as firmly as his sword, Lorcan smiled back. He had seen what Sidorio was as yet blissfully unaware of.

Obsidian had heard Sidorio's rantings and was making his way swiftly across the deck—in his anger, easily dispatching several of Sidorio's squad en route.

"I suggest we let Grace be the one to decide whom she does and doesn't want in her life," Lorcan said, watching Obsidian approach, sword raised.

"A father knows best," Sidorio said, shaking his head and puffing out his chest smugly as he made a jab at Lorcan.

Lorcan stepped neatly to one side as Obsidian brought his sword up against his rival's neck. The look of surprise on Sidorio's face was something to savor.

"Turn around, renegade," Obsidian commanded. "I will not be cheated of my fight with you."

Sidorio was quick to recover. "Nor I with you!" he exclaimed, turning to face his ancient foe.

As Obsidian and Sidorio squared up to each other, Lorcan hastened across the deck, taking stock of the overall situation. It was bad. *Really* bad. Many Nocturnals and donors had fallen, and the predominance of serge uniforms proclaimed the full extent of the dominating Vampirate force.

Lorcan caught sight of Oskar once again. His donor was now locked in one-to-one combat with a figure Lorcan recognized as Stukeley, Sidorio's joint deputy. In the split second it took to assess the situation, Lorcan felt equal parts pride for his donor's extraordinary bravery and fear for Oskar's life. Letting out a roar, he charged at Stukeley, causing the Vampirate to turn away from Oskar and defend himself.

"Aha!" Stukeley cried out with pleasure as their swords clashed. "At last, a worthy opponent. Though you might just wait while I finish off this mortal."

"I'll finish you first," Lorcan cried, his sword once more meeting Stukeley's and leaving his adversary in no doubt as to the threat.

"Go!" Lorcan commanded Oskar. Gratefully, the donor ran off as Lorcan took over from him.

"I'll give him his due," Stukeley said. "He fought well for a mere mortal."

"You were a mortal not so long ago," Lorcan said.

"Have you conveniently forgotten that, or have you been brainwashed by Sidorio and Lola?"

Stukeley shook his head. "We don't go in for brainwashing on *our* side, Commander. We leave that up to you and your masked captain."

"He's not masked anymore, in case you hadn't noticed," Lorcan said gruffly. His blade met Stukeley's and they parried back across the deck.

"Masked or not," rasped Stukeley, "he'd better watch out — Sidorio will make mincemeat of him!"

"It's Sidorio who had better watch out," Lorcan snarled. "Obsidian is a far more powerful Nocturnal."

"Pah!" Stukeley spat onto the deck between them. "There's no such thing as Nocturnals! You're a *Vampirate*, Furey, no different from Sidorio and me — only you're the self-hating kind, just like your pathetic excuse for a captain."

Stukeley made a fresh lunge at Lorcan. He was incredibly fast. Lorcan swerved to his side in the nick of time.

"Very good!" Stukeley nodded approvingly as they held each other's gaze once more. "You have more fight in you than I'd expected."

"You have no idea!" Lorcan cried, launching himself at Stukeley once more. "I'll finish you off and then turn my attentions to your pal Johnny. Where is he, by the way? I can't see him in the melee."

"Johnny?" Stukeley shrugged. "His mission is very cut

and dried on this occasion," he said. "He only has one target in his sights." He smiled. "I wonder if you can guess who that is?"

There was no need for Stukeley to say the name. When had Johnny's target been anyone other than Grace? Lorcan felt a terrible ache in his head and a chill race along his spine. He had to dispatch Stukeley and find a way to get to Grace. His eyes darted over Stukeley's shoulder, looking for Oskar. He had a momentary thought that he could send Oskar to warn her. But where had Oskar gone?

Suddenly Lorcan felt a searing heat coming from his shoulder. Glancing down, he saw that Stukeley's sword had sliced through his uniform and penetrated his skin.

Stukeley drew back his sword with evident satisfaction. "*She* really is your Achilles' heel, isn't she, Furey?"

"No," Lorcan said, preparing his own attack. "Not my Achilles' heel. The love of my life. And I'll do whatever it takes to protect her."

⌒⌒⌒

Johnny pushed open the cabin door to find Grace staring at him in shock.

"What are *you* doing here?" she asked.

"I came for you," he said. "Don't be alarmed, Grace. My brief is to escort you to *The Blood Captain*, unharmed. Sidorio has plans for you."

"I'm not interested in his plans," she said. "And I'm not going anywhere."

"You have no choice," Johnny said, not without a certain kindness. "This battle is all but won. The Vampirates outnumber the Nocturnals by at least three to one. Sidorio is certain to overpower Obsidian and claim *The Nocturne* for our fleet. The war is coming to an end. Well, this phase of it at least. The southern quadrant is locked down, and then we move on."

"No!" Grace cried.

"Yes!" Johnny persisted, reaching out his hand. "Face facts, Grace. There's nothing you can do about it."

Grace took his hand in her own. "I'm sorry," she said.

Johnny looked askance at her. "What do you have to be sorry about?"

"This," she said, expertly pinpointing the pressure points in his hand and watching him instantly slump to the floor, unconscious.

She stared at him for a moment, his words ringing in her head. *The war is coming to an end. There's nothing you can do about it.*

Wasn't there? Well, she'd be the judge of that.

———

"Take a look around you!" Sidorio commanded Obsidian. His neck bore the wounds Obsidian had lately inflicted on him, but the cuts were already beginning to heal. "See your pitiable crew falling to the deck around you. You couldn't ask for a more perfect symbol of your dwindling power. Your time is over, *Captain*." The last word was spoken with the deepest irony.

"No." Obsidian shook his head. He had sustained lacerations, but these too were closing up as the enemies circled each other once more.

Sidorio laughed mercilessly. "There's no sense in denying it when it's clear as night. I came here with a mission to decimate your crew and I've already exceeded that ambition. They're falling like autumn leaves." He smiled. "It won't be long before I've sent you and every last member of your crew to oblivion and taken *The Nocturne* as part of my fleet. Though I think it's time we changed its name to something more... gutsy."

"Is that what this is about?" Obsidian asked. "Is that what's behind this war? Your petty need for revenge because I exiled you from this ship?"

Sidorio smiled and shook his head. "No," he said. "This war is about so much more than that." He had a sudden vision of Lola and their twin boys as he lifted his sword again. "This war is about who controls the oceans."

"I never set out to control anything but this ship," Obsidian said as their swords met. "I tried to provide a refuge for vampires who—"

"Spare me the sermon!" Sidorio cried, his sword

clashing against Obsidian's. "I've heard it all before. How you wanted to create a refuge for *the outsiders among the outsiders*—*yadda, yadda, yadda*. It's old news, grandpa—it's all a gigantic con!"

"No!" Obsidian shook his head. "It's true. Whether *you* believe it or not is of no importance."

"You created a prison ship for lost Vampirates," Sidorio cried, stalking Obsidian with his sword, pushing him backward. "You and Mosh Zu Kamal intended to keep us in your thrall, to build your own power base and make the rest of us bend to your ridiculous rules. Whoever heard of vampires who don't drink blood? It's perverse!"

Obsidian shook his head. "We never cared for power," he said. "We wanted Vampirates to have a choice—to be able to rise above their base appetites and find ways to make meaningful use of their immortality."

Sidorio's mouth twisted into a snarl once more. "You think that hiding yourself away on a ghost ship and restricting yourself to one furtive drink of blood each week is meaningful?" His eyes widened. "You really do think that, don't you?"

"Tell me," Obsidian said, his face up close to that of his rival. "What's *your* idea of a meaningful existence?"

"This!" Sidorio exclaimed. "Claiming new ships, establishing supremacy over the oceans, throwing over this tyranny of pirates we've all been living under for as long as we can remember and bringing the oceans under *our* control." Once more, he thought of Lola, Hunter, and

Evil. "It's time to usher in a new sea power—now that's *my* definition of meaningful."

Obsidian's eyes met those of his arch foe. They were filled not just with hatred but with a certain sadness, too. "How can you find meaning in so much destruction?" he asked.

Sidorio shrugged, his eyes flashing fire. "Guess we'll have to agree to disagree, eh? I've never been given to lengthy conversations, like you and your kind. Why don't we just settle this once and for all? And not like wannabe pirates, but like true Vampirates." So saying, he threw his sword up into the air and leaped at Obsidian, fangs extended.

Lorcan watched in horror as Obsidian was thrown against the deck. He was already lying there himself, the tip of Stukeley's sword pricking his own neck. Stukeley's boot bore down on Lorcan's arm. In his hand, he still gripped his own sword, but it was useless as he found himself unable to counter Stukeley's greater strength.

His enemy's sword felt cold against his neck. But there was a deeper coldness flooding Lorcan's heart and bones. Around him, he could see the potent signs of defeat. And now he could feel the pitiful truth of it spreading within him. *A ship of losers.* Those had been Sidorio's words. *A weakened, dying force.* Coming from Sidorio, such words had seemed like empty bravado. Now they appeared, heartbreakingly, to be true. The deck was littered with fallen members of *The Nocturne*'s crew.

Lorcan felt Stukeley's boot pressing down again. The pressure was sufficient that, at last, he let go of his sword. Looking up, he saw Stukeley smiling with satisfaction. Lorcan couldn't bear to look at him. He turned his head and saw Sidorio pinning Obsidian down upon the deck and bearing down, fangs directed at his rival's neck. How had it come to this? Lorcan's thoughts turned to Grace. He thought of the moment her blood had flowed into his. He thought, once more, of their fleeting kiss. He had feared that kiss might be their last; it seemed now that it was.

Doubtless, Johnny had found her. Lorcan could only hope that somehow Grace might awaken within herself the power that he and Obsidian had lacked, but he was suddenly filled with doubt. It appeared that they had completely underestimated the powers of their enemy. Maybe it was simply the wheel of fate turning, but, if so, it was a brutal new order that was poised to be ushered in.

He felt a fresh stab of pain in his shoulder and realized that Stukeley was reopening the wound. "Just in case you start repairing yourself," Stukeley said coldly.

Lorcan stared up at Stukeley's face. He caught a glimpse of his rival's brutal sneer, then the Vampirate's features began to grow distant. It was as if a mist now separated them. Feeling the deepening pain in his shoulder, Lorcan had no doubt as to what now lay ahead. Still he felt a terrible sadness flow through him as the fog thickened around him. He wanted to cry out, for everything he had lost—everything they had all lost—but it seemed that even this form of release would be denied him as the fog of oblivion drew him more completely into its stifling embrace.

38

THE FOUR CARDINALS

Lorcan's eyes were closed and, for a time, everything was still and silent and peaceful. If this was his final journey, then perhaps it was not nearly as bad as he had feared. Summoning up the courage to open his eyes, he found that he was still encircled in mist, but it was not as thick as before. He could make out the red-stained deck boards around him. Could it be that he was still on the deck of *The Nocturne*, that he hadn't been transported to some other place? As the mist thinned, he saw a little farther. He realized that his arm—which had been trapped under Stukeley's merciless boot—was now free, his sword within his grasp once more. But how? And why was everything so still and quiet?

Glancing up, Lorcan saw something even more curi-ous. Stukeley was still standing above him, but he was now surrounded by two men and a woman—none of them familiar to Lorcan. The Vampirate did not move. It looked as if he were still alive but frozen somehow. One of the men glanced down at Lorcan and smiled. Suddenly, Lorcan felt sensation again in his shoulder. His numbness gave way to a fresh wave of nausea. He saw the stranger lifting Stukeley's sword away. Despite the intense rush of pain, he could feel the fibers deep beneath his skin fusing back together. Now he was in no doubt. This was not oblivion. He had, somehow, been saved. The second of the two men reached out his hand to help Lorcan to his feet while the woman crouched down and returned his sword.

Standing up, Lorcan saw drifts of fog moving across the deck. He realized that it must have encircled not only him but the entire deck of the ship. It was thinning now and he began to make sense of what was happening right across the deck. The Vampirates had been disarmed and their swords turned against them by a fresh influx of men and women. Though the newcomers' faces were unfamiliar, nonetheless Lorcan recognized some kind of union with them, as if they were from the same tribe.

His eyes skimmed the deck, seeking out each of his comrades, Nocturnal and donor. Those who had fallen earlier in the battle still lay motionless, and Lorcan sensed that their stories were at an end. But, as the wisps of remaining mist streamed across the deck, like coils of muslin, Lorcan watched others rise up to their feet again.

At last, his anxious eyes located Obsidian, who, to Lorcan's great relief, was now standing tall at the center of the deck. Lorcan began making his way over to join his leader.

In front of them stood Sidorio. He, too, was surrounded. But now Lorcan saw that it was not merely the *threat* of force that had held the Vampirates in abeyance. His hands were raised before him, as if pushing against an invisible wall. It seemed as if there were a force field around them. It glowed indigo in the darkness of the night.

As Lorcan reached Obsidian's side, he saw further movement across the deck. At first he thought it was more of his comrades, come to determine for themselves what miracle had happened here. But then he saw the most mysterious sight his eyes had ever borne witness to. Three imposing figures were making their way toward the center of the deck. One came from the starboard side; the next from the prow; the third from the port side. They were each clad identically in masks and capes. Their attire was exactly that which *The Nocturne*'s own captain had formerly worn, before he assumed the identity of Obsidian Darke.

The three figures came to the center of the deck and stood before Obsidian and Sidorio. If Lorcan looked on them in wonder, he saw that Sidorio registered their arrival with even greater surprise.

Though Sidorio was still held firm by whatever force

field had been thrown about him, he was still able to speak.

"Who are you?" he asked of the new arrivals, his voice full of wonder.

There was silence for a moment. The capes of the three masked captains billowed in the breeze, the material sparking here and there with indigo light. Then they began to speak—with just one voice. It was a familiar whisper, reminiscent of lapping waters.

"We are Cardinals North, East, and West. Together with Cardinal South, we provide safe harbor for Nocturnals across the oceans."

"Cardinals?" Sidorio grunted, his voice now devoid of its former respect. "Are you some kind of religious sect?"

"No." Lorcan found himself answering the question. "They each represent a cardinal point on the compass."

"That is correct." The Cardinals nodded, then spoke again. "We are the four leaders of the Nocturnal fleet. Each of us takes responsibility for one cardinal point on the compass."

"North, East, and West," Sidorio said, finding he could move his hands, but only within a certain radius. "So where is Cardinal South?"

The three Cardinals did not answer his question but moved to stand beside Obsidian, who shook his head slowly at Sidorio. "You always were a little slow on the uptake," he said, "but surely this isn't beyond your understanding."

"*You*," Sidorio said. "You're Cardinal South."

"I am..." Obsidian suddenly faltered, his eyes turning from Sidorio to the three masked captains at his side. "Or, at least, I was."

There was another pause, in which all that could be heard was the movement of the ship's sails and the Cardinals' capes, blending with the ocean breeze and the churning of the waters deep below. Then the three Cardinals spoke once more. "It is a very long time since the four of us have been in one place. We come together now in order to give you a clear message." Though the masks covered their eyes, there could be no doubt the three were addressing Sidorio. "This conflict is over. Go back to your ships and start dismantling your war machine. You and your kind will never gain dominion over the oceans."

Sidorio shook his head, then attempted to lunge forward at Obsidian. The force field around him was too strong and he found himself further humiliated.

"Admit your defeat," the Cardinals continued. "Take your crews back to the ships you have plundered and never think to set foot here, from where you were exiled, ever again."

As the Cardinals finished speaking, Lorcan glanced across the deck, looking for the reactions from both the crew of *The Nocturne* and Sidorio's own force. It seemed that everyone was poised, waiting to see what Sidorio would do next. Lorcan's eyes turned back to his erstwhile comrade, the first rebel Vampirate and now commander in chief of the empire of night.

Still imprisoned, Sidorio lifted his head to the skies and let out a roar. The sound was deafening. It seemed to echo not only across the deck but out over the oceans and back again. Lorcan realized this was no war cry; this was a cry of disappointment and abject defeat. Now Sidorio lowered his head and called across the deck. "We are defeated," he cried. "Back to the ships!"

At these words, the force field around Sidorio disappeared. Lorcan saw that the same had happened to Stukeley and all of Sidorio's followers, who had been held in paralysis across the deck until the renegade admitted defeat.

Now the surrendering army began its way, as if hypnotized, across the deck. Only then did Lorcan see that there were no longer three ships surrounding *The Nocturne* but six. And each of the three ships that had lately arrived bore the same strange winglike sails he had come to know and love. He smiled to himself at the confirmation that he was part of a greater force.

Sidorio watched his forces drifting away, then turned back to Obsidian once more. "I underestimated you," he said. "I won't make that mistake again. Though, just so we're clear about this, I'd have won the night if you hadn't summoned reinforcements."

Lorcan smiled ruefully. No one would have expected

Sidorio to be gracious in defeat, and he had not disappointed.

Obsidian glanced from the three Cardinals back to Sidorio. "I didn't summon them," he said, at length.

Sidorio's eyes narrowed. "If that's true, then who did?"

"I did," came a voice from behind Lorcan. Grace walked up to join the group gathered at the center of the deck. Turning, thrilled beyond measure to see her, Lorcan smiled. His smile froze as he saw Johnny, following in her wake, looking as dazed as his comrades as he joined the lines flowing off the deck back onto the rebel ships.

As Grace took her place next to Obsidian, Sidorio smiled at her. "My all-powerful daughter," he said, with obvious pride. "If only I could have persuaded you to join my side, this conflict might have had a very different outcome."

Standing beside Obsidian and the three masked Cardinals, Grace seemed in possession of a new authority as she responded to Sidorio. "My powers are a gift beyond measure," she said. "I will never use them for wanton destruction."

Sidorio gazed at her thoughtfully, perhaps still thinking of what might have been. Behind him, the line of his disembarking crew had come to an end.

"It's time to go now, Father," Grace told him. There was a measure of mercy in her voice.

Sidorio nodded. He seemed about to say something but thought better of it. Instead, he turned and joined the exodus.

Lorcan reached out and squeezed Grace's hand. He was gratified she did not resist. She might be some incredible — and growing — force of nature, but, when all was said and done, she was also his girl.

The surviving crew of *The Nocturne* seemed as dazed as Sidorio and his troops. They had now all risen to their feet, above their fallen comrades, to watch as the enemy ships set sail into the dying night. Lorcan knew that each and every Nocturnal and donor had hoped for victory in this fight, but none could have anticipated this outcome.

"Captain." Lorcan addressed his comrade. "The night is beginning to fade. We must tend to our dead and injured swiftly and get the crew belowdecks once more."

"Yes," Obsidian agreed. "Please give your orders, Commander Furey." Standing there, between Grace and the three Cardinals, Obsidian seemed trapped in a force field of his own, though there were no indigo sparks to bind him.

Lorcan sought out his deputies and the cleanup of the deck began. Already, his head was full of practical issues. The ship had been stormed at the outset of the Feast. The surviving Nocturnals were now in greater need of blood than ever. Once the cleanup was complete, they would need to resume the Feast or, at least, the sharing. But with many casualties sustained, the established pairings of Nocturnal and donor had been wrecked. It was an unholy mess, but, he reminded himself, at least this was an end to the conflict. Whatever challenges lay ahead, they couldn't be worse than what they had lately endured.

Satisfied that everything was under control, Lorcan began making his way back to the center of the deck. As he did so, a hand reached out to him. Glancing up, Lorcan saw Oskar and smiled.

"You fought well tonight," he told him. "You did all that was asked of you and more."

Oskar smiled, but only briefly. Lorcan's donor usually lapped up any praise, but it was entirely understandable if the intensity of the night's events had taken its toll on his usual high spirits. He realized that Oskar was looking at him curiously.

"You've taken blood from someone else," Oskar said. There was a look of hurt and panic in the donor's eyes. Then he turned and hastened inside. Lorcan reached out a hand to reassure him, but they were separated by the movement of others. The crews brought by the three Cardinals were making their own way back to the three ships. Oskar disappeared behind the stream of Nocturnals.

The exodus of the three other Nocturnal crews was as swift and seamless as that of Sidorio and the renegades. Soon the crews stood ranked across their decks, like statues of warriors lit silver by the moonlight. They appeared to be waiting for their captains to join them.

The three Cardinals were no longer ranked in a line. Instead, they were clustered, facing Obsidian, as if the four of them were indeed points on a compass. Grace stood to one side. Lorcan found his way over to her and stood beside her.

"You did a wonderful thing tonight," he said.

"No." Obsidian spoke without turning toward them. "She did a foolish thing."

Lorcan was amazed at his words, and even more stunned as Obsidian turned his angry face toward them both. "I warned you many times that we had no allies upon which to call. But you chose to ignore me."

"What do you mean?" Lorcan retorted. "If it wasn't for Grace, we'd have certainly been defeated by Sidorio and his rebel army. As it is, we have sustained more losses than ever before in this last battle."

"That is your perspective, Commander Furey," Obsidian said. "Not mine." He turned back to address the three Cardinals. "I apologize for my comrades. I'm sorry that you were summoned here tonight."

Cardinals North, East, and West answered in their strange, united whisper: "It is not on your comrades' behalf that you should apologize, Cardinal South—or whatever you now care to call yourself." Their capes sparked with light once more. "Any blame in this matter must be carried by you and you alone. You broke the ways of our ancient code and enabled rebellion."

Despite being spoken in a whisper, their words were no less brutal.

"I knew you would feel that way," Obsidian began, only to be swiftly interrupted.

"It is not a matter of feeling but of fact. You have consistently broken the code."

Obsidian's voice was cracked as he responded. "I have always tried to do my best as captain of my ship. To provide sanctuary to the outsiders among the outsiders, as was our ancient accord."

The Cardinals were merciless. "You overstepped the bounds of your power. You confused being captain with being a god. You are too much in thrall to humanity. Your role, like ours, was to care for Vampirates who needed haven. Yet you remain fascinated by mortals, though they are frail and transitory in comparison to us. You made yourself weak by allowing yourself to become a vessel for the lost souls you gathered like flies to your web. You failed to contain the threat on board your ship and within your quadrant. And, instead of turning to us, you sought the help of Mosh Zu Kamal. It was he, no doubt, who persuaded you to remove your mask and take a human face. At that point, you ceased all entitlement to the name of Cardinal South. And now — now you have entered an alliance with mortals! How could this have ended anything but badly?"

"I had to change," Obsidian said, a note of pleading in his voice. "I felt the world, *our* world, changing, and I had to respond." He shook his head. "The rest of you haven't faced a rebel like Sidorio on board your ships, within your quadrants."

There was a moment of silence, then the Cardinals resumed. "Sidorio is not the biggest rebel on board *The Nocturne*. You are! You chose to disregard the old ways —

the ways that have ensured peace for many centuries. You endangered not only the Vampirates in your quadrant but those across the oceans as a whole." The Cardinals paused. "And so, when we were called to help you, we came. But we come only once."

Obsidian bowed his head. "I repeat," he said, his voice retaining a stubbornness and pride, "that it was not I who called you here tonight. You have my word that your help will not be called upon again."

Lorcan exchanged an anxious glance with Grace as the Cardinals made their response.

"Call or do not call. We have our own quadrants to attend to. Next time yours is under threat, you must face the consequences alone."

Obsidian nodded. "We understand one another."

"It is time for us to depart," the Cardinals said. They moved into an approximation of a circle, reaching out their arms until the tips of their gloves met. A mist began to rise around them and their capes began to spark once more. It rapidly became hard to distinguish one figure from another. Then a fog of incandescent light enveloped them. It was a light so bright that both Lorcan and Grace covered their eyes. When they opened them again, the Cardinals had vanished and so, too, had their three ships.

Now Obsidian, Grace, and Lorcan were alone on the ship's deck. Above them, *The Nocturne*'s sails flapped and crackled with light. It was as if the ship had been restored of its dwindling energy. Only the darker stains upon the red deck boards indicated that a terrible battle had taken place here tonight.

"We must go inside," Obsidian said, his head bowed. "The light is on its way." He strode away from the others without meeting their eyes.

Lorcan turned to Grace and saw there were tears on her cheeks.

"Grace, whatever Obsidian says, you were amazing tonight," Lorcan told her. He reached out and pulled her toward him. "By reuniting the Four Cardinals, you defeated Sidorio and pretty much single-handedly brought this terrible war to an end."

"Then why does it feel like I've lost everything?" she asked. "Why is Obsidian angry with me?"

"You've become so powerful," Lorcan said. "He used to be your mentor but it's clear your powers now outstrip his. The prophecy said that you and Connor would win this war, and so you have."

Grace shook her head. "The prophecy said that one of us would die. I don't think this war is over, and if Sidorio and Lola attack again, we're on our own. There are no more allies to reach out to. What if I played this card too soon?"

Lorcan brought her closer. "We don't need any more allies," he said. "They won't attack again. This war ended tonight. You saw the look on Sidorio's face. It's over, Grace. And it's all thanks to you."

Grace brought her head to rest on his shoulder. "I really

wish I could believe you," she said. "But I can't, Lorcan. I just can't."

He held her in his arms, trying to bring her comfort. But suddenly, in her head, she heard that whisper again. It seemed that the Three Cardinals had one further message for her.

You are right, child of the prophecy. This was not the end, but it approaches fast. Our work is done. The rest is up to you and your twin brother.

39

THE ACE IN THE HOLE

"This is *not* the end!" Lola cried. She was standing on the bridge of *The Blood Captain*, her eyes dark with fury, her fists clenched white. "This war is not over until I—that is *we*—say it is."

"I'm just as frustrated as you are, my darling," Sidorio said. "We all are." Standing behind Lola, his arms tentatively around her waist, he glanced over her shoulder at the sea of troops massing below them on the main deck. He shook his head dolefully, then turned back toward Johnny and Stukeley, both of whom looked battle-weary. "We underestimated the powers of the Alliance," Sidorio continued. Lola's head was still turned away from him. She shook it sharply, stubbornly. Sidorio nodded at Mimma. "You were there, Captain Didio," he said. "*You* tell her. Maybe she'll listen to you."

As Lola slowly turned around, Mimma valiantly entered the fray. "It was all going to plan—in fact, even *better* than that—until the Three Cardinals arrived," she confirmed. "Then everything changed."

Lola addressed Sidorio in plain exasperation. "I don't understand how you could have traveled on *The Nocturne* so long and not know there were other ships in the fleet."

Sidorio shrugged helplessly. "Darke—even before he became Obsidian Darke—was very practiced in the art of keeping secrets." He sighed. He was tired, bitterly disappointed, and in need of a good rest. The worst of it was admitting to Lola he had been outmaneuvered by his old adversary. And she had received the news no better than expected. Even now she was staring at him intently.

"What is it?" he asked, unnerved by the ferocity of her gaze.

"I've just realized something," she said, snapping her fingers, her eyes widening as if she had emerged from a trance. "The cards foresaw the coming of these Three Cardinals!"

"What cards?" Stukeley called disdainfully from across the room. "What on oceans are you going on about?"

"Last night," Lola said, with strained patience, "as you all hurried into battle without me, I was in need of some distraction. Nathalie suggested that we amuse ourselves by consulting the cards. And very interesting they were— though now I see that I somewhat misread them."

"With respect, Lola," Stukeley said, "we've just suffered

a massive defeat and we have three crews champing at the bit down there"—he pointed down to the main deck—"awaiting a debrief from us. I rather think we have bigger matters to discuss here than playing cards."

Lola stared at him coldly. He was grating on her even more than usual. Perhaps it was time to take care of him, but, for now, she had other, more pressing concerns. "How little you know," she said, then directed her attention to Sidorio once more. "Husband, the very first card I turned was the Four Cardinals! In readings, I have always taken the card to reflect the points on the compass and so, naturally, I interpreted it to mean that our empire was expanding and victory would soon be ours." Her hands began moving excitedly. "I had no idea that there could be another meaning of the Four Cardinals."

Stukeley tried to attract Sidorio's attention. "Captain, we really should work out what we're going to tell the troops."

Sidorio raised his hand, his eyes still on Lola. "Tell me about the rest of the reading, darling."

"The next card I drew was the Vanishing Angle," Lola said. "This I construed to mean that we have pushed the Alliance to its very limit."

"We certainly did that tonight." It was Johnny who spoke now. The others' eyes turned to him. "Like Mimma said before, everything was going *better* than planned until the Three Cardinals showed up. Seems to me like we forced Darke to pull an ace out of the hole."

Stukeley rested his hand on Johnny's shoulder. "Even if that's true," he said, "it was an awesome ace. We can't go up against those guys again. They've shown us they're invincible."

"On the contrary," Lola said, "the fact that Darke was forced to call on outside help shows the Alliance is at breaking point." Her eyes blazed with rediscovered zeal. "The cards were right! We *are* on the verge of victory."

"The darkest hour is the one before the dawn," Sidorio said knowingly, his eyes meeting Lola's. Once more, there was accord between husband and wife.

Lola smiled and nodded. "Speaking of dawn, let me tell you about my next card..."

Before she could continue, the door to the bridge was flung open and Olivier strode inside. "I'm sorry to interrupt you all," he said, "but I have sad news to share."

"What now?" Sidorio asked, despairingly.

"The Alliance has shut down five of the Blood Taverns," Olivier said. "Evidently the pirates conducted a coordinated series of raids today."

The Vampirates were shell-shocked at the news—none more so than Sidorio. His eyes meeting Olivier's, he rasped just one word: "Lilith?"

"Taken into custody," Olivier said.

"They're shutting down our world," Johnny said glumly. At his side, Mimma nodded.

"No!" Lola cried, drawing all eyes back to hers. "Who needs blood taverns when we have boatloads of pirates still to drain? They're trying to put the frighteners on us, but we're going to come back stronger than ever. We need to start planning the next battle."

"There isn't going to *be* a next battle," Stukeley said. "Now we know what the Alliance can conjure up, it would be suicidal to take them on again so soon."

"You are many things, Captain Stukeley," Lola said, "but I never had you down as a coward."

"I'm not a coward!" Stukeley protested hotly. "I'm a realist."

"Semantics!" Lola said, waving her hand dismissively in the air and striding over to Sidorio. She looped her arm through his. "You're not ready to throw in the towel just yet, are you, darling?"

Sidorio exchanged an awkward glance with Stukeley, then turned back to Lola. "Of course not!" he said. "We fight on!"

Stukeley frowned and shook his head. He remembered the early days of Sidorio's rebellion, when he had seen the Vampirate leader manipulated by another rebel by the name of Lumar. That had ended badly and Stukeley had a feeling this was going to end worse — for them all.

"Just supposing," he addressed Sidorio, "that we *do* launch a fresh attack on the Alliance, what exactly are you going to tell the crews?" He pointed down at the restless hordes gathered below. The troops were weary, wounded, and in need of answers.

"I'm not going to tell them anything," Sidorio said, decisively. "You are!" Lola nodded approvingly as Sidorio continued. "You're going to tell them that this war is not over. That they need to start feeding today so that their blood is primed and pumped for the biggest battle they've ever seen." Sidorio turned from Stukeley to the others. "Stetson, go with him. You, too, Captain Didio. You're all captains now. It's time you stopped depending on me and Lola to make everything happen around here."

"And what, pray, are you two going to do?" Stukeley inquired.

It was Lola who answered his question. "We need to start distributing supplies from the blood cellars. I want every last one of our foot soldiers' stomachs so full of blood, they'll be absolutely unstoppable."

Arm in arm, Sidorio and Lola strode toward the exit. The two commanders of the rebel Vampirates were united once more.

The metal door of the bridge clanked shut after them, its echo filling the tinny surroundings of the bridge. The three remaining young captains stared at one another.

"Well, I may as well be the one to say this." Stukeley broke the silence. "This plan stinks!" He turned to the others for support. "Come on, you guys. You saw what we were up against last night. Sid and Lola might fancy a suicide mission, but, tell you what, it's a no from me."

"Wait!" Mimma implored him. "I know you'll say I'm

biased, but I tend to agree with Lola when she says we've pushed them to their limits."

Johnny stepped forward, nodding. "Me, too."

Stukeley shook his head. "You're like her puppets, all of you. And Sidorio's the biggest puppet of all." Exasperatedly, Stukeley shook his head. "Well, fine, if that's the way you feel, *you* can deliver that message to the troops." He strode to the door.

"Where are you going?" Mimma asked.

"I don't know!" Stukeley said angrily as he pushed open the door. "Maybe I'll have a long soak in a hot bath!"

Johnny started to go after him but Mimma reached out her hand. "Leave him," she said. "He'll come around. I'll have a quiet word with him later if need be. I can be very persuasive, you know."

Johnny grinned. "I'm sure you can." His expression changed to one of anxiety. "Sidorio tasked all three of us to address the troops. He'll be furious when he finds out Stukeley disobeyed his orders."

Mimma smiled soothingly, shaking her head. "He doesn't need to find out," she said, reaching for the door. "Come on, Captain Desperado. You and I are perfectly capable of doing this ourselves. Sid and Lola clearly want us to step up to the plate. I'm ready. Aren't you?"

Johnny hesitated for a moment, then nodded and followed her out through the door.

"Here you are!" Nathalie said. "This should take the edge off." She sauntered over to where Stukeley stood beside Hunter and Evil's bassinets and handed him a glass.

"Thanks," he said, swigging a gulp, then glancing down again at the two babies, making funny faces at them.

"So, what prompted this visit?" Nathalie asked. "Not that I'm complaining, but I'd never have predicted that you were inclined toward child care. You're not thinking of applying to be their manny, are you?"

"Manny?" Stukeley looked blankly at her.

"Male nanny," Nathalie explained with a grin.

"No!" Stukeley laughed and shook his head. "But after everything I've been through tonight, I just thought that spending time with these little guys might help restore some sense of sanity."

Nathalie smiled. "I know exactly what you mean," she said, gazing at the two little bodies wriggling in their cots. "Would *you* like kids some day?" she inquired. "With Mimma, perhaps?"

Stukeley shrugged—now wriggling himself, taken off guard by her question. "I don't know," he said. "I guess I never really thought it was an option for me."

Nathalie nodded. "Me neither, but if it worked for Lola and Sidorio, why not for you guys, too? For what it's worth, I think you and Mim would make delectable babies!" Smiling at the thought, she reached out her hand to little Evil. He squealed with delight and gripped hold of her finger with both his hands. "Ouch!" she exclaimed.

"That's a tight grip! Just wait until he gets a sword in his hand!"

"It won't be long," Stukeley said. "I'm sure Sid and Lola have big plans for these two."

"Oh, yes." Nathalie nodded. "The world is their oyster. These little guys will be running us ragged, you can bet on it. I wonder if they'll even remember that Auntie Nat changed a thousand of their diapers when they're running the empire." She smiled and shook her head, rolling her eyes.

Stukeley's smile froze upon his face. These two little kids might look innocent enough now, but Nathalie was right. They stood to take their place at Sidorio and Lola's sides. He and Johnny would no longer be Sidorio's deputies. It was bad enough being edged aside by Lola, let alone by two rug rats who couldn't even control their own bowel movements. He made another face at Hunter, provoking a fresh burst of giggles.

"You're really good with them," Nathalie said. "You must visit us more often!"

Stukeley turned away from the babies for a moment and focused instead on his adult companion. "Are *you* their nanny?" he asked. "I get the impression you spend an awful lot of time with them."

Nathalie shrugged. "I do what I can. I promised Lola that they wouldn't be left alone at any point. Not after what she read in the cards last night!"

Greatly interested and keen to learn more, Stukeley leaned in closer. "Lola certainly does love the cards, doesn't she?"

Nathalie nodded, pursing her lips. "But she was in quite a state after what we found out about little Hunter here."

"What exactly *did* you find out?" Stukeley asked her casually, glancing back down and winking at the helpless brat.

Nathalie was tickling the baby's tummy. "Lola turned the Death card and then three others—the Healer, the Lost Buccaneer, and Orion, also known as the Hunter."

Stukeley quickly processed this latest information as Nathalie continued. "Lola's got it into her head that death is coming for Hunter. It absolutely terrifies her." Nathalie's eyes were wide as she turned to Stukeley. "You know the babies have really changed Captain Lockwood. As strong as she is, if anything happened to Hunter or Evil, it would completely and utterly destroy her."

There! There was the solace that Stukeley had been waiting for. He truly hadn't expected to find it here, but wasn't there some kind of saying about wisdom springing from the mouths of babes and fools? Well, Nathalie certainly wasn't a fool, and the babes hadn't exactly spoken to him, but... close enough. He heard Nathalie's voice inside his head—and it had never sounded so sweet. *If anything happened to Hunter or Evil, it would completely destroy her. Completely destroy her. Destroy her. Her.* The thought of

Lola Lockwood-Sidorio's destruction was the most pleasing thing in the world to Stukeley. Already his brain was working overtime.

"We must take very good care of these little guys," Nathalie said, in her soft, warm voice.

Stukeley nodded, reaching his own hand down into the crib.

"Yes indeed," he said. "We mustn't let the precious little devils out of our sights."

"You were rather magnificent up there, Sid," Lola said as they made their way along the corridor to the blood cellar. "Though I really do think you need to pull Stukeley into line."

"I know," Sidorio said. "And I will. Let's just get through the next battle and then we'll review our key personnel. Reshuffle the cards." He glanced down at her. "Does that sound like a good plan?"

Lola nodded. "A very good plan indeed," she said, dipping her hand into her pocket for the key to the cellar door.

"My only sadness," Sidorio continued, "is that Grace and Connor won't come back to our side. Then our family—our empire—would be complete."

Lola nodded carefully, thinking of the last few cards she had turned. "I wouldn't worry about it overmuch, darling." Why worry when Jack Tar was stalking the Healer *and* the Lost Buccaneer? Soon Grace and Connor would be written out of the story for good. And about time, too! Death might also have Hunter in his sights, but the cards had given Lola notice of this, and she had heeded their warning. Nothing bad was going to befall little Hunter. Lola smiled. "I have a feeling everything is falling into place."

"Do you really think so?" Sidorio asked her.

"I know so," Lola said, key outstretched as they reached the door. Her tone faltered. "What's this?"

The door was ajar and her boots appeared to be stepping not onto dry floorboards but into centimeters of liquid. With a sense of awful foreboding, Lola pushed open the door and strode into her beloved cellars. Sidorio heard her piercing scream and rushed inside to join her.

It was a terrible sight to behold. The cellars had been completely vandalized. Bottles lay emptied and smashed. Blood of many distinct vintages gushed over the floor and seeped down into the deck boards, unsavored. On the far wall, painted in blood, were the words:

YOU'VE LOST THE WAR!

Sidorio watched as Lola fell to her knees, her ruffled skirt now fully immersed in the sea of blood. "No!" she cried out, lifting her hands out from under the pool and running them dementedly through her hair. She was covered, head to foot, in blood. She looked uncharacteristically helpless as she turned to him, eyes showing the deep pain of this brutal assault on everything she had worked so hard to create. But there was something undeniably beautiful in the sight of his wonderful wife doused head to toe in the blood of those she had assiduously slaughtered, before filtering and decanting it into bottles. Bottles that now lay smashed all around her, like so many broken dreams.

"How could they do this?" she rasped, shaking her head. *What kind of animals are we dealing with?*"

Sidorio waded determinedly toward her, his boots sloshing through the blood, and reached out his hand to hers.

She was trembling. He had never seen her like this. Few people would ever think of Lola as being vulnerable, but Sidorio was privileged to know better. Lola was deeply vulnerable when it came to the things that truly mattered to her: her comrades; her precious wine; her sons; and, doubtless, her husband.

He held her by the wrist and drew her up to her feet once more. "They'll pay for this," he said.

"What if we *did* underestimate them?" Lola asked. "How could they have gotten on board to do this? And away again, too?"

"Those aren't the questions you should be asking," Sidorio said.

"No?" Lola looked at him, anxious for answers.

"I'm over being the underdog in this war. I've had it up to my ears with pompous pirates and blood-fearing vampires. I'm done with hearing Obsidian Darke's sanctimonious sermons and then bearing witness to random acts of violence like this." Sidorio locked eyes with his wife and comrade. "*They* are the ones who have underestimated *us*. Not the other way around."

"What are you saying?" Lola asked, reaching out and resting her elegant, bloodied hands on Sidorio's shoulders.

Sidorio smiled. "This war ends tonight. Whatever it takes. No one is going to stand in my way. I've been more than patient, but no more Mr. Nice Vampirate. This time, the gloves are off."

Lola at last managed to raise a half smile. "I love you, Sid. I hope you know that."

He nodded, smiling happily at her. "I know," he said. "I had you at hello. Now come on, Lola, let's bring the troops down here to feast and then we'll go blow the Alliance into smithereens. What do you say?"

For once, Lola Lockwood-Sidorio was silent. Any more words seemed utterly redundant after all the beautiful things he had said.

40

PROTOCOL NINE

Down in the vaults below the Rotunda at Pirate Academy, a meeting was under way in Room 13. It was a special meeting of the key personnel of the pirate and Nocturnal Alliance, convened in the immediate aftermath of *The Nocturne*'s successful dismissal of Sidorio and his rebel forces.

"Well," Ahab Black said, "let me be the first to congratulate you, Commanders Darke and Furey. You certainly saw off that punk Sidorio in no uncertain terms."

"Thank you, Commodore Black," Lorcan said, nodding graciously, as — at his side — Cheng Li squeezed his wrist. On Lorcan's other side, Obsidian remained silent.

"Though, I must say," Black continued, "I'd feel happier about breaking out the Federation champagne if you had actually and conclusively destroyed both Sidorio and his harpy of a wife."

"Hear, hear!" agreed Trofie Wrathe enthusiastically. "But surely, comrades, the termination of Sidorio, Lola, and the other Vampirate leaders is the next phase of our strategy?"

"Is it?" asked René Grammont. "That sounds like an expensive proposition. As I recall, when we last met, the war chest was running perilously low."

Ahab Black cracked a thin smile. "Worry no more on that score, René. We have lately received a sizable donation from our newest captain, Connor Tempest."

There was hubbub around the table at both aspects of this news. Jacoby and Jasmine exchanged a surprised glance, then turned to Cheng Li, who nodded but said nothing.

"Let me be sure I understand you," Trofie Wrathe addressed Commodore Black. "You made Connor Tempest a Federation captain? I don't remember us being consulted about this. And, according to Federation protocol, at least six members of the executive council must endorse all nominations for captaincy."

Black was unfazed. "Difficult times call for decisive action. As commander in chief of the Federation, I invoked article 224b. Connor's a fine young pirate, and his investiture sounds just the right PR note to the rest of the fleet." He smiled. "Moreover, as Connor has signed over a sizable chunk of his inheritance from Molucco, we're now firmly back in the black...no pun intended!"

Trofie remained incredulous. "I didn't realize we were in the business of selling captaincies these days."

Barbarro reached out and placed his own hand over her golden one in an attempt to pacify her. She angrily snatched it away.

Now Pavel Platonov spoke up. "This addition to our finances is undoubtedly fortuitous. Yet I share the concern of Captain Grammont. This war has already proved costly—in every sense. I see no need in prolonging our engagement or committing further expenditure if the threat from the Vampirates has, as I understand it, been neutralized."

Now Lisabeth Quivers entered the fray. "Is it true, Commodore Black, that the full Alliance fleet is making its way into this very harbor tonight?"

Ahab Black was only momentarily derailed by this question.

"My word, Captain Quivers, your sources are impeccable. Yes, I gave the order for all ships to gather here."

"Are you deciding everything unilaterally these days?" queried Trofie. "Because, if that's the case, why are we here at this godforsaken hour and not sleeping in our beds?"

"Why did you summon the fleet?" Captain Quivers asked Black.

"For a rallying call," Black said. "I want to punch home the message that we've won the war. Tomorrow we'll parade Connor Tempest in front of them, announce his investiture, and outline the next phase in our strategy."

"Which is what?" inquired Barbarro. "To send out

every last Alliance captain with a price on Sidorio and Lola's scalps?"

Black grinned once more. "Well now, that wouldn't be the worst idea in the world, would it?"

"I agree," said Moonshine Wrathe. "We should go after the Vampirates, and not just the demon duo. We shouldn't rest until every last one of the ships they hijacked from us has been taken back—just like *The Diablo*."

"With respect," René Grammont interjected, "that's fine rhetoric, Captain Wrathe, but there is a price tag attached to every Alliance vessel pursuing the Vampirates."

"Not only that," Cheng Li spoke now. "But if we further antagonize Sidorio and Lola, we could start up the war all over again."

"It's not like you to advocate mercy, Commodore Li," said Black.

"I'm advocating *caution*," Cheng Li said. "I'm as concerned about this situation as the rest of you, but I don't think there are any easy answers."

"I completely disagree," interjected Kirstin Larsen. "Surely this is blindingly simple? We *must* have a decisive end to the war."

Cheng Li remained calm. "Why don't we ask Commanders Darke and Furey how *they* feel it is best to proceed? After all, they both know Sidorio far better than any of us."

"Hear, hear!" Captain Quivers agreed.

Along the length of the conference table, all eyes turned to the two Nocturnal leaders.

At last, Obsidian Darke spoke. "I regret to say that I do not believe the threat from Sidorio is over."

"We have our answer!" Ahab Black punched the table. "I don't know what further prompting the rest of you need. We cannot rest easy until this threat is completely neutralized. We have the ships and the money. It's time to crank up our war machine to the max."

"We have a worrying skills shortage," Barbarro interjected. "Need I remind you all that this war has seen unprecedented levels of pirate fatalities?"

"On the Nocturnal side, too," Cheng Li said.

Ahab Black nodded, facing Obsidian Darke once more. "All in all, my friend, it's a pity you didn't call on these mysterious allies of yours somewhat sooner."

Darke did not rise to the bait. There was, momentarily, silence within Room 13. It seemed that there would be no easy answers. Cheng Li glanced at the clock on the wall. It was already well into the early hours. At this rate, they'd be lucky to have reached an accord by sunrise.

"Shouldn't you be down below in the Alliance bunker?" Grace asked Connor, pointing to the floor of the Rotunda. "After all, you are a Federation captain now."

Connor shrugged. "Aren't you the Alliance's leading

healer these days? You've earned your place at that table just as much as I have."

Grace considered his words. "Perhaps. Still, I'd much rather be here with you. We've spent far too much time apart, don't you think? We didn't even get to spend our birthday together. That was a first."

He nodded thoughtfully and glanced upward. They had left the lamps of the Rotunda unlit, but still Grace and Connor were bathed in a watery blue light—the result of the moonlight filtering down through the colored glass in the building's domed roof. Grace saw that Connor was staring up at the cases of swords belonging to some of the greatest pirates the world had ever seen. She knew they had fascinated him since the very first time they had visited Pirate Academy. He gazed up intently for a time, then his eyes slowly returned to her.

"Hey," he asked. "What's in that satchel of yours?"

Grace unzipped the bag and removed from it the book she now carried with her at all times. She'd been wanting to tell him about it since the moment she discovered it. Now seemed as good a time as any.

They stepped toward each other, directly beneath the cluster of swords. Grace held out the small book and Connor took it, holding it up to the light so he could read the words on the cover. "*The Way of the Dhampir*." He glanced up at Grace questioningly.

"It's a guide," Grace said. "It was blank when I found it, but it talks to me."

Connor looked askance at Grace, then back at the closed book. "It talks to you?" he said. "What about?"

"It answers questions no one else can answer," Grace said. "Have a look. I'm interested to know if it works for you, too." She stepped closer. "Open it and ask it a question. You don't even need to say the words aloud."

Not so long ago, Connor would have dismissed this as one of Grace's fantasies, but experience had taught him to take her at her word. He opened up the book and, with a soft sigh, focused on the blank pages before him.

Grace had walked over to stand beside him and watched over his shoulder as text began appearing on the page.

Your time as a dhampir is coming to an end.

They both stared at the page, then Connor's hands began to tremble and he dropped the book to the floor.

"Oh, Connor," Grace said sadly. "I'm so sorry."

"Don't be," he said, turning to face her. He was smiling. "I'm trembling, but it's with relief, I think. I'm not like you, Grace. I can't accept this thing I am. There's nothing I want more than to stop being a dhampir." He smiled broadly at her. "Your magic book has given me the best news I've had in ages."

It dawned on her that he didn't understand that the book was telling him that he would be the one to die. Because surely that was what the words meant—the time of the prophecy was drawing near and now it was revealed which one of the twins was going to be sacrificed. Grace felt bereft. As much as she had feared her own death, now she realized that the idea of Connor's dying was far worse. She felt as if she had betrayed him somehow, by failing to tell him sooner about the prophecy. But, truly, was it something they had any power to change?

Grace couldn't even face looking at her brother. Seeing the book lying there on the floor of the Rotunda, she knelt down to retrieve it. As she did, more words began to appear before her.

The time of the prophecy is now.

"No," she said. "No. I'm not ready."

"What does it mean, Grace?" Connor asked, at her side. "What prophecy?"

She couldn't speak. She couldn't be the one to tell him he was going to have to die to bring peace to the oceans.

"What prophecy?" Connor persisted. "Grace, you have to tell me."

⤙⤚

Down in the bunker, Cheng Li glanced at the clock once more. *Tick-tock. Tick-tock.* Would this meeting never end?

"We're not getting anywhere," Kirstin Larsen said, speaking, it seemed, for the majority of the assembly.

"Can I make a suggestion?" Moonshine asked. "We're a democratic organization, aren't we? Why don't we just put this to the vote?"

There were murmurings around the table, largely, it seemed, in favor of the suggestion. Then two things happened in quick succession. Ahab Black raised his hand to restore order. Then there was a hammering on the door to Room 13 and a breathless Bo Yin pushed it open.

All eyes turned to her. Suddenly everyone was quiet. Something told them that she brought news of the utmost seriousness.

"The Vampirate fleet is making its way to Pirate Academy," she said. "Kally brought the news."

Cheng Li glanced at the clock once more. "But this is madness," she said. "It's scarcely more than three hours until sunrise."

Ahab Black's expression was grim. "You're right, Commodore Li, but I don't think we require much further evidence that Sidorio and Lola are mad."

"Or," Lorcan sounded a note of warning, "extremely confident."

"How can they be?" cried Barbarro Wrathe.

A din of voices began to bubble up again.

Cheng Li addressed Ahab Black. "You need to invoke Protocol Nine," she said.

For once, he did not protest but simply nodded. "Consider it invoked." He rose to his feet and addressed his comrades. "Sound the attack sirens! Every captain needs to get to their ship!" He turned to Bo Yin. "Tell Kally and the intel team to get word to Sanctuary that we need medical backup." Bo Yin nodded, remaining admirably calm as the commander in chief of the Pirate Federation continued to bark orders at her. "And get them to warn the rest of our fleet that they are sailing into a battle zone." As Bo Yin raced off to execute his orders, Black continued to reel off commands. "All senior students to go to their assigned ships, juniors to gather in the bunkers..."

The sirens echoed in the vast dome of the Rotunda. The noise caused the bank of swords above their heads to tremble and agitate.

"We're under attack!" Connor cried, scrambling to his feet. "I have to get back to *The Tiger*."

"Wait!" Grace implored him.

He shook his head. "This is Protocol Nine, Grace. We all have to move fast."

"But there's so much we need to say to each other," she said. "Especially now that you know about the prophecy."

Connor shook his head once more. "We can't talk now. We both have important jobs to do." Seeing Grace's desolate expression, he added, "Maybe it's better this way."

Grace was trembling. Was this the beginning of the end? How were you supposed to say good-bye to the brother you might never see again?

She felt him hug her. She was numb but, as he released her, she managed to get out two words: "Be careful!"

After he'd gone and she was alone in the Rotunda, she berated herself for not saying something more meaningful. She realized it was futile. There were no words to reach across the terrible chasm they now faced.

She was still holding the book. It was open in front of her. As she glanced down, tears spattered onto its pages, staining the paper. Then she saw words gathering again, even over the tear marks. The book was speaking to her once more. But what could it possibly have to tell her?

It is time for you to enter the realm of the dead.

She experienced a sudden tremor of shock, then a strange form of relief. Then confusion. Did this mean that it was her, not Connor, who was destined to die? Her heart was racing as further instructions began to appear right before her eyes.

41

THE DESCENT

Johnny stood side by side with Stukeley at the front of *The Redeemer*. The night air was heady with expectation. To their port side was Mimma and her crew on board *The Calabria*; on their starboard, the vast hulk of *The Blood Captain* with Sidorio at the prow. Johnny knew that *The Vagabond* was on the other side of *The Blood Captain*, though for now the larger ship restricted his view.

"Isn't this amazing?" Johnny turned to Stukeley, his eyes bright. "Look up ahead! Are those the lights of the Pirate Academy?"

Stukeley shrugged. "That's right, pal. Our suicide mission is almost upon us."

Johnny frowned. "Don't talk that way. We're both coming back from this."

"I wish I shared your confidence," Stukeley said, "but

Sidorio has lost the plot. We were roundly defeated last night. The only reason we're back for more is because Lola's precious wine cellar was breached. She's always been a bad influence on him, and this time she's pushed him right to the edge."

"You think?" Johnny's face grew suddenly anxious.

Stukeley nodded. "Look at the sky, man. You can read it as well as me. It's only hours until dawn."

"This battle will all be over by the time the sun rises," Johnny said. "I can taste success." His eyes skimmed the fire beacons that marked the perimeter of the Pirate Academy harbor.

"Now, you're clear on your own mission in this?" Stukeley said.

Johnny nodded. "When the battle heats up, I slip onto *The Vagabond* and steal the babies."

Stukeley nodded grimly. "Still feeling confident?"

Johnny grinned. "Hey, I was a cattle rustler, remember. Stealing is my thing."

Stukeley gazed at his friend, wondering if it was the right moment to remind him he'd been caught cattle rustling and killed for it. On balance, not, he decided. He needed Johnny to deliver the goods tonight.

Johnny's expression changed suddenly. "I'm comfortable with the stealing part. But do I have to kill them? I know we need them out of the way, but killing babies is a first even for me."

Stukeley lowered his voice, intent that no one on his

crew overheard this conversation. "Johnny," he said, "you have to get rid of Hunter and Evil or there's no kind of future for us. You know that as well as I do. This crazy battle is the perfect smoke screen."

"I know that, but do I have to kill them?"

Stukeley's eyes met Johnny's. "I don't much care *what* you do with them. Throw them into the ocean or give them away. Just make sure that when the battle ends and the smoke clears, that nursery is empty and there's no way back for those kids."

Johnny nodded. "Okay, I understand, *hermano*. But wouldn't it be simpler to have another go at killing Lola?"

Stukeley shook his head. "Too dangerous," he said. "But if you take away her precious kids, she'll be a broken woman. And we have to break her, Johnny. You get that, don't you?"

Johnny nodded, his eyes turning once more from his comrade to the fire beacons, which seemed to be floating nearer and nearer. "I get it," he said. "I don't like it, but you can depend on me. I'll do what has to be done."

※

On board *The Nocturne*, the crew was moving back into attack positions. At least tonight there had been some warning and the Nocturnals had had a chance to feed. Still, Lorcan was fearful that this was one attack too many and too hard on the heels of the last. He was growing tired of this. This wasn't the life he had chosen. He'd risen to the challenge far better than he had expected—to protect the people he loved and their way of life—but fundamentally he was a peaceful person. He didn't know how much longer he could go on. He had never felt closer to the edge of the abyss. The sleep of oblivion was starting to appeal to him, had there not been so much at stake.

He hammered on Grace's cabin door, scarcely believing that once more he was about to say good-bye to her, perhaps for the last time.

"Come in!" came a voice, but it belonged to Oskar, not Grace. Already feeling a deep sense of disquiet, Lorcan pushed open the door.

The sight before his eyes only made his heart hammer faster. Grace lay motionless on the floor of the cabin. It looked as if she had fallen, though she had sustained no obvious wounds. Lying close by her was the precious book she had been carrying around with her. Its pages were open and flapped as if there were a breeze, though the air in the cabin was perfectly still.

"What's going on?" Lorcan asked Oskar.

"I don't know!" Oskar said, shaking his head. "I found her like this."

"What does this say?" Lorcan asked, crouching down before Grace's book. One of Grace's forefingers lay across the book as if keeping a page open. Lorcan reached out his own hand above hers to still the butterfly motion of the pages. At last, he could read what was written on the page. *"It's time for you to enter the realm of the dead.* No!" His frantic eyes met Oskar's.

"It's okay," Oskar said. "I just checked her pulse, and she's definitely breathing—but slowly, like she's sedated or in some kind of trance. I can't seem to wake her."

Lorcan looked at Grace's beautiful face. She seemed peaceful at least. He turned back to Oskar. "Look," he said, "I have to get going. I don't want to be anywhere but here, but I have no choice. You understand, don't you?"

Oskar nodded.

"Will you stay and look after her? Do what you can to bring her back around."

"Of course!" Oskar said. "You know I'd do anything for Grace—for both of you. As long as you're sure you can spare me from this battle?"

Lorcan did not hesitate. "You're a great swordsman, Oskar, but I need you right here, taking care of Grace for me. I can't go into this battle unless I know she's in safe hands."

Oskar nodded. "You have my word," he said. "I won't leave her side."

⸺ ⸺

The Alliance ships were moving swiftly into the battle zone, out beyond the harbor, in an arrowlike formation. Connor stood at the stern of *The Tiger*, looking back at the ships following in its wake. Every one of them was a legend. Moving behind them in a line were *The Diablo*, captained by Moonshine Wrathe with Cate Morgan as his deputy; *The Typhon* captained by Moonshine's father, Barbarro, with Trofie Wrathe as second-in-command; and *The Nocturne* under the dual command of Obsidian Darke and Lorcan Furey. Beyond those three ships came four more legendary vessels: *The Inferno*, captained by Francisco Moscardo; *The Muscovite*, captained by Pavel Platonov; *The Seferis*, captained by Apostolos Solomos; and *The Kronborg Slot*, captained by Kirsten Larsen. Behind them, Connor knew, were more legendary ships and equally legendary pirate captains.

There was a tangible sense of history in the air tonight as the last of the fleet made its way through the academy arch. Connor reminded himself that he was going into this battle as a captain himself. He could never have expected this when he had first journeyed to Pirate Academy, first sat at the table with these pirating legends. What an incredible journey he had traveled in the past year. He did not yet have his own ship — Ahab Black, currently directing operations from his bunker, had promised him one would be ready soon. Connor wasn't so sure. Perhaps, if what Grace had told him was true, this would be his one and only battle as Captain Tempest. Strangely, the thought was not a source of pain or terror. He felt almost preternaturally calm, though his senses were heightened. He realized he was the living embodiment of *zanshin* — the warrior's consciousness, which had been drilled into him at Pirate Academy and subsequently perfected through real-life conflict.

Turning his eyes forward, Connor could see the ominous lights of the enemy fleet stealing closer. It was a vast armada—made up in large part of ships stolen from the pirates and crewed by converts, both willing and unwilling. It was time to end the fearful empire Sidorio and Lola were building—with no loftier goal than spreading chaos and dark dominion over the oceans. They had to be stopped—here and now. Connor shivered and knew it was more from anticipation than fear. This was not the first time he had gone into battle against Sidorio or Lola. But he couldn't shake the feeling that tonight's battle was different. Somehow he knew that none of them would come out of this night quite the same.

He had another brief flash of his recurrent vision. Jasmine's cries and the sight of the sword embedded in his chest. The horrified faces of his comrades. He pushed the vision away. Every pirate—every pirate captain—went into battle in the certain knowledge that this could be his or her last. Connor was no exception. He thought fondly of those pirates who had gone before him—Porfirio and Molucco Wrathe, Commodore John Kuo, Bart Pearce. He was proud to be following in the path they had charted. If he died tonight, he doubted very much they'd hang *his* sword in Pirate Academy, doubted they'd even remember the name of the young pirate captain who fought once and once only. It didn't matter. When all was said and done, it was more than enough simply to have played his part.

His thoughts turned to Grace, knowing that aboard *The Nocturne*, she, too, was preparing to play her part. They had each come so far, though their journeys had been markedly different, since they first set out from Crescent Moon Bay almost a year ago. Connor was unaccustomed to praying, but now he closed his eyes to say a silent prayer for Grace's safety. If he did lose his life tonight, she would have to journey on for both of them. He wanted her to do so in peace, not in pain. He needed her to know that, whatever happened, he accepted his fate.

———

Grace stood in the lamp room of the lighthouse, looking down at the waters of Crescent Moon Bay, then out across the familiar seascape. Below, the ocean waters were high and rising, but it was still a long way down to their churning surface. She knew what she had to do. Stepping forward, she opened the door and walked out onto the balcony, savoring the familiar silhouette of the coastline one last time. She thought of the many previous times she'd been up here — with Connor and with Dexter. Then, unable to defer the moment any longer, she climbed up onto the balcony railing and dived down into the ocean, giving herself over to her fate.

Her descent was rapid, but this did not diminish the

magnitude of fear that rushed through her. It wasn't only fear for herself. The fate of so many others depended on her mission proving successful.

This was unlike any of her previous astral visits. This time, she could still feel the icy chill as she shot down through the surface of the ice-cold water. It was as if she had somehow split into two. The air was forced from her lungs. Then the swirling waters began to move her about, carrying her back up to the surface. No! She needed to go *down*, not *up*! She was completely at the mercy of the ocean and grateful to feel the undercurrent begin to suck her down. Her descent gained such momentum that she instinctively closed her eyes. The motion shifted and she felt her body spinning as if she were being carried through a vortex. Once more she was fearful that somehow she had gotten this wrong, even though she had followed the book's instructions to the letter. As she felt her body come to rest, she hardly dared to open her eyes.

Before the fear could take any deeper hold on her, she opened them—but onto pitch blackness. What her eyes could only suspect, her feet now confirmed. She had reached the ocean floor.

As her eyes grew accustomed to the darkness, she began to distinguish rough shapes. Then she saw what she had been searching for—a line of incandescent light barely visible in the distance. She knew in her gut it must be the door. She began swimming toward it, gratified to find the light growing stronger as she did.

Fish swam past her as she continued on toward the door, but they were not the kind of fish she was used to seeing—the rainbow-bright creatures who lived closer to the surface waters. These were as dark as their surroundings, their shapes simple, as if rough-hewn by a beginning carver. It felt to Grace as though she had not only descended to the floor of the ocean but back to a more basic world. She swam on.

As she reached the door, the light that ringed it illuminated the surrounding environs, though, actually, there was not much to see. The terrain was barren in the extreme, offering little sustenance for the creatures that had swum alongside her. The door was in the face of a vast rock and to one side was a painted sign, the words of which were now legible.

JACK TAR'S CAVERN. COME INSIDE! WE NEVER CLOSE.

Grace moved toward the door, her wet hair swirling about her face. Even her own flesh appeared ghostly in the ethereal light. Her hand rested on the heavy iron door, which looked as if it might have been salvaged from a shipwreck.

At her touch, the door opened with a creak. Grace had expected the interior of the cavern to be underwater, too, but, as she crossed the threshold, she found that it was dry and airy inside. Her hair and clothes were also now dry. Turning back, she saw the wall of ocean water that stopped at the entrance, as if held back by an invisible force field. The fish were stuck within it and could only stare back at her in mute wonder.

"Close the door! For goodness' sake, love—close the door! You're letting in a terrible draft!"

Grace obediently closed the heavy door as a lady pirate passed her with a grateful nod.

"Welcome to Jack Tar's!" said the woman, in a friendlier tone. "The company's grand and the drink is plentiful—but I'd stay away from the house cocktail until you've got your bearings!" With a wink and a giggle, the woman bustled on her way.

Grace stepped forward, finding herself awestruck by her surroundings. She wasn't sure exactly what she had expected of Jack Tar's Cavern—perhaps simply a deep underwater version of Ma Kettle's Tavern. In a way, it *was* like Ma's, but far bigger. And where Ma's was a rickety wooden building that always gave you the impression it might imminently collapse into the sea, Jack Tar's was a rock structure, as vast and solid as a cathedral. Stepping forward, Grace realized she was on a central landing, from which stone stairs stretched both up and down, left and right. She moved along the landing, trying to take it all in. Seeing—and hearing—hordes of pirates carousing in the room below her, she decided to continue down the stairs. As she made her descent, rough archways in the rock opened onto cavelike rooms, each filled with pirates lounging, drinking, playing cards, or singing chanteys. There were caves as far as she could see in every direction. It felt as if Jack Tar's Cavern might stretch across the entire ocean floor.

The downstairs bar was even more crowded than it had seemed from above. Up ahead, Grace could see the bar itself—a vast circular structure that seemed to be on two or three different levels. Clustered around the bar on every level were rows of pirates, lining up to refresh their tankards and those of their mates. She needed to find a way to get everyone's attention but, glancing around, realized just how difficult this might prove. They were all so engrossed in their conversations, games, and sing-songs. She couldn't blame them. They had earned their leisure. She had wondered, before entering the cavern, if the dead pirates' wounds would be visible, but mercifully this appeared not to be the case.

"Haven't seen *you* here before," said a gap-toothed pirate at her side. "Are you a new arrival?"

"Just visiting," Grace said.

The pirate laughed at that. "Just visiting, eh? I've heard *that* one before! Look around, missy—everyone is *just visiting*!" He headed off to join the clamor for the bar, laughing as if at some private joke.

Grace stood her ground, wondering again just how she was going to attract the attention of all the thirsty and gregarious denizens of this cavern.

"Grace? Is that you?" She heard a familiar voice coming closer. Turning, she found Bart Pearce at her side.

"Bart!" He looked just as she remembered him in life. As tall and strong and handsome as ever.

Bart smiled at her. "I thought I heard your voice, but I didn't like to think it could be you." His eyes flashed with sadness.

"It's okay," she said, realizing his mistake. "I'm not dead."

Bart's eyes narrowed. "Are you sure, Grace?" he said. "They say only the dead can enter Jack Tar's."

"Truly," she said. "I'm here on an astral visit."

"Okay..." he said, not totally understanding, but taking Grace's word for it.

Now Grace became aware of other eyes turning curiously toward her. "You look well, Bart," she said. "You look like you're at peace here."

He grinned and shrugged. "You know me, Grace. Happy-go-lucky. I always reckoned on a short life but a merry one. And this place, these crazy folks, well, it's all quite an unexpected bonus!" He turned momentarily as another pirate squeezed him on the shoulder and offered to buy him a drink. Grace smiled to herself. It was clear that Bart Pearce was every bit as popular in Jack Tar's Cavern as he had been at Ma's.

"Now, look," Bart said, turning back to her. "If you're not dead, what on oceans are you doing down here?"

"I need your help," Grace said. "Not just you, but all the pirates down here—or as many of them as are willing to bear arms again."

Bart's face showed concern. "Have things got that bad up above?" he asked. "I mean, we hear reports from all the newcomers, and, lately, there have been a *lot* of newcomers."

Grace nodded. "It's bad," she said. "Sidorio's armada outstrips the Alliance's now. His troops outnumber ours. He's just suffered what should have been a decisive defeat, but he's intent on one more push. We can't let him win. There's too much at stake."

Bart nodded. He looked reflective for a moment. "You know, Grace, we depend on new arrivals to bring us the news from above, but, I swear, the ocean itself has begun to weep for this war." His expression grew more determined. "What can we do?"

"I need you all to come back, one last time. I know you're at peace here and I wouldn't ask if it wasn't absolutely necessary. Will you come and join the fight?"

Bart didn't flinch. "Of course!" he said, then looked down woefully at his side. "Only I don't have my sword anymore, Grace. Those sentimental buggers up there strung it up in a case at Pirate Academy, so I hear."

"Yes," Grace said, smiling reassuringly. "Don't worry, Bart. Your sword will be waiting for you. The same goes for Molucco and any of the others who are missing theirs, too."

"You want Molucco, too, eh?" Bart grinned, remembering perhaps Grace's former animosity toward Molucco Wrathe.

Grace nodded purposefully. "I want Molucco *and* Porfirio Wrathe." Her eyes ranged about the vast cavern. "I want every last pirate here to come back up tonight."

Bart nodded in understanding. "Out of my way, lads!" he bellowed, pushing his way toward the old ship's bell that hung over the bar. He grabbed the chain and rang the bell loudly.

The chimes echoed up and down the huge cavern. Hearing it, the pirates ceased their chatter and turned, expectantly, toward the bar. Bart leaped up nimbly onto the counter.

"Sorry to interrupt your revels," he said, "but our help is sought in the war raging up above." His words seized everyone's attention. Grace glanced up to see attentive pirates leaning across the stairway and craning their necks from the most distant corners to see and hear better as Bart continued.

"We all know from the reports coming in nightly that the situation has been bad for a while. Things have come to a head tonight, it seems, and the Alliance needs us to go back to join them in one last battle. The future of piracy—the future of our oceans—depends on its outcome." Bart exchanged a glance with Grace, his eyes bright with purpose. He lifted his head up proud and strong and raised his hand high in the air. "All those who are ready to join me, cry 'aye'."

Nothing could have prepared Grace for the deafening cry. It echoed through the cathedral-like cavern and lingered for what seemed like minutes. The show of support and solidarity drew tears from Grace's emerald eyes.

Bart glanced down from the bar counter. "Reckon you have your answer, Grace. Now, jump up here beside me and tell us all what happens next."

42

WOUNDS

It happened simultaneously. The four vanguard Vampirate ships—*The Blood Captain*, *The Redeemer*, *The Calabria*, and *The Vagabond*—smashed into the three lead Alliance vessels—*The Diablo*, *The Tiger*, and *The Typhon*. Wood splintered as the ships crashed into one another. As the members of each crew experienced the shock waves, Sidorio let out a roar. "Now!"

The captains of each Vampirate ship flew up into the air, followed in their wake by their troops.

Sidorio and his crew thudded down onto the deck of *The Tiger*, where Cheng Li and her team were ready to do battle.

"Remember!" cried Sidorio, making his first swift kill. "This is the ship of Vampirate assassins. Take them down!"

"Eyes on the prize!" commanded Cheng Li, spearing an unsuspecting Vampirate. Moving on, she called out to her comrades, "Destroy Sidorio and the whole Vampirate house of cards collapses."

Now the two crews interlaced as surely and brutally as the prows of their ships.

Lorcan saw Sidorio fly through the air and land on *The Tiger*. The lead pirate vessel was now wedged between *The Blood Captain* at the fore and *The Nocturne* at the aft. The Vampirate armada had begun circling the Alliance fleet. If Sidorio took *The Tiger*, *The Nocturne* would be the next ship in his sights. But it wouldn't—it couldn't—come to that. No crew was better prepared to see off Sidorio than that of *The Tiger*.

As Lorcan watched Stukeley, Mimma, and their teams spill onto *The Diablo*, he felt Obsidian Darke's hot breath at his side. "I'm going after Sidorio," Darke said. "You're in command of *The Nocturne*. Do whatever is necessary."

With that, Darke sprinted to the prow of the ship and vaulted onto the stern of *The Tiger*. Lorcan shuddered as he glimpsed Sidorio far in the distance. He wondered how long it would take before the two old foes squared up to each other one last time.

Lola and her crew had landed on *The Typhon*. "Good to be back, eh?" She grinned at Marianne and Angelika, at her side.

"Aye, Captain!" chorused the two Vampirates as they sprang into action, swords aloft.

"It's great to be out of the nursery and in the heart of the battle," Lola cried to Nathalie as she used her lethal crossbow to slay her first victim. Nathalie kicked away the fast-desiccating Nocturnal, enabling Lola's gloved hand to swiftly retrieve her precious silver arrow.

"Nice one, Captain!" declared Nathalie. "At this rate, we'll have the cellars restocked in no time!"

The vast deck of *The Typhon* was alive with action as Lola's crew penetrated deep into the pirate ranks. But they had met their equal in Barbarro and Trofie's expertly trained pirates. It was going to be a close-won battle.

As she made a fifth kill, Lola glanced up and caught Trofie staring at her from the other end of the deck. There was pure visceral hatred in Trofie's eyes.

"Don't worry, Goldfingers!" Lola called. "I'm working my way back to you."

Trofie Wrathe raised her aconite-dipped silver sword. "Bring it on, Banshee!" she yelled as she pushed through the melee to tackle her black-hearted nemesis.

From on board *The Diablo*, Cate saw loathsome Lola. She dearly wished she was on *The Typhon* now so she could plunge a silver sword straight through the vixen's cold, dark heart. Payback for Lola's felling of Bart. Hopefully, Cate would have this satisfaction before the battle was through, but, for now, she had business to attend to defending *The Diablo*.

Mimma and Stukeley and their teams were each enjoying an early run of success on opposite sides of the ship. The deck boards were littered with their victims and drenched in warm pools of blood. Gazing at the sea of red, Stukeley was sorely tempted to lap it up. Maybe later—as a pick-me-up.

"Nice swordplay," said a familiar voice behind him. "But then you always were one of the best, Jez."

Stukeley spun around hastily to find Cate braced for attack.

He smiled at his worthy opponent. "That's not my name anymore," he said. "Don't play head games with me, pirate. They won't work."

Cate gritted her teeth. "The only head game I have in mind for you is decapitation."

"Touché!" Stukeley cried as their swords clashed. "We used to be pals! What changed, I wonder?"

Cate launched herself in the air, executing a move Lorcan had assiduously coached her in. She landed in front of Stukeley, her sword jabbing his chin. "You became a megalomaniac bloodsucking demon," she said.

"You say that like it's a bad thing!" Stukeley exclaimed.

Shrugging, Cate lifted her foot and booted him several meters across the deck. That felt good!

On the other side of the ship, Mimma had found her way onto the rigging and was hovering there, poised to jump down onto her next victim, Moonshine Wrathe.

"Oh, surely you can do better than that!" he said in bored tones. Without turning, he employed his sword to slice through the rigging and brought her tumbling to the deck in front of him.

As Mimma scrabbled back to her feet, Moonshine shook his head. "Well, you're certainly pretty, for a demon. But I'm a captain now. Don't I merit one of the big fangs rather than the backup squad?"

Mimma was angry now, her pride hurt. She hissed at him, her mouth already stained with the blood of his erstwhile crewmates. She spun her sword ominously toward Moonshine. "How's about I turn you into a pirate kebab," she said, "and then feast on your blood?"

"A charming proposition!" Moonshine declared, preparing to defend himself. "But no more kebabs for you today, methinks. Terrible for the cholesterol, you know!"

Seconds later, their swords were engaged and the backchat ceased as they let their weapons do the talking.

On board *The Tiger*, Connor was notching up one victory after another. He had never felt more completely in the combat zone. As his latest victim fell before him, the deck suddenly opened up and he could see Jasmine, Jacoby, and Bo Yin all holding their own against Sidorio's crew. Connor swelled with pride. If there was any ship and any crew that was going to turn the tide tonight, it was this one. He could see Cheng Li up at the stern, fighting in her usual exemplary fashion. And now she was joined by Obsidian Darke. The leader of the Nocturnals had barely set foot on deck when he started cutting a swath through Sidorio's troops. Darke had never seemed so pumped up and ready for the fight.

In the center of the deck, Connor identified the target they all wanted — Sidorio. The Vampirate leader was being given a good fight by Nada, one of *The Tiger*'s most able pirates. *That's it*, Connor thought. *Just keep him in play. Just keep him there until I make my way through this next rank of Vampirates. Then he'll have the fight he really wants.* He just hoped neither Cheng Li nor Obsidian beat him to it.

Lola and Trofie's swords clanged together once more, the blades reflecting the enmity in each woman's eyes.

"Nice try!" Lola said dismissively. "But I've come back for your hand tonight and I don't intend to leave without it."

"Maybe it's your turn to leave here limbless," Trofie said as her sword whipped through the air toward Lola's shoulder. Lola moved aside, just in time, but Trofie's sword nicked Jacqueline, who was fighting beside her.

Jacqueline's wound swiftly sealed but her ire had been stoked and now she, too, turned her attention to Trofie as Nathalie took her place. Lola and Jacqueline were both stalking her with malicious intent.

"Seems like I'll be getting my wedding bouquet back after all," Lola sneered.

"Think again!" cried Barbarro, descending from the crow's nest and landing between the combatants. He took advantage of his surprise arrival to skewer Jacqueline, who fell to the deck boards, her body buckling in response to the poison on his sword.

Though shocked to have lost such a close ally, Lola kept her focus—still stalking Trofie. Now it was Lola Lockwood-Sidorio who faced two adversaries as the captain and deputy captain of the ship looked for an opening to effect their long-harbored desire for revenge.

Johnny tentatively pushed open the door to the nursery and stepped inside. This was going to be easier than he'd thought. Up ahead were the two bassinets, with nothing and no one standing in his way. But, as he strode up to them, he found they were both empty. His first thought was that someone had beaten him to it. Relief flooded through his bones.

"Johnny?"

He turned slowly, to see Holly walking into the nursery. She had one of the babies in her arms. Where was the other one?

"What are you doing here?" she asked, already suspicious.

"I've come for the babies," Johnny said. So far, so truthful.

"Why?" Holly asked, drawing the infant in its swaddling clothes more closely toward her.

"Captain's orders," he said.

Holly's eyes narrowed. "Which captain?"

Johnny ignored the question. "Which little fellow is that, anyhow?" he asked, stepping closer. "Hunter or Evil?"

"It's Evil," Holly said, as Johnny's hands reached out for the child. "Hunter's not here."

"Where is he, sugar? I need them both."

"Why?" Holly asked again, steadfastly refusing to let go of Evil.

"I told you before." Johnny smiled sweetly. "Captain's orders. I'm taking them both to safety." Both Vampirates clutched at baby Evil now. The infant, not surprisingly, began to wail.

"Give him to me, Holly."

There were tears in her eyes, too. "I can't, Johnny. You have to go."

"Please don't make me do something I might regret."

"I'd give my life for these babies," Holly said through her tears.

She just got out the words before Johnny's silver dagger pierced her clean through the heart. As she slumped to the floor, Johnny retrieved baby Evil from her arms. "I'm sorry, sugar," he said as Holly's body writhed in rapid response to the toxic silver blade. "But you left me no choice. Now tell me where baby Hunter is."

She shook her head, clearly in pain. "Never. I won't..." Her head turned to one side and a glazed look came over her eyes. Then the silver began to work its way deeper into her system and her flesh began to burn.

"Come on, little Evil," Johnny said, clutching the crying babe to him. "It's okay, buddy. You're coming with Uncle Johnny." He shook his head. "If only you could talk, you could tell me where your brother is."

"Are you looking for Hunter?"

Johnny hadn't heard any footsteps, but now he found the threshold to the nursery was blocked by Olivier, who nonchalantly carried Lola and Sidorio's other baby in his arms. Smiling at Johnny, Olivier glided into the room, carrying Hunter over toward the twin bassinets. Olivier was about to lower Hunter into his crib but seemed suddenly to think better of it.

Turning, Olivier wrinkled his nose. "I smell burning," he said. Glancing down, he caught sight of Holly and shook his head at Johnny.

"Oh, dear, Cowboy. Was that really necessary? That bighearted girl was rather keen on you, you know." He hugged Hunter more closely to him. "Now then, I think you had better tell me just exactly what's going on."

～⌒～

The Nocturne had been infiltrated on port and starboard by members of the rebel Vampirate crews coming over from the sterns of *The Diablo* and *The Tiger*. Lorcan and his squad raced into position to defend the ship. Lorcan worried about what this meant. Had Sidorio and his comrades won out? Were the other two ships now overtaken by the Vampirates? As he watched more of the rebel crews leaping across, his blood ran cold. Had the unthinkable finally happened?

Suddenly, Lorcan felt a hand on his shoulder. Reflexively, he turned and saw Mimma standing, grinning, in front of him. The hand remained on his shoulder, but as he moved, it slid down his front and fell to the deck in front of him.

"Don't you like my gift?" Mimma said. "It's freshly severed. I had a little suck on the arteries on my way over."

Lorcan glanced with revulsion from the severed hand to the equally repellent Mimma.

"Let's play a little game, shall we?" Mimma said. "It's called guess whose hand it is . . . or, rather, was!"

"No games," Lorcan said, preparing to charge at her.

"Johnny told me you were a no-fun zone, and he was right," Mimma said, leaping into action. "Well, if you won't play, I may as well just tell you. It's your mate, Cate's. See what I did there, Furey? *Your mate, Cate!* I'm a poet!"

"That's *not* Cate's hand," Lorcan said with a shudder.

Mimma shrugged. "Maybe it is and maybe it isn't! And maybe I just dispatched her to a better place and maybe I sent off that Moonshine bloke along with her."

"You're full of talk," Lorcan said. "Why don't we see if you can walk the walk?"

Mimma winked at him. "You're on! I've heard all about your fancy moves. Let's see if you live up to all the hype!"

❧ ❧

Not far away from where Lorcan fought, Grace opened her eyes and found herself inside her cabin, looking up into Oskar's face.

"Thank goodness!" he cried. "Grace, I've been *so* worried about you."

Grace seemed disconcerted. She raised herself up on her elbows and looked curiously about her surroundings. Below her, she saw the open book. As she lifted her hand, the writing swiftly dissolved.

Breathing rapidly, she looked up at Oskar once more. "Did I succeed?" she asked. "Have they arrived?"

Oskar shook his head slowly. "You're not making sense," he said. "You've been out cold for almost an hour."

"No," she said. "I've been on a journey—a mission to fetch reinforcements."

Oskar shook his head. "You fell," he said. "And I think you may have concussed yourself. Wait! Don't get up too quickly. Let me check your head for wounds."

43

THE LOST BUCCANEER

"This is the last of them," Captain Quivers told Captain Grammont as she shepherded the junior class through the wooden doors into the Rotunda. Lisabeth Quivers looked back across the lawns of Pirate Academy, out past the harbor arch, to the mass of ships locked in conflict. She realized that she could no longer tell which belonged to her comrades and which to the enemy armada.

"Quick now!" Captain Grammont addressed the students, leading them across the floor of the Rotunda. "Onto the platform! Okay, that's enough for now."

The impromptu elevator began its descent to the subterranean bunker. There were excited looks on the young kids' faces; it seemed that even during times of stress, there were small pleasures to be derived. The rest of the class lately ushered in by Lisabeth Quivers stood by, eagerly awaiting their own turn on the elevator.

As the platform returned to draw level with the mosaic floor, Captain Grammont beckoned over the next group of students. As he did so, there was a sudden clinking noise overhead. Looking up, Grammont saw that the cases of swords were vibrating. He couldn't help but wonder what might prompt such unusual movement. Dark thoughts of incendiary devices on the roof crossed his mind but he gritted his teeth and maintained his sangfroid.

Captain Quivers's eyes had also been drawn up to the glass cases. Their movement was becoming more and more agitated. Determined not to alarm her young charges, still she exchanged an anxious glance with Captain Grammont. They were all standing directly beneath the rattling cases. The cases had begun to strike one another now. Glass chimed on glass, sending out a discordant sequence of notes, which made an ugly music with the ever-present wail of the "under attack" sirens.

"Should we..." Captain Quivers began. Before she could complete the thought, the cases suddenly shattered and shards of glass rained down from above.

"Run, everyone!" Grammont cried. "This way!"

The kids screamed, racing for cover. The falling glass was the least of it. As the cases broke, the hundred or more swords contained within them began their own descent. Razor-sharp steel and silver began hurtling down toward the students.

Captain Quivers pulled two of the youngsters within her grasp out of the danger zone. She saw Grammont do the same from the other side.

But then, the strangest thing of all happened. Before the swords could reach any of the pirate apprentices, the weapons vaporized before their very eyes.

"What the . . ." began Grammont, from the sidelines.

"But how?" asked Captain Quivers, her arms tightly hugging the students she had rescued.

Mercifully, miraculously, they had escaped with only minor cuts and grazes. Now they all looked on in wonder.

"Where did the swords go, Headmaster?" asked one of the young students.

Captain Grammont was unable to answer. He just shook his head.

◄—✦—►

On the deck of *The Tiger*, Bo Yin and Jasmine were fighting side by side at the rear of the ship. As they each dispatched their latest victims, Jasmine turned to her young protégée. "You're doing great!" she exclaimed.

"Thanks!" Bo flushed with pride. She was having fun, momentarily pushing aside all thoughts of the stakes of tonight's battle and enjoying implementing all her expert training.

Bo Yin and Jasmine looked along the length of the deck. During the course of the fighting, it had thinned out because of the casualties, but now it was suddenly full again.

"Do you see what I see?" Bo Yin asked.

Jasmine nodded. Her first response was alarm. Where had this new crew sprung from? She wasn't aware of any new ship pulling up alongside.

"Jasmine!" Bo Yin said. "Look around the deck." Her tone was full of wonder.

Jasmine soon understood why. The deck had suddenly been infiltrated by new combatants. But the new fighters had not arrived from any ships, conventional or otherwise. They were utterly familiar.

"There's Osbert," Jasmine said, "who died five months ago. And Bima. We lost her when we took back *The Diablo*, remember?"

Bo Yin nodded. "That's right, but she's back again— and she doesn't seem to have lost any of her combat skills."

Jasmine's eyes were wide and her heart was racing. "I don't know how this happened, Bo, but our dead have come back to join the fight."

They watched as a Vampirate's sword passed clean through one of the new arrivals. The dead pirate swiftly staked the Vampirate for his troubles. Jasmine turned to Bo Yin, awestruck.

"It's as if the swords of our dead crew members are even more lethal than ours!"

"Yes," Bo agreed, elated. "But it's not *just* our ship's dead, Jasmine. See that guy over there? He's Chang Po. A complete pirate legend. He once ran the Red Flag Fleet with Cheng I Sao. Look, she's fighting alongside him! I read all about her in my dad's history books—she has much in common with Captain Li."

Jasmine gasped. "You read about them in history books? Can this really be happening? Have the dead come back to help us win this battle?"

Just then, Jasmine saw a familiar figure materialize right before her eyes.

"Commodore Kuo!" she exclaimed.

"At your service!" said the commodore with a smile. He rested his hand on her shoulder. Jasmine's eyes turned to his hand. How could the swords of the enemy plow uninterrupted through the bodies of the dead pirates and yet she could feel John Kuo's hand as if it were live flesh? He smiled at her now and it seemed that he had read her thoughts.

"Only our enemies cannot touch us," he said. "Now don't let me put you off your game, Deputy Peacock. I've been hearing such good things about you."

Renewed with energy and purpose, Jasmine and Bo raced back into the fray, supported on all sides by their comrades, old and new.

On *The Diablo*, Cate was concerned. She hadn't seen or heard Moonshine for some time. Not since he'd been drawn into combat by Mimma. Cate feared for the fate of *The Diablo*'s captain but there was nothing she could do while she was still embroiled in her duel with Stukeley.

She felt a sudden stab of pain in her leg. Glancing down, she saw blood pooling through a slit in her leggings.

"You took your eye off the ball, there," Stukeley reprimanded her. "Rookie mistake."

He was right. She was angry with herself. "It won't happen again!" she said, launching into another intricate series of moves, devised in partnership with Lorcan.

But this time, though the moves themselves were impressive, somehow Stukeley guessed the angle she was coming from and cut off her attack before she had launched it.

"Is that the best you've got?" he taunted her. "After all the time, effort, and money you've put into developing a revolutionary combat strategy, I expected more."

"I've got plenty more tricks up my sleeve," Cate said bullishly. Hopefully, he'd buy it. The truth was, she was short on tricks, imagination, and raw energy. Jez Stukeley had always been an exceptional fighter, and it seemed that now that he had supernatural abilities to throw into the mix, he was in another league altogether. One completely beyond her own.

Gritting her teeth, she threw herself back into the fight, but, once again, he swiftly neutralized her attack. "Someone's running low on gas," he said, smiling through extended fangs. "Not long now and I'll be tasting your blood, Cate."

The repellent thought made Cate shudder. She readied herself for his attack, but something had thrown him off his mettle.

"Impossible!" he rasped. His gaze was directed beyond Cate. She didn't dare turn and follow his stare. It was too dangerous.

But she felt a reassuring hand on her shoulder and heard a familiar voice in her ear.

"Thought you could do with some help, Catie!"

Bart! Could it really be Bart? She must be imagining it—perhaps a sign that she was close to the end. But then he stepped past her and drew his sword against Stukeley— one buccaneer against the other. Stukeley was as dazed as she was. Impossible as it was to conceive, Bart Pearce had come back from the dead to fight one more duel.

Barbarro and Trofie were just about holding their own against Lola, though she was now backed up by Nathalie, Angelika, and Camille.

"Face it, pirates!" Lola crowed. "You're outnumbered." As her comrades fell into a tight formation around her, Lola reached out her hand and grabbed Trofie by the golden wrist, her other hand lifting her sword toward Trofie's swanlike neck.

"No!" Barbarro cried.

Lola laughed at the frail mortals. She was still laughing

as a pair of hands reached from behind her and threw her roughly to the side. Simultaneously someone pushed forward and, in swift succession, knifed Angelika and Camille. The two dead Vampirates fell to the deck, contorting as their bodies began to burn. Lola was stunned—what weapons could have such an effect?

As Trofie stumbled forward, Barbarro reached out to catch her. He found himself gazing up at his two dead brothers. Both Molucco, who had dealt with Lola, and Porfirio, who had dispatched her two aides, looked decidedly pleased with themselves.

They both extended their swords toward Barbarro's. The tips of the two pirate captains' swords struck against each other. They stood there, waiting—it seemed—for Barbarro to join them. At first, he stood rooted to the spot, mouth agape. Then, still unable to form words, he raised his sword and felt the metal's connection with the two other blades.

"Just like old times!" Molucco declared.

"Yes," Porfirio agreed. "We always did depend on one another to get us out of scrapes! One for all..."

"...and all for one!" Molucco said, laughing loudly.

The familiar sound, which Barbarro had never thought to hear again, delighted him more than he could put into words. "But how can you be here?" he asked.

"If anyone has a score to settle with these bloodsuckers, it's the Brothers Wrathe!" Porfirio said.

"Too right!" agreed Molucco. "I've got a particular cowboy Vampirate in my sights!"

"Don't forget the harpy!" Trofie said, staring into the empty space where Lola had stood only a moment ago. "Where did she get to?"

"She can't have got far, *min elskling*!" Barbarro cried, grabbing his dear wife's hand and gazing in wonder at his beloved brothers. "Come on, let's finish off these demons—together!"

Johnny wasn't sure quite why he felt compelled to tell Olivier everything. It was as if the older Vampirate had administered a truth serum, though he had had no opportunity to do so. Maybe it was simply a reflection of Johnny's guilty conscience. There was something of the priest in Olivier's demeanor. Perhaps it was this and this alone that elicited Johnny's willing confession.

"It was Stukeley's idea," he continued. "He wants to break Lola's spirit and eliminate the threat to our position in the Vampirate hierarchy."

Olivier nodded, seemingly unshocked by Johnny's confession. "I understand," he said. "Heaven knows, I'm familiar with the frustrations of playing second fiddle."

"You are?" Johnny said, wondering how he could take Hunter from Olivier.

"Why, yes," Olivier said. "You could say I've made a career out of it."

Johnny stepped toward Olivier. Olivier might ooze authority, but Johnny was young and virile, and he had a silver dagger still concealed about his person.

But this time, things didn't go his way. As he reached for the dagger, he found it was missing, and, glancing around in his confusion, he saw that miraculously it had made its way into Olivier's clenched fist. Baby Hunter was still tucked securely in the crook of Olivier's other arm. Olivier was smiling.

"Now look, Cowboy, I'm going to talk fast because you don't have much time. But no more tricks, you understand? I'm a dhampir, you see. Rhymes with vampire but infinitely more powerful. Your little friend Grace—she's one, too, more's the pity, but we'll let that lie for now. I'm the one calling the shots here and now." He smiled. "I've listened to your story and I'm sympathetic to your predicament, truly I am. These two mewling babes do present a threat to your future career and, as it happens, also to mine."

Johnny found himself grinning. You just never knew when the wheel of fortune was going to turn back in your favor, but it sounded very much like Olivier was going to cut him a deal.

"I shall permit you to take one of the infants," Olivier continued. "Lola charged me with looking after baby Hunter so I'm sure you'll understand my reluctance to let him out of my sight." He brought his finger to the tip of Hunter's nose, then looked up again, smiling serenely at Johnny.

Evil was wriggling in Johnny's arms. Johnny held him close, his eyes still fixed on Olivier. "You're going to let me take Evil and . . . get rid of him? And you won't tell Lola?"

Olivier made a mime of zipping his lips. "Mum's the word!" he said with a smile.

Unable to believe his good fortune, Johnny decided to waste no more time. He strode toward the door, hugging Evil close to his chest.

"Whatever you plan to do with him," Olivier said, "you might want to avail yourself of one of the lightboats currently idling in the waters just below. You'll be much less visible than if you run across the decks."

"Thank you," Johnny said, feeling genuinely in Olivier's debt. "I'll pay you back for this."

Olivier nodded. "Yes, you will," he said. "Now, listen once again, Cowboy, as I elucidate—*that means explain to you*—the price of my silence."

Cheng Li had realized the impossible was happening and that her crew had been joined not only by their slaughtered comrades but also by some of the leading stars of the pirate firmament. There was no time to dwell on how such a miracle had occurred. Once, not long ago, she would have dismissed the possibility if she had not witnessed it with her own eyes. Now, she was hard put not to stand back and marvel at the sword skills of Chang Po and, in particular, Cheng I Sao. But there was no time to stop and stare. The dead pirates had evidently come back for a reason—to make the difference in this mother of all battles. She needed to capitalize on this miraculous gift and go send Sidorio to his final resting place—though, truly, rest was the very last thing she wished for the self-styled King of the Vampirates. Feeling flushed with murderous intent, Cheng Li set off toward the center of the deck, the true incarnation of evil in her sights.

But, before she could reach him, one of his cronies leaped out across her path. She could have screamed with frustration, but if she had to fight one more duel to claim the jewel in the Vampirate crown, so be it. But, as she lifted her sword, she saw in front of her a wondrous sight.

A face she had stared at every day of her life, whether in flesh or in pictorial form, appeared before her. And the body it was attached to leaped into action and attacked her Vampirate adversary from behind. As the demon fell at her feet with a thud, Cheng Li found herself reunited with the man who had haunted her dreams and nightmares—Chang Ko Li.

"Father!" she said, her voice never more rich with wonder.

"We have waited a long time for this meeting," Chang Ko Li said. "But our reunion must be deferred a little longer, my wondrous daughter. You are commander in chief here and I only came to help clear the path for you." He lifted his sword and pointed toward Sidorio. "Go now. Make history!"

Her heart pulsing with light, Cheng Li raced past her father and into the duel she had been hungering for for so long.

━ ⌒ ━

"Don't cry, little fella," Johnny told Evil as he lowered him into the lightboat, which, true to Olivier's word, was idling in the waters beneath *The Vagabond*. All about them were the sound and fury of the battle, but, strangely, as Johnny let loose their moorings, it was almost peaceful down here.

"There," Johnny said softly as their boat drifted away in the shadows of the vessels above. "We're going on a little journey, see?" He smiled down at the wriggling, giggling baby. "Well it's a little journey for me, but quite a major one for *you*. Uncle Johnny has a big ol' surprise for you. Yes, he does!"

━ ⌒ ━

At the rear of *The Tiger*, Connor saw Cheng Li racing toward Sidorio, who had taken up position near the ship's mast.

"No!" Connor wanted to cry. If anyone was going to take out Sidorio, it had to be him, not Cheng Li. But his own way was blocked by several of Sidorio's crew. He'd have to unleash a spree of violence such as he never had before in order to make it.

As he weighed both his odds and his strategy, he was dismayed to see that Cheng Li was not alone in closing in on Sidorio. It appeared that both Obsidian and Jacoby were closing in on the Vampirate leader, too.

Connor's decision had been made for him. A killing spree it was!

Lorcan was still sparring with Mimma when he saw Grace and Oskar running toward them.

"Stay back!" he cried out to his comrades. Mimma misunderstood.

"I can't kill you from a distance!" she cried, preparing to lunge.

Lorcan was wrong-footed, his attention distracted by Grace's sudden appearance, but as Mimma hurtled toward him, he saw that her threat had been neutralized. A sword had been plunged into her back and she was tumbling, arms scrabbling, stricken with panic, toward the deck. Her head came crashing down against the deck boards.

Grace stepped forward to retrieve her sword.

"You?" Mimma said, staring up at Grace in shock. "How could you, Gracie? I'm your friend, remember?"

"The name's Grace," she said, withdrawing Grace O'Malley's sword from Mimma's flesh. "And don't be over-dramatic. I haven't dealt you a fatal blow—yet. Look, see how your wound is already beginning to heal."

Mimma glanced down and saw that Grace was right. She looked up again to find Grace still standing threateningly over her. "If you ever attack my boyfriend again, the outcome will be much worse for you, understand?"

Mimma nodded slowly.

"It's time for you to leave this ship now," Grace continued, glancing up at the sky. "Dawn is on its way."

Mimma saw the truth of Grace's words. Other members of her crew had already reached *The Calabria* and had steered the ship around. Now she leaped from *The Nocturne*, across to safety.

After she and her cronies had departed, Lorcan turned to Grace. "Thank you!" he said. "Not just for saving my life but for all these fresh allies." He gestured across the deck, where the dead pirates were catching their breath, having turned the tide of the battle. "I take it that it was you who brought them back?"

Grace smiled, nodding. "Yes," she said. "Yes, I did." Her eyes were bright. "I went to Jack Tar's Cavern and asked for their help. Oh, Lorcan. We're going to win this war, aren't we? It's going to end here, tonight. And neither

Connor nor I need to die because I've already been to the realm of the dead and made it back! The prophecy has been fulfilled and we're both safe."

Lorcan had never experienced greater relief.

Oskar grinned at him. "Quite a catch, your girlfriend, by all accounts."

All Lorcan could do was nod.

—◦—

Sidorio smiled as he faced his three adversaries—Cheng Li, Jacoby, and Obsidian.

"Who wants to die first?" He grinned. "I know, let's take it in order of seniority." He waved his sword at Jacoby. "You, blondie—you're not even a captain, are you?"

Jacoby was unabashed. "It's a mistake to be so hung up on status," he said, making a charge at Sidorio. He landed a clean strike on Sidorio's arm. A deep gash opened up in the Vampirate's flesh.

Sidorio was surprised but not perturbed. Already, he could feel the fibers of his arm knitting themselves back together. As he stared back at Jacoby, he saw the kid was grinning at him. And he saw that the kid had fangs.

"You've got promise, Vampirate," Sidorio told him. "But you're on the wrong team."

"No, I'm not," Jacoby retorted. "Your group tried to recruit me once but I declined. I'm a Nocturnal, *not* a Vampirate."

His arm now fully restored, Sidorio shook his head. "There's no such thing as Nocturnals. There are just pirates and Vampirates. Anything else is just deluded."

"There's no one more deluded than you." It was Obsidian Darke who spoke now. "You always thought you were better than the rest of us. You even thought you were better than Julius Caesar, though he was the first one to kill you."

"The first?" Sidorio asked, his eyes once more taking in the hateful sight of Obsidian Darke.

"That's right!" Cheng Li said, stepping closer. "Caesar was the first, but now you're going to be dispatched by one of us to a second, more lasting, kind of death."

Sidorio laughed. "It's three of you versus me, but the odds are still in my favor."

As he spoke, he lost sight of Obsidian. He had to assume that the bloodless Vampirate had sneaked around him. Time to take care of one of the flunkies, then he'd dispatch Obsidian Darke to his ultimate torment.

With fire in his eyes, Sidorio lunged at Cheng Li. But, at the last second—having successfully wrong-footed his opponents—he turned and directed his sword toward Jacoby. "Die, Nocturnal!" he cried, burying his sword deep in the young man's chest.

It was only as the body fell to the deck that Sidorio realized his mistake. Jacoby had jumped clear of the attack, but a fourth adversary had come into play.

Sidorio looked down in horror as he saw Connor, his

own son, impaled on his sword. Connor's blood was pooling on the deck, his eyes already distant.

"You've killed Connor!" Cheng Li yelled at him, shocked and outraged.

"No!" Sidorio cried, feeling his own heart cracking into a million shards, his head splintering with never-before-known pain. Not Connor! But his eyes told him the unthinkable was true. He, Sidorio, had killed his own dear son.

44

GOOD-BYES AT DAWN

Sidorio was frozen to the spot above Connor's fallen body. From three sides, swords now pressed against his neck—from Jacoby, from Cheng Li, and from Obsidian. Sidorio was trapped but still he managed to cry out to his son.

"Open your eyes, Connor!"

Meanwhile, Jasmine called to her comrades. "Come... Captain Tempest. He is wounded! He needs urgent medical assistance."

Connor's eyes opened but her relief was short-lived. His eyes seemed different to her somehow—focused somewhere far off.

Jasmine fell to her knees at his side. "Connor!" she cried. "Connor! Stay with me!" Seeing the pool of blood fanning out from underneath him, she glanced up at

Cheng Li. "There's so much blood...I'm not sure how much longer he can last."

Jasmine's hands moved across Connor's chest, then she steadied herself and drew Sidorio's sword out from Connor's chest. As she cleared the entry wound, Connor's blood spattered up onto her face. Instinctively, she closed her eyes. When she opened them again, she saw that Connor's eyes were now closing. "No," she cried. "Don't go, Connor. Don't go!"

Her words seemed to take effect. His eyelids fluttered and briefly opened. She leaned over him, placing her hand against his cheek. But then his eyes began to close once more, and, somehow, she knew that they were never going to open again. She gazed up at Cheng Li, feeling utterly bereft.

"I'm so sorry, Jasmine," Cheng Li said, her own voice deep with emotion. "But there's nothing more we can do for him."

Rising to her feet, Jasmine spat at Sidorio. "You monster!" She had never felt more pain, nor felt more intensely the desire to inflict it. Seeing the tips of her three comrades' swords pressing into Sidorio's thick neck, she cried out, "What are you waiting for? Send him to oblivion!"

As she finished speaking, the air was suddenly riven with the sound of screams. They filled the sky. It was disconcerting at first, but then the pirates understood. The screams were sirens, coming from the Vampirate ships.

One of Sidorio's last remaining crew members called

out to him from the edge of the deck. "Sire, we must retreat! Dawn is coming!"

"Save yourself!" Sidorio responded. "I can take care of myself!"

With a worried expression, the Vampirate nodded and jumped ship.

"Dawn?" Jasmine confronted Jacoby. "You have to get inside. Now! I'll take your place." She extended her own sword to Sidorio's neck as Jacoby, with obvious reluctance, stood down.

"That's it! Run away, little *Nocturnal*," Sidorio sneered. "Run to safety!"

Irritated in the extreme, Jasmine pushed her sword deeper into Sidorio's flesh. He flashed her a murderous look but was powerless, for now, to do anything more.

———

"That odious sound is the Vampirates' call to retreat," Lorcan told Grace, on board *The Nocturne*. "You were right, my love. The war is won!"

Grace punched the air with delight. "I knew it!" she said. "I can't wait to see Connor again and tell him we're going to be okay."

Lorcan hugged her. "I need to clear the deck of our own crew before it gets any lighter," he said. "I'll come and find you inside."

She nodded, flushed with relief and exhilaration as she saw the enemy ships filling up in preparation for their urgent retreat. She leaned against the deck rail, thinking of everything she and her comrades had accomplished. This victory had been hard-won.

"Grace!" said an urgent voice, close behind her. It was immediately familiar but it wasn't Lorcan, nor Oskar. Turning, she found Johnny at her side. In his arms was a bundle, which, on closer inspection, looked very much like a baby.

"Johnny!" Grace exclaimed. "What are you doing here? It's almost dawn. You should be safe inside."

"I know," he said. "We don't have much time, but I needed to see you."

Grace nodded, leaning closer toward him. "Is that one of Lola's twins?" she asked.

"His name is Evil," Johnny said. "Would you like to hold him?" He didn't give Grace a chance to decline before thrusting baby Evil into her arms.

"Poor baby!" Grace said as the infant made himself comfortable. "As if the odds weren't already stacked against him! What kind of a name is Evil?"

"You can change it if you like," Johnny said.

Grace glanced up at him. "What do you mean?" She gazed at him intently. "Why did you bring him to me?"

"I stole him," Johnny said. "Stukeley wanted me to kill him." He shook his head. "I couldn't do that, Grace. But I had to get him away from Lola and Sidorio. He'll have a better chance at life with you." His dark eyes met hers. "With you and Lorcan, I mean."

Grace's eyes narrowed. "You want me and Lorcan to bring up Lola's baby?"

Johnny nodded. "I would have brought them both to you if I had the chance, but Hunter...well, I couldn't get Hunter away. But you can save this little guy. You'll do it, won't you, Grace? You understand why he needs to be kept away from them?"

She nodded with grim conviction. "Everyone is better off away from those two. But Johnny, *you* should stay, too. Leave that world behind. Come with this baby to *The Nocturne* and make a fresh start. Obsidian and the others will welcome you, I know they will."

Johnny considered her proposition for a moment. Then he shook his head. "The die is cast for me," he said. "I have to get back before the light scalds me. But I'll sleep a little more easy knowing I did something good at last."

He stepped closer in order to directly address baby Evil. "Be a good boy for your new folks," he said. "Or you'll have Uncle Johnny to answer to!" Grinning, he turned back to Grace. "I'd best get going now."

Grace looked into his eyes imploringly. "Please stay," she said.

He shook his head again. "I appreciate the offer, truly I do. It just wouldn't work out, Grace, not for any of us."

A tear escaped from Grace's eye. "I really wish I could help you," she said. "Ever since I met you, I've wished I could find a way to help you change. There's so much goodness inside you, but you just can't seem to see it."

Johnny was genuinely moved. "You'd best stop right there," he said, "or I'm going to start blubbering myself." Letting out a sigh, he resumed in a more pragmatic tone, "There is something I need from you before I head back. Do you happen to have in your possession a book? Some kind of magic book about being a dhampir?"

Grace frowned. "No," she lied. "I don't."

"I really need that book," Johnny said, a note of pleading in his voice.

"I did have it, but I gave it to someone else," Grace said. "Someone who needs it more than me." Before Johnny could make a further appeal, Grace nodded toward the sky. "If you're going, you need to go right now," she said.

Johnny saw that she was right. "I hope to see you again sometime, once all this dust has settled." He leaned over and kissed her tenderly on the cheek. "Remember, Grace, the ride is far from over."

Then he stole away into the night, leaving Lola and Sidorio's baby already sleeping peacefully in her arms.

———

"Where is he?" Lola cried, running along the corridor of *The Vagabond*, Nathalie at her side. "Where is he?" Each cry more desperate than the one before. "Can you see him?"

"There he is, Captain!" Nathalie cried, pointing out through the porthole toward the deck of *The Tiger*.

As Lola came to a stop beside her, Nathalie opened up the porthole so that their view was no longer impeded by its smeared surface. Now Lola stepped forward and saw the terrible truth—Sidorio, her dear husband and father of her twins, commander in chief of the empire of night, was trapped on the deck of the enemy ship.

"Come away from the window!" Nathalie urged her. "The light!"

A single tear fell across the black-heart tattoo around Lola's eye. "How can you tell me to step away from the light when you see the predicament Sidorio is in?" She remained at the window, watching with horror as the light grew more golden. Dawn was imminent now. She saw the light stalk hungrily across the decks of the pirate ships, swiftly overpowering their sails and rigging.

Her eyes returned to the deck of *The Tiger*, watching in mounting horror as the light began to steal its way from the prow to the center of the deck, where Sidorio was effectively pinioned by his three captors.

———

"Let's destroy him!" Jasmine repeated.

"No," Cheng Li said. "We'll simply allow the light to do its work." She glanced across at Obsidian Darke, seeking his agreement. He nodded.

They stood there, their three swords pressed into Sidorio's neck, as the light crept across the deck toward them. Suddenly it was upon them, bathing Jasmine and Cheng Li's face with welcome warmth. Obsidian Darke kept his head bowed. He might be able to endure the light, but still it was not something he welcomed. He kept his face fixed on Sidorio's.

As light fell on Sidorio's forehead, the Vampirate grinned and lifted his face, as best he could, to meet the sun's rays. He laughed, his eyes turning from Cheng Li to Obsidian. "You see. I'm just as powerful as you now. The light can do me no harm."

Jasmine was the first to notice that the tip of her sword, still plunged into Sidorio's flesh, had begun to glow red. It was as if the sword was being heated from within Sidorio. She turned to Cheng Li, wondering if she had noticed, too. Cheng Li nodded discreetly, then turned her eyes back to their captive.

Sidorio's expression had faltered. He appeared far less cocky now. In fact, he looked as if he was in considerable pain. There was fire coming from within him. The skin on his face and the exposed parts of his body rapidly darkened, cut through with traces of fire, like embers. Already, his face had started to disintegrate—no more than ash floating away on the ocean breeze. There was a sudden splintering as his shoulder detached from his body and fell to the deck, breaking into a thousand tiny pieces.

"No!" Lola cried out, still watching the nightmarish scene unfolding on the opposite deck. She lifted her crossbow and swiftly loaded it with a single silver arrow. "I'm going to make Obsidian Darke pay for this. Pathetic excuse for a Vampirate that he is!"

Lola aimed the crossbow sight through the open port-hole at her unsuspecting target. With a guttural cry, she sent the silver arrow flying through the air and onto the deck of *The Tiger*.

Perhaps it was the infinitesimal movement of *The Vagabond*; perhaps a sudden gust of ocean breeze; or perhaps simply the maelstrom of Lola's own emotions. Whichever, her aim was a little off, and the arrow sailed clear past Obsidian and deep into the heart of Cheng Li.

"No!" Cheng Li cried, falling toward the deck. "Not yet! There's so much more to do!"

Her fall was broken by a pair of strong arms, which reached out from behind her. They broke her fall and lowered her gently down onto the deck boards, but still the hands kept hold of Cheng Li.

"Don't worry, daughter," whispered a voice in her ear. "You're safe now."

On the deck of *The Typhon*, Barbarro shook his head with relief and delight. "We did it!" he said. "Together, we won this."

"Yes," Molucco said, squeezing his brother's shoulder. "Another victory for the Brothers Wrathe!" He turned to Porfirio. "We should be getting back, don't you think?"

Porfirio nodded. "I think so."

"Wait!" Barbarro said, reaching out to Molucco. "Moonshine is on *The Diablo*, brother. Let me call him over so he can thank you in person for giving him the chance to be captain. It's been the making of the lad."

Molucco smiled. "I knew he'd pull through," he said. "There's a lot of me in that kid, I always thought."

Now Trofie addressed her erstwhile brother-in-law. "I have to ask you this," she said. "If you have such a high opinion of Moonshine, why did you apportion the majority share of your inheritance to Connor Tempest?"

"Trofie!" Barbarro exclaimed in shock. "This is hardly the time..."

"I have to ask," Trofie repeated. "When will I get another chance, *min elskling*?"

Unfazed by her question, Molucco shrugged. "It felt like the right thing to do," he said. "Moonshine has all the advantages of *your* wealth and status. I thought Connor deserved a leg up." A strange look came over his eyes. "It doesn't really matter now."

"On the contrary," Trofie said. "It matters very much."

Porfirio turned to Barbarro. "We really should say our good-byes now, brother."

"Won't you stay until I can get word to Moonshine?" Barbarro asked. "He'd love to see you again, and I'd so like you to meet him now that he's all grown up."

"I would have liked that, too," Porfirio said with evident sadness, "but it's not possible. Jack Tar's is calling us back." He turned to Molucco. "Come on, brother, the clock is ticking. We must take our leave."

Molucco nodded. The two brothers hugged Barbarro and Trofie good-bye. There were tears in Barbarro's eyes as he finally released Molucco.

"We'll see each other again," Molucco said.

"Not too soon, I hope!" Trofie said.

Porfirio and Molucco laughed at that. "Quite right," Molucco said. "Not too soon—for all our sakes!"

━━━ ⌒ ━━━

Bart and Cate stood together at the deck rail of *The Diablo*. They had stood there many times before, but they both knew this would be the very last time.

"I have to go now," Bart told Cate, stroking her cheek. "But before I do, there's something I want to say to you."

She looked up at him, her eyes already filled with tears. "I wish I could come with you. I wish I had died tonight—"

"Cate! Darling Cate, you have everything to live for. Please don't live a life of regret or dwell on what could have been. Know that I loved you, and always will, but open up your heart so that you can let someone else in."

"It's too soon," Cate said, shaking her head. "You're a bloody tough act to follow, Bart Pearce."

"Fair enough." He grinned. "I wouldn't want you to get over me in a heartbeat. In fact, I don't want you to get over me at all, but I *do* want you to get on with your life." Then his expression changed. "I'm sorry, Catie, but I really do have to go now." He opened his arms and drew her into a lingering embrace.

As they reluctantly parted once more, Bart took Cate's hand in his. His eyes lit up with surprise and delight. "You're wearing my gran's wedding ring! How on oceans..."

"Connor found it and gave it to me," Cate told him. "He told me the question you were going to ask me."

Bart shook his head, beaming broadly though his eyes were wet. "No flies on that Tempest kid, eh?"

Cate nodded, smiling.

"Well." Bart looked suddenly at a loss. "I'm rubbish at good-byes, and there is no harder good-bye than this." He began to turn.

"Wait!" Cate said, reaching out her hand. "I know you have to go and I know I won't be seeing you again anytime soon. I want you to know that I heard what you said and

I'll do my best." She nodded. "It may take some time, but I'll do my best, truly."

Their gaze met once more and the love in both their eyes was luminous.

"And that question you never got around to asking me..." Cate lifted her finger, so that the light of the new morning caught the beautiful ring. "Just in case you were in any doubt, my answer would have been a resounding yes."

"Yes!" Bart cried, smiling and punching the air as he began to fade from view.

John Kuo helped Cheng Li back onto her feet. She surveyed the deck, wondering where Jasmine and Jacoby had got to. Though the battle was only just over, her head was already buzzing with thoughts of what she should do next. Ahab Back would want a detailed debrief, no doubt, and she would have to organize a fitting memorial for Connor. So much to do, so little time—just like always!

She turned to Commodore Kuo. "John," she said. "It was so wonderful to see you again, and fight alongside you, but now I have to get back to my crew."

Commodore Kuo smiled at her softly as Chang Ko Li joined him at his side.

"Your crew is going to be just fine without you," said Kuo. "Jasmine and Jacoby will do you proud."

"Without me?" Cheng Li asked, confused for a moment. Then it dawned on her. "John, am I dead?"

He nodded. "I'm afraid so," he said. "I thought you realized when the pain went away."

Cheng Li shook her head. "No, I just assumed I'd made a remarkable recovery." She sighed. "Well, this is quite a blow, I must say." She turned to her father.

"It's always a blow," he said. "And, doubtless, you'll be thinking of everything you had yet to achieve."

Cheng Li nodded. "Yes," she said. "But how did you know?"

The corners of Chang Ko Li's eyes crinkled. "Not far from the tree falls the fruit," he said with a smile. "But in time you will come to see that your achievements were many and your place in the annals of pirate history is assured."

"It is?" Cheng Li's eyes brightened.

Both men nodded and then extended their arms toward her, ready to lead her away from the deck of *The Tiger* and toward her next big adventure. Cheng Li found herself walking down through the ocean itself, arm in arm with her father and her mentor. She stole one last lingering glance at her beautiful ship, then turned to find John Kuo and Chang Ko Li both smiling serenely at her. Together, the three pirate legends disappeared beneath the silver waves.

SEVEN
DAYS
LATER...

45

NEW BEGINNINGS

MA KETTLE'S TAVERN

"No words," Barbarro said, "can do justice to what we have all experienced these past seven months—the wounds we have sustained, the losses we have endured. We came perilously close to losing not just this war but our whole world." He looked out across the tavern, his dark eyes full of woe. Ma's was full to the rafters with pirates tonight, just like the best of the old days. But no one made so much as a sound and all eyes were trained on Barbarro, standing on the small stage in the center of the tavern.

"But we won," he said, a smile creeping across his face. "We came together as an incredible force—an unprecedented alliance between the pirate world and the realm of the Nocturnals—and we won! I want you—each and every one of you—to remember how you're feeling tonight. I want you to pass on the story to your children and grandchildren and their children. Remind them of the war that we had to fight for our sakes but, more important, for theirs. But, more than anything, I want each of your hearts to be filled with pride at what we have all achieved."

There were tears in his eyes as he finished. Trofie stepped across the stage and took his hand as a wall of noise erupted from all around. Pirates were standing on their tables and chairs, clapping their hands, stamping their feet, and cheering at the pirate captain. Of the three Brothers Wrathe, Barbarro was the least given to public speaking. He stood there, greatly humbled by the response to his few inadequate words.

When the clamor finally subsided, Barbarro raised his hand aloft.

"Thank you, my dear friends," he said. "And now, I would like to call up Deputy Jasmine Peacock to say a few words about her lost comrades."

As Barbarro beckoned to her, Jasmine felt Jacoby squeeze her shoulder supportively, then release his hand so she could walk across to the stage. She realized she was trembling. It was a short distance in steps but it felt like the longest journey of her life.

As Jasmine joined Barbarro on the stage, the captain and his wife stepped aside. Jasmine looked up, feeling awe-struck by the number of faces gazing at her expectantly.

What if she let them down? But, in that moment, some rare alchemy occurred and her fear somehow gave way to a calm energy. She knew she had the support of each and every pirate in that room. They were willing her to succeed.

"When Captain Wrathe asked me to say a few words tonight, my first reaction was no," she began. There was a ripple of warm laughter across the pirate ranks. It was reassuring. Jasmine fixed on Jacoby's face. He gave her a nod. "But, when I gave it some thought," she continued, "I knew that I wanted to stand up and speak briefly about two of my lost comrades, Captain Connor Tempest and Commodore Cheng Li."

At the mere mention of their names, there was thunderous applause throughout the tavern. Jasmine waited patiently until, once more, a hush descended throughout the tavern and all eyes were trained upon her.

"It's very simple, really," Jasmine said. "They were two of the bravest, most dedicated pirates you could ever hope to meet. They came from strikingly different beginnings. Cheng Li was born into a famous pirating family and, like many of us, was educated at the Pirate Academy. Connor, on the other hand, only came into the world of piracy by chance, exactly a year ago tonight." She sighed. "I wish he could be here to mark that anniversary. I wish they were both here. Every choice of word feels like a cliché under these circumstances, but I can't help thinking that these two bright lights of our universe were taken away from us much too soon."

"Hear, hear!" came a voice from the crowd. It was Lisabeth Quivers's familiar cut-glass tones.

Composing herself, Jasmine glanced about the tavern once more. "I do not intend to dwell on my personal losses. I know that every one of you has lost valued comrades and dear friends through this war. Tonight is a time for celebrating not only our success in achieving this victory but also the enduring friendships we made along the way. I will never forget Cheng Li or Connor. I am confident that their names will be spoken of in our circles for many years to come. But, as important, they will live on in my heart as I know your lost comrades will in each of yours."

She couldn't help the sob that came as she reached her last words. It didn't matter. She had gotten through this, said what she had come here to say. The response to her brief speech was even more rapturous than to Barbarro's. Jasmine stood, rooted to the spot, as applause and cheers came at her from every angle. Embarrassed, she began walking off the stage, but Barbarro gestured for her to remain and it seemed churlish not to do so.

Jasmine scanned the crowd for her dearest friends and comrades. Somehow, seeing their faces made it all a bit less overwhelming. She saw Ma Kettle herself and Sugar Pie waving and cheering at her. Then her eyes met those of Lisabeth Quivers and René Grammont, who stood at the front of the pack of captains who doubled up as teachers at Pirate Academy. She nodded in gratitude at their applause, then found herself breaking into a smile as her eyes turned to where Moonshine Wrathe stood, with Cate on one side and Bo Yin on the other. All three were cheering loudly. She hoped she had spoken adequately on their behalf about the comrades who had touched all their young lives.

Jasmine's eyes moved on — past Commodore Black, who had ceased clapping but nodded at her formally as their eyes met — until, at last, she found Jacoby again. No one was clapping or cheering her more loudly than he was. For a moment, she felt guilt at the complex emotions she had experienced for Jacoby and for Connor. Then, she felt her spirits lift. All that was in the past now. Tonight was a new beginning. A time to honor lost comrades and then to begin again, anew. She didn't know what lay ahead for her, or for any of them, but she was confident that together they would embark on exciting new adventures. Together, there was no need to be afraid.

THE VAGABOND

"This end is not *the* end," Lola declared, pacing up and down her cabin. She stopped abruptly and turned to face her comrades. "This hasn't been in vain. We may have lost this bout, but we'll be back." She wasn't sure whose benefit these words were for — her own or the surviving members of her crew? Now that Sidorio was gone, she was commander in chief of the Empire. They were, she knew, all looking to her to lead them forward, but she had nothing left to give. Feeling cold and rather claustrophobic, she scanned the room, wondering if any of them could sense just how lost she felt.

If anything, the others seemed grateful for the end to the current conflict and for the time and space in which to come to terms with their losses. They seemed calm in a way she found to be utterly at odds with her own tortured state of mind.

Nathalie was sitting on the chaise, reading a picture book to baby Hunter. "We're all going on a pirate hunt," she heard Nathalie recite. It was the boy's favorite.

Olivier sat opposite, smiling and refreshing Mimma's glass. Stukeley and Johnny, who had only lately arrived in her cabin, were still standing in the doorway, chatting quietly. The room was full of people, but it was full of the *wrong* people. Where were Jacqueline and Holly? Where were Angelika and Camille? Where were Sidorio and Evil?

Lola began to shake. Her first thought was that she was in need of a drink. She reached for her glass and lifted it to her lips, but her hand was shaking too much and the glass slipped through her fingers. It fell to the floor and shattered, dark blood pooling on the Persian carpet below. Ordinarily, the loss of an antique glass and a stain on her fine carpet would have upset her deeply, but these were no more than trifles in the present scheme of things. She didn't make any move to clear up the debris; she just stood there shaking uncontrollably. She had never felt more empty or alone.

To her surprise, she saw Stukeley making his way toward her. She was even more surprised when he folded his arms around her. "You're not alone," he said. "Whatever you might think, however you might be feeling, you are not alone."

She had never been in such close physical proximity to Stukeley before. He was somewhat shorter and leaner than Sidorio, and he was surprisingly strong. As their bodies met, she drew fresh strength from his. She felt a wave of calm flowing through her. When he gently released her, she nodded gratefully. "Thank you," she said.

"We're all here for you, Lola," he said. "And we all share in your loss. Sidorio was like a father to me."

His intent, no doubt, was to comfort her, but the mere word *father* made her turn toward Hunter. Seeing him, sitting happily on Nathalie's knee, reaching out with his pudgy little hands to the pictures on the page of his book, Lola couldn't help but think about her other son. She turned back to Stukeley.

"I need your help," she said.

"Anything," he readily agreed. "You can count on me, Lola."

"I cannot do anything, I cannot go on, until I have found my other son," she said. "I intend to search the seven oceans for baby Evil if that's what it takes."

Stukeley nodded somberly. "I'll be there, with you," he said. "Every step of the way." He paused. "But you need to be prepared for the worst. We may never find Evil. Whoever took him may already have done the unthinkable."

Lola's eyes clouded and she shook her head. "He's alive," she said. "I'm certain he's alive." Her hand came to rest over her heart as her eyes met Stukeley's once more. "A mother knows," she said.

JACK TAR'S CAVERN

Cheng Li made her way across to the bar. How many nights had it been since her arrival here? She had lost count. She was still coming to grips with the size of Jack Tar's Cavern. At first she had thought she'd be restless, eager to return to the fray, but, strangely, this was not the case. Ever since her arrival here, in this vast cathedral-like cavern, she had felt something new. A sense of peace, perhaps.

As she waited to order drinks for herself and her father, she turned and found a familiar face at her side.

"Captain Wrathe," she said with some formality.

He smiled. "Why don't you call me Molucco?" he said.

"All right," she agreed, though whether she could pull this off was another matter indeed.

"So, how are you settling in?" he asked her.

She nodded. "Very well, thank you, *Molucco*." The word wasn't quite so strange on her tongue as she had anticipated. "It's a very relaxing kind of place, isn't it?"

Her companion grinned and nodded. "Very relaxing," he said, his eyes taking in the room. "And you're never lost for good company down here. As I was just saying to Eddie Teach—"

Before he got started on what promised to be a lengthy anecdote, Cheng Li cut him off. "Can I get you a drink?" she asked.

He smiled agreeably. "Why thank you. I won't say no to a Dark and Stormy."

"Coming up!" she said as she reached the front of the queue.

"Yes, young lady. What'll it be?"

Cheng Li opened her mouth, but no words came out. Her attention had been distracted by a face across the bar. There was someone she had been looking for ever since her arrival in Jack Tar's Cavern. And now, at last, she saw him—right across the bar from her.

"Connor!" she called across the vast circular bar. "Connor, it's me! Cheng Li!"

The young man turned toward her, prompted by nudges from those at his side. In a flash, she saw that though he was of a similar age and build, it was not Connor. Her heart fell. She saw that she had lost the bartender's attention now, too.

Molucco pushed through to stand beside her. "You thought that lad was Connor Tempest, didn't you?"

"Yes," she admitted dolefully. "I've been searching for him ever since I arrived here, but I can't seem to find him. I suppose Jack Tar's is a bigger place than I realized, but, even so..."

Molucco reached out and put his hand on her wrist. It was the kind of gesture that previously might have enraged her, but now it merely silenced her as she lifted her eyes to his face. He was looking at her with genuine kindness and patience.

"Connor Tempest isn't here," he said.

AT SEA

Connor and Grace sat in the small boat making its way across the dark velvet waters.

"Just like old times, eh?" he said with a grin.

She nodded. "Just like old times."

They had already left the coast behind them and were out in the ocean waters. But the vessel was steady and making good progress through the night. Grace watched as Connor busied himself expertly with the ropes.

"When did you first realize you could split in two?" Grace asked him.

Connor continued working on the ropes as his face turned toward her, illuminated by the full moon. "It first happened during the recapture of *The Diablo*." He paused, trapping a bit of rope in his mouth, as he knotted another section. "Then, Jacoby and I had this fight," he continued. "Over Jasmine, of course, and it happened again. So I knew, going into the last battle, that it was a possibility." He came to join her at the center of the boat again. "After what you told me about the prophecy, I knew it was my destiny to fight Sidorio. But I was down at the other end of the ship. I couldn't get to him—not by conventional means—before Cheng Li and the others beat me to it. When the split happened, one of me was able to speed to the center of the ship, while the other one jumped overboard to make my escape."

Grace nodded. "Did you know that the one taking on Sidorio was destined to be killed?"

Connor's eyes met his sister's. "Yes, I think so. I've foreseen my death several times. The pieces of the jigsaw seemed to fit. That's why it seemed a good idea for my other self to get the hell out of there and wait out the rest of the battle." A dark look clouded his face. "My only regret is the hurt I've caused to Jasmine, Bo Yin, and the others."

Grace smiled reassuringly. "Perhaps it's better this way. After all, you are going to disappear from their lives for quite some time."

He nodded. "Yes, according to your book, it'll take seven years. Seven years of wandering the world, encountering no one I know, and I'll rid myself of the dhampir gene." His eyes were bright. "When I come back, I'll be a mortal again."

Grace felt a rise of emotion at his words. The thought

of being apart from him for seven years was hard to bear. But she knew how much he yearned to become mortal once more. If this was what it took to bring her brother back a sense of peace, it was well worth it.

"It's *your* book now," she said. "I want you to keep it with you during this time away. It will comfort me greatly to know you're not completely alone."

"Thank you," he said, sliding closer toward her. "I'll come and find you, you know," he said. "The moment my seven years are up."

She nodded, determined not to cry. "You better!" she said. "And just think what adventures you'll have to tell me about then."

"Yes." He nodded. She could see how filled with conviction he was for this fresh journey.

"I'd better go," she said. "Someone's knocking on my door."

"I think I can guess who that might be!" Connor grinned. "I wish I could have been there for the wedding—nice dress, by the way—but it's better like this."

Grace nodded. All things considered, he was right.

"And I wish I could hug you good-bye properly!" Connor added.

"That's the problem with these astral visits," Grace said. She brought her hand to his cheek and, though it did not make conventional physical contact, still the gesture comforted them both. "Travel safe," she said.

"You, too!"

Grace watched as his eyes turned back toward the ocean. It shimmered with reflections of the moon and stars. Comforted that her brother's future was now assured, Grace exited the boat and returned to her cabin on board *The Nocturne*.

〜

The knocking at her door had grown louder. She jumped down from the bed and opened it. Darcy Flotsam floated into the room, looking more beautiful than ever before.

"Oh, Darcy!" Grace said. "Jet Jetsam is a very lucky man!"

Darcy flushed with pleasure. "I'm the lucky one, Grace. I never thought this night would come. And now, of course, I'm a bundle of nerves!"

"Come here!" Grace said, grateful that she could hug Darcy for real. As she held her close, she thought once more of her brother, making his way on the beginnings of his seven-year odyssey.

"What are you thinking about?" Darcy asked her. "Or rather, who?"

"Connor," Grace admitted.

"Of course," Darcy said, her face suddenly grave. "I understand."

"But look." Grace wiped away her tear. "This is your night, Darcy. We've waited a long time for it, and there's something I want to do for you."

"What's that?" Darcy inquired, intrigued.

Grace reached up her hands and unclasped the chain around her neck. Catching the locket she had been given by Connor many months earlier, she held it out toward her friend. "Something borrowed," she said. As Darcy glanced at her in surprise and delight, Grace added, "It seems about time I lent you something of mine!"

As Grace was fastening the locket around Darcy's neck, there was another knock at the door.

"Come in!" cried Grace.

"We're all ready for you!" Lorcan said, hovering at the cabin door, looking off-the-scale handsome in his tuxedo and Grace's favorite ice-blue cravat.

"Oh, no!" Darcy cried. "You mustn't see me! It's bad luck!"

Lorcan laughed. "Now, now, Darcy. You're marrying Mr. Jetsam, remember? No more bad luck for you." He took her in his arms.

"Of course," she said. "How silly! See what a state I'm in?"

"You look very beautiful, Miss Flotsam," Lorcan said. "Just think—that's the last time I shall call you that. From now on, you'll be known as *Mrs.* Jetsam."

"Yes." Darcy smiled. "Yes, I suppose I shall." She seemed calmer now. Over her shoulder, Lorcan grinned at Grace. "Speaking of beautiful...Grace Tempest, you are a picture to behold!"

Grace rose to her feet. "Why, thank you," she said as he

stepped forward to kiss her. It began as a brief brushing of their lips but soon developed into something more.

"Come on!" Darcy said. "People, we have a wedding to get to. Mine!"

Lorcan and Grace broke off their kiss, laughing.

"Off you go!" Grace pushed him away playfully. "We'll see you up on deck."

Lorcan nodded. "It's a beautiful night," he said. "The stars have all come out for you, Darcy." He turned to go, then had a fresh thought. "Oh, and Tempest, a word to the wise..."

Grace was busily gathering up the edges of Darcy's train. "Yes?" she said, glancing up at Lorcan. "What is it, *Furey*?"

Lorcan grinned. "Just so you know, I've put down good money on you catching the wedding bouquet. I trust you won't let me down!"

As he winked at her, Grace thought his eyes had never looked so blue. They were eyes you could never tire from looking at—as deep and constant and infinite as the ocean itself. In her head, Grace heard a familiar whisper.

So it ends, so it begins.